Learning to Love

Praise for *Learning to Love*

"Women's fiction has a rising star in Sheryl Browne. Her novels cut straight to the heart and if you're looking for a totally engrossing read that will make you cry as well as laugh your socks off then look no further ..."
Matt Bates, Fiction Buyer WH Smith Travel

"*Learning to Love* is fast paced and engaging. Not only does the romance sizzle but we see family life in all its shades of grey sprinkled with humour and sadness, and there is an element of suspense and fear. What a combination!"
Jera's Jamboree

"Deals with loss & betrayal in manner that lifts it far above an average 'chick lit'. This book goes on my top ten reads of all time!"
Nikki's Books4U

"Sheryl Browne's great style of writing brings us real characters in believable, moving yet amusing scenarios. *Learning to Love* is no exception to this and is another brilliant book from such a talented author. *Learning to Love* mixes just the right amount of humour in with a more serious outlook on life. It's about family, as beautifully chaotic as they can be, and it's about overcoming the obstacles life throws your way and finding love in the right place. It's an addictive, gorgeous read."
Sophie Hedley – Reviewed The Book

Learning to Love

Sheryl Browne

Where heroes are like chocolate – irresistible!

Printed and bound by Clays Ltd

Acknowledgements

Those who know me will know that this book was written whilst I was caring for a loved one. THANK YOU readers. I could not have done it without you. Thank you, too, to all the lovely people at Choc Lit and Matt Bates, Fiction Buyer at WH Smith, who loved the book so much he took a quote from it.

A special thanks goes to the Tasting Panel readers who passed the novel and made this all possible: Sandra F., Alexa H., Vanessa O., Siobhan K., Linda Sp., Isabelle, Claire W. and Rosie F.

Chapter One

Catapulted from sleep by what he slowly remembered was the ancient boiler firing up, David Adams checked his alarm and then, '*Dammit*,' threw back the duvet and shot along the landing. Poised to press down the handle on his son's bedroom door, he debated, and then knocked and waited. 'Jake, clock's ticking,' he called. 'Time to get up.'

Shivering in only his boxers, David curbed his impatience and wondered again what had possessed him to rent an Edwardian townhouse in a tiny village, which retained many of its charming period features, including an antiquated plumbing system he'd come to hate over the two days he'd been here. There was the 'spectacular' view, of course, which the estate agent had assured him people would die for. Blowing out an icy breath, David glanced through the high sashed landing window to where the distant peaks of the majestic Malvern Hills were eclipsed by a charcoal grey mist, and concluded that if they'd viewed it from where he was standing, they very probably would die – of hypothermia.

Jake was right. The place was a dump. And David was deluded, thinking he might do a better job of parenting here than he had in Oxford. So, why were they here? For his son's sake, David reminded himself, that's why he'd made the decision to take the position at Hibberton Health Centre. So he could start afresh. Work locally, while Jake attended the nearby school; and try to rebuild his relationship with his son.

'Jake,' he called again, not really expecting an answer. The most Jake had offered by way of communication since he'd picked him up from his aunt's yesterday was the odd monosyllabic grunt, much as he'd done every time David had visited him there. He couldn't blame him. If he were Jake, he wouldn't have much to say to someone who hadn't been much of a father either.

Swallowing back the bitter taste of regret, David tried again. 'Jake, come on. Get showered and dressed, please, or we'll be late.'

No response.

Despairing, David squeaked the door open. 'Jake?'

Apparently determined to ignore him, Jake remained mute, moodily stuffing his feet into his trainers, his hair tousled from a fitful night's sleep.

Awake most of the night himself, thanks to rattling pipes and creaking floorboards, David had heard Jake tossing and turning. 'Come on, small fry, move it. Don't want to get a black mark on your first day, do you?' he said, trying to cajole him.

That worked. Eye contact nil, the boy bent to scoop his T-shirt from the floor and then attempted to push past David to the landing. 'Jake!'

Standing his ground, David tried to inject some authority into his voice, but his ten-year-old son's reply was an impudent, 'What?'

Noting Jake's now openly mutinous scowl, David sighed and stood aside.

'Go and get washed,' he said, an argument on the boy's first day at a new school being the last thing he wanted. Thanks to a mix up with the keys to the house, Jake was already starting partway through the week, also midterm, which wasn't ideal. With his aunt about to embark on a new career, though, David really didn't have any choice. She'd already put her life on hold for the best part of a year to look after Jake until he'd sorted himself out, and leaving him home alone while he orientated himself with the surgery before starting next week just wasn't an option. 'You'll need a clean shirt,' he suggested as Jake shuffled grudgingly onwards.

'Don't have none,' Jake retorted, without a backward glance.

'Any, Jake. And there are plenty of clean shirts in the dresser. I put them there last night. I'd like you to put one on, please.'

'And I like this one,' Jake imparted, before disappearing into the bathroom to slam the door shut behind him.

Great. David raked a hand through his hair. Jake was testing him, he knew. Wearing his insolence like a suit of armour, all his emotions stuffed safely inside.

'You have to wear a white button front shirt, Jake. You know you do. And shoes, not trainers!' David called after him, and then sighed, frustrated. He wished he knew what to say that didn't incite the very argument he was trying to avoid, wished he knew how to reach him. Being there for him might be a start, he decided, steeling his resolve to make that his first, and only, priority: one-on-one quality time with his son. If only he could get to the place where Jake actually wanted to spend time with him, doing whatever ten-year-old kids ... David's thoughts screeched to a halt as a reality check hit him head on.

He didn't know what Jake did.

Due to his own inexcusable behaviour, he and his wife had been separated before Michelle's accident and after her death he'd agreed it would be better for her sister, Becky, to move into his home and look after Jake until he'd got her estate in order and sorted out his own affairs. Becky was between jobs and, although grieving the loss of her sister, she was happy to take care of Jake. What with selling the family home, then with house and job hunting high on the agenda, his visits to his son had become sporadic over the last few months, and now, almost a year later ... he had absolutely no idea what Jake was currently into, he realised. Yes, he knew what films he liked, the cinema being the safest bet when he had seen him. But what music or computer games were cool, David had no clue. And, other than Big Macs or popcorn, he didn't even know what food his son enjoyed. He needed to bridge the gap somehow.

Maybe he should get him a dog? Jake had wanted one,

been desperate for one, before … before his world had been blown apart. What must be going through his mind? David wondered. If his own nights were filled with waking nightmares, what demons must be haunting Jake's dreams?

Curbing his thoughts before they ventured too far down that dark road, David sucked in a breath and attempted to focus on the here and now. He couldn't realistically fit in walking a dog, though, could he? Training it. With Jake to look after and with a new job to start, he was going to be pushed for time as it was.

Feeling defeated before he'd even got started, David headed back to his own room, wondering what he should make Jake for breakfast. He'd barely touched the pasta he'd offered him last night.

Burger and chips, maybe?

Still pondering, David reached for the curtains hanging precariously in the huge bay window. The agent had laughingly referred to these depressing brown and tangerine floral things as retro. He needed to get new ones. The place needed cheering up. The natural wood flooring could hopefully stay, but the '60s nylon carpet had to go.

'Grrreat!' David closed his eyes and silently counted to five as the 'retro' curtains pooled at his feet, complete with rail.

Oops. Andrea pulled her gaze away from the semi-naked male torso in the bedroom window opposite. Quite a tasty torso, too. Pity the window ledge interrupted the view. Hiding a smile, she stepped quickly away from her own window in order to spare her new neighbour's blushes, who was now gathering up armfuls of curtains. Oh, dear. Well, it was comforting to know hers wasn't the only household where pandemonium reigned in the mornings.

'Problem?' she asked as she turned, noting her partner's obvious exasperation with her lack of skill in the sock sorting department.

'No, not really.' Blowing out an elongated sigh, Jonathan tugged on his mismatching socks. 'It's just … I don't understand your desire to take off in another direction. I mean, selling second-hand clothes is hardly an entrepreneurial business idea, Andrea, is it?'

'I am not selling second-hand clothes.' Miffed, Andrea ignored his dishevelled Colin Firth-ish appearance and headed for the en suite. The damp tendrils of hair tickling his forehead looked the part, but the open shirt didn't really work with striped boxers – and odd socks. 'They're second-chance designer, for your information.'

'Well, that'll make all the difference, won't it? Move over, Victoria Beckham. Make way for Hibberton's very own high-flying supplier of designer.'

'Hah, hah. Sarcasm, Jonathan, is the lowest form of wit.'

'Look, Andy,' Jonathan paused, and groaned, probably realising his normally precision pressed trousers weren't, due to a slight malfunction in the trouser press caused by a misplaced doll's head, which was beautifully pressed. 'I'm not being sarcastic. I'm being realistic. You're not superwoman. You can't single-handedly set up a shop selling used clothing, designer or not, and expect it to take off.'

Damn. Andrea went cross-eyed in the bathroom mirror. And there was me about to slip into my sparkly skirt and cape. 'Not single-handedly, Jonathan.' One eye on the clock, Andrea dragged a face-wipe down her face, careless of wrinkles. 'Eva Bunting owns the property I'm looking to rent, and—'

'I know,' Jonathan cut in, now sounding irritated. 'I am her investment adviser, Andrea. She's absolutely loaded.'

Andrea poked her head around the bathroom door. 'What, serious money, you mean?'

'A fair whack. Her great-grandfather made a fortune setting up one of Malvern's first water cure clinics. He was raking it in. Eva benefitted from the lot, lucky old bat.'

'Ah, well, that would explain why she's letting me have it at a low rent, initially anyway. Oh, that reminds me, she said you forgot to ring her. She needs to release the funds from her investment with you to get the renovation work underway, apparently. Could you do it today, do you think?' Andrea skidded from the bathroom to the wardrobe.

'*Hell*,' Jonathan cursed and sighed. 'Sorry. Slipped my mind. I'll do it later.'

'She's going to be renting the top floors out as living accommodation,' Andrea went on, not quite able to contain her excitement now her dream seemed to be coming to fruition, 'but she's offered me the shopfront for peanuts. It's ideally placed, opposite the Cup Cake Café. You know, next to Tiny Tots, the bespoke babywear shop? And I'm not just thinking designer, by the way. I'm thinking vintage: wedding dresses, evening wear; anything retro, which is currently cool.'

Flipping quickly through coat hangers in hope of inspiration, Andrea turned from the wardrobe, dubiously eyeing her camel coloured harem pants, which were definitely retro, but possibly not cool. Ah, well, teamed with her new wedge ankle boots and with her camel cape coat over, they'd just have to do.

'Sally has some to-die-for sixties and seventies stuff for me,' she continued, grabbing the opportunity to share her plans while she had Jonathan's attention, 'plus a vintage Harvey Nichols ball gown, which is totally divine. Ooh, and an absolutely fabulous Mary Quant dress. And Nita has a real treasure trove of Victorian hair accessories. You should see the burlesque feather adornments she has. They're amazing.'

'Yes, well, I still don't understand,' Jonathan muttered moodily. 'Why on earth would you want to get involved in what is basically going to be a cottage industry when you've already got so much on your plate?'

'It is not going to be a cottage industry.' Andrea twanged a shirt-style blouse from its hanger. 'It's an attempt at doing something different, more fulfilling. And I know it's going to take up a little more of my time initially, but …'

Oh, what was the point? Jonathan seemed determined to be dead set against it. But she so needed a change of direction. Personal satisfaction aside, work-life balance dictated she needed to make changes. With three children, two of whom were throwing themselves heartily into the truculent teenager phase and one into everything toddler, and a mother who would try the patience of a saint lately, there was no balance. Her 'plates' were skew-whiff and her balls were dropping all over the place. Andrea knew she might never replace her income from her teaching job. But then, didn't she pay a good portion of her salary out on childcare for Chloe anyway?

'Typical,' Jonathan muttered, glancing despairingly down at his shirt. 'Missing button.' He sighed. 'I don't suppose you've got time to …' he trailed off as Andrea cast him a withering look.

'Of course,' she said, her brow knitted pseudo-sympathetically. 'Why don't you whip the shirt off and I'll sew one on while I'm feeding Chloe and loading the dishwasher?'

'Uh-oh, move over, Dougal.' Jonathan glanced up sheepishly. 'Make room for me in the doghouse.'

There followed a timely, frenzied yap yapping, which ritually accompanied siblings at war in the mornings.

'You might be in luck. I think Dougal may be about to vacate it in favour of the rescue centre.' Andrea's mouth twitched into a smile. Why were they arguing, she wondered. Now of all times, when, after living together for four years, and producing a child, they'd finally decided to seal their relationship? She didn't want to fight with him, despite his presumption she'd popped out of the womb wielding a needle. It was just so … pointless.

'I don't blame him. We'll just have to stick a sign outside saying "Beware of the Kids" instead. That should make intruders think twice,' Jonathan replied with a smile back and Andrea remembered that was what she'd first loved about him, his easy smile. The twinkle in his eye when he'd laughed. The way those liquid brown eyes had darkened with desire the first time they'd kissed.

He'd made their first intimate touch easy, unhurried and unselfish. But that was Jonathan, so amicable and laid-back she'd almost fallen over him on the way to the bedroom. Where had that Jonathan gone, Andrea wondered. Their lovemaking seemed perfunctory lately, almost as if the honeymoon was already over.

He was tired, she supposed, working as hard as he did. They both were, but Andrea couldn't help thinking there might be more to Jonathan's moodiness than he was letting on. Could it be that he was running scared of change? The transition from footloose and fancy-free to full-time father of three must be daunting.

'Mum!' Sophie bawled along the landing, right on cue. 'He's done it again!'

'What?' was her brother's innocent reply. 'I only brushed the dog's fur.'

'Yes! With my hairbrush,' Sophie pointed out loudly. 'Give it back, retard! Mum, tell him!'

'Give it back, Ryan,' Andrea shouted. 'Now. And stop teasing the dog!' She paid lip service to her lipstick, twisted her own tangle of unruly hair up in a topknot, and tried to get her mind into teaching mode.

'Yeah, give it back, derbrain,' Sophie yelled, 'or I'll thump you.'

'Ooh, save me. She's gonna kick ass,' Ryan drawled wittily.

'You two have one second to retreat to your corners and get ready, or I'll bang heads together,' Andrea threatened.

'Huh, wouldn't make any difference to dumbum. He hasn't got a brain,' Sophie muttered, padding back to her bedroom to close the door with a resounding bang.

'Kids, hey?' Jonathan sighed. 'Who'd have 'em?'

'Um, us?' Andrea suggested, nodding towards their bed. 'The lump under the duvet is yours, I believe.'

'For my sins.' Jonathan glanced at the toddler-shaped lump, then his watch. 'Er, I don't suppose ...'

'... I could drop her off at the nursery on my way in? Don't tell me, you've got an early appointment.' Andrea tugged back the duvet to reveal a tangle of sausage arms and legs and a headless Igglepiggle.

'Yes, sorry. Key client.' Jonathan shrugged apologetically as Andrea heaved her bleary-eyed lastborn into her arms. 'And sorry about ... Well, not understanding. It's just that I don't know why you want to take something else on board when you've already got your hands full.'

'Ten out of ten for observation, Jonathan. Come on, sweetie.' Andrea kissed the top of Chloe's soft downy head and breathed in pure fragrance of baby. 'Let's put your CBeebies DVD on while Mummy makes breakfast, shall we?'

'Curl flies,' Chloe mumbled sleepily into her shoulder.

Andrea smiled. Ooh, how she loved this little body. She'd never imagined having another child. Now, though, she couldn't imagine life without her. 'We're all out of curly fries, darling. How about big, fat Marmite soldiers, hmm?'

'You've already got a full-time job. A proper nine-to-five job with a decent income.' Jonathan followed Andrea to the landing. 'Why do you want to faff about—'

'Because I need to, Jonathan.' Andrea scooped Sophie's discarded leggings from the landing floor and headed for the stairs, hands fuller.

Jonathan trailed down the stairs after her, hands free. 'Why?'

Andrea eyed him despairingly over her shoulder. 'Fle-xi-bi-li-ty, Jonathan.' She felt inclined to spell it out. 'As for income, childcare is extortionate, as you very well know. And day care for Mum is almost non-existent. I don't have any leeway at the moment and I need some.'

'So being your own boss is going to allow you to be flexible?' Jonathan laughed wryly behind her. 'I don't think so.'

Andrea stepped over Ryan's Reeboks and a backpack illegally parked on the hall floor. 'Well, I do. Mum can stay with me during the day for a start, which will give her a sense of purpose, rather than patronising her by doing things for her because she's a bit—'

'—nuts,' Jonathan finished bluntly.

'Forgetful.' Andrea scowled. 'And Chloe can go to nursery part-time rather than full-time. It can work,' she insisted as Jonathan continued to look sceptical. 'I'm going to work at making it work ... after I've sewed your buttons on and knitted you a new pair of socks, of course.'

'Andrea, you've got three kids.' Jonathan splayed his hands in despair.

'Oh, Mu-um,' Sophie whined from upstairs. 'Gran's locked herself in the bathroom again.'

'Gosh, *three*? I wondered where all the little voices were coming from.' Andrea puffed out a sigh and deposited Chloe guiltily on her playmat in the lounge, along with the entire soft toy cast of *In the Night Garden*.

'Pants! She's going to make me late, again.' Sophie stomped back to her bedroom, making sure to slam the door behind her once again.

'And a mother,' Jonathan reminded Andrea of the cause of Sophie's distress.

'This, Jonathan, I am aware of, funnily enough. Do you think now you've done a body count and realised how full my hands are, you could help out a little, possibly?'

Giving Jonathan a weary glance, Andrea marched on to the kitchen, where Ryan greeted her cheerily, 'Morning, Mother dearest. And how are we this bright new day?'

'Morning, Ry— Oh.' Andrea eyed the chaos where once was a kitchen, skirted around a pair of Sophie's platform shoes, narrowly missed the dog dish plonked mid-floor, and trod on the dog instead. 'Hell! Sorry, Dougal.' She winced as the little Yorkie emitted a startled yelp and then skidded for the safety of his basket.

'Oh, that good, then?' Ryan gave her an all-too-knowing look. 'Come on, little guy.' He plucked up the dog to nuzzle him cheek-to-cheek. 'I'll help you type a letter to the RSPCA. Nasty Mummy.'

'He's a Yorkshire Terrier, Ryan, not a child,' Andrea reminded him as her macho seventeen-year-old son, who wouldn't be seen dead kissing his mum, proceeded to snog the dog. 'And stop kissing him, for goodness sake. You'll catch something.'

'I know he's a Yorkshire Terrier, Mother. This is why he's too short to reach the keyboard, aren't you, Dougal? I take it you two are having a nice civilised conversation again, then?' Ryan observed drolly, casting an inscrutable glance at a retreating Jonathan as he did.

'Ryan, get breakfast and get gone, please,' Andrea answered her son evasively.

'Definitely arguing,' Ryan surmised, plopping the dog down, and heading across the kitchen in search of sustenance.

'No, we are not. We're talking.' Andrea cuffed her son's lopsided coiffure as he waited for the contents of the fridge to speak to him. 'And before you make any smart remarks about my deficient domestic goddess gene—'

'Toast.' Ryan sighed. 'Again.'

'Correct. Top of the class. And put an extra slice on for Chloe, please.'

'Aw, Mum, why me?'

'Funny that,' Andrea mused, wearing her best mystified expression, 'I ask myself that every day – while I'm cooking, cleaning, washing, ironing ...'

'Because you're a mother, Mother,' Ryan supplied helpfully. 'It's in the job description.'

'Such a wit. Don't strain anything buttering the toast, will you? I'm off to sort Gran out.' Andrea gave him a no-nonsense look as she groped in the cutlery drawer for the means to vacate the bathroom.

'Scary.' Ryan arched an eyebrow as Andrea walked purposely towards the stairs, carving knife in hand.

Jonathan also looked rather alarmed as he emerged from the cloakroom to grab his car keys from the top of the hall cupboard. 'Bit drastic, isn't it?' he commented, nodding at her lethal weapon.

Andrea blinked, attempting amused, but probably looking demented. 'Golly, another comedian. I'm so glad you all find living in a madhouse so hilarious. Don't you strain anything either, will you, running for the getaway car?'

'I'll try not to.' Jonathan smiled wanly. 'Er, I'd better go.' He slid desperate eyes towards the door.

'Yes, you'd better had, before I do.' Andrea trooped on up the stairs, bracing herself outside the bathroom, before tapping on the door. 'Mum, could you undo the bolt, please?'

'Bye,' Jonathan called from the hall.

'Mum!' Andrea hammered. 'Will you please open the door!'

'Bye, darling. Have a nice day. See you at the restaurant at eight for our date night. Love you,' Jonathan answered himself, and closed the front door quietly behind him.

Lord, please give me strength. Andrea eyed the ceiling and then squatted to slide the knife between door and frame. 'Mum, do you think you could turn the lock anticlockwise for me?' she asked patiently.

'Have,' came the short reply from inside.

'Well, try ag— No, Mum, anti ... Thank you.' Andrea addressed Dee's odd slippered feet.

'Fangled.' Dee narrowed accusing eyes at the door. 'Can't be doing with newfangled things.' She bustled past as Andrea

12

crawled up the bath. 'And you know I can't see a thing without my glasses.'

'Mum, your glasses are on your ... ' Head, Andrea would have said, had her mother's bustle not turned to a miraculous near sprint. How was it, she wondered, that a woman with arthritic knees could skip so lithely downstairs when it suited?

Andrea sighed tolerantly. Her mum would rather be in her own little riverside cottage, she knew, free to use her own bathroom and come and go as she pleased. If only her comings and goings hadn't become forgetful meanderings, worryingly so with the water only yards from her front door. Poor Dee. She'd been devastated when it had been sold back to British Waterways for renovation. She so missed her independence. Andrea reined in her impatience and trudged down after her mother, to meet Ryan looking weak and willowy as he sloped from the kitchen.

'I've made the toast,' he informed her, his shoulders in droopy abused child mode. 'I'm off to college now, before I'm too worn out to do any work.' He paused to wipe a theatrical hand across his brow, then peered panicky into the hall mirror lest his uber-cool emo cut had a single hair out of place.

Andrea cocked her head to one side as, hair crisis averted, Ryan turned relieved to the front door. 'Ryan,' she started cautiously, not wanting to damage his delicate teen ego, 'you do realise you're showing an awful lot of, um, bum?'

'Yes, Mother.' Ryan swaggered onwards, an abundance of underpants on show above his belt. 'It's called fashion sense.'

No sense, more like. Rolling her eyes heavenwards, Andrea started back to the kitchen and then almost had a heart attack as Ryan poked his head back around the doorframe. 'Um, talking of fashion sense, thought you should know Gran's out front in her wellies and nightie.'

Chapter Two

Uh, oh, more problems. Andrea noted Jonathan was still there, poking about in his engine as she shot down the drive, Chloe and Igglepiggle in her arms. 'I thought you'd gone,' she said as she passed him.

'I haven't. She has,' Jonathan mumbled, from under the bonnet.

Andrea stopped. 'Sorry?'

'Nothing.' Jonathan surfaced and gave her the briefest of smiles. 'No good trying to make a fast getaway if the getaway car's given up the ghost, is there? This isn't working, Andrea,' he dropped the bonnet and turned to face her, 'is it?'

'So get it fixed,' Andrea suggested, puzzled as to what she was supposed to do about it, short of a motor mechanics course – at midnight, by candlelight. What on earth was wrong with the car anyway? It was barely past its warranty.

'I wish I could.' Jonathan nodded past Andrea, with a sigh. 'She's over the road, scaring the new neighbour.'

'Oh.' Andrea glanced anxiously over her shoulder to see the man who'd got in a tangle with his curtains emerging from his house. Obviously he was wondering what a slightly dotty old lady in wellies and nightie would be doing wafting about on his drive. 'I'd better go and get her before she damages neighbourhood relations.'

'Andrea, it's not working.' Jonathan caught her arm as she turned. 'We have to make alternative arrangements.'

Andrea narrowed her eyes as she realised the look in his eyes was telling her he was talking about something more serious than a dodgy carburettor. 'What alternative arrangements?' she asked warily, hoisting Chloe higher in her arms.

Jonathan shrugged and looked towards Dee, who, were it not for the winceyette nightie, could be mistaken for a traffic warden, and was circling the new neighbour's car with slit-eyed suspicion. 'Andrea, I think we should—'

'I have to get Mum, Jonathan. We'll all freeze without our coats on,' Andrea cut in. She had a sinking feeling she wouldn't want to hear what Jonathan thought. 'Back in a sec.'

Turning away, Andrea dashed across the road before Dee did irrevocable damage.

'Sorry,' she apologised, her friendliest smile plastered in place as she skidded up the drive opposite, where her new neighbour was looking anything but neighbourly. 'She gets a bit—'

'What?' The man – up close he was tall, dark, and seemingly humourless – glanced at her askance. His eyes were blue, Andrea noticed, ice cool and agitated.

'My mum,' Andrea started again. 'She gets a bit confused.'

'Right,' he said shortly, and checked his watch.

How rude. Andrea bristled inwardly as he looked inscrutably back at her. 'I apologise if she bothered you.' She forced a smile and tried to hang on to her miniature Houdini, who had dropped Igglepiggle and was so determined to get back to Jonathan, she almost wriggled out of her jim-jams.

'In a minute, baby,' Andrea promised, bending to scoop the decapitated toy from the ground, in the absence of any forthcoming assistance from her neighbour.

'I thought I'd better come over and explain in case you thought she was about to steal your personalised number plate.' Igglepiggle retrieved, Andrea glanced in the direction of his shiny BMW soft top.

'I see,' he said, parting with a whole two more precious words.

He obviously did have a basic grasp of English, then.

Pity he hadn't got a grasp of rudimentary good manners. Unimpressed, Andrea looked him over surreptitiously. His tie was askew, she noticed, and he was unshaven. Designer stubble? Or was he just a worried man in a hurry, which might explain his attitude problem. She noted the greying hair at the temples, which was definitely an asset on this man, who was good-looking if one liked the moody, silent sort.

'Sorry, I'm waffling and we haven't even met properly. Andrea,' forging on, she introduced herself, determined to be civil even if he wasn't. 'Andrea Kelly. This is my mother, Deirdre. As I said, she gets a bit—'

'Your licence is out of date,' Dee said on introduction, having finally acquainted glasses with nose. She slid accusatory eyes from his windscreen, where his presumably out of date tax disc was displayed, to look him up and down. 'And your shoes need cleaning.'

'Um,' Andrea tried to keep her face straight, 'sorry. She gets a bit muddled sometimes. She really doesn't mean—'

'Obviously,' he said, cutting her short. With which, he gave her a curt nod and turned away.

Ooh! How utterly … Andrea's fuse fizzled as he walked to his front door without even a backwards glance. Disbelieving of his arrogance, she was about to turn away when a young boy stepped out of the house, still in his pyjamas.

'Jake.' The man stopped in his tracks. 'Get back inside!' the man, who was clearly the boy's father, said.

The boy just looked at him. His expression was insolent, Andrea noted, but he was clearly upset.

'Jake!'

The boy glanced at Andrea, whose heart twisted inside her as she noted his red-rimmed eyes.

'Now, Jake!' his father shouted, his face turning white with palpable fury. 'Last warning!'

Dropping his gaze, the boy turned reluctantly back inside.

'Get your uniform on, get breakfast and make sure you're ready to go, Jake. Or else ...'

Or else what? Andrea wondered, her tummy tightening inside her, as he closed the front door. She had no idea what was going on here, but whatever it was, this man seemed dangerously close to losing it. Concerned, she looked towards the house. It could have been Ryan at the same age, impotently trying to stand up to his bullying father. Andrea had been here, watching a similarly heart-breaking scene, before she'd finally asked her children's father to leave. He'd struck out, once too often. Would this man? Had he already? Is that what the charged atmosphere was all about?

'UFO,' Dee imparted out of nowhere as Andrea turned, troubled, back to her house. 'Unattached Fit Object,' she clarified, seemingly oblivious to the scene they'd just witnessed. 'You shouldn't play too hard to get, darling. You're not getting any younger.'

Andrea glanced back. 'He's an arrogant bully, if you ask me,' she said, wishing she'd said something. At least asked the boy if he was all right. 'I have no idea what any woman would see in him.'

'Makes two of us,' Jonathan said moodily as Andrea trooped back towards the house, Dee in tow.

'Two of us what?' Andrea eyed him curiously.

'Unattached men.' Jonathan shot Dee a less than amused glance.

'And if she has any sense, you'll stay that way.' Dee gave him a long disparaging look back. 'My daughter might not be in her prime, but she's not desperate, you know. Or daft.'

Thanks, Mum. Andrea eyed the skies. 'I am, actually,' she said, nodding at Dee's disappearing back, then offering Jonathan a sympathetic smile.

'Me too.' Jonathan didn't smile back. 'Andrea, about ... what we were discussing ...'

Andrea felt immediately uneasy. 'Which was?'

'Alternative arrangements. For Dee, I mean. I was thinking some kind of care, may—'

'Care?' Andrea stared at him, incredulous. 'She's my mother, Jonathan. She's cared for me all my life. Do you propose I just abandon her to spend the rest of her days in some godforsaken care home because she gets a bit confused?'

'No, I …' Jonathan stopped and sighed. 'I care, Andrea. I'm your fiancé.'

Unofficially, Andrea didn't point out. He hadn't actually put the ring on her finger yet. 'Which doesn't give you the right to lay down the law,' she did feel inclined to point out.

'Quite.' Jonathan plunged his hands in his pockets and glanced at his shoes. 'So, assuming our time together, or lack of, doesn't matter in the great scheme of things, what about your kids, Andrea? Don't you think they deserve a little more of your attention?'

'I do know they're my kids.' Andrea tethered her temper and tried to placate Chloe, who was definitely getting fractious now. 'One third of them is also yours, Jonathan. I'm sure Chloe would be delighted if you spent more—'

'Look, Andrea, I know I need to pull my weight more, and I'll try. But I can only do so much with my own business to run. It might look as if all I do is organise a few client meetings and, hey presto, I make money, but it's not that easy.'

'It was your choice to give up management and go into investment planning, Jonathan,' Andrea reminded him, resisting the urge to also remind him that she'd supported him every step of the way. 'And you are making money, aren't you?'

At least he said he was. He was all for moving house and booking holidays six months ago. Thinking about it, he hadn't been so keen to spend money recently though.

'Jonathan, do you have a problem we're not sharing?'

Andrea studied him carefully. If there were things he wasn't telling her, whether to save her from worrying or to save face, then she needed to know.

'Yes. No. I ... Of course I'm making money. And, no, I don't have any problems we're not sharing, apart from ... It's stressful, Andy. We're already stretched way too thin. And now you're proposing some hare-brained scheme about starting a shop?'

'It's not hare-brained.' Andrea stared at him, bewildered. She struggled to hold onto Chloe, whose little feet were reaching determinedly for the floor. Why did she have to keep trying to explain? Did he have any idea how stressful teaching was nowadays? Granted, starting a business would be hard work, but was it really so wrong to want a change of direction before it was too late? She wasn't intending to stop working altogether and put her feet up.

Did he want her to? Andrea scanned his eyes. Would he prefer her to be a stay-at-home wife, brush up on her Delia and serve his clients gastronomic delights? She couldn't. Wouldn't. She could never be entirely dependent on a man, he knew that.

'I've played it by the book all my life, Jonathan, mostly to support other people,' Andrea let it hang, hoping he might understand. 'I still have people to support, I'm aware of that,' she went on, alluding to Chloe, whom she loved with her very bones, but who wasn't planned at the end of the day, 'but now I want to do it in a way that fulfils me. Why do you insist on putting me down?'

'I'm not putting you down. You've just got too many balls in the air. It's a fact.'

'Right.' Andrea felt her hackles rising. 'So let's look at the facts, shall we? Woman multitasks because she has to: fact. This is fine. Woman multitasking includes taking a slice of time for herself, this is not fine: fact.'

'There are only twenty-four hours in a day, Andrea.'

'Which is why I don't want to spend eight of them doing something that no longer interests me. I need a change of direction. I can do this. I want to. Why do you think I can't?'

'Because there's not enough of you to go around as it is!'

'There might be if you'd help out more!' Andrea snapped, and then nipped hard on her bottom lip. She was doing exactly what she didn't want to do, arguing. Because he wanted to? She looked back into his eyes, eyes which had changed somehow, from tranquil to tumultuous, truculent even. Why? Was he that scared of change? Did he want to take off in another direction?

'I know there's not enough of me to go around, Jonathan,' Andrea said quietly. 'But that's the whole point, don't you see? I need to get a little piece of myself back for me.'

'Fine, whatever,' Jonathan acquiesced with a shrug, but his eyes were still set to do battle. Mustering up a smile, he trailed a finger down the length of Chloe's nose, which had her back in wriggle mode in an instant, hands outstretched and whimpering, 'Want Dad-dee.'

'Later, baby,' Jonathan promised, planting a kiss on her soft peachy cheek. 'Daddy has to go to work, but I'll bring you some sweeties back. How's that?'

'Choclat,' Chloe said, somewhat subdued by the promise of sweeties.

Andrea searched Jonathan's face, trying to work out what it was he really wanted. His classic good looks seemed more chiselled somehow. He looked older, but still young for his age. Five years younger than her, she reminded herself, making him eligible marriage material for many less encumbered women. What was he doing with a woman with three children whose only hope of seeing a size ten again was to look at her daughter? 'I'd better go.' She glanced down and then back. 'We'll talk later, yes?'

20

Jonathan looked at her, as if he was going to say something, but stopped himself short. 'Yes, fine.' He smiled, but it was a half-hearted attempt, Andrea could tell. 'I've got a late appointment, so I'll meet you at the restaurant, assuming we've someone to keep an eye on the kids, that is?'

Andrea decided not to incite yet more argument by insisting that Ryan, though so laid-back he was almost horizontal sometimes, was perfectly capable of babysitting Chloe, had they asked him, and certainly didn't need babysitting himself. 'Sophie and Ryan are out, if you recall,' she repeated what she'd told him when they'd made the weeknight restaurant booking, which apparently suited Jonathan's evening appointment schedule. 'As I also mentioned, Mum and Chloe will be over at Sally's watching animated films. She's only just back from visiting her mum, but she's usually reliable, so ... we're good to go.'

Jonathan nodded, still not looking exactly overjoyed, Andrea noted. 'See you later, then.' She forced a smile and turned quickly away, a peculiar knot in her stomach as she wondered whether he'd rather not see her later.

How does she do it? Sally wondered, noticing Andrea heading back to her house as she emerged from her own cottage two doors down to deposit a recyclable. How did a full-time teacher with three children always manage to look so fantastically put together when her clothes were thrown on? Literally. Sally had watched Andrea select her outfit in awe on the odd occasion she'd called for her to walk to school, rummaging blindly in her wardrobe, her mind on her family, then tugging on whatever came to hand.

The result: casual, yet sophisticated with minimal effort. Who else their age in the village could wear retro Oxfam and get away with it? Her make-up would be minimal, too, Sally knew. She sighed and turned back to her door. No blending foundation, eyeshadow, or blusher for Andrea. 'Until someone invents a one-pot potion one can apply whilst one pees, my face goes au naturel, broken veins, blotches and all,' she'd said once. The amazing thing was Andrea wasn't conceited. She was just plain pretty. 'Effortless,' Sally's husband had once observed, his eyes roving over her as Andrea had circulated at her birthday party, 'like she's not trying too hard.'

'Yes, well, a woman whose man obviously adores her wouldn't need to try too hard, would she?' Sally had retorted, watching peeved over her drink as Jonathan had walked up behind Andrea to plant a soft kiss on the nape of her neck, naturally, as lovers do. She hadn't meant to be bitchy. Andrea was her friend. A good friend, but the thing was Sally had been trying to compete with the twenty-something slut she absolutely knew Nick was having an affair with at the time. She couldn't hope to, of course, not without surgery.

Dragging a hand over her own blotchy face, Sally tried to quell a pang of jealousy at Andrea's apparent happiness. Things weren't quite as picture-perfect as the fulfilled mother and baby scene would have one believe, Sally was aware. Chloe's rosy cheeks were more to do with teething problems than contentment, Andrea had said a while back, confiding that, though she loved Chloe fiercely and never regretted for a second having her, sometimes a toddler on top of two teenagers seemed one child too many. Sally tugged in a shuddery breath, her hand straying to her midriff.

She wished Andrea hadn't confided, at least not that particular snippet. She'd regretted it immediately, distraught that she'd been so careless of Sally's feelings around pregnancy and motherhood. Andrea was like that, sympathetic and thoughtful.

Sally wished she'd been able to confide in Andrea then that her sham of a marriage had reached the tit-for-tat stage.

That in some misguided attempt to get Nick's attention, get anyone's attention, she'd offered herself like a tart on a plate to the first man who'd noticed her. She'd toyed with the idea of telling Andrea, but her pride wouldn't let her – and she'd been hoping, she supposed, that her marriage might survive.

It hadn't, of course, because apparently she'd ended it. Hah! She follows her husband on a business trip she knows damn well is all pleasure and *she'd* ended the marriage? Sally's anger rose afresh, like bile in her throat she couldn't spit out. Just as it had when she'd caught him red-handed.

She'd met her illicit lover that same night, in her hotel bar. After watching – like some sad heroine in a rom-com – Nick engaging in oral foreplay with his little tramp as he'd entered her apartment, Sally had returned to her hotel to try to wash the pain from her heart. She'd noticed him after a while, the man she'd met earlier when checking in. He'd seemed pleasant and easy-going. He was definitely easy on the eye. And there he was again, apparently also on his own. She'd joined him. Why not? she'd thought, several wines bolstering her confidence. He'd been amiable, receptive. And she used him, shamelessly. Yes, she had needed to be reassured, desired. Oh, and how. They were ships that passed in the night, that was all. She'd convinced herself of that as she slipped silently from his room the next morning. Two lonely people seeking brief solace from the storm of their respective rocky relationships. No one would ever know but her.

She hadn't wanted anyone to know then. She'd still wanted Nick. She'd even considered sharing him. Nick hadn't wanted her though. Sally swallowed hard. Had she really thought so little of herself?

When he had found out, when she'd blurted it out in her anger and frustration during the awful row they'd had a week ago, he'd packed his bags and left and she'd run to her mother's for a shoulder to cry on. In truth, she was glad he knew. She'd wanted him to be angry, distraught, destroyed. Even then, she'd been clinging to the hope that another man finding her attractive might rekindle her husband's desire. Pathetic. She'd handed him his get-out card. Nick's reaction had been to finally, cruelly, crush any hope she might have had.

One mistake she'd made. One tiny mistake, her pain driving her. 'Can you really blame me?' she'd asked him.

Oh, yes. The adage 'it meant nothing' only applies to men it seems. 'Women don't do emotionally detached sex. They give themselves body and soul to a man,' Nick had spat, quoting back what she'd told him when she'd discovered the nauseating truth about his affair when it had first started. She'd been hoping to make him see how deeply he'd hurt her, sleeping with his slut, even when she'd been pregnant.

The look in his eye had been one of utter contempt. Sally stifled a sob as she recalled how he'd banged furiously around the bedroom, crashing drawers and slamming cupboards, stuffing clothes in bags, as if he were the injured party.

And then, he'd gone. Permanently.

What comes around goes around, Sally supposed, her heart wrenching afresh as she stood in the cold light of a new day feeling lonelier than she'd ever felt. 'Cheaters' don't change their spots, she should have known. Nick had been married when she'd met him, after all. All he'd ever really wanted was an affair, uncomplicated sex, carnal desires satiated, no strings. It had been satiating too. Hot hungry sex, fired by the illicit thrill of it. Lips eagerly seeking each other's, tongues searching, limbs entwining. The piquant taste of forbidden fruit as he'd made urgent love to her. And then, the bittersweet taste of tears when he'd left.

Sally hadn't been able to let him go, though. She'd been far too addicted to the man, too intoxicated by his touch to give him up. She hadn't had to try too hard to keep him back then. She'd been younger. She'd loved him. She'd wanted him, and she'd won him. Nick had eventually left his wife and his children. He hadn't wanted more children. She'd known that, too, deep down. Shackles with which to tie him down.

Sally heaved out a sigh that came from her soul, and then squeezed her eyes shut tight, to no avail. The tears came anyway. Great, dollopy tears, rolling down her cheeks to splat onto her breast, no matter that she'd already sobbed until she'd retched dry tears and thought she simply couldn't cry any more.

It had been hard finally realising she had lost him. Sally ran a hand over the soft round of her tummy. It had been harder still losing her baby.

Chapter Three

Sophie emerged from Andrea's en suite in her Cheeky Monkey slippers and her 'Do I look like a morning person?' T-shirt, which she'd pulled on over a zebra print bra and pants set she wasn't sure her mother would approve of. Fashioning a towel into a turban around her hair, she padded along the landing, then stopped and did a double take. 'Gran!'

She gawked as Dee slinked from her bedroom to bop along the landing, with not bad rhythm, Sophie had to concede, for an old grinkly.

'Gran!' Sophie yelled again as Dee bopped on. 'Oooh, Gran!' Stomping after her, Sophie patted her firmly on the shoulder. And if she died of fright, serve the dotty old bat right. What was she doing, wearing *her* crocheted sequined top and cardigan? Unbelievable!

Dee twizzled around to beam Sophie a smile. 'Yes, dear?'

Sophie circled a finger at Dee's midriff. 'What's this?' she enquired after the attire her gran had obviously stolen from her wardrobe to complement her own purple velour jogging bottoms.

'Sorry?' Dee blinked, the epitome of innocence.

Sophie rolled her eyes. 'I said—'

'Can't hear you, dear,' Dee shouted, pointing a finger of her own to indicate Sophie's iPod earphones stuffed in her ears.

'I don't flipping believe this. I SAID …' Sophie plucked up the hem of the top between thumb and forefinger '… what … are … you … wear-ring?'

Dee glanced down. 'Oh, this old thing.' She flapped a dismissive hand. 'I've had it for ages.'

'Old?' Sophie almost had apoplexy. She'd blown all her birthday money on that top, along with her bra and pants set. It was brand new.

'My grandmother's,' Dee imparted, a nostalgic glint in her eye. 'It's hand crocheted, you know.'

'It's not.' Sophie folded her arms and agitatedly tapped a monkey-faced mule. 'It's New Look and it's mine.'

'Pardon, dear?'

'I said … God!' Reaching up, Sophie twanged an earphone from under her gran's curls. 'I said … it's mine!'

'Is it?' Dee said over the Black Eyed Peas drifting from the iPod.

'Yes! And so is the—'

'Could have sworn it was mine.' Dee dropped her puzzled gaze to the top.

'Well, it's not,' Sophie pointed out, not very patiently, patience not being her thing. 'Now, could you take it off, please? I have to go to school. Like, today?' Even with a free period first lesson, she was *so* going to be late.

At which point Dee plucked up the hem of Sophie's cardigan, arms splayed each side, and started swaying, startlingly. 'They're buzzing.' She nodded knowledgeably, then emitted a noise like a slow-dying fly.

Sophie curled a lip. Gone, she thought. Gaga. Mind has officially left the …

Dee cut Sophie's speculation worryingly short. 'I'm a bee,' she sang, turning on the spot like an inebriated ballerina. 'I'm a bee on the next level. I'm a bee rockin' over that bass treble,' she sang on, accompanying the lyrics she was obviously listening to – and tottering forth.

Towards the top of the stairs.

'Mum! Quick!!' Sophie bawled as Andrea came through the front door. 'Gran thinks she's got wings.'

Andrea deposited Chloe in the hall and charged up the

stairs – to find her normally obstreperous daughter arm-in-arm with her grandmother, both doing a waltz on the landing.

Morning pandemonium over and crisis averted, thanks to Sophie's quick thinking, Dee, Chloe and Andrea were finally fully dressed and on their way, though she was running very late, unfortunately. Thank goodness Nita, on work experience in the school office and, frankly, invaluable, had managed to get someone to cover registration for her. Well, almost fully dressed. Andrea glanced sideways at her mother, and then bemusedly down at her feet. Drizzle on the air and damp underfoot it might be, but Dee was now determinedly eschewing wearing her wellies in favour of slippers. Ah, well, it was only a short walk to Chloe's nursery, and from there a few yards up to the drop-in centre and at least the slippers were easy on her mother's bunions.

'Morning, Eva,' Andrea called over to where Eva was hard at work on her prize vegetables in the front garden of her little half-bricked cottage as they passed by. Gosh, she was always at it, Hibberton's very own eco-warrior. 'Don't overdo it, will you? Don't want you straining anything.'

Eva, a robust woman with cheeks the colour of ripe tomatoes, straightened up and scraped back a wisp of steely-grey hair. 'Oh, I'm as strong as an ox, my dear,' she assured her. 'Bit of hard work never hurt anyone.'

Dee, walking on Andrea's inside, peered around her. 'Should have been a sergeant major,' she observed of the redoubtable ex-headmistress.

'Mum, shush.' Andrea glanced sideways, hoping Eva hadn't overheard.

'Well, she gets on my pip with her silly war effort mentality, as if growing mouldy old vegetables is going to save the planet. She'd have us all growing cabbage and swash up the trellis if she had her way. Once a schoolteacher, always a bossy boots, I say.'

'Ye-es. Thank you, Mum.' Andrea smiled flatly, aware of her mother's propensity to forget her daughter was a schoolteacher, and hoisted Chloe higher in her arms. 'And it's squash.'

'What's squashed?' Dee glanced at her, puzzled.

'Not squashed. Squash, the vegetable growing up the … Never mind.' Andrea stopped as Eva wiped her muddy hands on her yellow outdoor trousers and came across, her stride purposeful, bar a slight dip to her dodgy hip.

'Andrea.' She nodded and offered her a bright but efficient smile. 'Any news on the SOGS campaign?' she enquired after their Save Our Green Space efforts, vis-à-vis the open space adjoining the school. Builders had already applied for planning permission for fifty residential properties. It would be a terrible shame to lose what was basically natural woodland – ergo a rich source of education for the children – but lose it they might.

'Oh, you know, gathering momentum,' Andrea said, a lie she couldn't hope to get past Miss Bunting, her very own beady-eyed headmistress as a child.

'Momentum, my eye,' Dee muttered to Andrea's dismay. 'Like a blooming bicycle without wheels, if you ask me.'

Andrea sighed and swapped Chloe to her other arm. She'd spotted Eva's sooty black cat padding along the pavement and was in serious wriggle mode.

'Sorry, Deirdre, I'm not quite sure I understand.' Eva laced her fingers under her ample bosom and eyed Dee patiently over her glasses. And managed to look rather superior, Andrea noticed, which would be bound to get Dee's goat up.

'The townsfolk couldn't be arsed to turn up,' Dee clarified, the emphasis on 'arsed' no doubt for maximum shock effect.

'Oh, I see.' Eva arched an eyebrow and looked disdainfully

down her nose. 'In which case, we'll have to see if we can offer them a little incentive, won't we? I think perhaps trying to give them a sense of pride in their community might work, don't you?' she suggested, her tone now definitely patronising.

'Yes. We could start by insisting on eyesores being removed from front gardens.' Dee looked Eva pointedly up and down.

'Wonderful idea,' Andrea interjected, before there were fisticuffs on the street. 'The community pride thing, I mean. If the planning permission goes ahead, maybe we could enlist some help turning part of the playground into a garden area?'

Eva looked delighted. 'Marvellous idea, my dear,' she said, reaching out to give Chloe's baby-plump cheek an over affectionate pinch, which would probably have the child apoplectic in a flash. 'Isn't it, my little munchkin?' Eva went on, producing a peapod in a mysterious manner from her pocket as Chloe looked on, obviously too surprised for spontaneous shrieking.

'It's magic,' Eva said of her peapod. 'It has jewels in it, see?' She unzipped it, popped a pea in her mouth and ate it. 'Ooh, yummy, scrummy in my tummy,' she sang.

Dee looked at Eva as if something had gone wrong, like her head. 'Would you like it?' Eva asked, holding the pod out to Chloe. 'It's a very special peapod but we can grow some more with lots of love and magic, can't we?'

Chloe, who had 'magically' ceased all fidgeting, glanced uncertainly at Eva, then shyly reached out, took the pod, popped a pea in her mouth and gleefully chewed on it.

'Unbelievable.' Andrea laughed. 'That must be the first time she's eaten a whole vegetable, albeit a little one. Thank you, Eva. You're a star.'

Eva glowed. 'It's all in the presentation, my dear,' she imparted, turning to cross the road back to her garden.

'Yes.' Dee glanced at the seat of Eva's yellow gardening trousers as she walked away, which had obviously had a close encounter with the fruits of her labours. 'Beautifully presented, my dear,' Dee observed – loudly – as she eyed the splotched tomatoes thereon smugly.

'Mum, stop it,' Andrea hissed, then almost disappeared inside her shoes as Eva turned back. 'Oh, Andrea …?'

Oh, Lord, she'd heard. 'Yes, Eva?' Andrea answered lightly.

'Do you think you could remind Jonathan to give me a call about my investment portfolio? Or drop by sometime? I need to make a withdrawal as soon as possible in regard to the works on the shop, you see.'

'Sorry, Eva. He was tied up in meetings I think.' Guessing he was under pressure, Andrea covered for Jonathan. 'I did mention it again this morning and he said he'd do it today.' Andrea smiled and steered Dee on, before she felt obliged to comment, no doubt inappropriately.

Dee didn't disappoint. 'As in a withdrawal from her account and straight into his, more likely.'

'Mum …' Andrea despaired. 'Her son's not that bad. Honestly, talk about lack of community spirit. Can't you two bury the hatchet and just get along?'

'*Me?*' Dee gasped, affronted. 'It was Hibberton's sad answer to Charlie Dimmock who started it, thinking she's an authority on everything just because she was a headmistress. Never missed an opportunity to tell me how to bring up my children.' Dee stuck out her chin indignantly. 'And look how her perfect son turned out. Only ever bothers to turn up when he's short of cash. Humph.'

'Don't Mum.' Andrea glanced back to Eva, now hard at work in the soil, which was, Andrea knew, Eva's way of filling the long lonely hours since her layabout son had moved out, only ever paying her a visit when he wanted something. 'It's not Eva's fault her son's like he is. We can't blame everything on our parents, can we?'

Dee opened her mouth, and then closed it again.

Her charges finally despatched, Chloe at the nursery and Dee at the drop-in centre at the village hall –which Dee, on first attendance, had promptly re-named drop-dead-in centre – Andrea headed back to pick up Sally before heading off in the opposite direction to the school.

Sally had said she was running late as well when Andrea rang. No surprise there. True, Andrea was late herself today, but she wasn't generally if she could avoid it. Sally, on the other hand ... Well, as an example to the children regarding timekeeping, teaching assistant Sally Anderson was not a good one.

Andrea tried not to mind though. Sally and she had hit it off immediately when she and her then fiancé, Nick, had moved to the village, in search of rural tranquillity and a cleaner, safer place to bring up her children, Sally had confided. Also confiding that she'd invited practically the whole village to her wedding because she was scared of being alienated in a community where everyone knew everyone.

Andrea smiled as she remembered how Sally had set about winning the locals over, the men with fluttery eyes and the women with compliments on their dress sense, as she walked up the path to Sally's cottage.

She knocked on Sally's front door, mulling over an idea as she did. Inviting Eva's participation might actually be a way to solve her playground garden problem. If the green space went, the children would definitely need some kind of alternative, and what better than a 'magic garden' where flowers and vegetables, rather than the current weeds, thrived? Andrea would love to see that underway before she left.

No answer from Sally. Andrea checked her watch, and then knocked again. And waited.

'Coming,' Sally finally called.

'Lord! Sally?' Andrea balked as Sally swung her door wide, her normally perfectly made-up face looking more like Eva's tomato-blotched bottom.

'Sally, what on earth …? Has something happened? Are you sick?'

'Yes,' Sally said in a little voice, her bottom lip quivering. 'Of men!'

Oh, dear. Another couple at loggerheads, it seemed. Andrea ushered her tearful friend inside. 'Come on, tell me all about it,' she said, wrapping an arm around Sally's shoulders as she guided her to the kitchen.

'He's left me,' Sally blurted, once seated at her recycled and lovingly waxed farmhouse table.

'What?' Andrea's mouth fell open. 'When?'

'Before I went to my mother's. We had a terrible argument and …' She stopped, and swallowed.

'But I thought you were—'

'Trying for another baby?' Sally gulped back another sob. 'I was. He wasn't so keen on the idea. Had a narrow escape the first time, obviously.'

That was awful! Sally had lost her baby at five months. She'd been desperate to get pregnant again. 'Oh, Sally …' No wonder the poor woman had taken off when she should have been at work. She'd obviously needed some space to try to come to terms with the end of her marriage. Andrea reached across the table to squeeze her friend's hand. 'I'm so sorry, sweetie.'

Sally nodded and dragged a tissue under her nose. 'He, um, did want one though, it turns out.'

'What?' Andrea stared at her friend, disbelieving. The man hadn't got someone else pregnant, had he? That would be too cruel.

Twisting her tortured tissue into a rope, Sally enlightened her. 'Well, a babe anyway. He's been bedding one on a regular basis,' she said, quite still now, apart from a slow tear sliding down her cheek. 'It started when I was pregnant. He denied it at first, of course, but ... Well, you just know, don't you?'

'I, um ...' Shit, Andrea reached again for Sally's hand – and quietly cursed Nick to damnation. How could he? Why would he? Sally was beautiful, elegant, talented. Andrea glanced around at Sally's also elegant home, individually and tastefully decorated with rescued pieces. What was the matter with the man?

Andrea tightened her grip on Sally's hand and waited, every conceivable curse wedged in her windpipe. It would do no good to voice them. Sally had probably thought and said them all. She didn't need anyone else reinforcing what a lowlife her husband was.

'Fresh fruit, I suppose.' Sally shrugged, but looked so desolate Andrea felt her own heart breaking inside her. 'Early twenties, from what I could see when he was drooling all over her.'

Andrea frowned.

'I followed him,' she answered Andrea's confused expression. 'He'd said he was away on business. *Hah!* More like doing the business. They were practically shagging on the street. Not a crow's foot or droop in sight, the little slut.'

Thus the Botox, which Andrea had suspected Sally had been having. Sally was desperately trying to iron out her creases to compete with her younger rival. Honestly, did she not know how attractive she was?

'No brain in sight either, presumably,' Andrea growled.

'Actually, she has a psychology degree,' Sally said lightly – troublingly lightly. 'I called her a bimbo and Nick kindly put me right on the subject.'

'She'll need to use her blooming psychology degree if she's

going out with a deceitful, two-timing, emotion-abusing bastard!' Andrea fumed, thoughts of not voicing her opinions flown out of the window. 'Ooh, how I hope he does unto his new not-so-dim young thing what he's done to you. On the other hand, poetic justice would be if she with the degree reversed the psychology and did unto him, the predictable little twerp!' Andrea finished on a humph.

'Well, Miss Kelly, I'm shocked.' Sally widened her eyes and attempted a wobbly smile. 'You're to stay after school and write out five hundred times, "I must not use such mild language when talking about adulterous rat-bag husbands".'

She squeezed Andrea's hand back. 'I'll be fine,' she said, not very convincingly. 'I'd rather live without him than live a lie with him.'

'I suppose,' Andrea agreed.

'Don't be surprised if you see him with half of his flat screen TV under his arm later, though, whilst clutching his vitals with his other hand. I don't think I'll be able to do dignified and calm very well.'

No, nor would Andrea, but … 'Later?' she asked, puzzled.

'He rang earlier to say he's coming back tonight for his share of our belongings, which obviously wasn't a great start to the day. So I thought I'd be absolutely fair about it and divide them up equal … Oh no, Andrea, your evening out! I forgot all about Chloe and—'

'Sally, it's all right. I can ask Ryan. He's fine about watching Chloe, honestly.'

Sally nodded. 'Don't suppose I'd be very good company anyway, would I?'

'You're always good company,' Andrea said firmly.

Sally smiled sadly. 'Pity Nick didn't think so.'

'We'll go out,' Andrea said, wishing there was something more she could say that would take Sally's pain away. 'We'll organise a girl's night and—'

'Pull a few men?' Sally enquired, with a hint of a twinkle back in her eye.

'Um, how about we pull them apart instead?'

Sally laughed. 'Sounds like a plan. Thanks, hon, for being there. Now, come on,' she hoisted up her shoulders and got to her feet. 'We've work to go to and a certain entrepreneurial someone's Second Chance Designer store to plan at lunchtime. Can't conquer the world if we're sitting here contemplating the meaning of men, can we? We have to make sure at least one of our dreams comes true. Talking of which, I have an exquisite Halston Heritage gown for your evening wear section. You can pick it up later. Just in case the adulterer decides he wants half of that, too, along with half of his flat screen.'

With which, Sally notched up her chin and headed off across her stripped and waxed floor with her head held high, leaving Andrea quite in awe of the strength of the woman.

Chapter Four

Running late, having come straight from the surgery, David abandoned the car on double yellow lines and sprinted for the school. He hadn't bargained on the school run being so stressful in a supposedly sleepy location. It was mayhem. Mothers driving four-by-fours like Formula One racing Ferraris. He could have sworn one came around the corner on two wheels spitting sparks. It would be easier to walk through the woods in future, he decided. At least then he wouldn't have the hassle of parking.

Raking a hand through his hair, he walked more calmly into the playground, knowing that Jake wouldn't be pleased to see him there, even on his first day. The kid had made it obvious he couldn't bear to be in his company for more than two minutes. David didn't blame him.

Swallowing hard, he tried not to look too obviously like a fish out of water, though he could see from the furtive glances and hushed whispers in the playground that that was exactly what he looked like. What he was: a single father, new to the village, and probably soon to be labelled not very sociable. He doubted he'd be swapping small talk at the village shop anytime soon. If there was one thing he was determined to avoid it was fuelling neighbourhood gossip. He'd done enough of that to last a lifetime, making Michelle's and Jake's lives miserable into the bargain. Sighing, David pulled up his collar against the biting wind, and hoped that Jake might at least acknowledge him when he came out of school. Not likely, he realised, after the disastrous start this morning.

'And-ee?' Nita's wheedling tone alerted Andrea to the question before it was asked.

'No,' Andrea replied adamantly, weary after an afternoon that started organising the grand total of two computers for the afternoon skills lesson, and ended in a double lesson of art. She'd grabbed Steph, the PE instructor, as she'd passed by the door and asked her to keep an eye on her class while she located the CD player for tomorrow's oracy session. With Nita's help, she'd found it, finally, and now her feet were killing her. The new boots had been a bad idea.

Grabbing another minute while she could, she plopped down in a chair in the school office to prise off one heel-blistering boot. The art lesson had gone well, though. The mural depicting seasons of the year had been an inspired idea, if Andrea did say so herself. The kids had thought it was cool anyhow, knuckling down to produce templates of bees and birds, foxes, hedgehogs, bugs and spiders against a backdrop of fluffy white cloud and seasonal foliage. It would make an amazing mural for the playground wall beyond the 'magic garden', given she did ever manage to turn it into anything other than a patch of weed.

'Pretty please?'

'All right, Nita.' Andrea sighed, resigned to the task of removal man. 'I'll see if I can get Sally to help out and save your bacon, but make sure you bat the beguiling eyes at some of the male members of staff next time desks need moving, hey?'

'I was going to. My eyelashes were poised, honestly.' Nita fluttered demonstratively. 'But then my mother rang.'

'Ah.' Andrea got the gist. Nita's mother could talk the hind leg off a donkey. Andrea had been in the office the last time she'd rung, watching amused as Nita plopped the phone down on the desk – her mother's tones still drifting therefrom – and leisurely wheeled her wheelchair over to the filing cabinet for a file.

'And I do try to tell her I'm at work, but there's just no pause between words. She's like, "Now-I-know-you're-busy-sweetie, but ..." and off she goes.' Nita threw her hands in the air in despair. 'What can I do?'

Andrea laughed, despite her sore feet.

'She's telephoned to remind me my cousin's coming over this afternoon. I won't be there, I tell her. *Whyevernot?* she says. I'm going to be working, I say. Sheesh, she says, you're only on work experience, Nita. What are they running there? A sweatshop? She'll stop at nothing to match me up with a suitable young man, I swear.'

'I'm sure she means well,' Andrea sympathised, with a tolerant smile. 'I'd better go and find Sally and ask Steph if she wouldn't mind dismissing my class.'

'Sorry, Andrea. I didn't mean to bang on. It's just that you're such a good listener and I don't have anyone else, what with two so-good-they're-golden brothers and a father who popped his clogs rather than risk saying boo to the goose that laid them.'

'There's nothing else for it, I'm going to have to get me a toyboy.' Sally sighed, contemplating the three desks they'd been volunteered to haul across the playground to the temporary Terrapin classroom.

Andrea blinked, astonished. She was all for Sally skipping the self-analysis and going straight for the bulk purchase of impractical raunchy lingerie stage, but wasn't she being just a teeny bit quick off the mark?

'Well, why shouldn't I?' Sally had obviously noted Andrea's bemused expression. 'I'm not ready to cast aside my plunge bra and man-trapper shoes for tan tights and fluffy slippers yet, you know?'

'No reason.' Andrea smiled, doubting Sally would be caught dead in tan tights and slippers, as she positioned herself to grab hold of one end of a desk.

'Precisely.' Sally positioned herself at the other end. 'If

he can have tender young flesh, then so can I. I don't need commitment, not any more. It's too painful. I need a man in his prime. A lean, keen sex machine, with rabbit inclinations in the bedroom.'

'Sally!' Andrea gawped at her. 'You're not going to become one of those panther people, are you?'

Sally laughed. 'Cougars, honey. You make them sound like Pan's People unleashed. And why not? Younger men aren't the domain of the Sharon Stones of this world, you know. I'm not nearly as near to my prime as she is anyway. If she can, I can.'

Andrea didn't doubt it. At just thirty-seven and looking a lot younger in Andrea's estimation, Sally could probably out-cougar most women. 'But what would you actually do with a toyboy?' she mused.

Sally arched an eyebrow suggestively. 'Um, now, let me think ...'

'I meant outside the bedroom, Sally. You're bound to get bored when you find his conversation is limited to football and bloke jokes.'

'Who cares?' Sally said as they negotiated their way down the corridor. 'Do I mind if his vocabulary's small as long as his—'

'Ahem!' Andrea coughed loudly as a stray pupil straggled past.

'—attention span isn't.' Sally smirked.

Andrea rolled her eyes despairingly. 'Bad girl.'

'I'm not getting any younger, though, am I, Andrea?' Sally went on more seriously as the two women, plus desk, progressed precariously down the school steps. 'Another relationship would be nice, but that's not going to happen anytime soon, is it? In any case, even if I was ready for one, I'm not sure I want to settle for a less than perfect love again. You know, I don't think Nick ever really—Oh no!'

'What?' Andrea asked, alarmed as Sally stopped abruptly and plonked the desk down in the junior playground.

'Nothing. I, um … Hot flush, obviously.' Sally flapped a hand in front of her face. 'I think I'll just go and get a drink of water.'

'Do you want me to come with you?' Andrea asked, concerned. Sally was looking most definitely peaky.

'No, I'm fine. You stay. Looks like we've a stranger in our midst.' Sally nodded quickly behind her as she hurried back to the school.

Andrea glanced in the direction Sally had nodded. Oh, no, it was him, Mr Obnoxious himself. An intimidating, aggressive man, if ever she saw one. Was he, though? Andrea was often too quick to jump to conclusions. It shouldn't really be any of her business, but then, the man's child obviously now attended the junior part of the school, which made it her business, even though she worked in the infant school. She might well have blundered in on no more than a family argument this morning, though. Children could drive you to metaphorical murder, Andrea was well aware of that, and the last thing she wanted to do was make waves if it was nothing more. But still, there was no doubt in Andrea's mind that this man was bad-tempered. Not that you'd guess it to look at him now, standing alone and obviously feeling awkward amidst the majority of women in the playground. And inviting all eyes, she couldn't help but notice.

'I tell you what,' a young mum close by said, coiffing her bob and nudging the mum next to her, 'I wouldn't throw him out of bed.'

Andrea shook her head as she watched the group of women gossiping excitedly and glancing towards him. Honestly, what was it about moody sorts that had women's hearts and eyelashes all aflutter? Yes, he was handsome, all buttoned up and broody in his dark overcoat and four o'clock shadow but, as Andrea could attest to, he had about as much charisma as Jack Nicholson, frozen to death in *The Shining*.

What luck that she had a man whose attractions were more than skin-deep. At least, she hoped she had. Andrea couldn't get Jonathan's half-hearted smile this morning out of her head. She couldn't blame him if he was having second thoughts. Would any man in his right mind want to share his lover with a mad mother, two teenagers and a toddler? A woman who didn't have the time to take on board his insecurities?

Or was it more that she didn't have the inclination to?

Confused, and somehow feeling a little exposed, Andrea headed back towards the school, aware of her neighbour in her peripheral vision, tugging up his collar, looking every inch like Heathcliff in a bad mood.

'So does he have a name, our Ben Affleck lookalike?' she overheard one eager mother ask another as she walked past.

'That's Doctor Adams,' another mother supplied importantly. 'He's the new general practitioner at the health centre,' she gushed on, enthusiastically imparting what was obviously the most exciting thing to hit Hibberton since Sincerely ABBA played the village hall.

'Is he now?' Eager mum sounded delighted. 'Well, I'd say he'd know which bits go where in the baby making department, wouldn't you?'

The local GP! Hell! She'd have to move surgeries. No matter how qualified he was vis-à-vis which bits go where in the baby making department, he was absolutely not getting a glimpse of hers. Andrea hurried on, making a mental note to check whether she was on his list as she did – and to check out young Jake's records in the office tomorrow. The boy seemed to be in the sole custody of his father. Why, Andrea didn't know. She couldn't help but wonder, though.

The bitter custody battle she'd had with Ryan and Sophie's father came to mind. The lies he'd told, attempting to rubbish her as a parent. Not because he'd wanted his children. Far from it, he'd been an uncaring, uncompromising man, who simply couldn't bear to lose. Was Doctor Adams of a similar ilk, she pondered, possibly using his good standing as a doctor to sway the courts?

'Excuse me, Miss ...?' a male voice said behind her, almost giving her a heart attack.

Zipping on her professional face, Andrea turned slowly around. 'Kelly,' she supplied. 'Yes?' She offered him a short smile, determined to be courteous, despite their awkward earlier meeting.

'David Adams,' he introduced himself, finally offering her his hand. 'I wanted to apologise for this morning. I was a little distracted, I'm afraid. Bad start to the day.'

'Oh, right.' Andrea nodded, noting the slight thaw in his gaze.

'Please extend my apologies to your, er ...' he hesitated, apparently distracted again as the junior bell rang, '... grandmother,' he finished, looking back at Andrea.

'Mother,' Andrea corrected him dryly. And that kind of blatant flattery, Doctor Adams, will get you nowhere, particularly with Dee, she thought, unimpressed.

Andrea yawned as she hurried from school to the Happy Hours nursery, where Chloe had howled and clutched at her skirt when she'd left her there this morning. And now, thanks to desk removal duty, she was late collecting her, again.

Damn. She tried to blend with the walls as she slipped inside. No dice. The nursery nurse greeted her with a scowl and a ready-coated charge. Andrea sighed as she trailed out, a bandaged Igglepiggle in one hand and a jiggling toddler attached to the other. A toddler whose expression had switched fast from hopeful to petulant now Andrea had said no to fast food for dinner.

'Want vlanilla.' Chloe dragged her feet, scuffing the toes of her Timberland toddler boots, which had cost Andrea an arm and a leg.

'We can't, darling. Ronald's ...' Andrea thought fast as to feasible reasons why McDonald's wasn't on the menu. '... poorly.'

Chloe knitted her little brow thoughtfully. 'Like Igglepiggle?'

'Just like Igglepiggle, sweetie.' Andrea crouched down to rub the bandage where once was a head.

Obviously gauging her mood, Chloe decided on a trade-off rather than a tantrum. 'Chips, then,' she said, glancing wide-eyed from under her eyelashes.

Andrea looked into eyes crystal clear with the innocence of childhood and wondered how anyone could possibly resist. 'Chips it is.' She smiled resignedly.

'Wiv ketchup?'

'Yes, with ketch ... Ooh!' Andrea stopped outside her drive. 'Bloody hell!' She gawped at the soft top BMW blocking it. What was he trying to do? Force home the fact that he was totally rude?

She was going to have to have a few words with the man-of-few-words, David Adams, she decided, her fuse fizzling as she turned on her heel, stepped off the kerb, and straight into the man himself.

'Whoops,' he said, catching hold of her forearms as she all but barrelled into him. 'Sorry about the car,' he added immediately. 'There's a water leak. Workmen are due out. I'll move it as soon as I can.'

'Thank you. That would be most kind,' Andrea said, her cheeks heating up at the thought of what she had been about to impart. 'Right, well, I'd better, um ...' Unsure what else to say, her concerns for his son being the only thing she felt inclined to discuss with the man, though preferably not in the street, Andrea waved a hand behind her.

'Right.' He nodded and managed a smile. Nice smile, actually. Yes, and one no doubt practised on many a susceptible female.

'Good night, Mr Adams,' she said curtly.

'And to you, Miss Kelly,' he said as Andrea turned abruptly away.

Well, that was just plain unfair. Sally couldn't help feeling miffed as she watched David Adams, who Nita had been desperate to give her the goss on when she'd gone back to the office, practically embracing Andrea. And what on earth had Andrea been doing gazing into his eyes? Checking for contact lenses?

Sally took a step closer to the window. As close as she dared in the Intrigue purple and noir raunchy lingerie she'd bought as a last ditch attempt at seducing her husband. Hah! That had worked. He hadn't even bothered to come home that night, obviously preferring the slut's seduction technique. She'd been thinking about taking the underwear back again, until her eyes fell upon the good doctor this afternoon. He who was now a new resident in the village, it seemed. And actually better looking than Nick with his dark hair and strong profile. Yes, Doctor Adams definitely had what it took in the genes department.

She ran her hands over the tight-fitting silken attire she tried on again for size, almost feeling David's hands trailing in their wake. Her heart might be broken, but her spirit wasn't. If anything, Sally was more determined than ever. As a teenager, her hormones flying all over the place, hadn't she swallowed back the hurt and told herself she was worth loving, even though her father – the one man who should have loved her enough to be part of her life – couldn't be bothered? Hadn't she been resolute in her efforts to make sure Nick became part of her life?

No, she wouldn't allow her husband's pathetic affairs with younger women to corrode her confidence, not now. Nick wasn't the only fish in the sea, was he? There were other men out there, David Adams for one.

She wasn't exactly ugly, was she? And her figure, despite the odd bump, was still good. Wasn't it? Sally's eyes flickered to her full breasts, which looked reasonably presentable, uplifted in all the right places.

Yes, David Adams might just have made an opportune appearance and Sally was sure he would like what he saw, assuming he could prise his eyes away from Andrea. Sally watched on, feeling more than a bit peeved now, as she noted him watching Andrea walk into her house. Having a good look, too, judging by the curious tilt of his head.

At least three repeated bloody hells from the mouth of her babe later, Andrea let herself in through the front door, where a cacophony of music assaulted her ears. Ryan was blasting ear-splitting indie from his bedroom, while Sophie was in pop mode. Despairing at her own children's adept ability to drive her to distraction, Andrea debated again David Adams and the obvious argument he'd had with his son that morning. Had it been just that, an argument? One of many possibly, which was, after all, perfectly normal when kids reached the age where they challenged a parent's authority?

Worried about how she should tackle it, whether she should, Andrea headed to the kitchen, where Dee, being more mature in her tastes, was blasting out 'Die Another Day', along with Madonna on Radio Two. 'I've so much more to do,' she sang, cavorting across the kitchen, dripping colander in hand.

'Hi, Mum,' Andrea said, pleased that Ryan had remembered to pick up his grandmother after college.

'Potatoes are peeled,' Dee said, dripping back again. 'And the washing's pegged out.'

Andrea deposited Chloe in front of her Burger Bar, fully equipped with chip fryer to encourage a healthy diet and a microphone, through which Chloe was able to demonstrate the new words she'd learned today. She then strolled across to glance in the saucepan, where she found the potatoes were indeed peeled, bar one or two, or ten. Ah, well, there were probably vitamins therein.

The washing was pegged out, she noticed through the window. Unfortunately, it didn't appear to be washed, but that didn't qualify as the end of the world either. Andrea smiled, despite her exhaustion, because Dee looked tickled pink to be doing what she'd been doing all her life, albeit in rather a hit-and-miss fashion.

'Good day at the drop-in centre?' Andrea enquired, seating herself at her own rescued kitchen table, which had been lovingly restored, but which wasn't quite so lovingly maintained unfortunately, bearing many a telltale scar of family at war at mealtimes.

'Marvellous.' Dee reached for the tenderiser and decimated the steak. 'Madge Riley stopped complaining and cheered everyone up.'

'Oh? How's that?' Andrea tugged off her boots before she went lame, then padded across her kitchen, which, with its homey smells, magnets adorning the fridge and hand paintings pinned haphazardly to walls, could never aspire to Sally's beautifully organised rustic simplicity, but which Andrea felt was truly the heart of her home.

'Curled up her toes, miserable old cow. Dead as a dodo.'

'*Mum.*'

'And that nice Walter Stevens asked me to have sex with him.'

Andrea cringed. '*Mum.*'

'Liven the place up a bit though, wouldn't it?' Dee chuckled, delighted with her wit, and walloped the steaks under the grill.

Delighted, though, wasn't how Andrea would describe her little darlings' faces when presented with the steaks.

'Want chips!' Chloe squealed, close to convulsion at the sight of bloody meat and two veg adorning her plate. Ryan curled a lip and headed for the fridge in search of bread and cheese, while Dee, oblivious to all, chewed, and chewed. So determined was she to digest, Andrea worried she might swallow her teeth.

'Sophie,' Andrea called again, 'your di—'

'—dead cow's on the table,' Ryan finished predictably.

'Thank you, Ryan.' Andrea sighed, awaiting Sophie's inevitable response as she sloped into the kitchen. Prompted once again by her own children's undoubtedly wearing behaviour, her mind wandered to David Adams. If she mentioned anything at the school, she could be making a terrible mistake. And if she didn't? She'd have to, she decided. At least then, the staff would be alerted to a possible problem.

'Ugh, that is soooo disgusting,' Sophie obliged. 'I'd rather starve to death.'

'Won't take long, will it, beanpole?' Ryan quipped.

'Ryan, enough!' Andrea warned. 'And Sophie, eat something, now please, or you stay home tonight.'

'God! That is so typical! Treat me like a child, why don't you?' Sophie clanged her chair out and plopped herself moodily down by way of response.

'I can't imagine why.' Andrea eyed her sulky fifteen-year-old daughter wearily. 'Don't worry about it, Mum. She won't eat fresh air lately without counting the calorie—' Andrea stopped, finding Dee looking not at all worried as she speared Sophie's steak from her plate.

Oh, the joys of mother/daughterhood. Andrea shook her head and went in search of curl fries for Chloe, hoping to convince her to eat a bit of 'magic tree' broccoli alongside them.

'Catchya later,' Sophie called coming down the stairs as Andrea presented Chloe with fries and broccoli, the latter cunningly disguised with lots of ketchup.

'Uh-uh. I just said, Sophie, you don't eat, you don't go out,' Andrea reminded her, watching despairingly as her far-too-cute toddler licked a green spear clean of sauce and then discarded it for another.

'I am eating. Later. Hannah's mum's doing lasagne.'

'Make sure you do. And make sure to be back by ten, Sophie. No arguments.'

'Okey-dokey,' Sophie replied cheerily.

Pardon? Andrea glanced curiously over her shoulder, and then did a double take as Sophie flashed past the kitchen door.

'Sophie!' Andrea skidded after her. Okey-dokey, indeed. 'Come back here!'

'Pants,' Sophie muttered, turning at the open front door to roll over-made-up eyes. 'What now? I'm late.'

'You have two choices, Sophie – you are either late, or you stay home, because you are not going out in those.'

Sophie bent to examine leopard print legs, which were topped with the wisp of denim she called shorts. 'What's wrong with them? They're leggings.'

'Yeah, but it helps if you've got legs-in them, chopstick,' Ryan said wittily, poking his head around the lounge door.

'Oh, ha-di-ha-ha. Very funny pigeon-chest.' Sophie gave him a ladylike sit-on-it sign. 'Why don't you go upstairs and fantasise about being a man.'

Ryan returned the gesture. 'I am a man, metal-mouth,' he informed her, now making fun of her braces, to Andrea's utter despair. 'This is why I don't have to wear gel-padded bras and pretend I've got boobs.'

'Ryan, be quiet!' Andrea snapped, wondering when her little darlings had turned into absolute monsters.

'Yeah, shut your mouth, muppet.' Sophie smirked, triumphant. 'Mum, I have to go.' She jiggled impatiently. 'I'll be late.'

'Sophie, get in, and get dressed, please. And, Ryan, one more word and you're grounded!'

'Oh, M-u-m, I've got nothing else to wear.' Sophie flounced past, wearing as close to nothing as was possible whilst passing as fully dressed.

Andrea eyed the swatch of cloth adorning her posterior despairingly. 'What about wearing the frilled hem skirt instead of the shorts?' she suggested, the skirt at least having enough material to decently cover her daughter's bum cheeks, ergo not making her stick out like a Belisha beacon in the town centre, which is where, Andrea suspected, Sophie would be doing her 'studying' with Hannah tonight.

'No way. That'll look totally uncool,' Sophie spluttered over her shoulder as she flounced on upstairs. 'Does your fashion sense die when you hit forty?'

'Thirty-eight, actually.' Andrea sighed, feeling a bit feeble and wondering whether her fashion sense had in fact died because, try as she might, she just could not understand her son's wish to go out with the top half of his derrière on show, and her daughter her bottom half.

Chapter Five

Andrea knew her son was in there somewhere with the alien that had taken over his body. Bless his Simpsons socks. After explaining her babysitting dilemma – and crossing his palm with a suitable amount of silver – Ryan's caring side came valiantly to the fore.

'No worries. Beyoncé's washing her hair anyway,' he said, magnanimously agreeing to stand in for Sally.

'Who?' Andrea asked ever-so-casually, assuming he meant his latest 'crush' at college. Also assuming he hadn't succeeded in enticing this one out on a hot date either.

'Beyoncé. Pop singer. You know, she wiv da cute booty?' Ryan waggled his eyebrows then wiggled his bottom as he headed upstairs, to which his skinny jeans were still miraculously clinging.

Not the current crush, then. Rolling her eyes, Andrea followed him up to look in on Chloe and found ten tiny toes parked on the pillow, along with her headless Igglepiggle, and Chloe's head the other end of the bed.

Andrea turned her around and made sure Chloe's Peppa Pig duvet was tucked well under her chin. She then watched for a moment; her baby's softly-curled eyelashes fluttered as her eyes chased her dreams. Innocent dreams, filled with wonder and magic, Andrea hoped. She planted a whisper-light kiss on Chloe's overripe cheek, then tiptoed out, closing the door quietly behind her.

She hated to admit it, but, though she was heartbroken for her friend, Andrea was relieved in a way that Sally wouldn't be available tonight. Sally adored Chloe without question but, the fact was, a toddler's sticky fingers and pristine art deco furnishings did not go well together. Sally had flapped her hand dismissively and said a bit of mess and a damp mattress didn't matter last time she'd babysat for her, but Andrea couldn't help thinking it did matter to someone who felt the need to fluff up cushions every time a seat was vacated. Chloe was better safe in her own bed, she decided, where a little accident wouldn't be the end of the world.

Right, a quick check on Dee, who was lusting over Jack Bauer in the 24 DVD box set, and all was well, apart from the fact that Andrea now only had precisely fourteen minutes and counting to get herself gorgeous to go and meet Jonathan – as gorgeous as anyone with a dead fashion sense could manage, of course.

Twenty minutes later, Andrea finally lurched through her front door flashing at least as much thigh as Sophie had earlier. Was it too much, she worried, glancing down at her spray can bodycon dress and wondering how on earth she got into it – more, how she was ever going to get out of it again.

Maybe foregoing retro in favour of raiding her daughter's wardrobe hadn't been such a good idea, after all, Andrea mused, as she teetered precariously towards her car in vertiginous heels, also Sophie's. Far from finding her alluring and sexy, which was the look she was trying for in light of their recent tiffs, Jonathan would think she'd either gone gaga or gone on the game.

Well, she couldn't go back now. She'd tried on everything of her own, apart from the actual wardrobe. She'd just have to go and hope for soft light ... Oh, no. Andrea closed her eyes and wished she was elsewhere as the front door opposite opened.

Damn. She swiftly about-turned. Of all the men in the village, why did she have to keep bumping into him? Whilst at a disadvantage? Naked this time. Practically. Andrea dithered on the drive, debating whether to dash back inside. Uh-uh. Just because she was wearing her daughter's clothes didn't mean she had to act her daughter's age and die of embarrassment if a man so much as glanced in her direction. Andrea wasn't about to let Doctor Adams dictate her state of undress.

So, why was she allowing any man to dictate what she did or didn't wear? Andrea wondered, as she teetered onwards towards her car, making a great show of ferreting around in her handbag as she did.

'Um, car keys,' she explained, jangling the obviously hitherto misplaced car keys from her hand, the other clutching her coat and wishing she had put it on and covered herself up.

'Right. Have a good evening,' he said, giving her a cursory glance and then turning to his car.

'Thank you.' Andrea felt a bit foolish and more than a bit annoyed with herself. She didn't like the man, so why on earth would she care that he'd barely glanced in her direction? Was her ego really that fragile? She sighed inwardly, despairing of a woman's propensity to judge herself on how a man looked at her, or didn't, and stepped up to her car, then stopped as she noticed his son following David Adams out, the child's expression and demeanour definitely that of a lonely little boy who was making sure to keep a distance between himself and his father.

Age and supposed equality made little difference. As far as Andrea could see a woman sitting alone in a restaurant still attracted all eyes. She wished she'd bought a newspaper, novel, knee-length skirt, anything that might make her look less like a desperate floozy who'd been stood up.

No, she had not. Jonathan wouldn't leave her sitting by herself in a restaurant, not without good reason, and certainly not without letting her know. He loved her. He'd said so a hundred times. Not so much lately, but that was because they didn't have time to speak, other than when they passed in the hall.

And he loved Chloe. He'd loved her ferociously from birth. She recalled how he'd cradled her in his arms, gazing down at the perfect wonder of her. How he'd confessed, his throat tight, that he'd kill to protect his newborn daughter. He would too. He'd never do anything to hurt her. Any of them. So where was he?

Andrea dawdled over her wine, a little lump in her throat becoming harder and harder to swallow as the minutes ticked by. Half an hour she sat, wondering how they could get back to where they were. She needed so much to talk to Jonathan. But how could she do that when …

He wasn't here? And he absolutely would be if he could be. She was sure. Had something happened? He'd been distracted this morning, to say the least, and the car had been … Oh God, no! Please don't let him be hurt or …

Gulping back her heart which was suddenly wedged in her windpipe, Andrea grabbed up her bag and scrambled in it for her mobile. 'Jonathan?' she said, confused when he answered. 'Where are—? Jonathan?'

Stunned for a second, Andrea pulled her mobile away from her ear and stared at it. He'd cut her off. Deliberately ended the call. Why would he? He'd known it was her. He'd know where she was too. They'd only confirmed it this morning, hadn't they? How could he have forgotten something as important as committing to their future together? Unless …

He didn't want to.

The urgent wail of a siren jolted Andrea from a dazed drive along the dual carriageway.

So, Jonathan had got cold feet, if Andrea's further unanswered calls and texts were anything to judge by. Right. Okay. She breathed in deeply and tried to compose herself. It wasn't the end of the world. There were always people worse off, families torn asunder by tragedy. Those sirens were a stark reminder of that.

Would Jonathan show up at home tonight? Would he even ring? Andrea swiped angrily at a tear and tightened her grip on the wheel, determined to drive herself safely home, whatever Jonathan was up to, wherever he was. At least she still had her family. People she loved and needed; who loved and needed her, far more than he.

Where would he go if he didn't come home? Did she even want him to, after this? Andrea wasn't sure. Of anything any more, other than Chloe being Jonathan's daughter and needing her father as sure as the desert needed the rain. He'd leave a huge gap in Ryan and Sophie's life too, if he had decided he wanted no part of theirs, albeit they weren't his flesh and … Andrea's thoughts were cut short as another fire engine squealed up behind her. She pulled in, offering up a silent prayer for the unfortunate souls the fire crew were rushing to, as the engine swept past in a haze of red and blue.

Still the sirens wailed. Eerily, like the shrill cry of a banshee. Andrea watched the engine speed into the distance as she followed in its wake, taking the same exit at the island. Her breath caught in her chest as the engine rounded another corner, preceding the exact same route Andrea would take to her home.

Two short roads from her house. Andrea's throat tightened.

Her stomach turned over. She could smell it, hot fumes on the air.

Sweet Mary, mother of Jesus, she could see it. An orange glow, soft against the night sky. Andrea's head reeled.

Her stomach plummeted. She tried to calm her racing heart and increased her speed. Damn it! She tried to concentrate as her tyres clipped the kerb, sucking in a deep breath, breathing out long and hard. It didn't help. As much as Andrea tried to tell herself it was coincidence. That just because the property they were hurtling towards was in her vicinity ...

One road from her own!

Oh no!

Panic flooded every vein in her body.

'No!' Andrea gripped the wheel hard, dread fast turning to sheer terror. 'Don't you dare! Don't you dare do this!' she screamed, looking heavenwards and ramming her foot down hard on the accelerator.

Andrea stopped praying as the car skidded to a halt, cold fear clutching at her insides now, forcing the air from her lungs, and chilling her blood to the bone. She climbed out. Legs like lead. Limbs reluctant and heavy, until her startled heart kicked back, hammering so wildly against her ribcage she could hear it.

And then she ran.

Dragging in fumes that seared the back of her throat, Andrea ran. Blindly swerving away from one set of arms, she was caught from behind by another, yanking her forcefully backwards, gripping her hard.

It wasn't happening. It was a nightmare. They were everywhere, men in uniform, running, shouting, dragging hands over rain-spattered faces.

Aiming hoses. Yelling instructions. Pouring water.

Broken doors, Andrea thought, watching her beautiful home burn in surreal slow motion before her.

Splintering wood.

She pulled in a breath. Couldn't breathe out. Shattered windows.

Dear Lord! Where were her children? Where was her

mother? Were they still inside? She moaned, a deep guttural moan from the depths of her soul. Then closed her eyes, and fought. Kicked and clawed, and tore at the hands restraining her, wrapped around her, holding her back.

She choked back a sob. And another. And then it came out. In one long scream, 'My babies! My mother! My children! Where are they?' Andrea struggled harder.

The man was saying something behind her. She couldn't hear him.

She wasn't listening. She wriggled. Her knees buckled. Andrea tried to duck under his arms.

He yanked her back. Held her tight, arms like a vice; the look in his eye as he twisted her around to face him, like molten metal about to ignite.

'They're safe,' he shouted. 'Listen to me,' he shouted louder, his hands firm on her arms, his gaze unwavering on hers.

Blue eyes, Andrea thought obliquely, her own eyes swimming out of focus. Ice cool and …

'They're all safe,' David Adams insisted, his voice still loud against the mayhem and machinery behind her, and urgent, and earnest.

Andrea scanned his eyes, pleading with her own. Please let them be … 'Oh no …' She caught a ragged breath in her throat; her chest filled up, and hot, impotent tears finally spilled over.

David eased her to him, as a violent sob shook her body.

And another. His own breath catching in his throat, which was dry and raw from the smoke, he pulled her closer, allowing her head to drop briefly to his shoulder. She didn't rest for long.

'I have to go to them,' she said, snatching her gaze back to his. Swiping at the tears on her cheeks, she stepped back and looked wildly around, her eyes wide and palpably petrified. 'I have to find them. Where—'

'Can you move back, mate?' one of the fire crew yelled, running urgently towards them. 'We need you out of the danger zone.'

David quickly reached out, his arm instinctively going around the woman's shoulders, easing her back towards him. She didn't look capable of standing, let alone walking. 'This way,' he said, shouting still, no choice but to with the bedlam surrounding them, but trying to inject some calmness into his voice now he was over the shock of seeing her careering towards certain death.

Steering her around towards his house and along the drive, he continued to talk to her, trying to keep her focus away from the fire. 'They're all fine, I promise,' he assured her again, pushing his open front door wide and making sure she stepped up, rather than tripped over the doorstep. 'They're upset, obviously, but—'

'Mum!' The daughter shouted, cutting him short as she hurtled down the stairs and all but cannonballed into her mother.

Thinking it might be appropriate, David stepped away as the woman hugged the girl hard to her. 'Sophie. Oh, thank God.' She squeezed her eyes closed over the girl's shoulder, trying unsuccessfully to hold back her tears.

'It was awful, Mum,' the daughter blurted, easing back and wiping a hand across her mascara-streaked cheeks. 'I came home early. Hannah went off with some spotty little dickhead from school, the absolute cow, so I came back and was in my bedroom with my earphones in,' she jabbered tearfully on as her mother looked more and more confused, 'and I didn't realise and suddenly there was smoke everywhere. I don't know how we would have got out if not for—'

'It wasn't me,' the old lady interrupted, wearing two

rollers in her hair and a worried expression as she, too, came down the stairs.

'Mum.' Sweeping her hair from her eyes, the woman blinked up at her, swallowing hard and dragging a hand under her nose.

'It wasn't me,' the old lady repeated, wringing her hands as she arrived in the hall to also receive a fierce hug from a woman who looked very much in need of a mother. 'I told that young man of yours, I didn't leave the pan on. I would say if I had.'

'Jonathan?' The woman looked around, bewildered, as if the husband, who'd been little in evidence, might materialise out of the ether.

'No, not *him*.' The old lady eyed the ceiling. 'Him.' She nodded in David's direction, who, feeling helpless to offer the emotional comfort they would badly need, was trying to debate how to get past the sooty ensemble and attend to the practicalities of having them here.

'He was very gallant,' the old lady went on. 'Though I'm not sure throwing me over —'

'Chloe? Ryan?' Andrea asked urgently. 'Where are —'

'Here,' Ryan said, appearing at the top of the stairs, a snuffling, hiccupping toddler in arms. 'We're good,' he assured her.

His throat didn't sound too good though. Noting the hoarseness, possibly from smoke inhalation, David looked the teenager over, concerned, as he came down to join them. The kid deserved a medal, he decided, but now might not be a good time to tell his mother why.

'We could use a drink, though, couldn't we, munchkin?' Glancing at David, Ryan arranged his face into a tremulous smile, for his mother's sake, David guessed, and then pressed a kiss to his little sister's overripe cheek.

'Uh, huh,' Chloe murmured around the thumb wedged

in her mouth. She blinked at her brother, and then arms outstretched, emitted a heart-wrenching sob, and reached out for her mother.

'I'll get some drinks organised,' David said, taking the opportunity as Andrea stepped forwards, to squeeze around behind her to the kitchen.

'I've got the sheets and stuff,' Jake called from the landing. 'Where do you want them?'

'My room. Thanks, Jake,' David shouted up, grateful that his own son had been mature enough to realise now wasn't a good time for them to be at loggerheads.

'What are we going to do, Mum? Everything's gone.' David stopped at the kitchen door, hearing Sophie wretchedly ask the question that would hit them all hard.

Turning back, he watched as the woman, Andrea, hugged her child closer and tugged in a long breath, as if steeling herself. 'We'll think of something, sweetie,' she said shakily. 'It's only a house. Just things. We've still got each other. Maybe we could go to a hotel. Have a little holiday, couldn't we, Chloe?'

'A holiday?' The girl gawked through her tears, incredulous.

Swallowing, Andrea nodded and indicated the little girl, obviously not wanting to upset her more than she already was. 'Just until we can sort out what to do next.'

She closed her eyes as she said that, clearly not having a bloody clue what she would do next.

David debated. He'd only just moved in, it wouldn't be ideal, but ... There was no way they were going to a hotel. The state they were in? He had no idea where the husband was, but for now ... 'Why don't you take them all upstairs?' he suggested, nodding in that direction. 'Jake's sorted out some extra bed linen and I'm sure we can rustle up a couple of spare toothbrushes and clean clothes of some sort.'

Andrea looked at him, her expression a mixture of relief and uncertainty.

'For tonight, at least,' David pushed it. He wasn't sure he could live with his already guilty conscience if he allowed this traumatised family to troop off to a hotel. 'The girls can take my room.' He glanced at Sophie and the old lady, who coiffed her curlers and beamed him a smile. 'Ryan can bunk up with Jake. I'm sure he won't mind.' He was actually pretty sure. Jake had definitely come up trumps in a crisis.

Andrea glanced at her bedraggled children, who hadn't got a coat between them, at her mother, who was dressed in nothing but her nightdress, and then back to him. 'Thank you.' She smiled falteringly and nodded.

'I'll bring some drinks up.' Watching another slow tear slide down her cheek, David offered her a sympathetic smile back. 'Tea and Coke all right?' he asked softly.

'And choclat,' Chloe added her preference, blinking huge beguiling eyes at him.

'One hot chocolate coming up.' David offered her a broad smile too, and turned back to the kitchen.

Chapter Six

Andrea heard David come into his lounge, once he'd finished helping the boys get organised upstairs.

'Okay?' he asked her gently.

Unable to squeeze a response past the tight lump in her throat, Andrea simply nodded and continued to stare stunned out of the window, her arms wrapped tightly about herself, as if she could somehow keep the emotion inside. The lights were rotating ominously now rather than urgently, casting blue shadows on the walls beyond her, each slow, rhythmic sweep sending a chill right through her. She couldn't believe it. Her whole life reduced to ashes in such a short space of time. Never had she felt so devastated and, even in a houseful of people, so utterly alone. Where was Jonathan? Why wasn't he here?

'I've brought you some tea,' David said. 'It won't help much, but it's warm and wet at least.'

His house, Andrea reminded herself, offered as a safe haven for her distraught family. Pulling in a breath, she tried somehow to pull herself together and at least appear grateful. 'Thank you,' she managed, turning to face him. 'For the use of the shirts, too. That was very kind of you. I'll make sure they're washed and returned obviously, as soon as I ...' realising she hadn't got a washing machine, hadn't got anything, Andrea swallowed back another hard knot of emotion and glanced down.

'No problem,' he assured her. 'Help yourself to anything you need. And as for the washing, don't worry. I think I've finally figured out how to sort the whites from the coloureds.'

He wasn't being flippant. He was trying to reassure her, that was all, but the concern in his voice ... Andrea wasn't sure kindness from this near stranger wouldn't release the stop valve and cause the tears she was trying so hard to hold back to spill over.

'How are they doing?' he asked after a moment, clearly not sure what else to say.

'Reasonably,' she answered shakily, attempting to be civil after all that he'd done. 'Sophie's tucked herself in with Chloe. To comfort her, in case she has nightmares, she said, but to be honest, I think it's Sophie who needs the comforting. Mum's worrying. She thinks we all think …'Andrea trailed off, her tummy physically clenching as she imagined the abject terror they must all have felt. 'I shouldn't have left them.' It came out barely a whisper.

'You couldn't have known.' David took a step towards her. 'It was an—'

'I shouldn't have left them!' She screamed it this time.

'Miss Kel … Andrea.' David moved closer, his expression a mixture of sympathy and apprehension. 'Blaming yourself isn't going to help. You can't keep them safe twenty-four hours—'

'I can!' Andrea took a step back, physically deflecting sympathy she didn't deserve. 'It's my job! It's what parents are supposed to do. Make sure they're safe, never scared or lonely or hurting.'

She fixed him with an angry, almost accusing glare and David glanced down.

'Oh God,' Andrea choked back a sob. 'I'm sorry. I've no right to be shouting at you. Absolutely none.'

'Shout away, if it helps.' David shrugged, and then moved again towards her. 'They're safe, that's the thing to focus on,' he said quietly. 'Try to ground yourself on that, for now.'

He was right. Of course he was. Closing her eyes, Andrea tried very hard to concentrate on what mattered above all else. 'Where's Ryan?' she asked, looking back at him.

'In Jake's room.' He smiled encouragingly. 'I'm not sure who's looking after who. I left him showing Jake how to use his new PlayStation 4. Ryan's putting a brave face on things, I suspect, but he seems okay. I'll keep my eye on him.'

Relieved, Andrea nodded. The man was a doctor. He would do that instinctively, she guessed, and was grateful for that one small mercy. 'How did it ...? The fire ...?' Needing to know, she started haltingly, and then stopped, as an involuntary shudder shook through her.

Obviously wary of invading her space, David hesitated and then tentatively reached to wrap an arm around her shoulders. 'They're not sure yet. It started in the kitchen, apparently. It might possibly have been a pan left on. Everyone was upstairs, according to your son. Your mother was doing her hair. Sophie had come in in a 'strop', it seems, and gone straight up to her room. Ryan had his earphones on, playing on his Xbox, he said, so he didn't hear anything, but as soon as he smelled smoke, he raised the alarm and then helped everyone get out. He's a good kid, Andrea. They all are. Hold on to that. I know it probably doesn't help much right now, but it could have been a hell of a lot worse.'

Painfully aware of how much worse, Andrea swallowed again. 'Did you ...?' She glanced questioningly at him. She hadn't noticed at first, but his smoke-blackened appearance indicated that he'd done more than stand outside watching her house burn.

David nodded, reluctantly, Andrea noted. 'With Ryan's help, yes,' he said. 'They were all out by the time the fire crews arrived.'

Not quite all. Andrea's heart sank. 'Dougal? Is he ...? Our dog. A terrier. He's tiny. Did he ...?'

David scanned her face. 'There's a chance he could have got out,' he offered. 'Run off scared possibly.' He stopped as a slow tear slid down her cheek, looking deeply apologetic.

He was trying to be tactful. Offer her a glimmer of hope. There was none though. If Dougal hadn't got out of the house ...

'It's okay to cry, you know,' he said softly, squeezing her shoulders. 'Therapeutic, so they say.'

Again, Andrea nodded, but wiped her tears away anyway.

'You should try to get some rest,' David urged her as Andrea glanced again towards the nightmare outside the window. 'I'll bring a jug of water and some glasses up. They might be thirsty if they wake in the night,' he explained.

From the effects of the smoke, Andrea gleaned he meant, and felt her heart twist all over again.

Realising Andrea was in the bathroom, David hesitated, and then headed to see Jake.

David swallowed back a little emotion of his own before going into his son's room. Jake had been pretty shaken by events too, but if his son wasn't talking to him, other than the odd sentence, at least he'd been listening in the aftermath of the fire. Doing everything David had instructed him to, helping him to sort out bed linen and towels, and then trying, as best a ten-year-old could, to take Ryan under his wing.

Jake was definitely one of the good guys. David just wished he could hold the boy's gaze long enough to communicate to him how much he appreciated him.

'Hey, how's it going?' he asked, after knocking on the door, then going on in to find the two boys with eyes glued to the screen and thumbs poised on hand-controls.

'Yeah, good.' Ryan peeled his gaze away to glance up at him and David could see there was definitely an element of bravado in there. He was still pale and, though his eyes were not as red as they were, they still looked irritated.

'Let me know if you have any shortness of breath, Ryan,' he asked him, 'or headache, okay?' He may not appear to have respiratory problems but he would have been exposed to carbon monoxide. David needed to keep an eye on that. The psychological effects would need keeping an eye on too.

Given the circumstances, David doubted the kid was quite so cool and laid-back as he seemed.

'Will do,' Ryan assured him, his attention back on the screen.

'So what's the game?' David followed his gaze, cocking his head to one side as a cross between a Gremlin and ET let out a blood-curdling cackle and thwacked some other reptilian creature with a club.

'Overlord II,' Ryan supplied.

'And it's about?' David asked, unimpressed as another gargoyle chased a doe-eyed seal across the screen growling, 'Die, sweaty fur ball.'

'Um, Overlords?' Ryan suggested, giving Jake a parents-are-past-it roll of his eyes. David wasn't too perturbed by that, though, when he saw Jake's mouth twitch into something resembling a smile. 'You have to destroy or dominate your way through a twisted fantasy world with an army of crazed minions at your command.'

'Ah.' David nodded. 'Not guaranteed to ensure a trouble-free night's sleep, then?'

The two boys looked sheepish in unison, but didn't look up.

'So, who does it belong to?' David enquired, knowing Jake was aware he'd have got a definitive no for an answer if he'd asked about purchasing it himself.

'Nathan.' Jake sighed audibly, casting David a bored glance from under his Bench cap as he did, which was worn back to front to facilitate seeing said destruction and domination, David supposed.

His cousin, who was older than Jake, and who should have known better than to lend it to him without permission. 'In which case, you can post it back to Nathan and stick to something more appropriate to your age, please, Jake.' David attempted to lay down the law, knowing that not to would be tantamount to telling Jake he could do what he liked.

'Yeah, yeah.' Jake shrugged, which basically meant he'd failed.

'Jake, turn it off, please.' David tried again, feeling torn, as he did perpetually lately. Did he stick to his guns? Or let Jake get his own way? Always there was the guilt; the fear that when the emotion finally surfaced, he'd be as poorly equipped to deal with it as he was to deal with the cause of it.

'Jake ...' David waited, feeling impotent in the face of Jake's open disobedience. 'Come on. It's way past your bedtime. You'll be tired tomorrow.'

Jake shot him a scathing glance. 'Like you give a stuff how I feel,' he mumbled.

David tugged in a breath. 'Turn it off, Jake,' he said, knowing that what he wanted to say – that he did care, very much – might elicit yet more contempt. Rightly so, probably, but now wasn't the time for a showdown, not with so many people here and emotions so fraught.

Counting silently to five, David waited, and then, when Jake didn't budge, he dragged a hand over his neck, debated, and walked to the window, feeling utterly defeated. Jake and he needed to talk, somehow, sometime soon, but it would have to be on Jake's terms, David knew that. It was Jake who needed to vent his anger, let go of his frustration. He wouldn't do that if David started in on him because of his own frustrations.

Stifling a sigh, he peeled back a curtain to check out proceedings opposite, noting that the fire was under control, which was good. And that the house looked pretty much uninhabitable, which most definitely wasn't. Selfish it might be, but with Jake apparently determined to see how far he could push him, David really did not need a refugee family in situ for long.

'It's half past midnight, Jake. People are tired.' He glanced back over his shoulder to meet Ryan's curious gaze, who was no doubt wondering how it was that a ten-year-old seemed to be getting away with outright insolence.

David offered him an apologetic shrug.

In response to which, Ryan parked his control to one side and stretched. 'I got The Simpsons game,' he addressed Jake, through a demonstrative yawn.

'Yeah?' Jake glanced languidly, but interestedly, sideways.

'Uh-huh. The graphics are nothing special, but it's pretty fun—' Ryan stopped, and blinked '—um, crispy,' he went on with a flat smile. 'Like toast.'

'Damn.' Jake shook his head, commiserating the loss of software in a world where gaming cred was all.

David ran a hand over his chin to hide a smile. 'How about you and Jake go into town and get a new one tomorrow after school?' he offered, glad that Ryan had picked up on the vibes and was obviously trying to bring the computer session to a discreet close.

'Cool. We could see what else they've got, while we're at it.' Ryan glanced questioningly at Jake as he got to his feet.

'Ye-ah,' Jake said, boyish enthusiasm bubbling to the surface for the first time in a long time, to David's relief. 'Nothing better to do,' he added, working now to make his tone more chilled adolescent than excited little kid.

'Awesome,' Ryan said, with another leisurely stretch, which had David quietly smiling again. The kid's jeans were hanging onto his hips for grim death. 'Right, time for bed, mate,' Ryan went on, through another yawn. 'Need to brush the pearlies, then get some zeds in. Things been a bit weird lately, y'know?'

'Tell me about it,' Jake empathised as Ryan sauntered manfully towards the door, giving David a conspiratorial nod as he went.

Taking Ryan's cue, David grabbed his chance. 'Time you got some zeds in as well, Jake,' he suggested.

Jake's expression went swiftly back to unimpressed. 'Yeah, right,' he muttered, shuffling reluctantly to his feet. Still, he had actually moved something other than his thumbs.

David hesitated for a second to make sure his son was actually heading for his pyjamas, then, 'Night, Jake,' he said, hopefully. 'See you in the morning.'

Guessing Jake wouldn't answer, David left him to it. Tomorrow was another day, he told himself. He'd try harder. There had to be a way to reach out to Jake. Though other than PlayStation bribery, David wasn't sure he knew of one.

Noting Ryan heading for the bathroom, he decided to tactfully check up on him. The kid might be acting as if he was okay, but David suspected it was just that, an act. Ryan was trying to be macho for his mum, as well as his credibility's sake. Come to think of it, where was the husband in all of this? Not here obviously. David pondered briefly. Working maybe? Not his business, he told himself.

'Sorry about your dog, Ryan,' he offered sympathetically. 'I tried, but ...'

'I know. I saw,' Ryan said, through a sharp intake of breath. 'Thanks.' His eyes flickered to David's and David read what was there. I appreciate it, but subject closed, the kid's expression said. Trying to be the man of the family in lieu of the actual man, Ryan was working hard at keeping the emotions in check. David got it.

'Do you need anything?' he asked diplomatically. 'Something to sleep in, maybe?'

'Nah, it's cool,' Ryan assured him, turning at the door. 'Prefer not to be restricted in bed, you know.'

'Right.' David nodded, trying to keep his face straight. 'I'll leave some boxers on the stair rail anyhow, just in case.'

'I could probably use a shave though.' Ryan dragged a hand under his chin.

Which was adorned with nothing but a few nicks, presumably from a recent "I shave, therefore I am a man", endeavour. David's mouth twitched into a smile. 'Left-hand side of the cabinet. Spare blades are in there, too.'

'Minty,' Ryan said, another slant on cool, David gathered. 'I take it you two have issues,' he added, nodding towards Jake's room.

'Er, yes,' David admitted. 'Some.'

'Most families do.' Ryan nodded maturely. 'Word of advice though, if I may?'

David glanced at the gangly teenager, turned father confessor and dispenser of advice, bemused. 'You may.'

'Go easy on the parentals.'

The …? 'Er, right. I'll try.' David glanced at the closed bathroom door as Ryan whistled on in.

'Parental rules,' Ryan informed him from inside.

Andrea lay listlessly on the spare mattress David Adams had thoughtfully supplied, her energy depleted after a fitful night's sleep. For hours she'd tossed and turned, listening to night noises, the dawn chorus, early-risers getting up and getting on with their lives, dogs barking. Not Dougal. Dougal didn't do confrontation. In the midst of excitement, Dougal's was a lively, spirited little yap. Sensing real danger, though, he'd turn tail, skid through the dog flap and hide behind a handy bush until the coast was clear.

Poor Dougal. Where was he?

Her arms wrapped about herself in an attempt to ward off the incessant shaking, Andrea tried to find the will to get up, go downstairs, get on with her own life.

What was left of her life.

She still couldn't believe it. She'd lost everything. The house she'd lived in since Ryan was born. Loved in, laughed in, cried in. The same house she'd made into a home and which she adored every messy room and dusty nook and cranny of. And now it was gone. She'd watched it burn. Then watched it burn again in her nightmares. Paint bubbling. Barbie dolls melting. Hand-paintings pinned haphazardly to walls turning to ashes.

70

The heart of her home, blackened and twisted and torn out. Her funny little gremlin dog, gone.

Dragging her hands over her face, determined to be strong – her family would need her to be – Andrea heaved herself from the mattress and pulled herself to her feet. David Adams had been right. The horrendous truth was she could have lost her family.

She choked back a fresh sob as she looked down at Chloe sleeping, a stubby thumb in her mouth, her other hand caught in a soft ringlet of curls at her cheek. At Sophie, lying on her back, one arm thrown over her head, squashing her new scary hairdo. Emo anime, apparently, inspired by futuristic Japanese games, Ryan had informed Andrea when Sophie had slouched in from 'shopping' last week, her blonde hair dyed black and purple and topped with a spiked crown.

Andrea had nearly had an apoplexy then. It didn't seem to matter now.

Purple, pink or rainbow coloured, her daughter was still beautiful.

She glanced at Dee at the foot of the bed, who'd tucked herself in, the only one properly attired in her winceyette nightie, but who had steadfastly refused to part with her teeth. That didn't seem to matter much either.

All they had to their names were the clothes they stood up in. Small wonder her mum had wanted to hang on to her teeth then, without even her handbag to put them in. Andrea knew she should be grateful they were all here, safe and together, but … It was just so bloody awful. She gulped back hard, shuddering at another stark recollection of hungry flames devouring her home.

How could she not feel bereft with all their worldly goods gone? And Jonathan, where was he? Yes, her mobile was out of action with no charger, but if he had tried to ring, on either landline or mobile, surely he would have realised something was terribly wrong and come …

No, maybe not. Andrea ran a hand under her nose. He'd stood her up, after all, for reasons which were becoming more apparent in his continued absence. Pity he hadn't decided to get trendy and become a commitment-phobe before having a baby.

Damn him! Where was he? Tucked up at his mother's? With someone else? Things hadn't exactly been good between them lately, had they? No, she would have had some inkling of that, surely? He obviously had got cold feet. How heart breaking was it that he'd deserted her on the very night her house had caught fire?

Andrea swallowed back the hurt.

His sheets would need washing, she thought obliquely, noting the stains deposited on David Adam's bed linen by her hot chocolate coated toddler and Sophie's cried off mascara, to say little of the state of her own crumpled pillow.

He'd been amazing. She couldn't even begin to contemplate what scenario might have greeted her last night if not for him. He'd saved her family – and she'd been on the brink of tearing his small family apart, no more than suspicion to base her accusations on.

Uncertain what to do next – of anything any more, her judgement of men, in particular – Andrea shivered in the cool morning air. Wondering what on earth she could wear, she rubbed her goose-pimpled arms under the sleeves of David Adams' shirt, which she wished was a bit longer. She'd much rather stay in something androgynous and comfortable, than struggle back into Sophie's spray can bodycon thing, which actually spraying on might make it more practical than getting into. She could hardly wear just the shirt, though.

Bathroom, she instructed herself. Hopefully a shower might make her feel at least half human. She'd think about clothes, or lack of, when she could actually think.

Tempted to steal the black leggings Sophie had finally gone out in, then thinking better of it since Sophie was very likely to go downstairs adorned in nought but the T-shirt also provided by their host, Andrea inched open the bedroom door and peered out onto the landing.

It smelled like bonfire night. The saddest bonfire night ever. Her heart plummeted afresh at the smell of burnt wood permeating the air, along with … bacon? She blinked. Crikey, she'd barely unscrambled her brain and their host for the night had started breakfast?

Checking the coast was clear, she made a dash for the bathroom, where she eventually got the endlessly clunking pipes to produce more than a dribble, then stepped under the shower and allowed the lukewarm water to wash her awake. Clean, if not exactly refreshed, she towelled herself down with one of a bundle of towels David Adams had generously left there and then realised she'd none of the other essentials one takes for granted either. No deodorant. Not a cosmetic or toiletry to her name. Andrea eyed what was presumably David's roll-on and then, deciding a guilty conscience was better than sweaty armpits, she applied a quick blob.

Finally, feeling marginally better, she tugged the shirt back on, padded quickly out, and … Ooh, hell … almost parted company with her skin.

'Morning,' David Adams said from the foot of the stairs, where, Andrea realised mortified, he might well have a lovely view of her bottom.

Damn. She skittered hastily on, throwing, 'Morning,' over her shoulder.

'There's breakfast downstairs, if you fancy eating something,' he called. 'And there's some jog pants over the stair rail. A bit on the large size, I imagine, but better than nothing.'

Andrea sighed. He had got a glimpse, then. Perfect.

Chapter Seven

'Better?' David asked when Andrea appeared in the kitchen ten minutes later, jog pants rolled up at the bottom and down at the top, shirt tied in a not very artistic knot in the middle.

Andrea nodded, offering him a grateful smile. 'Yes. Thanks. You're very organised,' she said, having noted that, although there were various boxes parked in the hall and the lounge, the man seemed to have most things in place.

'The house came furnished, so there wasn't too much to do, thank goodness.' He glanced at her. 'But then, you'd probably know that.'

'Yes.' Andrea nodded and glanced down, reminded that she wouldn't be spying on him from her bedroom window again. She didn't have one.

'Hope the plumbing didn't keep you awake?' he asked, obviously trying to make conversation. 'Boiler's a bit past it, I'm afraid.'

'No, not really.'

David arched an incredulous eyebrow.

'I was awake anyway.' Andrea shrugged.

David nodded, understanding, and went back to grilling the bacon, stirring the beans, burning the toast. 'Damn!' he cursed, shaking his also burned fingers.

'Can I help?' Andrea asked, stepping forwards.

'No,' David said quickly and rather brusquely.

Startled by his tone, Andrea stepped back.

'Sorry. Sorry.' David looked immediately apologetic. 'It's just ... I prefer my space, you know? Thanks, anyway.'

'That's okay,' Andrea said, but she couldn't help but be reminded again of his fast temper. 'I'm the same in my own, um ...' she trailed off, studying her toes and trying hard not to think of what was burned in her kitchen. 'We'll be out of your hair just as soon as I can get something sorted out,' she offered, aware that having her family descend on him uninvited must be as awkward for him as it was for her.

'Right,' David said, placing plates on the kitchen table, along with a handful of cutlery, coming back for juice, catching the unburned toast, dropping a slice. 'Shit!'

He shoved that in the bin and tried again.

'I'll go over to my ... the house later,' Andrea went on as he carried a dish laden with bacon to the table. 'Survey the damage and see what can be salvaged.'

'Bad idea.' David headed back again to the hall. 'Jake. Breakfast!' he shouted up the stairs. 'Now, please.' He gave Andrea a brief smile as he came back to the kitchen. 'He'll be late. School, you know.'

'Yes. Yes, of course.' Andrea managed a small smile back. It was business as usual for the rest of the world, she supposed, even if her world had ground to a disastrous halt. 'I'd better ring in.' She sighed wearily. 'Tell them what's happened, though I imagine the village drums will have conveyed the news by now.'

David smiled wryly. 'I expect so, but feel free to use the phone anyway,' he offered, finally managing to produce edible toast that stayed on the plate.

'Thank you. I will, if you don't mind. I don't have my mobile charger. It's ... You know.' Melted probably, Andrea thought miserably.

She glanced at the ceiling, almost wishing he wouldn't be quite so hospitable. Her previous judgement of him may well have been hasty, the man was being terribly kind, but she didn't want to be his houseguest any more than he wanted her family camped there, she imagined.

'What's a bad idea?' she asked, since he hadn't elaborated.

'Going back into the house before it's been checked out by

the fire safety officer. Too risky. The insurance assessor will have to go in, too, presumably. Might be best not to disturb anything yet.'

He was right. Of course he was. So, what on earth did she do? Go shopping in his jog pants? Go to school in them?

'Black or white?' David asked after her preference to coffee as Andrea blinked back a useless tear.

'White. Thanks. Ten thousand sugars … for energy,' she said, drooping across to the table.

'I have some stuff you might be able to use,' David said, seating himself opposite, checking his watch, one eye on the door to the hall.

'Sorry?'

'Clothing.' He shrugged, seemingly uncomfortable. 'Things you could wear until you get yourself sorted out.'

Andrea looked at him curiously. 'Well, I'd be glad of anything, obviously. I'm sure the jog pants look wonderful on you, but … um …' she trailed off awkwardly as Ryan came into the kitchen, apparently his usual witty self.

'Put him down, Mother. Children present,' he commented drolly, stretched and yawned, and then scratched his armpit as he headed to the table.

'So I see.' Andrea arched an eyebrow at his Homer Simpson boxers.

'What?' Ryan followed her gaze. 'Can I help it if someone has immature dress sense?'

'Jake bought them. A Christmas present, a while back,' David explained, glancing down, quite obviously embarrassed.

Oh, dear. So they were his, then. And Jake had bought them for him? The Jake she'd seen wouldn't be excitedly buying Christmas presents for his dad, which might indicate the wide gulf between them was due to recent events.

'Cool, cooked breakfast.' Ryan stopped yawning in order

76

to facilitate stuffing a rasher of bacon complete into his mouth.

Andrea was about to admonish him when Jake himself wandered bleary-eyed into the kitchen. 'Not hungry,' he mumbled, sloping to the fridge to extract a pint of milk.

'Uh-uh,' David issued a warning as Jake tilted the bottle towards his mouth. 'Sit and eat, please. And I mean eat, Jake. No arguments.'

'Not hungry,' Jake repeated, eyeballing his father defiantly, whose jaw tensed somewhat, Andrea noticed.

'Better do it, mate,' Ryan interrupted the almost indiscernible standoff as father and son locked eyes. 'Don't want to invite the wrath of Dad, do we? Not if he's coughing up dosh so we can hit the shops later? In any case, you'll need your strength if I'm going to beat you at Superior Challenge.'

'Yeah, right.' Jake's mouth twitched into a smile. 'In your dreams, mate.' He parked himself next to Ryan and reached for the juice, his eyes again flickering moodily over his father as he did.

Andrea glanced at David, wondering what his reaction would be, and then cringed as Dee marched in, still dressed in her winceyette nightie and her chest puffed up indignantly. 'Who's had them?' she boomed, turning suspicious eyes on Ryan.

Ryan splayed his hands innocently. 'What?'

'Teeth, boy. Teeth.' Dee pointed a finger at her mouth and all became clear, to Andrea anyway. Ryan had 'borrowed' his gran's teeth last snowfall, to give Chloe's snowman a smile.

'Mum, they're in your—' Andrea was about to point out where she'd left them for safekeeping, when Dee interrupted.

'They're not!' She took a step forward, tripped over her nightie, and then hoisted the hem up. 'The glass is empty,' she imparted, raising the glass of water Andrea had left on

77

the bedside table as irrefutable evidence. 'You're chewing very well.' Dee turned her slit-eyed gaze on David.

Actually, he was more choking than chewing, Andrea noticed, concerned, as David coughed heartily and reached for his juice.

'Mum, stop it!' Andrea hissed, getting to her feet. 'He has his own teeth.' She tried not to look at Ryan, who was doing a rather impressive Bugs Bunny impression. 'Why would he want yours?'

'Exactly.' Dee nodded triumphantly, leaving the audience to draw their own conclusions, presumably.

David knocked back his juice, coughed some more, then looked at Andrea as if he'd been caught up in a world gone quite mad. Then diplomatically looked down, as Sophie wandered in, her spikes bolt upright and her legs on show up to her knickers under one of his shirts.

'Sophie!' Andrea glanced despairingly from her mother – who was looking at David menacingly now – to her daughter.

'What?' Sophie blinked panda eyes and looked the picture of innocence.

Andrea sighed. 'Clothes, Sophie! Put some on.'

'I haven't got any clothes to put on,' Sophie retorted, hands on hips, and her head going from side-to-side as she spelled out her point.

'Go!' Andrea gave Sophie a no-nonsense glare and pointed to the door, and then shot off her chair as Chloe wailed from the landing, 'Mum-my, wanna wee-wee.'

'What on earth are you doing, Sophie?' Andrea snapped as she bolted towards the hall. 'You don't leave toddlers alone at the top of the stairs with no baby gate.'

'D'oh.' Sophie stuffed her tongue belligerently against the inside of her lower lip. 'We don't have a baby gate, though, do we?'

'You are going to be in big trouble, young lady, if you

don't watch the attitude,' Andrea warned her, disappearing through the door to take the stairs two at a time.

'Well, that's really different, innit?' Sophie's sulky reply drifted up after her. 'Blame everything on me, why don't you?'

'Grow up, metal-mouth,' Ryan retorted. 'Give Mum a break and give it a rest.'

Andrea scooped Chloe up, torn between being grateful to Ryan and giving him hell for making fun of Sophie's braces in front of people.

'Shut it, muppet,' Sophie growled from below.

'Says she with the cartoon hairdo,' Ryan replied smartly.

At which point Jake joined in. 'Weirdo.'

'Jake, enough!' Andrea heard David warn him. 'And you two ...' he paused, obviously trying to moderate his tone. 'Why don't you both give your mum a break, hey? She has a lot on her plate.'

Andrea wasn't about to judge him badly this time. Glad for his intervention, she reached to pluck her little one up from the landing as silence prevailed. Almost.

'Gran, geddoff! They're in your mouth.' Sophie's peeved tones followed Andrea to the bathroom as she carried Chloe there.

Too late, unfortunately. Wonderful. Ah, well, little catastrophes Andrea could cope with. She gave Chloe a whoops-a-daisy smile, decided her first port of call would have to be the Tiny Tots shop, and then swilled out Chloe's *Fifi and the Flowertots* trainer pants in the sink.

Though where would she hang them to dry? She glanced around the bathroom. Lots of man-stuff scattered about, but no handy hooks or indoor clothes line.

'Mummy, upsies.' Chloe jiggled, arms outstretched as Andrea squeezed as much water from the garment as she could.

'One minute, sweetie,' she promised, grabbing the opportunity for a quick call of nature herself, on the basis that time to pee was of a premium.

'Mum-my.' Chloe jiggled some more, desperate to be picked up as there was a knock at the bathroom door.

Typical! Andrea twanged up her own drawers and wondered whether to just drown herself in the bath and be done with it. She took a deep breath, breathed out, then picked Chloe up and hugged her tight.

'Mummy loves you bigger than the whole world and all the stars, baby,' she whispered, sure being even mildly irritated with her family was dreadful after what had happened. Shaking off the icy tremor that ran the length of her spine, Andrea grabbed Chloe's pants from the sink and pulled open the door.

'Everything okay?' David stood on the landing, hands in his pockets, an expression of mild irritation tempered with concern on his face.

'Perfect,' Andrea assured him, dredging a smile from the soles of her feet.

'Just a suggestion,' he shrugged, taking in her attire and Chloe's handheld wet pants, 'but why don't you do some shopping online? You could probably get next day delivery on most things, and the insurance should cough up, assuming you have household insurance?' He glanced at her questioningly.

Andrea blinked at him as if he'd just sprouted a halo, and then nodded, dumbly. Why on earth hadn't she thought of that?

'There's a desktop in Jake's room, but you might prefer to rest up a bit and use my laptop in the lounge.'

Andrea found her voice. 'Rest? Chance would be a fine thing.' She smiled and hoisted Chloe higher in her arms.

He smiled back, properly this time, amazingly. Nothing

too earth-shattering or face altering, but definitely a proper smile.

'There's a clothes airer in the utility, if you need it, and the clothes I talked about are in the spare room.' He nodded towards a room at the end of the landing. 'Sorry I couldn't offer you the bed in there last night, but it's pretty chock-a-block with stuff.'

Oh. So, if Ryan had bunked up with Jake and the rest of her family had taken over his bedroom, where had he slept, then?

'Which is why I ended up on the sofa – and grouchier than usual. Sorry about that.' David smiled again, a self-deprecating smile this time.

'Oh, Lord, you shouldn't have done that, Dav ... Mr Adams. We could have camped in the lounge.'

'No problem. The sofa converts to a bed. And it's David, the name. Might as well dispense with formalities now we're sleeping on top of one another. Er, I mean ...' he trailed off, looking a touch embarrassed.

Andrea laughed – she couldn't help herself – and extended her hand around Chloe to re-introduce herself. 'Nice to meet the nicer side of you, David. And thank you ... for everything.'

She was grateful, truly, more than he could ever know, for his hospitality and his bravery. He might have burned his fingers on the toast, but his forearm looked to Andrea as if it had been licked by flames. She was still worried for his son – something was terribly wrong between them. She had no idea where the mother was or what the man's circumstances were, but whatever had caused the dreadful rift between them, her own past experiences had coloured her judgement of David Adams, of that Andrea was sure.

'Do you have something for that?' she asked, concerned that he might have been too busy with everyone else to attend to himself.

'Sorry?' David followed her glance down. 'Oh, yes, thanks. Be a poor show if I didn't, wouldn't it, my being a GP?' David shrugged it off with a smile.

'How did …?' Andrea wondered how he'd come to be so close to the fire, though she wasn't sure she wanted to know.

'The, er, dog.' He shrugged again, awkwardly. 'I looked for him, but …'

Andrea nodded and swallowed back the tears that welled up inside her. 'A very courageous GP, I think,' she said softly.

David hesitated, his eyes searching hers for a second, before he dropped his gaze. 'Depends on how you measure courage.'

'And a very busy one, I imagine.' Noting the flicker of guilt she'd seen there, the body language, Andrea sensed it wasn't a subject he wanted to pursue. 'I'll book us into a hotel for tonight and leave you in peace,' she said, sure he'd be desperate for his space.

He eyed her quizzically. 'Not a lot of point ordering next day delivery then?'

'Oh.'

'Stay,' he said, 'until you can sort yourself out properly at least. You might need to be on hand for the insurers anyway.'

Andrea debated. It wasn't a begrudging offer, made out of politeness. She could see he was genuinely being kind. And she knew it made more sense than booking into a hotel without a scrap of luggage, but still … 'Well, if you're sure?'

'I wouldn't have offered if I wasn't.'

'Thank you,' she said again, her heart warming to this man she'd thought an arrogant bully. 'It really is very kind of you.'

'It's no problem,' he assured her, turning towards the stairs. 'Oh,' he turned back, 'is your husband working away or something? It's just that he doesn't seem to be—'

'He's not,' Andrea said quickly.

David cocked his head curiously to one side.

'Neither my husband, nor around, just now,' Andrea elaborated, not sure why she'd mentioned the husband bit, other than she felt utterly deserted by Jonathan.

David nodded, looking somewhat pensive, and then headed off downstairs as the doorbell rang.

The first of many concerned well-wishers, Andrea suspected, knowing how fast news travelled in the village. She held Chloe tight and, wet undies still in hand, made to follow him, supposing she'd have to face them sooner or later.

'Andrea!' Sally exclaimed, bustling past a very surprised looking David as she spotted Andrea coming down the stairs. 'Honey, I am so, so sorry.' Sally blinked up at Andrea sympathetically. 'I tried to get to you last night, but the firemen had everything cordoned off and ... Oh, Andrea, I can't believe it. It's so awful. Eva said everyone had got out all right, but ... How are you, sweetie?'

Sally threw her arms around her as Andrea reached the hall, stood back to look her over and then, 'Good God, Andrea. You look just like one of the Teletubbies. What have you got on?'

Chapter Eight

'So, how are you?' Sally asked, Chloe in arms as she followed David into the kitchen.

David took a second to answer. 'Er, good, yes.' He turned from where he was retrieving a plastic cup from the drainer, to look her over curiously. 'You?'

'Oh, fine, you know.' Sally smiled. 'All things considered.'

David nodded contemplatively. 'Good.' He gave her a short smile back and then turned to extract milk from the fridge.

'I live over the road.' Sally nodded toward her cottage as he turned back.

'Oh, right.' David knitted his brow. 'I didn't realise.'

'I gathered,' Sally said, noting his awkward expression. 'I would have popped over, but with everything going on ...'

David nodded again, his attention now on pouring milk into the plastic cup. She hoped Chloe didn't spill it all over herself as they did not have a sipper cup, obviously.

Sally waited expectantly then, still no comment forthcoming from David, she turned her attention to Chloe. 'Well, this is a surprise, isn't it, Chloekins, hmm?' she said jollily. 'You and your mummy moving in with the good doctor?'

David glanced towards the stairs, where Andrea had gone up to find something to make her look 'a little less cuddly'.

'This would be because her house burned down, I suspect,' he pointed out, looking Sally quizzically over again as he turned to put the milk back in the fridge.

Honestly, it was like wading through molasses, Sally thought peeved. Would the man not speak to her? Look at her, properly?

'God, I know,' she said quickly. 'Isn't it dreadful? I honestly couldn't believe it. I saw Andrea arrive, poor thing. She looked absolutely terrified. I tried to get to her but the firemen wouldn't let me past. And then, well, I saw you were with her, so ...' Sally trailed off, aware that she might have sounded a bit flippant, which she hadn't meant to be.

It was a terrible, awful thing to have happened. Sally was truly devastated for her friend. There was a tiny part of her, though, that wished David hadn't been quite so fast to offer Andrea refuge at his house. But then, that was obviously the kind of person he was, caring. And brave: risking his own safety to help Andrea's family escape the inferno. He was undoubtedly a good man.

'She could stay with me, you know. I wasn't just offering because I felt obliged to,' Sally went on, feeling a bit put out that Andrea had declined her offer just now. She'd said Sally's cottage was too small, which Sally supposed it was, with only two bedrooms. The bit that upset Sally, though, was that Andrea thought the mess the children would make of her elegant furnishings and décor would drive Sally to move out.

She'd said it jokingly, without really thinking about it, which Sally couldn't blame her for – Andrea would have so much on her mind – but still, it did hurt. Andrea, above all people, must know that Sally craved the mess children might make.

'I'm sure she knows it was a genuine offer,' David assured her. 'Can I get you some tea, coffee?'

'No, no thanks. I have to get to school.' Sally's mind was still on Andrea's housing problem. 'I suppose there's always The Swan or the Travelodge in town until she can get fixed up. Actually, thinking about it, I'm sure there's a house to rent on Hibberton Road. I could pop by the estate agents for her and—'

'I'm not sure she's had time to think about anything much

yet,' David said before Sally had finished. 'She's fine here for now,' he added, handing Sally the cup of milk to give to Chloe and Chloe a chocolate biscuit.

'Oh?' Sally glanced at him, feeling a bit put out. 'Well, yes, of course. I'm sure she is, if that's what you've both, um ...' She hoisted Chloe higher in her arms, who was now busy stripping chocolate from the digestive with a long length of her tongue. 'It's just that I thought with you only having the three bedrooms ...'

'We're managing,' David assured her. 'The boys are okay in Jake's room. Andrea's in the master bedroom.'

'Oh,' Sally said again, trying to keep her tone ever so casual, whilst smiling to stop herself from licking the excess chocolate from Chloe's outstretched palm.

'It is a bit of a squeeze ...' David went on, turning to wet a wad of paper towelling, as Sally tried to digest what he'd just said about the sleeping arrangements '... with Sophie, Chloe and Andrea's mother in there as well, but it's manageable with a spare mattress on the floor. And I can decamp from the sofa and use the spare room, once I've cleared it out.'

'Splendid idea,' Sally said delightedly as he walked across to attempt to find Chloe's face under the chocolate. 'The spare mattress,' she clarified, lest David get a glimpse of a green-eyed monster. He didn't know that much about her and possessive and stupidly jealous wasn't how Sally wanted him to perceive her. 'And if it all gets too hectic and you need a bolthole, we can always crack open a bottle and cosy up at my place, can't we?'

'Er, yes, maybe.' David scanned Sally's face, his expression inscrutable, and then turned his attention back to Chloe.

Good Lord. Sally sighed inwardly. Did she have to spell it out? Hello, Doctor Adams, I'm inviting you for more than wine. Do you think you could summon up at least a smidgeon of enthusiasm?

'Though I'm assuming your husband might not be too thrilled at my cosying up?' David eyed her questioningly.

Aha, so that was it. Sally felt a huge surge of relief. He was worried about being caught in flagrante by an enraged husband; that was all. Phew. Sally didn't think her brittle self-esteem could have coped with him turning her down flat.

'He won't,' she assured him, with a sad smile as she gave Chloe some milk before putting the cup down. 'He left me, three being a crowd in a marriage, to quote Lady Di.' She swapped a now wriggling Chloe from one arm to the other. 'He's moved on to pastures new.'

'Oh?' David's eyes flicked towards her. 'I'm sorry.' He offered her a smile of commiseration. 'Here, let me,' he said, reaching to relieve her of the chocolate-coated toddler, Chloe now wanting 'downsies'.

'Oh, it's fine. I won't miss him. We weren't compatible anyway. It was bound to happen.'

'It's still hard,' David's tone was soft. He studied her for a second, genuine sympathy in his eyes.

Oh no, don't. Sally glanced quickly down. Kindness – especially from a man – would set her off in an instant. She'd rather he be mean and moody. 'Damn. Chocolate,' she said, noting a stain breast level. 'All over my blouse. Now I'll have to go home and change.' Sally dabbed at the smear with her fingers, annoyed – with Nick for leaving her, and with David for feeling sorry for her, when she wanted him aroused by her. Mostly annoyed with herself for being annoyed with Chloe. What on earth was the matter with her?

'My fault,' David said, setting Chloe carefully down on her feet. 'Should know better than to let a toddler loose with chocolate.'

'No, no. It's not,' Sally insisted, marvelling at how paternal he seemed. How patient. 'It's just …' She squeezed her eyes shut, forcing back a tear. 'Oh no, I can't believe I'm doing this. Poor Andrea, here she is, homeless and heartbroken, and here's me feeling sorry for myself.'

'I think that's called being human,' David said kindly. 'Whoops, hang on a sec.' He moved quickly to close the kitchen door before Chloe went a wandering. 'Come on, little one. Let's do some drawing with Jake's special pencils, shall we?' He lifted her back up and carried her to the table, reaching for a pad and crayons from the work surface as he went.

'Dougal.' Chloe smiled gleefully. 'Draw doggy.'

'Certainly.' David glanced ruefully at Sally, whose heart seemed to be melting along with the chocolate. He really was a nice man, more caring by far than Nick had ever been. Perfect father material.

'Now,' he sat Chloe gently in a chair and popped paper and crayons in front of her, 'you sit there, while I get Sally a cloth, and then we'll make a really good drawing, okay?'

'Iggpiggle.' Chloe, having apparently changed her mind as to the content, resolutely plucked up a pencil.

'No problem.' David nodded obligingly. 'Give me two minutes. Iggpiggle?' he mouthed, obviously mystified as he walked back towards Sally.

'Igglepiggle,' Sally repeated. 'CBeebies *In the Night Garden*,' she enlightened him. 'He's blue with red sticky up hair and carries a red blanket. I think you need to watch more daytime TV.'

David eyed the ceiling. 'Hopefully not.' He reached for more towelling and handed it to Sally.

'Thank you.' Sally smiled through a sniffle. 'And for offering me a shoulder. I'm not normally the falling apart sort, but … You know.'

'It's allowed. Perfectly normal. Other people's traumas often trigger latent emotional responses to our own.'

Sally dabbed at her cheek and nodded, then swallowed. 'I feel so bloody selfish.'

'Don't.' David reached out and squeezed her arm. 'Feeling upset after the events of last night, on top of losing a partner, for whatever reason, isn't unreasonable.'

Sally stared at him in wonder. He's genuine, she thought giddily, her heart swelling as she noted the compassion in his searching blue eyes.

'Doesn't mean you're selfish or bad, just flesh and blood.'

Oh, I'm definitely that, Sally thought, her flesh tingling at his touch. 'Thank you.' She smiled. 'In case I forgot to mention it, your bedside manner, for your information, good doctor, is quite exquisite.'

Sally saw a flicker of apprehension now in David's eyes as she stepped towards him.

He was right. It was chock-a-block in here. Andrea blinked against the semi-darkness once inside the spare room, then walked across to draw back the curtains. The bed was covered in stuff, but not leftover jumble from a house move, as she'd expected. There were clothes. Many clothes, all women's and folded so neatly Andrea didn't like to disturb them: sweaters, T-shirts and jeans, much like those any thirty-something woman would wear, much like her own.

Oh, no. Andrea closed her eyes, realisation finally dawning. There'd been no bitter custody battle. Jake wasn't suffering the fallout of an acrimonious divorce. He was lost and he was lonely because the poor child was grieving the loss of his mother. And David? Could she have ever been more wrong?

Berating herself, Andrea gazed around the room, noting several painted canvasses leaning against the far wall. Tentatively, feeling as if she were trespassing, she walked across to look through them. There were abstracts, some representational. Life drawings too, which were amazingly sensual and extremely well drawn.

Did his wife produce these?

They were beautiful. Passionate. Andrea looked for the artist's signature. Michelle Adams, it read, painted in italic script, soft and flowing, yet bold and strong.

Was that the measure of the woman? Andrea wandered across to peek in the wardrobe, where slightly bohemian, yet exquisitely pretty, summer dresses nestled with stylish skirts and smart blouses. Soft and feminine, yet bold and strong, Jake's mother, the woman who had shaped the child's formative years. David's wife.

Andrea felt she almost knew her, yet couldn't possibly. What had happened to her?

She wiped away a tear.

Padding across to the bed, her gaze fell on a photograph frame on the bedside table. She picked it up and studied the portrait therein. This was her then, Michelle, unquestionably. Jake had his mother's eyes, deep blue, lively, intelligent eyes, where David's were ice-blue almost, and often unreadable.

Jake had David's colouring but his features were more his mother's: delicate, but in a way that would look handsome on a man, showing him to be sensitive. David's features were more rugged. He was the kind of man that wouldn't look out of place climbing a mountain, where his son might be better placed in an art studio.

He might well be climbing a mountain, Andrea thought sadly, David and Jake both; most likely having days where even getting out of bed would seem like an uphill struggle.

Her heart breaking for them, Andrea placed the photograph carefully back on the table, and then selected the simplest garments she could find, lest it be too painful a reminder, for both father and son.

She hadn't noticed any other photographs adorning the house, she realised, other than those gathering dust here in the spare room along with the clothes. Why was that? she wondered, pulling on a plain tracksuit. True, David had only just moved in but she'd noticed ornaments on display, albeit a bit haphazardly. Surely one or two of these photos should be on display alongside them? She didn't know how recently they'd been bereaved, but judging by Jake's behaviour, it couldn't have been all that long ago. It seemed early days yet to have tidied their memories away.

Did Jake have a photograph in his room? He should have. Andrea knew from the loss of her own father, along with the course she'd taken to enable her to help kids through bereavement in school, that Jake needed to know it was all right to grieve the loss of his mum, to celebrate her life and keep whatever he needed to out in the open, for as long as he needed to. She'd ask David about it, when the time was right, she decided. First, she needed to at least offer the man her condolences.

He'd never imagined he would be, but David couldn't have been more grateful to have a toddler throwing a timely tantrum in his kitchen, and a teenager, sulky or otherwise, to hand her over to. Where Sally was concerned, David realised he might have a problem. One he could never have envisaged in a million years. So much for making a new start.

He'd just have to deal with it later. Right now, he needed to concentrate his attention where it should be, on his son. Buttoning a clean shirt as he went, David headed for Jake's room. He hadn't had a chance yet to talk to him about his new school, mainly because Jake had given him the silent treatment when he'd picked him up yesterday. And since then ... Well, he could hardly blame Andrea, but pandemonium all around pretty much put a stop to private conversation.

Bracing himself, he knocked and waited, and then, on the basis that Jake probably wouldn't invite him in, pressed the handle down and went in anyway.

Jake was parked in front of his flat screen watching some animated DVD.

'Hey,' David said.

Jake said nothing.

'We didn't get a chance to talk yet, about your new school.'

No reaction.

'So, how did it go, Jake? Your first day?'

Jake shrugged, arms folded, essential Bench cap pulled way down, eyes under there somewhere fixed firmly on the TV.

David tugged in a breath and tried again. 'Make any new friends?'

Jake sighed, audibly. He didn't avert his gaze.

So far, so good, thought David, dragging a frustrated hand over his neck. 'Do you like it, Jake, the new school?'

More silence.

'I thought being a smaller school it might be easier for you to make new friends,' David pushed on, recalling with overwhelming sadness at how his son had withdrawn, almost visibly, when he told him about Michelle. He hadn't cried. He'd known his mother was ill, Michelle had talked to him quietly, as only a mother could, preparing him for an uncertain future, but maybe he'd never really expected her to die. Maybe he just couldn't accept that she had.

Damn it. It was all maybes. Jake didn't talk about it. Wouldn't talk about it with him anyway. He'd confided in his aunt, possibly because he knew, as Michelle's sister, she would understand his grief. Telling her how much he missed his mum, every single minute of every single day. Crying out in his sleep, according to Becky most nights since his mother had died. David had heard him, too, the night before last, his first night alone with him. Jake, obviously not wanting any comfort David might try to offer him, had feigned sleep when he'd gone in to check on him.

David couldn't blame him. He swallowed back the heavy taste of guilt, born of his own culpability in Michelle's death. If only he'd been there. Glancing towards the window, where a fresh deluge of rain spattered against the glass, David tried not to dwell on it because it crushed him all over again every time he did, and he'd be no help to Jake feeling like that. He couldn't have saved her, ultimately. David knew that, deep down. Jake might realise it too, though it didn't look as if he'd confide in David anytime soon – if ever.

He couldn't blame him for that either. The fact was he hadn't been there for Michelle way before the accident. As a doctor, yes, for all the good that could do, but emotionally … He'd bailed out. He knew that much was true. Jake did, too. How could he forgive his father that?

He didn't deserve forgiveness. He'd turned his back on the two … No, three people who most needed him, when they most needed him because he'd been too scared and inadequate to offer the boy's mother the support she desperately needed. How the hell was he supposed to explain that to a ten-year-old child? Tell him how sorry he was that he'd been incapable of focusing on anything but his own self–centred pain. He couldn't. He'd tried, several times, stumbling over useless words.

And failed.

Jake didn't want to hear it. Didn't want to talk to him at all. David understood why, though it didn't hurt any the less. He hadn't needed the counsellor at his last surgery to tell him you don't just go through stages and that was it, grief over. It might become more manageable after the sheer desolation at the beginning. You might pass through so-called stages, move on, accept it eventually, but you could never deny it. Grief had a habit of washing over you when and where you least expected it, David was well aware of that. His own grief was bad enough, but Jake's … The boy was probably grieving twice over, for the loss of his mother, and for the loss of the father who, in his mind, had deserted them both.

David wanted Jake to know it was okay to feel it, to express the hurt, the anger. That grieving was as unpredictable as life and couldn't be packaged up and packed away. He wanted to help Jake not to forget, if only he knew how. To recall the good stuff, not just the bad, to be able to talk about it with him. How he wished Jake and he could talk.

He glanced at Jake again, recalling vividly the look of adoration that once shone in his son's eyes, when Jake had trusted him, laughed with him, as kids should with their fathers. 'What's it to be,' David would ask him on the drive home from Jake's regular Friday football practice, 'Rachmaninoff or Radio One?'

'Old man music, I suppose.' Jake would have indulged him whilst shaking his head, denigrating his dad's sad taste in music.

David would give a wry smile and then play Rachmaninoff's 'Piano Concerto No. 2' at full volume, windows wide and not giving a damn about anything or anyone. David wished the kid would denigrate him now. Say something, no matter how banal.

Shout at him. Anything.

Realising Jake wasn't going to utter even a word, David gave up and turned to the door, knowing that if he tried to physically reach out to him, Jake would shrug him off – and that's what hurt most of all, the fact that he couldn't even hug the boy, when Jake so badly needed him to.

'We really should stop meeting like this. People will talk.' Andrea smiled coming out of the spare room to meet David on the landing.

David sighed, feeling ragged inside. 'I needed to get changed,' he said, forcing a smile back. 'Sally, she, er, got chocolate on my shirt.'

Andrea blinked at him, clearly bemused.

'Chloe, that is, got chocolate on Sally's shirt. Blouse, I mean. I took Chloe off her and—'

'Got in a mess?' Andrea suggested.

'Definitely.' One hell of a mess, David thought ruefully, still reeling from the shock of Sally's impromptu kiss. Damn it. He shouldn't have allowed that to happen. Allowed any of it to happen. David pulled himself up, looking at Andrea looking at him. Her pretty green eyes scrutinising his very thoughts, he felt.

'Your mother was in the bedroom when I went in, unfortunately,' David attempted to change the subject. 'I was half out of the shirt before I realised. She thinks I'm out to have my wicked way with her now.'

Andrea laughed. 'She's hoping, you mean. Just watch she doesn't sink her wandering teeth into parts of your anatomy when you walk past her.'

'I'll be on my guard,' David assured her, his eyes involuntarily travelling over her. It suited her, the tracksuit. The trainers obviously fitted her too. He was glad she'd chosen something innocuous that didn't scream Michelle, for Jake's sake. Would Michelle have minded him doing this? Offering this woman her clothes? His hospitality?

David thought not. She'd probably congratulate him for finally finding the courage to be there for someone in a crisis.

'I'd better go and put some washing in. We're all out of shirts.' Offering her another smile, he turned for the stairs, wishing he could turn back the clock and do things differently. Allow Jake to be the child he should be.

'No work then?' Andrea asked conversationally.

'I'm not due to start until next week. Jake's aunt cared for him for a while before the move, but now ... Well, I need to give him a little more of my time, you know? The surgery has a locum covering for me, so ...'

Andrea nodded, understanding.

'I said he could stay at home today, by the way. It seemed unfair to make him go to school with so much going on around here. I hope Miss Kelly doesn't disapprove?'

'Absolutely not. He'd feel pushed out if he was packed off while my tribe get to stay at home. We'll all get back to normal soon.' Andrea shrugged hopefully. 'Somehow.' She stepped towards him and briefly placed a hand on his arm. 'David, I just wanted to say I was sorry, about Michelle. Your loss. I didn't realise.'

David shot her a quizzical look. Michelle? Where had she ...? Ah, the paintings. She'd obviously seen them. She hadn't known Michelle. How could she? Nor then, by association, what a bastard he'd been.

'Don't be.' David closed his eyes briefly. The woman taught at Jake's school. She should know, he supposed, at least some of why there was a gulf the size of an ocean between him and his son. 'I ... let her down.'

'Oh.' Andrea nodded, obviously not sure what to say. 'Well, none of us are perfect,' she started sympathetically. 'We all make—'

'Badly,' David added, reinforcing the fact that sympathy for him would be sympathy wasted. 'I wasn't there for her ... before she died. Jake, he, er ... He has some issues, as you can probably—' David stopped, looking past Andrea to where Jake stood in his doorway, his complexion ashen, his expression as if he'd run full-force into a goalpost. 'Jake?' David moved quickly towards him, but Jake moved faster, stepping back swiftly into his room.

'Jake!' David ground to a halt outside the slammed door.

'Go away!' Jake shouted from inside. 'I hate you!'

David placed his hands either side of the doorframe, every muscle in his body tense with frustration and anger. 'Damn it!'

Chapter Nine

'How is he?' Andrea asked when David came into the lounge, after several failed attempts to communicate with his son through the closed door.

'Still in his room.' David ran his hand over his neck, looking exasperated. 'Won't come out. Won't let me in.'

Ryan glanced up from *The Simpsons* on TV. 'Do you want me to have a go?' he asked. 'See if I can get him to talk?'

David glanced at him. Hopefully, Andrea noticed. Also noticing how totally exhausted the man looked. As if he hadn't slept properly in months. Yes, and given what he'd just confided, he possibly didn't deserve to.

The man had obviously been with someone else. That's what Jake's anger was all about. But then, as unpalatable as it seemed, it was hardly a hanging offence, Andrea supposed. And, as much as some background information might be helpful in regard to Jake, the details really were none of her business. Andrea cautioned herself not to poke her nose in where it wasn't wanted and turned her attention away from David, who seemed to look more dejected by the second, to Ryan. 'Do you think he might talk to you?'

'Dunno. Might. I could offer to take him into town now, if you like, rather than later? Do man stuff, you know?'

'Boy stuff, you mean,' Sophie muttered, from where she sat curled up in the armchair, fiddling idly with her hair.

'Thanks, Ryan.' David smiled, visibly relieved. 'That'd be great.'

''S'no big deal,' Ryan said as if it were indeed no big deal, which of course it was. Trawling the town centre with a 'kid' in tow could seriously curtail Ryan's 'pulling' power. Not that Andrea had seen much evidence his pulling endeavours had succeeded thus far.

''Course, I might need some dosh,' Ryan suggested nonchalantly as he got to his feet.

'No problem. How much?' David asked, reaching into his pocket before Andrea had time to protest.

Ryan shrugged his shoulders under his 'Undercover Genius' T-shirt. 'Dunno. Thought we might get a PlayStation game appropriate to his age.' He eyed David interestedly.

'Get a couple.' David plucked at least fifty pounds in notes from his wallet.

Ryan held out his hand, delighted. 'Cool.'

'No wait.' David stuffed the notes back. Ryan looked less delighted.

'Take my card.' David handed Ryan a bank card instead. 'Get whatever you need from the cash machine. You'll need a change of clothes, while you're there.'

'Stunning.' Ryan nodded approvingly. 'Do I get the number?'

'1515. Memorise it and then eat it.'

Andrea opened her mouth to say something when David stopped her.

'Not conscience money,' David said, turning to Andrea as Ryan popped the bank card hilariously between his teeth and scooted for the door. 'Necessary purchases,' he pointed out. 'Particularly if it means Jake will talk to Ryan. We can settle our differences later. Yes?'

Andrea heaved Chloe higher in her arms and studied him. She wasn't sure they had any differences, other than those on the subject of doling out money so readily. She should object, out of earshot of Miss Moody-Spikey, but the look in David's eyes was one of quiet desperation just then. Whatever he'd done in the past, he was trying to do right by his son, Andrea was now sure of that. He might have challenged her to dislike him, but she doubted she could dislike him as much as he seemed to dislike himself.

She nodded, albeit reluctantly. He was right. Clothes were necessary purchases. She needed to get Ryan and Sophie back to college and school and Chloe to nursery as soon as possible. They needed normality right now. And she needed some space to sort herself out. Speak to the insurance company for a start, if only she could remember who they were insured with. Insurance had always been Jonathan's department, him being 'in the business'. Andrea chose not to dwell on why Jonathan wasn't here to damn well deal with it. She'd think about that when she had time to think. She'd just have to pay David back as soon as she could. And if the computer game could ignite a spark of enthusiasm in Jake ...

'Oi!' Sophie shouted after Ryan, cutting Andrea's thoughts short. 'Bring the remote back, muppet!'

'I'll just, er ...' Possibly to avoid getting caught in the crossfire, David nodded and headed towards the hall as Ryan wandered back in.

'Thought you said *The Simpsons* was for kids.' Ryan tossed Sophie the remote, then sauntered back out with a smirk.

'It is,' Sophie informed him, notching up the volume. 'Gran wants to watch it.'

Andrea winced at the mention of Dee. She'd forgotten she'd got a mum. 'Kitchen. Defrosting the oven,' Sophie supplied, then dutifully obliged as Andrea handed her Chloe.

Defrosting the what? Andrea dashed for the door, then stopped. 'Sophie?'

'Huh?'

'Sorry about being a bit snappy. It's just—'

'— not PMS. It's you?' Sophie finished, glancing sideways at her. ''S'okay,' she offered grudgingly. 'Shit happens.'

Definitely. Andrea shook her head, deciding to ignore the

bad language in favour of not berating her daughter, yet again, and skidded to the kitchen, where Dee was floating about in her nightie looking quite at home.

Andrea waited while she filled up an ovenproof dish with boiling water. 'Um, Mum,' she started hesitantly as Dee parked the kettle and plucked up the oven gloves, 'why are you defrosting the oven?'

'The oven?' Dee glanced at her, puzzled. 'Don't be ridiculous, darling, the oven's self-cleaning,' she informed her despairingly. 'I'm defrosting the freezer before we all get semolina.'

Andrea held her breath until Dee got the dish safely in place in the freezer, which did look like the North Pole after a blizzard, Andrea had to admit. 'Salmonella, Mum,' she corrected her as Dee turned back, looking pleased with herself.

'No, thank you, darling. I like a bit of cod, but salmon gets under my palate,' Dee said sweetly, then boomed, 'Do you mind? I've just cleaned that!' as David stepped into the kitchen.

David froze mid-step and glanced at Andrea, obviously baffled.

'The floor.' Andrea nodded towards his feet, which Dee was making evil eyes at.

'Oh, right.' David scratched his head and stepped back. 'Great. Thanks. I think.'

Lord, at this rate the man would be checking himself into a hotel, or a mental institution very soon.

'Mum's very house-proud,' Andrea offered by way of explanation for her mother's preoccupation with cleaning his house.

'Bit of dirt never hurt anyone,' Dee imparted, bustling over to yank the dishwasher door open. 'Germs, however, do.' She threw the tea towel into the dishwasher, banged the door closed, then turned to give David a meaningful stare.

David looked as if he didn't know which way to turn. 'Sorry,' he offered embarrassedly. 'I rented the house furnished. I haven't had much time yet to—'

'Now,' Dee said over him, dusting off her hands, 'have you cleaned your skirting boards lately?'

'Er, no,' David admitted, looking shamefaced. 'I'm not sure if someone cleaned the house before we moved in. I've organised a cleaner but she—'

'Well, they ought to be sacked,' Dee huffed, and then strutted across the kitchen to run a finger along the skirting board. 'I think you'd better show the young lady to me when she arrives,' she suggested, offering the evidence of the servant's slovenly ways for David to see.

David sighed melodramatically. 'Unbelievable. You just can't get good staff nowadays, can you?'

'Precisely.' Dee looked at David for the first time with the merest hint of approval and then strode purposefully past him into the hall.

Andrea smiled, realising that he was indulging her mother, rather than despairing of her or making fun of her, as Jonathan might.

David eyed the ceiling good-naturedly and then smiled back at her, but still there was an immense sadness about him.

Andrea held his gaze, feeling for him, though she wasn't sure why.

'Do you think she's noticed the cobwebs yet?' David's gaze travelled worriedly upwards again, after a second.

Andrea laughed. 'Oh, dear, she can be a bit much, can't she? Sorry about that. Mum gets a bit confused. It can be quite amusing, but …' She paused, wondering how much to say. How he'd react. Would Doctor Adams be of the opinion she should put her mother out to grass for the sake of the people around her and for her own sake?

'A bit of a handful, as well, sometimes?' David finished astutely.

Andrea felt her shoulders physically droop. 'Yes,' she admitted, with a tired nod. 'She tends to get a bit muddled. Wanders off occasionally, too, and then gets lost, you know?'

'Trying to find her way home?' David suggested.

Andrea thought about it. 'Yes,' she conceded, realising that Dee's wanderings often did take her in the direction of the canal. It hadn't occurred to her before, but the riverside cottage might well be where her mother was headed. The place Dee still thought of as home even though Andrea had explained to her many times that it had been sold. She dearly hoped she didn't wander too far that way – a fresh worry surfaced – now that it was actually under renovation.

'It's symptomatic,' David said sympathetically. 'Dementia is an unkind condition, short-term memory loss, meaning the past is more real than the present, inertia, mood swings. The cruellest part though, I imagine, are the periods of absolute lucidity.'

Andrea closed her eyes and pulled in a breath. 'She is aware, a lot of the time,' she said quietly. 'She's not muddled up Dee. She's my mum, there for me, like she's always been. Do you see? And then we'll talk, and laugh, and—' Andrea stopped, wishing people could understand. There might come a time when she couldn't cope, she knew that. But, for now, she could. More importantly, she wanted to.

'At least she can laugh,' David offered reassuringly. 'And you can laugh with her. Can't be all bad.'

Andrea smiled.

David did too. 'She seems happy enough.'

'Yes.' Andrea's smile broadened. 'Yes, she is,' she said, comforted by the fact that this near stranger seemed to understand that for as long as she could, Andrea wanted to grab every bit of happiness for her mother, not rob of her of what dignity she had left.

'And I think I can live with my shortcomings in the housework department being pointed out.' Again, David rolled his eyes affably.

Andrea scrunched her eyes closed. 'Sorry,' she said, peeling one eye open. 'She does get a bit carried away sometimes. Misses her own little cottage much more than I imagined she would.'

David nodded. 'Just bricks and mortar to some, but a lifetime's memories for her.'

'Yes.' Andrea studied him curiously, wondering why he'd worked so hard at appearing to be obnoxious initially.

David glanced down, then back. 'I do have a cleaner, starting next week hopefully, but it's not a problem if your mother wants to go wild with the duster meanwhile,' he said, with an unconcerned shrug. 'The place could do with a good spring clean anyway.'

'It'll be more like a cat lick and a whisper.'

David looked at her, confused.

'One of Mum's sayings, meaning: a quick surface clean rather than getting down to the nitty-gritty. She's a bit hit-and-miss, I'm afraid, but I don't like to take jobs off her. She finds that patronising, you know?'

David obviously got the gist. 'Fine by me. She can clean away as hit-and-miss as she likes, as long as she doesn't look under the chairs in the lounge.'

Andrea shuddered. 'Oh dear. Make yourself scarce, if she does.'

'I'm on my starting blocks.' David laughed, and there was a definite twinkle in his eye this time, making him more human and accessible.

Andrea studied him, trying to work out what circumstances had brought him here, a widower obviously torturing himself with his past.

David looked away first, glancing down again and then

towards the hall, relieved probably, that he'd been saved from further scrutiny by the doorbell.

'You're staring,' Nita informed David, who was looking at his callers bemused.

It was more likely to be Eva than Nita who had flummoxed him though, Andrea suspected. Eva was standing behind Nita's wheelchair brandishing a huge courgette. The woman beside her, draped in faux fur and with a bunch of aubergines pressed to her fulsome breast, was also rather alarming.

'Are you waiting for us to die of hypothermia, or are you going to invite us in?' the woman asked bluntly.

'Er?' David glanced over his shoulder at Andrea, who shrugged apologetically. Nita, who only worked Monday to Thursdays on her work placement, had obviously wanted to check Andrea was okay, which was kind.

'Yes, of course,' David said, smiling uncertainly and standing aside.

'Well?' said the woman.

'Sorry?' David now looked extremely confused.

'Are you going to help her in, or leave her on the doorstep?' the woman went on curtly.

'By her she means me,' Nita clarified, with a roll of her eyes. 'And she obviously thinks you're a weightlifter. What do you want him to do, Mum?' she craned her neck over her shoulder to eyeball the woman. 'Carry me over it?'

Ah, so this was Nita's mother. No wonder Nita was looking so pained. Andrea tried not to laugh as the woman proceeded to look David up and down as if he were a prime cut of beef. 'Hmm?' she said interestedly, her eyes pinging wide.

Nita sighed exasperatedly. 'Mum, no.'

'I don't suppose you're single, are you, by any chance?' the woman asked, predictably, judging by Nita's now mortified expression.

'Oooh, Mum, will you just stop with the fishing expeditions.' Nita scowled. 'I'm seventeen years old! I'm probably only half his age.'

'What? I'm not.' The woman stood ramrod straight, her chin tucked in indignantly. 'I only asked him if he was single. I wasn't necessarily trying to net him for you, Nita.' With which, she gave David another lingering perusal, beamed him a smile, then waltzed on in, leaving her daughter on the doorstep.

'Meet my mother, Dorothea. Thea for short. Greek translation for gift of God,' Nita offered in her wake.

'I'd rather not,' David mumbled.

'Ditto,' said Nita. 'Don't suppose you fancy sweeping me off my feet, despite Mother having first dibs on you, do you?'

'No problem.' David mustered up a smile. Then, as if it were second nature, he bent down to allow Nita to wrap her arms around his neck and lifted her into his own arms – which had Andrea, once again, quite unable to reconcile this obviously caring man with the uncaring one he'd insisted on presenting.

She wished she knew more about his circumstances. Jake clearly needed someone to talk to, but she couldn't help thinking David Adams needed to confide in someone too. Chance would be a fine thing, she sighed, stepping down to help Eva in with Nita's wheelchair.

'I can manage,' Eva assured her, already having competently tipped it back and aimed it at the doorstep.

Andrea didn't doubt it. 'I know. I just ...' A cold shudder running through her, Andrea paused, glancing past Eva to the blackened ruins of her house, the ashes of her life.

'Quite fancy running in the other direction?' Eva finished, parking the chair in the hall. 'I don't blame you. Doctor Adams is probably contemplating bolting out of the back door. Come on,' she said, turning to wrap an arm around Andrea's shoulders and steer her around, 'one day at a time, my dear. You'll get through this. We women do, you know. Meanwhile, we have a man in our midst whom I suspect may need rescuing.'

She nodded up the hall and Andrea couldn't help but smile as Nita's tones drifted back. 'Just don't let your eyes linger anywhere near my boobs,' she heard her warn David, as the two negotiated the lounge door. 'She'll be knitting baby boots and booking the font before you can blink.'

Oh dear. Andrea laughed out loud as Eva manoeuvred the chair after them, looking like a land girl about to till the soil in her dungarees. 'We're making moussaka,' she informed Andrea enthusiastically over her shoulder. 'Thea's idea. Rather a splendid one, I thought. Community spirit and whatnot, what ho?'

Andrea knitted her brow and trailed after her. 'Um, Eva, it's really very kind of you, but we're homeless, not starving,' she pointed out.

'Yet,' added Thea as Andrea went into the lounge, from which Sophie swiftly exited, a horrified expression on her face and Chloe safely in her arms.

'You've moved in with a man, darling,' Thea went on as if it were perfectly obvious what she was talking about. 'Clearly you'll be needing a good square meal inside you.' With which Thea deposited her aubergines on the coffee table. 'Look at you, nothing but skin and bone,' she observed, looking Andrea over.

Andrea smiled wanly, torn between being flattered and hugely embarrassed.

'Moussaka,' Thea added decisively, following the aubergines with onions and tomatoes produced from her handbag. 'Building bricks of life, my late husband always said, may he rest in peace.'

'Finally,' Nita muttered as David lowered her onto the sofa, a smile playing at his mouth.

'From my own mother's traditional Greek recipe, of course.'

Andrea looked doubtfully at the courgettes and carrots Eva added to the pile.

'Bit of home-cooked will soon put the roses back in your cheeks,' Thea said, bustling across to tweak Andrea's apparently pale cheek. 'Give you strength to rebuild your broken home, you poor girl.'

Andrea, wincing from the rather over-affectionate tweak, didn't like to point out that she wasn't actually thinking of rebuilding her home personally, with or without moussaka-shaped building bricks.

'We're all pitching in,' Eva pitched in. 'We're going to be with you every step of the way. There's a collection going on door-to-door as we speak.'

'Oh.' Andrea was now extremely doubtful. She didn't want her neighbours feeling obliged to hand money over on her behalf. She'd have the insurance, eventually, if she ever had time to contact them.

'Don't look so worried, my dear,' Eva said, patting her forearm. 'We're only asking for clothes. I don't suppose there'll be much in the way of vintage, but we'll think about re-stocking for the shop when we've sorted out the essentials.'

'No.' Andrea sighed inwardly, thinking about the stock she'd lost, the 1920s Japanese silk kimono, a late 1960s gold brocade trouser suit, the 1960s Radley Moss crepe mini-dress Sally had found in a charity shop, along with the 1950s Eriko thee-quarter length coat. The '70s Gucci bags. The '80s silver sequined jackets ... All unique. All irreplaceable. All gone, along with her Second Chance Designer dream. She hadn't even got a home, she reminded herself, fear and dread for the future twisting inside her. Stock for the shop was way down on her list of priorities, but still it hurt to have her dreams ended in a puff of smoke.

'Meanwhile,' Eva went on as Andrea swallowed back a hard lump in her throat, 'we're selecting the best of the cast-offs for you to sift through for your family, and the rest is going towards a grand jumble sale to start up a bit of a kitty to help refurnish your house.'

'Oh.' Andrea blinked at her, taken aback. 'Thank you, Eva,' she said, overwhelmed, in every sense of the word.

'That's what neighbours are for, my dear,' Eva assured her, giving Andrea's arm another comforting little pat, then striding purposefully back towards the hall. 'I'll just go and get the éclairs and then we can all settle down and discuss our plan of action.'

'Eclairs?' Andrea arched an eyebrow at Nita, who only yesterday was bemoaning the size of her bum.

Nita shrugged blamelessly. 'What's a girl supposed to do?'

Andrea shook her head, feeling as bewildered as David looked. 'Sorry,' she mouthed as he walked towards her to the hall, looking ever so slightly cross-eyed.

'No problem,' David repeated his stock phrase. 'I'll just go and prescribe myself some Prozac.'

Chapter Ten

'Thought you'd want to know Ryan and Jake are off out,' David said, coming into the kitchen where Andrea was making tea and wondering whether to invest in an urn.

'Ryan managed to talk him out of his room, then?'

'Yes, amazingly,' David said, obviously relieved. 'Not sure Jake's going to be talking to me any time soon though.'

'Catchya lata,' Ryan interrupted, poking his head around the kitchen door. 'By the way, you do realise there's a Women's Institute meeting in the lounge?'

Andrea swapped amused glances with David. 'It's the Save the Kellys Committee. Whatever you do, don't get too close to the door or they'll whip you in and knit you up a sweater.'

'We're outa here.' Ryan retracted his head in a flash. 'Come on, Jake,' his wary tones drifted back from the hall, 'let's go catch the bus, before they start hugging us and ruffling our hair.'

'Stick close to Ryan, Jake, and do as he says, okay?' David called after them.

Jake didn't answer, and David looked utterly crushed.

Andrea guessed why. Most children that age wouldn't have let that comment pass without an 'I'm not a kid' retort. Some retort. Jake, it seemed, wasn't talking to his father at all.

'I take it he didn't know?' she asked quietly, pushing the kitchen door to, once the boys had left. 'About your, um, indiscretion; assuming that's what it was?'

David searched her eyes, seeming to debate, and then nodded tiredly. 'Indiscretion,' he repeated, his mouth curving into a sad smile, 'quaint way of describing destroying three people's lives. Four people's.'

He stopped, tugging a sharp breath, as if the memory

physically pained him. 'I'm not sure. He, er ... He knew something was wrong. Heard Michelle and me ...'

'Arguing?'

David nodded, glancing away. 'Michelle ... She was ill. Leukaemia. Lymphatic. I didn't handle it very well. Her decision, I mean.'

Decision? Andrea's heart lurched. 'To?' she gently urged him on.

David breathed out. 'She ... Michelle, she was pregnant. She decided against therapeutic abortion. And she insisted on delaying anti-leukaemic treatment until the third trimester for the baby's sake. It wouldn't have made a great deal of difference to her life expectancy in the long term, but in the short term ...'

All this David said with his eyes fixed to the floor. 'I wasn't there for her,' he went on tightly. 'I should have been.'

He glanced up at last, such anguish in his eyes, Andrea felt utterly wretched for him. He'd lost his wife and his child?

'I'd better go.' He looked quickly away again. 'I have some reading to catch up on. I'll be in the study, if you or the Kelly Committee need anything.'

Feeling utterly devastated for him, Andrea watched David walk away, his hand going through his hair, visibly hurting. Of course he would be. Whatever he'd done, with or without details of where he had been when his wife needed him, Andrea realised she had no right to judge him. Because, no matter the abrasiveness she'd first encountered, it was obvious the man was carrying his guilt around like a lead weight.

It was too soon for him to consign it to history, undoubtedly, but David Adams needed to try to forgive himself in order to move on. As did his son. How could they do that when they'd both separately erected brick walls?

She'd take him some tea, Andrea decided. It probably wouldn't help much, but it might send out the right signals, that she wasn't about to despise him, no matter that he'd seemed to want her to. So he wasn't perfect. Was anyone? Was she?

After a quick check on Chloe, who was napping in David's bed, oblivious to the chaos all around, bless her mismatching pyjamas, and then Sophie, who was washing her hair, Andrea tapped on the door to the study. Then waited. Then wondered whether to go on in when David didn't answer. She tapped again.

Still nothing. Andrea was about to step away from the door when he opened it. 'I brought you a cure-all cuppa.' She offered him a smile. 'It's got its work cut out I know, but, well, it's warm and wet, anyhow.'

He looked at her, seemingly unseeing for a second and then gave her a short smile back. 'Thanks,' he said, reaching for the cup.

'No problem.' Andrea assured him, holding his eyes.

Eyes where dark shadows danced. Those of a man, Andrea realised with a jolt, who might actually have been crying? She stared at him, feeling the despair which seemed to emanate almost palpably from him now.

'David, if you ever want to ...' she started, and then stopped as her mum's not-so dulcet tones drifted up the hall.

'Eva Bunting, get out of my kitchen immediately!' Dee bellowed. 'And take that furry fleabag with you!'

Referring to Thea and her faux fur, Andrea assumed, despairing.

David smiled bemusedly. 'I think the Kelly Committee have taken over the kitchen.'

'Lord help us.' Andrea rolled her eyes and dashed off to referee.

'Deirdre, my dear, don't you think you might be getting a little paranoid?' Eva asked Dee across the casserole pot they were fighting over. Eva had a hold of one handle, Dee hung onto the other and both, it seemed, were reluctant to let go.

'Paranoid, pffffffff! Don't try to distract me with your long words and privileged education, Eva Bunting, you great fat ...' Dee looked Eva up and down, taking in her dungarees distastefully. '... lesbian, you!'

I don't believe this. Andrea turned back to her pan, whammed the flame up under it and threw another batch of aubergines in, careless of the instructions on Thea's recipe to fry gently.

'For your information, it wasn't privileged, Deirdre,' Eva supplied plummily. 'Mummy scrimped and saved to put me through university, actually.'

'Well, for your information ...' Dee tugged the casserole pot towards her. '... this mummy scrimped and saved to put her daughter through university, too.'

'In which case, my dear ...' Eva gave the pot a tug back in her direction. '... we have something in common, don't we?'

'That's as maybe, but not ...' Dee tugged the pot back again. '... my casserole pot!'

'Girls, girls,' Thea said, whisking egg yolks heartily, oblivious to the danger of the ingredients already in the casserole pot ending up all over the floor, 'stop with the arguments, or you'll spoil our lovely lunch.'

Our? Oh, no, please! Andrea's eyes sprang wide. They weren't intending to stay, were they? Uh-uh. Absolutely not. David would barricade himself in his study and stay there. And Andrea might blooming well join him.

'All done!' she trilled, turning the 'darkly' browned aubergines over and dousing the gas.

'It is not,' Eva declared.

'Not what?' Dee eyeballed her over the pot.

'Not your pot. It's the doctor's.'

'What doctor's?'

'Doctor Adams.' Eva eyeballed Dee back. 'This is the doctor's house.'

'Oh, no it isn't,' Dee huffed, giving the pot another tug.

'Oh, yes, it is,' Thea chipped in, coming across to pluck the lid off the pot. 'He lives here,' she announced as she scraped the aubergines in. 'He's upstairs in the shower, right now as we speak.'

Dee knitted her brow. 'With Andrea?' she asked, turning to blink mystified at Andrea.

'No, dear.' Eva sighed. 'Andrea's not in the shower, is she? She's here.'

Dear Lord, please beam me up. Flushing down to her décolleté, Andrea opened her scrunched eyes to see Thea bustling back from the work surface with the sauce.

'Uh-uh. Enough!' Andrea shouted over Thea's revelations that she wouldn't mind sharing a shower with Doctor Adams. That sauce was hot. And those two dotty women were still clutching that pot.

'Thea, thank you so much for all your help, we really appreciate it, but I think Mum and I can manage from here,' Andrea suggested, her tone slightly more subdued, if a little demented.

'Oh, it's no bother.' Thea waved away her concerns with the flap of an extravagantly bejewelled hand. 'We only have to season it and then pop it in the oven and—'

'It's ever so kind of you, Thea, but I think we'd rather—' Andrea started.

'—then we can all put our feet up with a nice sherry and watch a DVD,' Thea finished. 'How does that sound?'

'Um?' Andrea opened her mouth and then closed it. And swallowed. The last thing she wanted to do was offend anyone, but ... She glanced desperately from Thea to a still miffed Dee and then to Eva. Then quickly at the floor as a long overdue tear plopped down her cheek.

'I think what Andrea's trying to say, Thea, without wishing to sound ungrateful for your sterling efforts,' Eva picked up shrewdly, 'is that she'd quite like her mother to finish the job.'

Andrea glanced hopefully back up.

'Deirdre's a bit of a dab hand in the kitchen herself, after all, aren't you, my dear?' Eva offered Dee a short smile and finally allowed her the pot.

'Thank you,' Andrea mouthed, relieved.

Eva shot her a quick thumbs up, then rounded up Thea. 'Come along, my dear,' she said, marching her towards the door, 'let's collect the daughter you left on the doorstep before she dies of boredom in the lounge, then we'll all scoot over to my place for a wee sherry, shall we?'

'Oh, by the way, I've rung the investment company direct,' Eva said, hanging behind as Andrea showed her self-invited guests out.

Andrea looked at her, puzzled.

'About my withdrawal,' Eva reminded her. 'I was assuming Jonathan would be up to his eyes, running around trying to sort out your affairs and whatnot?'

Andrea nodded awkwardly. 'Yes, most likely,' she mumbled evasively.

Eva glanced at her askew, no doubt wondering about the vagueness of her answer. 'They're going to ring me back,' she went on. 'Apparently they're having a spot of bother matching up my policy number with my investment, or some such nonsense. Computer glitch, so they say. Good old-fashioned cock-up, if you ask me. Do you know, they even had the cheek to ask me if I was quoting the correct policy number? Fortunately, I had my own list of investments in front of me so I gave them short shrift there, I can tell you.'

'Oh, right. I'll, um ...' Andrea searched for something to say other than actually Jonathan's suffering a slight malfunction too. As in, forgotten I exist.

Eva held up a silencing hand. 'No, no. Don't trouble him, my dear. You both have more than enough to worry about, and I'm sure I'll catch him around.'

Andrea wasn't quite so sure she would. She nodded anyway and, with supreme effort, arranged her face into a smile. She'd been keeping the emotion in check, just. Speculation as to Jonathan's whereabouts, though, might have her dissolving in a heap on the hall carpet. She couldn't do that. Couldn't allow herself the luxury of going to pieces, no matter how therapeutic David Adams thought tears might be. Not with the children to think about.

'I'll pop back later,' Eva promised, stopping at the front door to give Andrea a reassuring, if rather firm, hug. 'I've got something that might cheer you up. I'll bring it with me.'

'George Clooney? Wearing nothing but a smile and bearing a chocolate éclair?'

'Ooh, how terribly naughty,' Eva exclaimed delightedly. 'But nice.'

She winked over her shoulder as she finally followed the rest of the Kelly Committee out.

Andrea closed the door behind her and turned to lean against it with a sigh as David came downstairs.

'That sounds like a sigh of relief.' He nodded past her to their departed guests and then looked Andrea over.

She was pale, he noticed. He wasn't sure she was up to a constant stream of visitors. He didn't doubt the neighbours' kind intentions, but if they weren't careful, the person they were trying to help might just keel over under the weight of their do-gooding.

She can't have slept much. Concerned, he stopped to study her more closely. She looked weary. Pretty, even with telltale shadows under her eyes, but exhausted. She was strong. David had no doubt about that. He'd been watching her, looking for signs of shock: tears, debilitating flashbacks – something he knew about on a personal as well as professional level. There'd been none, other than long sighs and momentary lapses in concentration.

Even then, she seemed to pull herself up and get on with things for the sake of her kids. David knew all about that, too. Still though, with three children, including one barely out of nappies, no possessions and her house burnt to the ground, David thought she must have a rod of iron running through her spine to still be standing upright.

'Is it safe to go in?' he asked, nodding cautiously towards the lounge.

'Safe-ish.' Andrea laughed.

And David found himself smiling, again. How the hell did she do that? Laugh when her world had fallen apart? Andrea Kelly, he was beginning to realise, was a bit of an enigma. Despite the chaos she'd brought with her, she was a bright spark in what seemed to have been perpetual gloom lately.

'As long as you don't mind Sophie snarling at you because her spikes won't stand up,' she added.

David furrowed his brow, confused. Andrea pointed at her head. 'No hairdryer.'

'Ah, right.' He nodded and took a breath. 'There's one upstairs,' he offered. He hadn't parted with anything of Michelle's yet. The dryer, amongst other things, might as well go to good use here, though, he supposed. 'It's in the, er …' Actually, he wasn't quite sure where it was. 'Tell you what, I'll go and find it.'

David started back up the stairs and then stopped, turning to swap wary glances with Andrea as the doorbell went again. 'Shall we duck?' he suggested.

Andrea pressed a finger to her lips. 'Shhhh,' she hissed, another laugh escaping her nevertheless. Yes, David most definitely liked that about her, a laugh that was infectious.

She should bottle that and sell it online. She'd make a fortune.

Andrea peeked over her shoulder at the opaque glass in the door. 'Drat. I think we've been spotted.'

'Damn.' David emitted a melodramatic sigh. 'Maybe we should get closed-circuit television out there. Then we can hide in advance?'

'Or a moat?' Andrea suggested.

'With a drawbridge,' David mused. 'And a gun in the turret. What do you think?'

'I think I should answer the door,' Andrea informed him, a twinkle in her eye David hadn't noticed before. This woman, he decided, was just what the doctor might order, a tonic, no doubt about it.

Sighing theatrically again, he saluted and turned back up the stairs. 'You're a braver man than I am. Good luck.'

'Did anyone ever tell you you're a little bit mad?' Andrea called good-humouredly after him.

'Frequently,' David called back, still smiling. Mad was about right, giving houseroom to a whole other family when his own family was so fractured, but he had to concede he was feeling a little less lonely in the midst of the madness.

Careful not to let his eyes linger too long on anything else in the spare room, he retrieved the hairdryer from a box under the window and started back down, then ... shit ... faltered mid-stairs as he noticed Sally in the hall.

'They cost me an arm and a leg when I bought them,' Sally was saying, passing a bag to Andrea, 'but your need is greater.'

'You shouldn't have, Sally, really ...' Andrea peered excitedly into the bag, her expression falling a bit flat as she extracted what looked like a baby-doll nightie '... you shouldn't have.'

'There's some underwear too,' Sally said, delving deeper

and bringing out black lace lingerie that had David missing the last step.

'Oops,' Sally said, flashing him a coy smile as he righted himself in the hall. 'They're hardly worn,' she went on, more to David than Andrea, a definite innuendo in her eye.

David noted the look and mentally kicked himself for not immediately telling Sally he just didn't feel the way he suspected she needed him to. He liked the woman, what he knew of her, but he couldn't envisage lying safe and satiated in her arms, talking late into the night of secrets and dreams. He doubted he'd ever want to smile quietly inside when she smiled. Laugh with her, like he had with Michelle, before the darkness crept into their lives. Like he felt he could with ... He glanced quickly at Andrea, feeling peculiarly destabilised.

'Aren't they, David?' Andrea was saying, asking a question David hadn't heard.

'Sorry? Oh, yes.' He reined in his confused thoughts and tried to focus his attention back where it should be. Or possibly shouldn't.

Bloody hell. He did a double take as he noticed the flimsy garment Andrea was now holding, bemused as to which bits might go where from the look on her face.

'I've revamped my lingerie drawer for something a little bit more raunchy,' Sally said, looking up at him from under her eyelashes.

More raunchy? A distinctly panicky feeling gripped David now. He risked another glance at Andrea. She met his gaze, a smile playing about her mouth.

'The other bag has some clothes in it for Chloe.' Sally looked from David to Andrea. 'I rang the girl who runs the nursery and she put the word out to the mums, and, hey presto, Chloe's going to be kitted out for the foreseeable future, as far as I can see.'

Andrea peered into that bag and pulled out a cotton-striped jacket that would certainly fit Chloe. There were pyjamas, a Dalmatian printed dressing gown, a little denim jacket, floral print dresses … 'I don't know what to say.' She looked at Sally, astonished.

'There's loads more stuff still at the village hall for the jumble,' Sally went on, obviously pleased. 'It's quite extraordinary, isn't it, the camaraderie between mothers? When they're not bitching about each other's kids in the school playground, that is.'

'Sally!' Andrea shot her a mock-scowl.

'What? They do.' Sally shrugged innocently. 'Okay, got to go and grab a quick sandwich before heading back to school. I'll see you later, hon.' She gave Andrea a hug and turned to the door. 'Keep the chin up, yes?'

With which Sally departed, teetering down the path on heels which surely weren't made for walking.

'Oh, dear.' Andrea chuckled as she closed the door.

'What's funny?' David asked warily.

'Sally. She's wearing her man-killer shoes. I'd watch yourself, if I were you. I think she might be out on a manhunt.'

'Er, right.' David dragged a hand over his neck, now feeling definitely panicky.

Chapter Eleven

Ankle accentuating or not, wearing stilettos to run around after a class full of seven-year-old children all day was definitely a bad idea, Sally decided.

Once inside her front door, she kicked the torturous things off and then padded straight to the kitchen in search of tea, all the time musing about what had happened at lunchtime. David still hadn't looked overly interested. Damn. Was it too much? Sally worried as she dunked a teabag. Had she come on too strong? Far from turned on, David had actually looked shocked when she'd produced almost her entire underwear collection. Some of the stuff she'd donated to Andrea wasn't exactly ready for the charity shop, but the whole point of producing it had been to prompt David into picturing Sally in it, with the toe-deforming stilettos, of course, which hopefully would do it for the good doctor.

Well, she'd just have to pique his interest, wouldn't she? All she needed were the right props, good wine, mood music, soft lighting. But how was she ever going to orchestrate it? How was she even going to get the man on his own when he suddenly had a houseful of people? She took a pensive sip of her tea and reached for a bag of crisps which she had a craving to eat by the big bagful lately. So, how was she going to get David Adams to make a house call?

Munching contemplatively, Sally headed for the lounge. Obviously she would have to come up with a way to get him on her home turf, where she could set the scene and they could talk without Andrea looking on. Talking of whom, it seemed to Sally that Andrea and David had been doing an awful lot of swapping glances when she'd called round, almost as if there was some kind of connection between them.

Crisps in hand, Sally curled herself up in the corner of her Italian leather art deco sofa, a comforting cushion clutched to her midriff. David had had a faraway look in his eye at one point. Sally had hoped he might be mentally undressing her. Now, it almost seemed ...

Hell! Had he been fantasising about Andrea in silk and lace?

Sally swallowed, then choked, then coughed up the crisp wedged in her throat.

Oh, no, no, no! She unfurled herself, and leapt to her feet. That wasn't fair. Andrea already had a man. If there was any connecting to be done with David Adams, it was Sally who was going to be doing it, damn it!

She was going to phone him. That's what she'd do. Right now. Strike while the iron was hot. Nip it in the bud. She had to do something.

Where was Jonathan, anyway? Sorting out their affairs, Andrea had said. What, from afar? Granted there wasn't much room at David's house, but surely Jonathan wouldn't want to be away from his family when their house had just burned down? Had they had a row? An irreconcilable difference of some kind? Had he not proposed, as Andrea had expected him to? He'd taken his time up until now, after all, and if he had evaded the issue again ...? Could it be that Andrea and he had agreed to some kind of separation? Her mind going into overdrive, Sally tossed the cushion arbitrarily behind her onto the sofa. Might Andrea be orchestrating her own plan – to make Jonathan jealous? Was that it?

That was awful. Terrible.

Relieved that she'd remembered to get David's number from Andrea should she need to contact her, Sally took two steps towards the phone and then turned back. Arbitrarily scattered cushions she simply couldn't live with.

Using a man like that. Dreadful. *Ooooh!* And that was

worse! Crisp crumbs – all over the Jean Renoir Ferrari-red sofa with contrasting piping.

Eeeargh! Grease! It would stain! Muttering, Sally turned on her heel and marched to the kitchen. Then back again with a soft cloth and beeswax leather polish.

'Damn,' she muttered, on her knees, dabbing delicately at the offending stain. 'Damn, damn, damn!' Cursing liberally, she worked the polish in, buffed it sparingly, and then cocked her head to one side to appraise the damage.

Phew. No unsightly blemishes in sight, thank goodness. The sofa was safe. The day was saved. And Andrea hasn't got a single stick of furniture to her name, you self-centred cow.

Swallowing guiltily, Sally plopped the cloth on her rescued Victorian chiffonier – then stopped, and swallowed back an altogether different emotion.

Hesitantly, she reached for the photograph album on the shelf of the chiffonier and flicked through the pages for the precious memory she kept there: her second trimester ultrasound scan. She found it and traced a finger lightly over the grainy image. The twenty week anomaly scan.

There were no anomalies though.

Apart from there not being an abundance of amniotic fluid around him, his little body had been perfect: limbs, hands, feet, fingers, toes. All accounted for. All perfect. So why had she lost him? Why had her baby's perfect little heart never beaten independently of her?

Sally wiped away a slow tear. She'd planned to have a four-dimensional scan later; moving images of him. She'd hardly been able to wait until the recommended twenty-six weeks. 'Never quite made it, did we, my angel?' she said softly, breathed out a shuddery sigh, and placed the scan back carefully.

How could Nick have been so utterly cruel, turning his back on her when she needed him most, abandoning her for some twenty-something trollop, as if what they'd had together meant nothing? Their child meant nothing. Damn him to hell. Gulping back a sob, she recalled the black, awful emptiness she'd felt after the birth, walking empty-handed away from the hospital, the desolation she'd felt knowing she was losing Nick too. Sally had decided she would have her baby, with or without a man. But preferably with.

It was time to make that phone call. Pulling herself up, she turned to the phone. And before she spoke to David, she'd speak to Andrea. Double-check she really was okay and be a friend to a person who was actually Sally's only friend, the one person who'd been there for her when she'd been so terribly down, instead of being a complete bitch because David Adams had appeared on the scene. Just because Andrea had been forced to move in with him didn't mean she had designs on David.

Did it?

Finding the number Andrea had given her next to the phone, Sally dialled and waited, determined to resist flirting with him in favour of speaking to Andrea first if David picked up. But she fluttered her eyelashes nevertheless when he did.

'David Adams,' he said, the timbre of his voice deep and sultry, like delicious, decadent, dark chocolate, immediately causing Sally's determination to waver and her pelvis to dip.

'Yes, hi, David,' Sally said, flustered as a soft flurry of butterflies took off in her tummy. 'How are you?'

'Fine,' David replied. 'Er, who are you?'

'Oh, whoops, sorry.' Sally laughed. 'It's me, Sally, she who gives in far too easily to her desires.'

'Ah,' David said, and paused, 'about that … things … in general,' he hesitated, during which time Sally's butterflies nosedived, 'I, er, think we might need to talk, Sally.'

'Talk away. I'm all ears,' Sally said, flippancy masking her apprehension.

'No, I, er ...' David paused again.

Oh no. Sally closed her eyes and clutched the phone hard to her ear.

'In private might be better, I think,' David went on, 'if that's okay with you?'

Private? Sally's mouth curled into a delighted smile. As in the two of them alone? Together? Yessss! She whooped silently. 'Of course,' she said quickly. 'No problem at all. Come on over now, why don't you?'

David went quiet again.

'No time like the present, after all, is there?'

'No, I, er, can't tonight. I've got some things I need to attend to,' David answered. 'How about tomorrow? About seven?'

'Great. See you then. I'll, um ...' Put the champers on ice, Sally wanted to say. '... make sure to pop the kettle on,' she said instead, on a softly-catchy-man basis. She'd pop the new Intrigue purple and noir basque on too, though, on a fishnets-guaranteed-to-catchy-man basis.

Excitedly, Sally rang off, and then remembered with a guilty pang that she'd completely forgotten to even enquire about Andrea.

Andrea was in the kitchen with Eva when the doorbell went yet again.

'I'll get it,' David offered, coming through from the conservatory, where he'd been listening to Elgar's cello concerto, which was beautiful, but a little reflective and melancholic, in Andrea's opinion.

'Thanks.' She smiled appreciatively, still holding the gorgeous silk crêpe de Chine 1920s wedding dress Eva had brought in front of her.

'Suits you,' David said.

'It's lovely, isn't it?' Andrea smoothed the dress over her

silhouette. It was Eva's mother's gown apparently, quite exquisite – and would be madly expensive to purchase.

'Are you sure?' she asked Eva, overcome by such open generosity. It was a wonderful gesture, offering the dress to help kick-start Andrea's Second Chance Designer collection, but she was concerned Eva might regret it.

'Positive,' David assured her, his eyes sweeping over the graceful, diaphanous outline. 'Cream is definitely your colour. So when do I get the pleasure of seeing you in it?'

He gave her another appreciative once over and then, smiling, headed for the hall.

'Good Lord.' Eva's jaw dropped. 'Andrea, my dear, you're not …' She moved closer, glancing nonplussed toward the door where David had just left. 'You and he are not …'

Getting the gist, Andrea laughed, astonished. 'No, we are not. We're just friends. I've only moved in with him temporarily, Eva. Honestly.'

'Who's moved in with whom?' asked Dee as she struggled in from the hall with the vacuum cleaner.

Eva dashed over to help her, despite her dippy hip. 'Andrea,' she imparted, 'moved in with the good doctor.'

'Has she?' Dee's eyes pinged wide, and then almost flew out on sight of the dress. 'You're getting *married*?'

'No, I am not,' Andrea stated adamantly. 'It's Eva's dress, Mum.'

'Humph, well no one in their right mind is going to marry Bunty, darling, are they?' Dee scoffed. 'And she's not going to fit into that tiny little thing, unless she has radical surgery.'

'Mum!'

'I'm just saying.' Dee smiled innocently and then walked in the opposite direction to Eva with her bit of the vacuum. Deliberately, Andrea suspected. 'It's Eva's mother's wedding dress, Mum. Eva has very kindly offered it as part of our Second Chance Designer collection.'

'We're thinking of advertising,' Eva picked up enthusiastically. 'We thought we'd invite people to bring along their glad rags, which we'd sell on for a percentage of, and, hopefully, they'll have a browse of the stock while they're there.'

Andrea smiled. Ooh, she was glad to have Eva on board. 'It's a splendid idea, Eva. We don't have much of a stock yet, but ...'

'We could start at home, right here in the village,' Eva went on, warming to her idea. 'Ask people to have a rummage in their wardrobes and—'

'Codswallop,' said Dee, rudely bursting Eva's bubble.

Eva stared at her. 'Beg pardon, my dear?'

'What's the point of collecting a load of old jumble when we haven't got room to swing a cat?' Dee rolled her eyes at Eva and then turned her gaze on Andrea. 'And why Bunty's help and not mine?'

Andrea blinked at Dee surprised. Oh, dear, was her mum jealous? 'It's not just Eva participating, Mum. It's a joint enterprise, remember? You're involved, too. We're going to run it to—'

'I have posh frocks.' Dee abandoned her vacuum and belligerently folded her arms. 'Whole wardrobes full.'

Andrea glanced mournfully at Eva and then dropped her gaze to the dress she was still holding to her.

'But you don't, do you, my dear,' Eva pointed out gently. 'They're ... Well, they're probably a bit wet, from the fire hose. But you never know,' she went on jollily, 'we might be able to salvage some of your stuff.'

'Oh, Mum ...' Andrea noticed her mum's eyes filling up, despite the petulant pout, and her heart ached for her. She wasn't feeling jealous. She was feeling expendable, vulnerable. Two homes lost in such a short space of time, and Dee so missed her own cosy little cottage. It was just so unfair. Silence ensued for a second, where Dee would normally have a sharp answer, until someone said from the doorway, 'I'll take a look for you tomorrow, Dee.'

Andrea's head snapped up. 'Jonathan?'

David tried to dismiss his feelings of disappointment as, intrigued, he looked over at the hitherto missing man in Andrea's life. Andrea's expression – which was more overwhelmed than overjoyed – added to his curiosity.

'Can I take your coat?' he offered, waiting for a discreet moment to step between the reconciled couple, who'd come into the hall to talk.

'Oh, yes. Thanks.' Jonathan nodded distractedly, shrugged out of his overcoat and handed it to him.

A wool and cashmere coat, David noted as he hung it on the coat stand, tastefully cut and reasonably expensive. As was the suit, which told David the guy was successful at whatever it was he did for a living.

'God, Andrea, what on earth happened?' Jonathan turned back to Andrea, looking bewildered as he stepped towards her.

Andrea stepped back a little. 'Jonathan,' she started, searching his face, her expression now one of incomprehension, 'I ...'

'What happened, Andrea?' Jonathan repeated urgently.

Her house burned down, sunshine, David thought scathingly. He couldn't help it. If the man was as concerned as his tone and demeanour might indicate, where the hell had he been?

Jonathan reached for Andrea's hands, which put David in the awkward position of having to stay where he was by the front door.

'There was a fire. It—' Andrea started, looking flustered.

'Good God, Andrea, I can see that much!' Jonathan cut in

sharply, which did nothing to endear him to David. Tense the man might be, but there was no call for condescension.

Jonathan breathed deeply, obviously trying to calm himself. 'Are you all right?' he asked.

Andrea nodded. 'Yes, I think so.'

'The kids?'

Andrea nodded again, all the while looking troubled. Looking at Jonathan as if it was him she was troubled by, which puzzled David.

He wasn't sure why, except ... In a world where there were no excuses any more for not being in communication with people, why didn't Jonathan know there'd been a major catastrophe that could have ended in tragedy? Which begged the question, where had he been? Even if he'd been away on a business trip, which the suit might indicate, he would have tried to contact his family, surely, and realised something was seriously wrong?

'Thank goodness.' Jonathan's body language relaxed some. He moved closer to Andrea, attempting to rest his forehead on hers.

Andrea did pull back then, noticeably. 'Jonathan, where have you been?' she asked quietly, scanning his eyes for answers.

Jonathan dropped his gaze. 'Not where I should have been.' He closed his eyes briefly, before looking back at her. 'I ... had an accident, Andrea. When you rang me, I—'

'*What?*' Andrea's expression was now one of alarm, swiftly followed by guilt. 'Oh my God.' She squeezed her eyes closed.

'It wasn't your fault,' Jonathan said quickly. 'Someone ran into me. I've been at the hospital since and I—'

'Hospital?' Andrea looked horrified.

'I'm okay,' Jonathan assured her. 'It was just a concussion.'

Must have been one hell of a concussion, David thought

cynically, as Andrea shook her head, clearly trying to assimilate.

'I did try to ring you, Andrea,' Jonathan insisted, 'as soon as I was able to. When I couldn't get you on the landline or your mobile, I was worried sick. I had no idea …'

It explained the business suit and the lateness in the day, David supposed, if he'd been taken to the hospital in it. Still, somehow, his story didn't ring quite true. Wouldn't he have tried to get hold of her at the school? Tried to find out if the kids were where they should be, whether Chloe was at nursery? David would certainly have done. And would a man's first priority on reaching the village to find his house a blackened shell be to poke around in the ruins before checking up on his family?

David doubted it. Even if one of the neighbours had told him Andrea and the kids were safe, he would have sought them out, surely, rather than go straight to the house, which he had. The guy's coat reeked of charred wood and smoke.

Andrea was wavering, David could see by her expression, now somewhere between shock and sympathy, but he didn't believe the man's story was the whole story. As a GP he'd learned to read the signs when people were lying: in need of a sick note maybe, or too embarrassed to say what the real symptoms were, possibly. Whatever, you learned to spot less than the truth, and Jonathan was telling it, which might well mean the man was bad news.

David narrowed his eyes. Had he cheated on her? Been cheating on her? No, he didn't think so. The guy looked as guilty as sin, but – he watched carefully as Jonathan folded Andrea into his arms – whatever it was he was guilty of, he did love her. That much seemed apparent.

David glanced down, struggling, he realised, with an uncomfortable pang of jealousy. He ran his hand over his neck and tried to dismiss it. He was envious of what this

Jonathan had, that was all, a whole family. Someone to come home and tell his troubles to. All of which David had had, until he'd chosen to throw it away.

And the man's family didn't actually have a home any more. David pulled himself up sharp. Talk about petty and judgemental. However neglectful Jonathan appeared to have been, it really wasn't his business. He should go, at least give them a little privacy. 'Do you mind if I, er …' He nodded past the couple to the lounge.

'Oh, sorry, David.' Andrea stepped quickly away from Jonathan, who was now looking David up and down, a quizzical look in his eye.

'David Adams,' David introduced himself. 'Nice to meet you.'

Jonathan shook the hand David offered, his expression communicating, right, and you're who, exactly? He couldn't blame him for that. The man had a pretty, witty, courageous woman in Andrea. David just hoped he appreciated her and didn't take anything for granted, only to wake up one day and find that he'd lost it.

'Jonathan Eden. Thanks for taking care of them,' Jonathan said, letting go of David's hand to drape an arm proprietorially around Andrea's shoulders.

'It's been a pleasure,' David assured him, squeezing past to the sanctuary of the lounge. You might be wise to take better care of them yourself in the future though, he couldn't help thinking.

Chapter Twelve

Sophie padded bleary-eyed from the bathroom towards the bedroom, determined to make the most of the weekend and crawl back into bed. She had loads of texts and Facebook messages to reply to, which she supposed she could do on David's PC, but ... later, she decided, going through the bedroom door. The prospect of luxuriating in the double bed without Chloe stuffing the new Igglepiggle Ryan had bought up her nose and Gran's freezing cold toes was just too tempting.

Yawning, Sophie turned to close the door, and then stopped. 'Er, Gran, what're you doing?' she asked patiently, with undertones of exasperation.

'Hiding,' Dee said, from her position pressed against the wall behind the door.

'Right.' Sophie sighed. 'Like, who from?'

'Him,' Dee imparted unhelpfully, and then peeled herself from the wall to march purposefully to the dressing table.

'Who?' Sophie twizzled around to follow her progress. 'David?'

'David who?' Dee asked, opening a drawer, stuffing something inside it, then extracting it again and stuffing it in her pocket. She then dragged the stool from under the dressing table over to the wardrobe, Sophie looking on, perplexed.

'David, the guy who lives ... Never mind.' Sophie shook her head, then puffed up her purple fringe in a baffled sigh as Dee perched herself precariously on the stool. 'Now, what're you doing?' she asked, peeved. So much for chillaxin'.

'Going home,' Dee announced, tugging a holdall from the top of the wardrobe.

'Gran, you can't.' Sophie yawned and headed wearily towards the bed.

'Oh, yes, I can,' Dee insisted, plopping the bag on to the floor and climbing creakily down after it.

'No, you can't, Gran. It's burned down,' Sophie pointed out as she peeled back the duvet, ready to dig herself bodily under it if that's what it took to get a little peace around here.

'Not that home. My home.' Dee plonked the bag in the space on the bed Sophie had made and then peered around, presumably for something to pack in it. 'Now, where are my clothes?'

'Ooooh! Gran! You've got no clothes.' Sophie slapped a hand against her forehead, utterly frustrated. 'They're in the house that got burned. And you haven't got a house because someone else has bought it! Now stoppit!'

'Have they?' Dee looked around the room as if the buyers of her house might appear from the ether.

Also looking watery-eyed, Sophie noticed, and felt a bit bad. 'They're renovating it, Gran,' she reminded her, more gently. 'Come and sit down, hey?' Sophie plonked herself on the bed and patted the space next to her. 'Take the weight off your feet, yes?'

'Well ... just for a minute, then. My bunions are playing up a bit, I must admit.' Dee shuffled closer and sat on the edge of the bed.

'Gran, I know you miss your home,' Sophie started hesitantly, 'but, well, you can stay here, with us, can't you, until we can sort ourselves out somewhere nice?'

'Oh, no, I can't do that.' Dee turned to look at her, her opaque blue eyes wide and aghast. 'He's going to do away with me. He might do away with Eva, too, if I don't hide it. She's an irritating cow, with her grow your own mentality, stuck in a time warp if you ask me, but I can't allow him to do that.'

Bloody hell, she really has lost it. Sophie knitted her pierced brow. 'Hide what, Gran? Who's going to do away with you?' she asked carefully. 'The doctor?'

She reached for her gran's hand, the tissue soft skin over which was almost translucent and mapped with blue veins. Sophie hadn't really noticed before.

'No, not him.' Dee looked at Sophie as if she were deranged. 'Jonathan. He's up to no good, that one. You mark my words.'

'Jonathan? Don't be daft, Gran. He's a bit shouty and moody sometimes, but he's all right.'

'Not,' said Dee, her chin set defiantly. 'And I'm not daft.'

Sophie adopted her best contrite expression. 'No, course not. So you gonna share then, or what?'

'Share what, dear?'

'No, Gran.' Sophie rolled her eyes. 'I meant, tell me why you think Jonathan's trying to do away with you.'

'He's being nice to me,' Dee said, with a resolute little nod. 'Made me a cup of tea and offered me a biscuit.'

'Rrrright.' Sophie flopped back on the bed.

'He's never nice to me,' Dee went on, regardless of her prostrate audience. 'He thinks I'm a dotty old bat. Wants to get shot of me. He knows I know, you know?'

'To a nice care home, Gran, where they have people to look out for you.' Sophie dragged her poor deprived-of-sleep body back up from the bed. 'He's not trying to do away with you, I'm sure.'

'So why is he being nice to me, then?'

'Because ...' Actually, Sophie had no idea. Jonathan, she had to admit, had about as much time for her gran as she did. 'Because we've all had a really traumatic experience, so he's trying not to upset us.'

Yes, that sounded about right. And Gran was, like, really, really old, so maybe Jonathan felt a bit guilty, since he did have a rant about how mental Dee was sometimes.

'Come on, Gran.' Sophie gave up on her snooze time and got to her feet. 'I heard the Save the Kellys Committee delivering stuff earlier. Let's go and get first dibs before Ryan nicks all the best stuff.'

'When did she ring them?' David heard Jonathan in the kitchen as he came down the stairs. Having spent the night on the sofa at his mother's, it seemed Jonathan was keen not to stay away from his family for too long. Now he was finally here, that was. For some reason David still couldn't shake the feeling that something didn't add up though.

'I'm not sure,' Andrea answered over her shoulder as she came into the hall. 'She was trying to move her investment withdrawal along in your absence.'

'Some technical error, probably,' Jonathan said. 'I'll pop around later and see her.'

'Do,' Andrea said. 'Eva might appear to be self-sufficient, but she is getting on a bit, Jonathan. I'd hate to think of her being passed around some call centre.'

'Good morning.' David caught Andrea's attention as she headed for the lounge.

'I'm not sure you'll think it's so good when you see the state of your carpet.' Andrea eyed the lounge door worriedly. 'It's covered in bags full of castoffs, I'm afraid. Mine for the dubious pleasure of sorting through.'

'Uh-oh.' David did his best to look serious. 'Better not let your mother loose with the Dyson, then.'

Andrea laughed. 'No. And you'd better not stand there for too long either. She'll be giving you a quick spring clean if she spots you.'

David smiled. 'I'll make sure not to.'

'There's coffee on,' Andrea said, heading off to her task. 'I would have started breakfast but ... ' she trailed off, throwing a mock-accusatory glance back at him.

'I like my space,' David finished. 'Remind me never to be territorial again.'

It was nothing to do with territory, actually, more to do with cooking breakfast together being too stark a reminder of family life as it had been. He hadn't been able to tell Andrea that yesterday, of course. Somehow, he felt he could now. He walked into the kitchen, still smiling. She was looking better, he'd noticed. Less tired. More bubbly. That was good.

Jonathan, who was seated at the kitchen table poring over some correspondence, didn't look quite so good though. 'Problem?' David asked, heading for a kick of caffeine to get the day started.

Jonathan glanced up. 'Rebuilding costs,' he said, kneading his forehead. 'Pretty steep.'

He'd organised an estimate then. From his hospital bed? 'But the insurance will cover it, right?' Biting back his cynicism, which was probably more to do with him not warming to the man, David took a good slug of coffee, then reached into the fridge for milk and bread, cereal and toast being all that was available until he sorted out shopping – and how many he needed to shop for.

Dumping the stuff on the table, he went to fetch cereal from the cupboard. 'You do have buildings and contents, I take it?'

'Sorry? What?' Jonathan looked up as David came back to the table.

'Insurance. I was just wondering whether you were adequately covered?'

'That's my line.' Jonathan gave him a short smile, shuffled his paperwork together and got to his feet. 'I run my own financial services company, so obviously I would be adequately covered, wouldn't I?' He reached for his cup, knocked back the dregs of his coffee and headed for the hall.

Watching him go, David sighed inwardly. Damn it, what

was the matter with him, reading something into the guy's every gesture? Wasn't he bound to be worrying about how to provide for his family and get them all back under one roof? It was none of his business. Any of it. And frankly, he didn't need or want to be embroiled in other people's problems. Hadn't he got enough of his own? David cautioned himself to get off Jonathan Eden's case. He was probably doing a hell of a better job supporting his family than David had done supporting his.

He couldn't avoid overhearing, though, as Eden shouted to Andrea, rather than going in to her, that he'd see her later. Clearly, he was now keen to be off again, for whatever reason. David debated what that reason might be on a Saturday. Something more important than sorting out practicalities with his family, presumably.

As in sorting out his affairs. Topping up the coffee filter, David shook his head, despairing of himself. The man was self-employed, ergo any paperwork he had pertaining to insurance detail would probably be in his office. No doubt Jonathan and Andrea had discussed it and, in any case, it had absolutely nothing to do with him. Flicking the switch, he headed after Jonathan into the hall. 'Jake, Ryan, breakfast's up!' he called up the stairs on his way to the lounge.

'There's toast and cereal in the kitchen,' he said, going in to find Andrea embroiled in her own problems: how to clothe her family from the contents of the charity bags, which immediately refocused his thinking.

As much as he would quite like his lounge free of Dee, who was currently solo waltzing around the coffee table wearing a circa sixties white taffeta dress, and ecstatic though he might be to reclaim his armchair and iPod station, which Sophie was currently plugged into, David wasn't about to push them to go anywhere until they were ready.

'How goes the battle?' He glanced to where Andrea was

sitting cross-legged on the floor, Chloe nestled in front of her, kitted out in a cap ten sizes too big and a scarf that would go twice around the village hall.

Andrea smiled. 'Wearily. Not much in the designer department, I'm afraid.'

'Anything worth salvaging?' David asked, wondering whether he could help in some way, though he wasn't sure he was really up for sorting through clothing, especially women's clothing.

'Wouldn't bother if I were you. It's all totally pants,' Sophie commented, iPod volume not at ear-piercing level then, David deduced.

'Bloomers, actually,' Dee imparted, skidding her waltz to an inelegant halt to hitch up her dress, where indeed were bloomers – big enough to fit Nellie the Elephant.

'Oh, that is sooo gross.' Sophie curled a lip at the sight of her gran's pale knees and reached for the TV remote.

'Mum, stop it!' Andrea hissed, her cheeks flushing – rather becomingly, David thought.

'Stop what?' Dee blinked innocently. 'I have my own drawers on underneath, all clean and well paid for,' she said, then, taking hold of her invisible partner, she continued to waltz.

Andrea closed one eye in a wince. 'Oh, Lord, sorry.'

'It's not a problem.' David smiled and glanced at Chloe, who clapped delightedly, and then almost disappeared under the cap, which plopped over her eyes.

'Whoops.' David decided he should consign his own worries to the backburner and do something practical. 'Here, let me help.'

'Thanks.' Andrea took the hand he offered and heaved herself to her feet. 'To be honest, I'm thinking the only way to sort through this lot is to tip it all over the floor.'

'Tip away. But you might want to lighten your child's

darkness first.' David nodded at Chloe, who, thumbs under her cap, was in danger of rearranging her nostrils as she tried to find her face.

'Dunno why you don't just bin the lot,' Sophie muttered as she flicked through the channels on the TV, one leg bobbing lazily over the arm of her chair.

'Right.' Andrea plucked an item of clothing from the upturned contents of one of the bags. 'So I'll chuck the Firetrap jeans Sally donated then, shall I?'

'Yerwhat?' Sophie's head twizzled on her neck.

Andrea glanced conspiratorially at David, who'd crouched down to reacquaint Chloe with her face. 'Along with anything else in this bag,' Andrea went on, holding up a carrier bag which obviously did house one or two coveted labels.

'Selfridges & Co? Like, wow!' Sophie was off the armchair and across the room in a flash. 'OhmyGod.' Her eyes grew wide, like a child's eyes falling on Christmas presents under the tree. 'OhmyGod! Warehouse stuff, look! And Armani cosmetics. This is so totally wicked.'

David glanced at Andrea, bemused.

'Wicked's in again, apparently,' she informed him.

'Ah.' David nodded, not sure he knew it had gone out.

'I am sooo made up.' Sophie jigged up and down, clutching the cosmetics to her chest – with which David assumed she would soon be 'made up', and then twirling on the spot as Dee danced around her.

David laughed, he couldn't help himself. 'I thought you said it was me who was mad.'

'Takes one to know one,' Andrea assured him, plopping a knitted beanie on her head. Turning to face him, she tugged the beanie close around her face, beamed him a smile – and completely took David's breath away.

She was beautiful.

Her red and gold hair tumbling carelessly around her shoulders and a smile so radiant, she could light up Blackpool on her own. 'You could give Julia Roberts a run for her money,' he said, feeling slightly off kilter.

'Do you know he's right, you could.' Dee gazed at her daughter and then turned to David with a heartfelt sigh. 'She'd make a wonderful prostitute.'

'Yes. Thank you, Mum.' Andrea's smile slipped a bit.

'Pretty woman,' Dee launched into song, oblivious.

Andrea rolled her eyes good-naturedly. 'Livin' on the street,' she picked up, giving her hips a cute little wiggle.

'Pretty woman, the kind I like to meet,' Sophie joined in, parking her make-up on the coffee table and then plucking Chloe from her nest of strewn about clothes to dance her around in a circle.

'Pretty woman, I don't be-lieve y-o-u,' Dee crooned on tunelessly, now cheek-to-cheek with Andrea.

'No one could look as good as you,' Andrea sang with gusto, all three women then launching into the instrumental bit in unison.

'Mur-cy,' Sophie finished in baritone tones.

David laughed out loud. 'Utterly mad.'

'Totally,' Sophie concurred, catching Dee's hand with her own free hand for an underarm twirl.

'As hatters.' Andrea plucked off her beanie, bowed, then beamed; and then straightened her face as she looked past David to the door.

David followed her gaze.

Damn. He cursed silently, noting the thunderous look on his son's face. There was a time and a place for carefree frivolity, and their lounge – with a whole other family, when Jake had lost such a huge part of his – wasn't it. Raking a hand through his hair, David walked over to him. 'Hey, Jake, how's it going? We were just ...' He stopped, searching for a way to explain. Andrea and her family were only there until their own house was habitable, but still it must seem to Jake as if she was trying to replace his mother.

'Sorting through the clothes people have kindly donated,' Andrea supplied, 'before Ryan's forced to go out chatting up babes in his less than cool boxers.'

Jake's expression didn't alter. He glanced at Andrea and then dragged derisive eyes back to David.

David placed a hand on his shoulder. 'You are going to get some breakfast, Jake, before you and Ryan go—'

Jake pulled away. 'Not hungry.'

Right. David blew out a breath. 'Jake, you either eat something, or you don't get to go into town today. Your choice.'

'Whatever.' Jake turned to walk towards the stairs, shrugging scrawny shoulders under his rugby shirt as he went.

'Jake!' David called after him.

'What?' Jake didn't turn back.

'The kitchen's that way. Get some breakfast, please,' David said calmly, though his patience was wearing thin. How the hell was he going to get Jake to talk to him, if they couldn't even communicate on a rudimentary level?

Jake did turn around then. 'Why?' he asked, his eyes holding a defiant challenge.

'Because I said so, Jake.'

'And what gives you the right to tell me what to do?' Jake demanded, his expression now bordering on hatred.

So here it was. Standoff time. Jake's fury about to be unleashed and David had no clue how to respond. 'I'm your dad, Jake,' he tried, sounding feeble, even to his own ears. 'If I ask you to do something, it's because I—'

'Care?' Jake gauged him through narrowed eyes. 'Yeah, right,' he sneered, and turned away.

'Jake ...' David counted silently to five. 'You either do as I say and eat something, or you're grounded.'

'Yeah, yeah.' Jake walked on up the stairs. 'Yadda yadda yadda.'

'I mean it, Jake.'

'Whatever.'

David tried very hard to remain calm. 'Jake, come back down, please.'

Jake stopped on the stairs, breathing hard, his shoulders tense. 'No,' he said shortly.

'Now, Jake!'

Jake whirled around. 'No!' He swiped a hot, angry tear from his face. 'I'm not doing anything you say! Why should I?' he shouted.

How David wished he could close the gap, climb the stairs, hold him. Tell the kid to hit him, kick him, whatever it took to make him feel better. 'Jake, come on ...' He took a tentative step towards him.

'Get stuffed!' Jake stopped him in his tracks. 'You don't care about me. You don't care about anybody. You didn't even care about Mum!'

David felt the blood drain from his face. He couldn't do this. He swallowed hard. Not here. Not now. In front of ... He glanced back at Andrea, his own breathing heavy. 'I ...' he started, shook his head and took another step forwards. 'Jake ...'

'No!' Jake yelled. 'You never cared about her. You never did that with her.' He nodded towards the lounge. 'Mum never laughed after she was ill when you were around. Never!' Jake's expression told David all he needed to know. Jake did hate him, with every bone in his body. He'd every right to. David knew it. And it hurt more than anything had ever done in his life.

'Let me try,' Andrea suggested gently as Jake turned on his heel and flew up the stairs.

141

David looked at her bewildered, incapable of coordinating his thoughts let alone his speech.

'We have a bereavement plan in place at the school,' Andrea explained. 'To help children like Jake cope. He might let me talk to him. You never know.'

'He's good in a crisis,' Andrea went on, talking to herself, as she had been for the last five minutes. Still Jake refused to acknowledge her, his expression stony, his eyes fixed to his PC, but so full of turmoil it wrenched at Andrea's heart.

'He has to use a satnav to find the kitchen, but he makes a mean Pepsi Max,' she went on, expounding her son's dubious culinary skills.

Still no response.

'A cup of tea is beyond him, unfortunately, which Ryan's always at pains to point out,' Andrea chatted on, 'he being a man and therefore incapable of multitasking, he says, i.e. putting teabags in the cups whilst boiling the kettle.'

Silence was Jake's answer.

'Of course, this is after he's hilariously balanced the kettle on his head, because I've made the fatal mistake of asking him to put the kettle on.' Andrea waited, wondering what on earth she could say that might at least elicit some response, however small.

Jake shrugged, then ... Yes! There it was, a definite upward twitch to his mouth. 'I'll go and see if he's managed to negotiate his way to your kitchen yet, shall I, before we dehydrate up here?'

Jake nodded. Definitely progress, Andrea thought, heading for the door. Pepsi Max and chocolate biscuits were probably not the balanced breakfast David had in mind, but at least Jake might eat something if she and Ryan joined him.

'He doesn't talk about her,' Jake blurted, behind her.

Andrea turned back. 'Do you want him to, Jake?'

Jake dragged his forearm hurriedly across his eyes. 'Uh-huh.' He nodded, obviously trying hard to force back his tears. 'He never says anything. It's like he's scared or something. Like the kids at school, where I went before. No one ever asked me about Mum after she died. No one ever said anything. They just looked, and whispered stuff to each other.'

Andrea parked herself back down next to him, as close as she dared without invading his space. 'Why was that Jake, do you think?'

Another shrug.

'Because they thought it might make you sad, possibly?'

'Maybe,' Jake acknowledged. 'The thing is …' he hesitated '… it does make me sad sometimes, really sad. But I want to talk about her. She was my mum.' He glanced at Andrea as if he couldn't quite understand why people didn't get it.

'I'm sure your mum knew you loved her, Jake. Mums do, you know? It's instinctive. We feel it in here.' Andrea placed a hand over her heart.

Jake's eyes slid towards her again. 'She said she was scared. Scared for him.'

'Your dad?' Andrea probed softly.

Jake nodded. 'She said she was scared for me, too, but that she knew that I knew she'd always love me and watch out for me. She didn't think he … knew she loved him, though.'

Andrea took a breath, her heart breaking for this little boy and his lost father. 'Adults don't see things so clearly sometimes, Jake.' She took a chance and took his hand. He didn't pull away. 'Sometimes emotions get in the way. Do you understand?'

Jake nodded again. 'Like anger?'

'Yes, anger. Hurt, sadness. Sometimes they stop you saying what you really feel.'

'I did tell her I loved her,' Jake confided, after a second.

'When she was ill, she tried really hard, you know?' He turned at last to look directly at Andrea, his eyes full to brimming. 'To make sure I was all right. Make me smile and stuff. She tried to make sure things would be okay for me and ... Dad, too, making lists of where things were and how stuff worked. I was kind of proud of her, you know?'

Andrea did know, absolutely. The sense of the woman she'd felt whilst looking through her things, even knowing how ill she was, Michelle Adams had been strong for her family, yet as gentle and caring as a mother could be.

'You know something, Jake,' she said, feeling humbled. 'There isn't a mum anywhere who wouldn't be proud of a son who could say out loud that he loved her.'

Jake pulled in a breath, his skinny chest puffing up. 'I'd like to tell people more about her, but ...'

'No one gives you the chance?' Andrea guessed.

'It's like everyone's pretending she never existed,' Jake said quietly.

'How about we make a memory box, Jake?' Andrea suggested, knowing that he needed to dwell, but on the good things, rather than the bad.

Jake squinted at her curiously.

'We'll make up a box of special things you can remember her by. Photographs, and such like.'

Jake thought about it and then nodded; a short, resolute nod. 'They're in the spare room,' he said, scrambling off the bed as Ryan came in with a tray laden with biscuits, essential sugar-high fizzy stuff and an actual cup of tea.

'And anything else you can think of, Jake,' Andrea said. 'Things that will help you to remember all the good times.'

'Her perfume. I've got some in my cupboard. It makes me remember her better.' Jake made a grab for his Pepsi. 'And Harry Potter,' he added, taking a slurp and wiping his mouth on his shirtsleeve as he headed on out.

'I'll give you a hand, mate,' Ryan offered, giving Andrea a knowing wink as he plonked the tray down. 'Not sure Harry Potter will fit in the box though,' he mused, heading after Jake, 'but …'

'Dimwit. I meant the book.' Jake's child-bordering-on-adolescent tones drifted back. 'Mum used to read it to me at bedtime.'

'Cool. Which one?'

'*Goblet of Fire. Prisoner of Azkaban.* Most of them, until she died. Have you read them?'

'Yep. Got them all,' Ryan said, cranking up his enthusiasm for Jake's sake. Bless his mismatching Simpsons socks. 'Or I did have, before the fire.'

'Aw, that sucks,' Jake commiserated. 'You could share mine.'

'Cool,' Ryan said, with rather less enthusiasm.

Chapter Thirteen

She was treading on delicate ground, Andrea knew, venturing to ask David why there were no photographs of his wife around the house; suggesting that Jake might need there to be. That he needed to hold on to his memories of his mother, rather than thinking he should consign her to history, as David seemed to have done; at least in Jake's mind.

David didn't answer at first. Hands thrust deep in his pockets, he distractedly studied the fireplace instead. 'I think I'll ask the landlord if I can strip it back; restore it rather than have it ripped out,' he said, nodding at the mahogany surround.

Sensing he needed some time, Andrea followed his gaze. He was right. It was beautiful. Original antique Edwardian, she guessed; a striking piece of furniture in itself.

David removed a hand from his pocket and dragged it slowly over his neck. 'I'm not sure why I didn't display the photographs,' he said eventually.

'Because you thought they'd be too painful a reminder for Jake?'

'To be honest, I wasn't sure.' He paused contemplatively. 'I knew he needed to think about her, talk about her, but if he wouldn't talk to me ... I suppose I thought Jake might think I was being hypocritical, pretending to miss her. To care, when I ...' he trailed off, glancing briefly at Andrea, and then away.

'You do miss her though.'

David swallowed. 'Every day.'

'You obviously cared about her a great deal,' Andrea probed gently.

David closed his eyes. 'I just couldn't bear the thought of losing her. Wasn't man enough to support the decision she'd made, once she was diagnosed. Acute leukaemia. What were the chances?' He shrugged hopelessly. 'There wasn't anything I could do about it. Nothing. I'm supposed to be a doctor and I couldn't do a damn thing.'

Swallowing again, he glanced at the ceiling, obviously trying to contain his emotions, so much like the little boy upstairs, who was so like his father. Andrea felt like weeping for him. She wished she could reach out to him. Penetrate the brick wall he seemed to have built around himself. But, as yet, she guessed, it was strictly no trespassing allowed.

'I knew, of course, what the chances were,' David continued, though it was obviously painful for him, 'one in every one hundred thousand. What I didn't know, will never understand, was why Michelle.'

'I'm so sorry, David.' Not knowing what else to say, Andrea offered him the standard words of condolence, which sounded inadequate, even to her own ears.

'Me, too. More than anyone can know,' David said quietly. 'I wasn't able to accept it,' he went on, tugging in a tight breath, 'the diagnosis, Michelle's subsequent decision to delay treatment. Anti-leukaemic drugs might not ultimately save her, she'd known that. But she could save the life of her unborn child. That was her goal.' He stopped again.

Andrea waited.

'And my response to her braveness?' David laughed bitterly. 'I ran away. Found any reason I could to stay late at the surgery. I wasn't there. When she needed me, I was ...'

'With someone else?' Andrea finished as he trailed awkwardly off.

David nodded wearily. 'A colleague,' he admitted, sounding as if the words might choke him. 'It only happened once, not that that makes it any more forgivable. Michelle and I argued, not surprisingly. Michelle turned to a friend, a friend who was also a neighbour, as it happened. Pretty soon, it seemed everyone knew our business, neighbours, acquaintances, friends; Jake's friends.'

Andrea nodded, understanding. 'Children can be brutal sometimes.'

'Can't they just.' David kneaded the back of his neck. 'We split, as you can imagine. Michelle's decision, not mine. Who could blame her? She tried to reach me ... when she realised ... she was losing the baby. She tried to get hold of me. She couldn't. I wasn't with anyone, not then,' he added, glancing quickly at Andrea again. 'I was on call. So, Michelle being Michelle, she drove herself to the hospital. She ... never arrived.'

'Oh, no, David.' Now she understood, his abruptness, his obvious anger. The guilt he seemed to carry around. But whatever the circumstances, whatever the reasons, if guilt were his punishment then hadn't he been punished enough?

'Jake would be right, wouldn't he?' David continued throatily. 'Hypocritical is exactly what it would be to stand a photograph on the shelf of the woman I deserted.'

He dropped his gaze, pinching the bridge of his nose hard with his thumb and forefinger.

Andrea hesitated for a second, and then reached out to risk a hand on his arm. 'Talk to him, David.'

David looked up at last, pain etched into his features, his very soul, it seemed.

Andrea offered him an encouraging smile. 'Yes, children can be brutal, but they do understand much more than we sometimes give them credit for.'

With some effort, David smiled back. 'Thanks. I'll try,' he promised. 'Not sure he'll want to listen, but I'll try.'

'Good.' Andrea gave his arm a reassuring squeeze, which prompted a loud cough from the doorway.

'Jonathan! You almost gave me a heart attack,' Andrea admonished him, stepping away from David. 'I didn't see you there.'

'Obviously,' Jonathan remarked deadpan. 'Sorry to interrupt. Sophie let me in. In case you wonder, she's taken Chloe to the park and Dee's tagged along, too. I didn't want you to panic, thinking she might have wandered off.'

'Oh, right.' Andrea nodded. 'Thanks, Jonathan. I've been a bit too busy to keep tabs on—'

'So I see,' Jonathan interrupted, pointedly. 'Do you think we could have a chat, Andrea? When it's convenient?'

Andrea frowned. 'Yes, yes of course. I, um ...' She glanced at David.

David glanced uncomfortably back. 'I'll go upstairs and check on the boys,' he said, giving Jonathan a polite nod as he left.

Chapter Fourteen

'Go and "check on the boys"?' Jonathan snorted derisively, once David had left. 'Well, well, looks like you've all become one big happy family in my absence.'

'What?' Andrea almost laughed. Was he serious?

Obviously, he was. She noted the look in his eye, which could easily outdo Chloe in the truculence department. 'Jonathan, what on earth are you talking about?' she asked, not quite able to believe he would be so paltry. 'David has very kindly allowed us the use of his house and we're all trying to get along as best we can. Do you have a problem with that?'

'No.' Jonathan shrugged moodily. 'It's just that David and you seemed to be getting along very well, that's all.'

Andrea's mouth dropped open. 'What?'

'The conversation you were having,' Jonathan looked her over accusingly, 'it looked very *cosy* from where I was standing.'

Yes, and how long had he been standing there? More to the point, why? And why this silly display of ruffled feathers? Wasn't there enough to be worrying about?

'We were talking, Jonathan. It's what people in close proximity generally do.'

'Yes, and it looked like a very intimate conversation to me. You were practically holding his hand.'

'Oh, don't be ridiculous,' Andrea snapped. She couldn't help herself. He obviously hadn't heard the whole conversation or he might be a little more understanding. In truth, she felt like bursting into tears. She was tired. Exhausted, in fact. And so very broken-hearted. She hadn't even found the courage to go over to her house yet, for fear of falling apart. She didn't want this. She wanted Jonathan to be strong and supportive, not petty and accusatory, however needy that might make her. She felt needy.

'Me, ridiculous?' Jonathan gawked incredulously. 'I'd say ridiculous is playing dress up and getting up close to David when our house has burned to the ground, wouldn't you?'

Andrea opened her mouth, and closed it again. He obviously hadn't left when she'd thought he had. Instead, he'd been loitering outside the lounge then, too. And, clearly, his nose was out of joint because she'd apparently been enjoying herself in the company of another man, while he, poor soul, was walking around with the weight of the world on his shoulders. Unbelievable. She stared at Jonathan, utterly speechless. 'Up close?' she spluttered, after a second. 'You really are serious, aren't you? Well, as it happens, David and I have become better acquainted, since it was David who helped the kids and Mum to safety, and then took us all in – in your absence.'

Her temper close to breaking point, Andrea eyeballed Jonathan angrily. 'If not for David, Jonathan, you might not have had a family to come back to. Did that thought occur to you?'

Jonathan studied her for a second and then nodded, shamefaced. 'Yes, of course it did.' He took a step towards her. 'Look, Andrea, let's not argue. I'm sorry. I didn't mean to upset you. I'm still in shock, I suppose. Finding out like I did. I mean, they weren't even supposed to be there, were they: the kids, your mum, when the fire started? I had no idea ...' Jonathan trailed off, with a sigh. 'Ignore me, I'm just a bit fraught, that's all.'

Andrea stepped back. 'So am I, Jonathan. A lot fraught. We don't have a home,' she reminded him, overdue tears now dangerously close to the surface. 'And what you choose to do about it is have a tantrum because you feel your ego's under threat?'

Andrea searched his face, disappointed and disillusioned. He had changed. He wasn't the Jonathan she knew. It was as if something was eating away at him, and Andrea had no clue what. When had he become so apparently uncaring?

'Excuse me. I think I need some air.' She notched up her chin and walked past him, determined not to give in to her tears, when the man who should be helping her hold it all together seemed to be emotionally missing.

'Andrea, don't go.' Jonathan caught her arm, his look now one of quiet desperation. 'I know I've been a bit off, but it's nothing to do with my ego being under threat. I might have lost you, for Pete's sake. That's the point, don't you see? I still feel I might lose you. I'm trying to sort things out, I swear. That's why I needed to talk to you. Damn it, Andrea, I've been trying to find a moment to talk to you since I came back.'

'In which case, maybe you should have tried harder, Jonathan, instead of sneaking about trying to catch people in some imagined secret liaison,' Andrea suggested, unimpressed by his agitated tone. 'I'd like to leave now, please.'

Jonathan sighed and let her go. 'You'd better stop by the park if you're going out,' he said, with a despondent shrug. 'Check on your mother.'

'I will be stopping by the park,' Andrea replied calmly, 'thank you. And since when did you care about my mother's welfare anyway?'

She hadn't meant to say that. She didn't want to hurl accusations any more than she wanted to hear them, but the fact was, he really didn't seem to care. Andrea gave him a despairing glance and then headed for the front door, to find David looking evermore uncomfortable in the hall.

It was obviously catching, Andrea thought, grabbing her coat and heading on out. They were all eavesdropping, David included. Though unavoidably, she supposed, blowing hot ragged steam on the air as she turned away from the house, from her own house, which she simply couldn't bear to see the destruction of beyond the blackened, soul crushing exterior. She'd been aiming to talk to Jonathan too, about his offering her a hand to hold while she ventured in. Fat chance with him still more missing than here now that he had finally turned up, and choosing to argue with her, rather than talk.

Breathing deeply, she tried to rein in her spiralling emotions. It wasn't Jonathan's fault they'd hardly had a moment together, she supposed. There was slim chance of privacy with so many people in one house, half of which was packed full of boxes, the other half in need of repair. Oh dear, she so missed her home. Had Jonathan made any headway with the insurance company? she wondered. He hadn't mentioned anything to her yet. But then, as he'd pointed out, he hadn't had much chance to mention anything, had he?

'Jake?' David knocked on his son's door. Would he answer this time? Probably not.

David reached for the handle, only to find the door yanked open by Ryan.

'Hi. How's it going?' David smiled at the gangly teenager, who, far from being the bad influence David had worried he might be, seemed to be sprouting a halo along with some actual stubble – and who David was hugely grateful to for looking out for Jake.

'Yeah, good. Just helping Jake sort some stuff out.'

'Oh?' David glanced past Ryan into the room, to where Jake sat cross-legged on the floor, no PlayStation control in sight, amazingly. 'What stuff would that be then, Jake?'

David waited, but took his cue when Ryan motioned him on in.

'Off to get some more Pepsi, mate,' Ryan said diplomatically. 'Want some?'

Jake nodded, but didn't look up.

'Back in ten.' Ryan drooped out, skinny fit jeans still clinging to his hips and looking every inch the typical allergic-to-anything-strenuous teenager, which belied his caring attitude. David owed the kid, that was for sure.

He owed Jake, too, big time.

David turned his attention back to his son, who was surrounded by a sea of photographs, he realised. Photographs of Michelle, from the albums in the spare room.

Cautiously, David walked across to stand by Jake's side. Then, hands in pockets, he waited again, wondering what to say that could even begin to heal their relationship. What would he want to hear, if he were Jake?

Sorry perhaps? Wholly inadequate, David knew, but it might be a start.

He looked down at his son, whose head was bent in concentration on his endeavours.

He needed a haircut. Needed a lot of things.

David closed his eyes as he noticed the bottle of perfume tucked in the corner of Jake's Adidas shoebox.

Michelle's perfume.

Because Jake wanted something to remind him of her.

'Need any help, Jake?' David asked softly.

Jake didn't answer. That was okay. David didn't really expect him to. He swallowed back a lump in his throat, then took a gamble, crouched down next to Jake – and silently waited.

Biding his time, he studied the photographs quietly alongside his son. 'You've chosen all the good ones,' he ventured.

Jake did respond then, somewhere between a nod and a shrug.

'Not many fun ones though.' David reached for a photograph. One he'd taken himself on what turned out to be their last time at the theme park together: Michelle, Jake in front of her on the log flume, both shrieking with laughter and soaked through to the skin.

Probably the last time she had laughed – with him.

David breathed in, hard. 'I did make her sad, Jake,' he said quietly. 'I'm sorry. I know it doesn't help much, but ... I wish I hadn't.'

Jake's head dropped even lower.

'She did laugh though, you know, Jake. With you.'

David placed the photograph carefully in the box. 'Alton Towers,' he said, 'summer before last. She laughed so much she had to dash to the loo, remember?'

Jake dragged the back of his hand under his nose.

'She couldn't have been that happy without you, Jake. You gave her the gift of laughter. That's something to be glad about. To be proud of.'

David stopped, his chest filling up as he watched a slow tear fall from his son's face.

David hesitated, then rested a hand lightly on Jake's shoulder. Jake didn't shrug him off.

'You won her a stuffed toy that day, do you remember? What was it? A tiger?'

'Tigger.' Jake finally spoke.

'That's right,' David said, his throat tight. 'Tigger.'

'She kept it in the car,' Jake picked up in a small voice.

The car she never arrived at the hospital in, David realised, overwhelming guilt slicing through him. 'She kept a whole family of furry friends in the car. I'm surprised there was room for her.'

Jake's mouth twitched into a small smile. 'She talked to them.' He glanced up at David, his huge blue eyes glassy with tears.

'That was the little girl inside her. The little girl you made laugh.' David squeezed Jake's shoulder. He actually felt like whooping. Like punching the air. Like picking Jake up and hugging him so hard ... Jake had looked at him. Full on. No anger.

David closed his eyes, relief washing over him. 'I have one of Mum's stuffed toys,' he said throatily. 'One she kept. Not Tigger, but ... Do you want me to fetch it?'

Jake nodded.

'Right.' David smiled. 'Back in two.' He dragged his forearm across his eyes as he headed for his own room. He had something else, too. Something he'd wanted to give Jake before, but somehow couldn't.

The antique locket he'd bought Michelle for her thirtieth birthday was in the bedside drawer. David collected it, ran his thumb over the engraved rose gold surface of it. If Jake needed something to remind him of his mother, this was it.

'Bedtime Bear,' David announced, joining Jake back on the floor. 'Your very first toy.' He handed his son the scruffy little white bear.

Jake laughed and David really did feel like crying then.

'I have something else for you, Jake.' He passed him the locket. 'It was very special to her,' he said gently as Jake's eyes fell on the photograph of himself inside it. 'She wore it right next to her heart. And that,' he went on as Jake looked at the lock of hair on the opposite side of the locket, 'is your hair and hers, entwined.'

Jake went very quiet.

'Okay?' David asked.

Jake nodded vigorously. 'Okay,' he said, around a sharp intake of breath. David reached out, ran his hand through Jake's unruly crop, and then allowed it to stray to his shoulder. He wanted very much to hold him, to reassure him. But Jake's body language was tense. It would take time, David knew, but maybe someday, Jake would let him back in.

Chapter Fifteen

Jake safe in his room with Ryan, David went in search of supplies. He'd take a tour of the village while he was out, he decided, something he'd avoided doing since he'd arrived, paranoia being his middle name. Somehow, it didn't seem to be dogging him as much the last few days. People were bound to gossip to a degree, Jake and him being new to the village and he a single dad at that. It was human nature, David supposed.

Feeling slightly more optimistic about the future, he nodded at one or two people as he walked. Passing Fleur's Flower Shop, he was almost tempted to go in and purchase a bouquet for Andrea by way of a thank you, but decided against it. Gesture of thanks, or not, it might well be misconstrued by Jonathan Eden, who was a troubled man if ever David saw one.

David pondered the remark he'd overheard the guy make before Andrea had gone out. He was still in shock, he'd said. Fair enough. He'd every right to be. It was what he'd said next that David had a problem with. 'They weren't even supposed to be there, were they: the kids, your mum, when the fire started. I had no idea ...' What was that all about?

Nothing to do with him was what. David pulled himself up, again. His paranoia was obviously refocusing on Eden. Naturally, the man would be shocked. Obviously he'd be troubled by the huge task of rebuilding their lives. Eden needn't trouble himself about David's intentions, however. No matter how attracted to Andrea he might be, he didn't intend to ... David almost stopped in his tracks. What was he thinking?

He wasn't. Clearly.

David tried to reel his thoughts back in, before he lingered too long on her breathtaking smile. The concern in her pretty green eyes; clear eyes, no condemnation there. There should have been. She was obviously a forgiving person, though David doubted he'd ever forgive himself.

If he really wanted to thank her, keep her as a friend – they'd been pretty thin on the ground lately – couldn't he help her out? Flowers might have been a nice gesture, but without even a vase to put them in ... It would mean helping Eden out, too, unfortunately. But then, the guy was Andrea's ... whatever he was. And David had liquid assets, money from the sale of his house that he hadn't touched. Nor did he need to with a fund already set up for Jake from his mother's insurance. He could do something, couldn't he? Give them a head start on getting their lives back together until their insurers paid up? David walked on, taking a side road from the High Street, his mind still on Andrea's situation, but his step faltering as he passed by the little red brick house between the pub and the post office. The door to which was ajar, he noticed.

The occupant of which was lying on the floor just inside it.

David wasted no time. One hand on the top of it, he was over the fence in two seconds flat.

'Eva?' He eased the door wider and crouched down beside her, gently squeezing her shoulder in hopes of a reaction. Nothing. Damn it. David pressed two fingers to the carotid artery in her neck. He found a pulse. He checked her airway, and was about to get her into the recovery position when she stirred.

David caught a movement behind him but stayed focused on the old lady. He needed her to open her eyes.

'Bloody hell,' Jonathan said, crouching down beside him. 'What happened?'

'Not sure.' David kept his eyes on Eva's, retrieving his

mobile from his pocket and passing it to Jonathan as he did. 'A fall, possibly. Ambulance,' he instructed Eden shortly.

'No,' Eva protested. 'I'm fine.' She tried to raise herself.

'Hey, hey, hold your horses, Eva,' David cautioned her. 'Can you move all right?'

'I'm trying to,' Eva replied haughtily, 'but I seem to have two burly men looming over me. Do you mind?'

'Not if you don't.' David smiled.

Eva's mouth twitched into a reciprocal smile. 'Saucy,' she said.

'I know.' David winked. 'Gets me into terrible trouble. Now, are you in any pain?'

Eva thought about it. 'No,' she said, after a second.

Good. She was answering sensibly. She definitely understood what he was saying, so she wasn't confused. And there didn't appear to be any life threatening injuries. Glad Jonathan Eden was there to witness, David bade Eva stay still while he checked for small broken bones, no obvious bleeding, or burns.

'Well, you appear to be in one piece,' he concluded.

'I could have told you that myself, my dear.' Eva allowed him to help her to sitting.

'You should still go to the hospital,' David advised her. 'You've been unconscious. You'll need to be monitored to find out the cause of it.'

'I fainted,' Eva informed him as the two men took an arm each to help her to her feet.

'That is still unconscious,' David pointed out patiently as they led her to the kitchen. 'And you still need to find out what caused it, Eva.'

'I know what caused it,' Eva insisted. 'Two factors, actually. Move over Kit-kit,' she instructed the cat comfortably curled on a chair, then allowed David to assist her down into it, while Jonathan put the kettle on.

'Firstly, I haven't eaten,' Eva went on, 'which you, as a doctor, would know causes light-headedness, and secondly, there was an intruder in the house.'

'An—?' David stopped as Jonathan dropped the tea caddy to the floor with the resounding clang.

'Sorry,' he said, quickly bending down to scoop up the spilled teabags.

'There was someone here?' David looked at Eva, doubly concerned now. She was an old woman. Who the hell would sink so low—?

'Most definitely. Upstairs,' Eva assured him, pointing to the ceiling. 'Must have slipped in through the back door while I was watering my garden out front. I didn't realise until I was sitting down in the lounge with my tea, and then ... footsteps, out of my room and along the landing, as clear as day.'

'You're sure it wasn't your cat, Eva?' David asked. He couldn't help wondering why an intruder would make himself known. Unless his intent was harassment, of course. In which case—

'Cats pad, silently, Doctor Adams. And though Kit-kit is a little overweight, I doubt she's heavy enough to creak floorboards.' Eva gave him a look. 'Anyway, I was saying, there was someone upstairs, so I waited until I was quite sure they'd passed by the lounge door to the kitchen, then stood up, quickly, as one would, rushed to the front door, the blood rushed to my head and whoosh, I fainted. Luckily, you were passing.'

'Very luckily.' David felt his jaw tighten. 'We need to call the police.'

'No we do not,' Eva said adamantly. 'I know who it was.'

'You do?' David cocked his head to one side, puzzled, whilst Jonathan apparently burned himself on the kettle, judging by his hand flapping and wincing.

'Yes.' Eva nodded. 'We do, don't we, Kit-kit?'

'And?' David bent to stroke the cat as it padded past, but the cat had other ideas, slinking aloofly out of his reach.

'Ooh, naughty Kit-kit.' Eva smiled fondly at the animal. 'Sorry, Doctor Adams. She's an unsociable beast. Doesn't like strangers, I'm afraid.'

'So I see.' David raised an eyebrow as the 'unsociable beast' purred loudly and wove a figure of eight around Jonathan's feet.

'Now where was I?' Eva asked.

'The intruder,' David prompted her.

'Well, I suspect it was—'

'Shit,' Jonathan cursed, missing the mug he was pouring water into in favour of the work surface.

'My son,' Eva went on, apparently unfazed as water dripped all over the floor. 'He's gone off the rails a bit, I'm afraid.' She glanced at David with a *c'est la vie* shrug. 'Probably looking for knick-knacks he thought I wouldn't miss.'

'Well, that's a relief,' Jonathan said brightly, too brightly, looking relieved as he finally managed to produce a whole cup of tea. 'It being your son, I mean,' he clarified, handing Eva a mug.

Eva gave him a disgusted look, no doubt fostered by his completely inept comment. 'Ye-es, isn't it?' she offered strangely.

Once he was sure Eva was all right, David decided to take his leave. He'd rather call the police, son or no, but, if it wasn't what Eva wanted … It was hard, David supposed, being her flesh and blood. And who was he to comment on the wisdom of parents?

'Now, remember, Eva,' he said, turning for the hall, 'keep those legs up high.'

'Ooh, you are cheeky, Doctor Adams,' Eva chuckled, 'but terribly nice. Isn't he, Kit-kit?'

David smiled. 'Spread the word. The "nice" bit, I mean.'

'Absolutely. I'll be down at the post office first thing on Monday.'

David didn't doubt it. 'And then to the surgery for that check-up, Eva. No excuses,' he said sternly.

'Oh, my, and authoritative with it. Be careful, Doctor Adams, you'll break hearts all over Hibberton.'

'I will be, Eva, scout's honour,' David said, playing along.

'Particularly with Kit-kit's. She's a sensitive soul,' Eva warned him as the cat, obviously having decided David was acceptable company, plopped off her lap to pad across and avail itself of his shins.

'I think Kit-kit's heart already belongs to another, Eva.' David smiled and bent to stroke the cat, glancing at Jonathan as he did, whom Kit-kit apparently hadn't considered the least bit 'strange', and who didn't seem to be a stranger to Eva's kitchen.

Odd, David couldn't help thinking.

'Right, I'll get off, Eva,' Jonathan said, placing his swilled cup in the dish rack and retrieving his coat from the back of a chair. 'If you are sure you're all right, that is?'

'Perfectly,' Eva assured him. 'But I thought, as you were already here, you might stay, Jonathan.'

Jonathan glanced quickly at David. 'I'd love to, Eva,' he said, looking less than enthusiastic. 'But I have to go—'

'To discuss my missing policy document,' Eva cut him short.

'Ah, right. Yes.' Jonathan nodded tightly.

'Jonathan's my investment adviser,' Eva addressed David. 'He looks after most of us baffled "oldies" of Hibberton. Has his offices on the High Street, don't you, Jonathan? Very posh.'

'Yes. Yes, I do.' Jonathan offered David a short smile on official business introduction.

'Specialises in Inheritance Tax matters,' Eva went on. 'He's very clever. I'm sure I wouldn't have a clue where my money would be safe without Jonathan's guidance.'

'Oh, right, I see.' David nodded, feeling less troubled by Eden's familiarity with his surroundings, yet still a little uneasy. Because of his own prejudices, David told himself firmly. 'Maybe I'll have a chat to you, sometime,' he suggested, trying to be at least halfway civil to the man.

'Anytime,' Jonathan offered. 'I'll let you have a card.'

'Do that.' David nodded his thanks.

'Right, so, you'll stay then Jonathan,' Eva turned back to Jonathan. 'It's just that I need to get my withdrawal under way.'

Pulling his attention away from David, Jonathan smiled at Eva resignedly.

'I've decided to inject some cash into Andrea's Second Chance Designer venture, Doctor Adams,' Eva confided. 'But keep it under your hat. I haven't had a chance to discuss anything but the original renovation works I'd intended with Andrea yet. She'll need some new stock, however, as I don't imagine any of the clothes she had, vintage or current, will be salvageable. Will they, Jonathan?'

Eva turned her gaze back on Eden, who looked distinctly uncomfortable. 'The insurance assessors have been in and they're ringing me back first thing next week, Eva. We'll know more then,' he said, with a short smile.

'Good.' Eva continued to look at him, though Jonathan's attention was now elsewhere. 'About time, too. The sooner they sort out the claim the sooner the poor woman can get on with her life. Homeless with three children, it's an abysmal situation to be in. No offence, Doctor Adams, but one's home is where one's heart is, don't you think?'

'None taken, Eva,' David assured her. 'And, yes, I do.' His home had more of a heart with Andrea and her family in it, he had to concede.

'Her heart's in her business venture, too, and she could make it work,' Eva went on determinedly. 'You only have to look at the way she dresses to see she has an eye for clothes. Or, should I say, the way she did dress, before all her worldly goods were burnt to a cinder.'

Eva glanced pointedly again at Jonathan, who'd moved on to plucking hairs from his trousers. 'I'm just glad she's in such safe hands,' Eva tacked on a touch cynically.

'Obviously.' David swapped glances with her, Eva's look telling him they were on the same wavelength. As far as David could see, apart from the few heartfelt words back at his house, Eden seemed not too perturbed that he'd lost all his worldly goods. That he might have lost Andrea.

'Anyway, that's why I've decided to chip in and help her get restocked.' Eva turned her attention back to David. 'Mum's the word though. I'm not sure Andrea would want me to be parted with my cash, would she Jonathan?'

'Um, sorry?' Jonathan's thoughts were still apparently distracted.

'My cash, Jonathan. Might we have that little chat, do you think?'

'I'll leave you to it,' David said, still trying – and failing – to get Eden's measure. This was the man Andrea was in love with? Surely he must have some redeeming features, though David was struggling to find any.

'Goodbye, Doctor Adams. Do give my best to Andrea,' Eva said with a smile.

At which, Jonathan shot him a none-too-friendly glance, David noted. Couldn't blame him for that, he supposed, Eva having just lumped the man's ... partner? ... fiancée? ... and David together.

'I'm sure Jonathan will pass on your regards, Eva,' he said, not wanting to cause any friction between Andrea and ... whoever he was, for Andrea's sake. 'Don't forget to make that appointment at the surgery.'

David gave Eva a no-nonsense look and left her to the care of her investment adviser. Maybe he could help out on the business front, David mused as he let himself out. Andrea's priorities, he imagined, would be to find a more permanent home for herself and her family until her own house was renovated, assuming it could be. Most of the expense for that would be covered by the insurance though, he assumed. Hopefully, most of the décor and furnishings could be replaced. Pity the missing dog couldn't be so easily replaced, David thought ruefully. He'd put some posters up, he decided. Maybe get Jake to help out, which would give them something they could do together. It might be a start.

He'd have another quick word with Eva, he decided. Check out where the actual business premises were and whether he could be of any practical assistance there. Intending to poke his head back in and ask her if he could drop by later, David turned back to Eva's, but stopped short of the front door when he heard Eva say, 'So, Jonathan, did you find whatever it was you were looking for?'

'The policy documents,' Jonathan said, with an audible sigh. 'I thought they'd be here, but no trace of them, I'm afraid.'

'I know. I've searched,' Eva stated categorically.

'Well, obviously you would, Eva, but you know, with age comes forgetfulness,' Jonathan replied patronisingly. 'Sometimes a second pair of eyes help, don't they?'

'I wouldn't know, Jonathan. I've only ever had one pair,' was Eva's droll reply. She sounded pretty much on the ball to David, whose uneasiness about Jonathan Eden was escalating. Had the guy actually come into Eva's house uninvited?

'So,' Eva went on, 'you thought you'd just let this second pair of eyes in through my back door without asking, did you?'

'I came down the back path from Mr Robinson's house,' Jonathan supplied. 'I did knock, but you were—'

'In the front garden.'

'Yes, I, um …'

'So you had a good look around for a document I'm absolutely sure I left with you, and then decided to let yourself out, also presumably through the back door?'

'Well, I assumed you were out, Eva. Obviously, I would have—'

'Made your presence known, if you'd realised where I was?'

'Yes, of course. I'd have made you a cuppa. You know I would, Eva. Now, about your investment, someone's cocked up at the company head office, I'm afraid. Nothing to worry about, a wrong bond number input or something. It might take a couple of weeks to sort out. I'm on it though, rest assured.'

'Hmm?' said Eva.

And well she might, thought David, now feeling extremely uneasy. Did Eden know the woman had taken a fall? That she was lying on the hall floor, possibly seriously injured?

Whatever, why the hell was Eva covering for him?

It was one of those muggy, damp mornings, a soft drizzle on the air that does absolutely nothing for a girl's hair. Not much caring, Andrea creaked open the school gates and slipped inside the playground. She was sweaty under her coat now, from the walk to the park, and then around the park searching fruitlessly for poor missing Dougal, as well as her now absent family. From there, she'd gone on to the village hall, where she'd eventually found Dee, with Sophie and Chloe, helping organise the bundles of donated clothes.

'For the jumble sale,' Thea had informed her, tossing knickers and bras efficiently on one pile and then turning her attention to the trouser pile.

'Oh, lovely,' Andrea had replied half-heartedly, then felt like an ungrateful wretch when Nita had wheelied by, her lap full of yet more clothing.

'We're having a raffle, too. And we're forming a think tank for more ideas to help you out until you get some insurance money,' Nita had said, parking herself at the trestle table to unburden herself.

Andrea should have stayed and helped, or at least put her Saturday to better use and gone shopping while her mum and her children were all happily occupied, Chloe up to her armpits in toys and Dee and Sophie sorting through bric-a-brac together, amazingly. There were so many things one needed when starting from scratch. Surely the insurance people could release some kind of emergency fund soon? She'd have to talk to Jonathan about it, though she really didn't feel much like talking, or rather arguing, with him, right then.

Andrea fixed her eyes down as she walked through the playground, and tried not to breathe in the acrid smell of burnt wood still permeating the air.

Shoes, she'd thought, when she'd gone online, only to wonder whether to buy trainers or boots, and this was before considering Ryan and Sophie's critical 'cool' footwear factor. There were toiletries to think about, potties and panties, duvets, toys and blankets, not to mention actual clothes. Andrea was truly grateful for her neighbours' efforts but, 'totally wicked' though Sophie had thought some of the donated clothes were, she doubted she'd be so thrilled at the prospect of second-hand knickers.

Where would she find the money to pay for it all until the insurers paid out? As for Jonathan and where they would be in the future … Andrea sighed heavily. In truth, she had no inclination to think about it. Jonathan's explanations about his whereabouts after the fire had sounded plausible, but vague somehow, and Andrea just didn't have the energy to go there. What she would quite like to do was crawl into bed and sleep, preferably to wake up and find the whole awful mess was no more than a nightmare. In the absence of a bed to call her own, however, she'd come to the school instead. Selfish though it might seem, she needed some space. Something to do, other than sort through castoffs, or curl into a ball and cry, which she'd come very close to doing.

Physical therapy might be better though, and far less destabilising to her children than a blubbering mother, she decided, discarding her coat and bending to clutch at a weed fighting for space amongst many on the patch of land Andrea wanted to transform into a garden. Determined, she concentrated her efforts on tugging the gangly plant from the ground, then puffed up her fringe and tugged harder; and then wiped her hands free of rubbery green leaves, the only things she'd succeeded in removing thus far.

Damn. 'It's you or me, Little Weed,' she growled, squatting to grab hold of it with both hands. 'And be warned I'm in no mood to give in.' She yanked at it, 'Oooh, come on!', and heaved, and … 'Eeek!' … keeled inelegantly backwards, plopping heavily – and painfully – to her hindquarters.

'Right! Now, it's war!' she muttered, narrowing her eyes and attempting to scramble to her feet, only to find herself being hauled up from behind by a pair of firm hands.

'Ouch, I bet that hurt,' the owner of the hands imparted.

'Not half as much as my pride,' Andrea grumbled, turning to face David, who obviously found her predicament hilarious, judging by the merriment in his eyes. Nice eyes, she thought, her own eyes reluctant to look away, not ice cool at all. Quite warm and friendly, in fact, now he'd let his guard down.

'I was passing,' he said, holding her gaze, which Andrea found peculiarly disconcerting. 'Saw this mad woman muttering to herself and trying to steal the plants, so I thought I'd better investigate.'

'I'm not trying to steal them.' Andrea looked away first, feeling more disorientated by the close proximity of his body than her spectacularly embarrassing tumble. 'They're weeds,' she explained, rubbing her assaulted rump. 'I'm trying to kill them.'

David laughed. 'What, with threats?'

Andrea folded her arms, which allowed her a little more breathing space between them, and cocked her head to one side, her expression she hoped conveying not amused, rather than inexplicably confused.

David did likewise, his expression highly amused. 'Not working really, is it?' he ventured.

Andrea's mouth twitched into a smile. She couldn't help it. Despite her bruised pride, bruised bottom, and her whole world falling apart, there was something about this man that made her feel … at ease with herself, somehow.

Or at least he had.

She doubted she'd have been dancing dottily around singing a duet with her mum in front of Jonathan, who would have thought her just that, dotty. David hadn't batted an eye. He'd even joined in and managed a whole actual laugh. He really was quite attractive. Andrea found herself appraising him again, taking in his soulful blue eyes, framed by unfairly dark eyelashes, his strong jawline, a hint of dark stubble thereon, which was undeniably sexy in a rugged-man sort of way, his mouth which far better suited a smile.

His torso was firm, long-limbed and well-toned, she couldn't help but notice as they'd passed on the landing. His hands elegant and strong, with clean fingernails; those of a doctor a patient might immediately trust. Yes, outwardly, all the qualities a woman would find extremely attractive. And inwardly? David Adams had learned the hardest possible way the immeasurable pain cheating and lying can cause a woman. He was a caring person. Andrea had seen that. A man who'd hurt someone he loved and was hurting because of it. Should he ever feel guilt-free enough to embark on another relationship, she was sure he would be sensitive to a woman's feelings. Her needs. Andrea's eyes strayed to his lips, soft and full enough to be sensuous on a man.

'Nice hair accessory,' David said, after an awkward second.

'Sorry?' Andrea continued to stare at him, her gaze seeming to be drawn to his.

'The, er, green foliage. Matches your eyes,' he joked, but there was a flicker of uncertainty in his expression.

She watched, transfixed, as he hesitated, and then reached for what could have been a hornet's nest in her hair, so little did she care. And when his fingers brushed her cheek, David Adams as good as electrocuted her on the spot.

Closing her eyes and panting out a surprised breath, Andrea stifled a ridiculous desire to turn her face to his touch, to feel his fingers tracing the curve of her cheek, her lips ... His mouth following in their wake, covering hers, his tongue gently probing and— she was fantasising about the man – right in front of him!

Andrea snapped her eyes open, to see David now studying her intently.

'It's er ...' He shook his head, as if bemused, then moved his hand through her hair to retrieve whatever was there, instantaneously sending another shockwave of pleasure right through her. 'A leaf,' he said, holding up the evidence. 'I thought you might panic when you pulled your sweater ... Ahem. Would you like a hand?'

Andrea blinked at him, now definitely disorientated.

'You have to dig them out,' David said softly.

'Sorry?'

'The weeds.'

Andrea didn't answer. Instead, she continued to study him. Searching his face. On hers, open confusion.

David mentally reprimanded himself. What on earth had possessed him to let his hand linger like that? Tempted him to lean forward and steal a kiss from those velvet soft lips, so breathtakingly beautiful when she smiled, so agonisingly sensual when parted like that, in surprise.

To wonder what Andrea would feel like in his arms, kissing him back? In his bed? He'd wanted to taste her, touch her. Explore every inch of her. He swallowed hard. He wanted to make love to her. This was more than needing the solace of a woman's touch. Needing to lose himself in the embrace of a woman. What he was feeling, David realised, with a jolt, was nothing to do with sex or lust.

He was in love with this woman.

But this woman was with another man. In love with another man – and completely out of bounds. There was simply nothing he could do about it. As much as David knew his chances of feeling this way ever again were probably nil, absolutely no way would he even test the waters. Break up another family? Traumatise Jake more than he already had? Cause chaos in Sophie and Ryan's lives? And what about little Chloe? Eden wasn't up to much in David's estimation, but to his daughter he would be everything.

Then there was Andrea. He was assuming an awful lot, such as the fact she might be remotely interested. Could she be? Had he seen … something … in her eyes, or was that just his own wishful thinking? And, if she was, wouldn't he break her bloody heart, too? That was one thing he was guaranteed to be good at.

'I know.' Andrea pulled his attention away from where it shouldn't be.

David squinted at her, sure she'd been reading every wrong thought in his head.

'By the roots,' Andrea went on, looking perturbed now. As if she would very much have preferred he keep his hands to himself.

David nodded, forcing a smile and telling himself he was a bloody fool. Her only interest in him was that she cared, because that's the kind of person she was.

'Are you okay?' he asked, thinking he'd rather apologise. But then, if Andrea had no inkling of why his hand had been reluctant to pull away, wouldn't she wonder what he was apologising for? 'You look a bit pale,' he said, groping for anything to say instead.

'Just cold,' Andrea assured him, wrapping her arms about herself.

How David wanted to wrap his arms around her. Pull her close and keep her safe. Do it right this time. But, of course, he couldn't.

Andrea's gaze faltered. 'Shall we have a bash, then?' She smiled uncertainly and nodded towards the patch of weeds. 'I think physical activity might be the only thing that will warm me up, to be honest.'

'Let's get some tools.' David nodded firmly, whilst working very hard not to imagine the kind of physical activity that might keep them both warm.

Chapter Sixteen

'I said, Andrea's made a start,' Eva repeated through the gap in Sally's door.

'On what?' Sally squinted out, her mind on other things, namely her preparations for her meeting with David this evening.

'The school garden project,' Eva imparted importantly. Her cheeks were flushed with excitement, Sally noted. Over a patch of weeds? She found that hard to believe. 'Andrea's at the school getting stuck in and I thought it would be a jolly good idea if one or two more of us lent a hand. Show a bit of solidarity and what not. What do you think?'

Sally sighed and pulled the door wide. 'You want me to dig, Eva?' she asked, holding up fingers adorned with nail extensions. 'With these?'

Eva considered. 'Well, a shovel might be better,' she decided, 'but I'm sure they'll do splendidly.'

'Not at five pounds a nail they won't,' Sally assured her. 'Sorry, Eva, but I'm feeling a stay-at-home-with-a-good-book mood coming on.' She was happy to help out. Given Andrea's awful predicament, of course she was. Going to school to dig a hole in the ground, though, wasn't on Sally's agenda today.

'Oh.' Eva looked crestfallen. 'Ah, well, never mind.' She shrugged stoically and turned to go. 'I'm sure Doctor Adams won't mind stepping into the breach and staying a bit longer. He's there now, I noticed, when I passed. Turning into a bit of a white knight, isn't he, our—'

'Give me one minute,' Sally said behind her, flipping off her slippers and stuffing her feet into Wellington boots.

'My, don't you two look cosy,' Sally shouted across the playground.

'Looks like we have company.' David glanced warily in Sally's direction as she slipped through the gate.

'It certainly does.' Andrea followed his gaze, pleased – and a touch relieved at the distraction. The air between David and her seemed so charged. Far from feeling cold when his arm had brushed hers earlier, her skin had practically sizzled. David was doing absolutely nothing to help, giving her such long, curious glances, Andrea was sure she'd sprouted a whole tree in her hair.

He was now giving Sally a rather worried look, she couldn't help but notice. 'Problem?' she asked.

'No,' David said quickly. 'Not really.'

But still, he looked like a worried man. Oh, dear. Perhaps she shouldn't have mentioned she thought Sally might be on a manhunt. David was now looking as if he wanted to dig a very large hole and get in it.

'Well, well, aren't we the chivalrous one?' Sally beamed David a smile as she walked towards them.

'Sally.' David smiled guardedly back. 'And Eva, what on earth are you doing? I thought I told you to keep those legs up.'

'Ooh, I bet he says that to all the ladies. I bet one or two of them would oblige, too, hey girls?' Eva chuckled and reached to give his already flushed cheek an over-robust pinch.

'Dressed for the occasion, I see, Eva.' Andrea noted the gardening belt around Eva's waist and leather knee pads adorning her dungarees.

'If I'm going to do a job, my dear, I like to do it well. Tools to hand and whatnot.'

'I'm not sure you should be doing jobs, well or not, Eva,' David said seriously. 'Not until I've checked you over.'

'Nonsense.' Eva flapped a dismissive hand. 'I'm perfectly fine, Doctor Adams, as we've already established. A little light-headedness never killed anyone.'

'Light-headedness?' Andrea turned to David, alarmed.

'Eva had a bit of a fall, but she's going to the surgery on Monday, aren't you, Eva?'

'Oh, I don't need to waste the doctor's valuable time. I'm perfectly—'

'Eva, I'm in the surgery on Monday. Either I see you there, or I pay you another house call, which will waste more of the doctor's valuable time, won't it?'

'Such a fuss,' Eva tsked, 'but if you insist. Now then, to the job at hand.' She moved swiftly on. 'We thought we'd help get you organised, didn't we, Sally?'

Andrea glanced from David to Eva, feeling quite overcome. 'I don't know what to say, Eva. Are you sure you're all right? I mean, all this can wait. I was really only … Well, trying to distract myself, I suppose.'

'As I said, I'm absolutely fine, my dear. I'm sure Doctor Adams means well, but he really is fussing about nothing. Now, come along, more hands make light work and all that.'

'Thank you,' Andrea said, in danger of blubbering all over again. She doubted she would have got through all this without Eva chivvying her on. 'I honestly don't know how I'll ever repay you for all your kindness, Eva.'

'I wouldn't say no to a chocolate cupcake and caramel latte,' Eva suggested, looking quietly pleased.

'Make mine a Sauvie B. I'm exhausted, and this was just pouring myself into my leggings this morning,' Sally put in, causing all eyes to turn to her legs, David's included.

'Right, move over, Andrea, you look frazzled. Let me have a go.' Sally stepped determinedly towards the patch they'd made little headway on.

'Sally, are you sure?' Andrea asked, worriedly perusing the rest of Sally's attire, a fur trimmed shell jacket, ivory in colour. 'It's very muddy.'

'Oh, you know me, Andrea, always the outdoorsy sort. Now, make way.'

'As long as it's bikini and martini weather,' Eva mumbled, behind her.

'Eva, shhhh!' Andrea hissed as Sally rolled up her metaphorical sleeves, placed the spade purposefully in the ground, pressed a foot on top of it, and made no impression whatsoever.

'Make that a large Sauvie B,' Sally said, gritting her teeth to try again.

'You'll need the hand hoe and a fork,' Eva informed her knowledgeably. 'And you'll need to get down to their level.'

She extended a hand, and David dutifully provided his own, allowing Eva leverage to lower herself to her knees.

'Hmm, looks as if we've quite a battle on our hands,' Eva observed, examining the foe at close quarters. 'Groundsel,' she said, picking up Andrea's plucked weed.

'Oh, I thought it was a dandelion.' Andrea furrowed her brow as she knelt alongside Eva. 'Mind you, I wouldn't know a cabbage from a rose.'

'Which is why I'm here, my dear,' Eva patted her thigh reassuringly, 'to identify our Senecio vulgaris or groundsel from our Taraxacum officinale or dandelion in order to eradicate them efficiently.'

David shook his head, bemused. 'I feel enlightened already.'

'Glad to be of help, Doctor Adams.' Eva smiled up at him, delighted.

Eva pointed her hoe at one or the other and David crouched down to join Andrea, who was paying proper attention, as Eva warbled on about annuals and perennials, and fluffy seeds being blown on the wind. 'Which is why we have to take every little bit of the root out,' she finished with a determined little nod.

'Absolutely.' Andrea nodded, equally determined.

'Wilco.' David saluted, he and Andrea then exchanging amused glances.

'We'll have a cuppa before we get stuck in,' Andrea suggested. 'I'll go and put the kettle on in the staffroom. Fancy one, Eva?'

'Ooh, lovely,' Eva said, already at work on what still looked like a weed as far as Andrea could see.

Disgruntled, Sally watched as David stood up and extended his hand to help Andrea up.

'So kind,' Andrea said, with a theatrical bat of her eyelashes, while Sally seethed quietly inside. They'd be finishing each other's sentences in a minute. What was the matter with Andrea, smiling and playing up to him?

'David?' Andrea asked. 'Are you up for a cup?'

'Great.' David smiled. 'Coffee please, if you have some. Black with—'

'No sugar,' Andrea finished. 'Got it. Sally, want one?'

God! 'No,' Sally said shortly, then pulled herself up and forced a smile. 'Thanks, Andrea, but I've not long had one. I'll give you a hand though,' she offered.

'No problem.' Andrea smiled, her oh, so, natural make-up-less smile, which had Sally's heart sinking into her Wellington boots. 'Stay and chat to David, why don't you?' Andrea suggested, heading off. 'Get better acquainted.'

'I'd love to,' Sally said cheerily. If only I could drag his attention away from you. Fuming silently, she looked at David, who was watching Andrea walk to the staffroom, her copper curls bouncing naturally behind her and still looking casual, yet sophisticated, with absolutely no flipping effort. She was wearing a man's shirt, for goodness' sake, and track bottoms. Couldn't the woman ever look the tiniest bit like a wardrobe disaster? Or at least put her coat back on and stop flaunting herself.

David wasn't just looking now, Sally noted, growing evermore peeved as she turned her attention back to him.

He was perusing. And Sally did not like it one little bit. This was just too much. Damn him. What was he playing at? Determined not to let him get a glimpse of her green-eyed monster, which was now practically spitting fire, Sally wet her lips with her tongue instead, and walked over to him.

'I'm going to help Eva on that side, just in case the poor dear exerts herself,' she said, doing her best to look saintly. 'I just wanted to confirm we're still on for tonight, though. I've cancelled my prior engagement, you see.'

'Oh,' David said, looking uncertain and Sally fervently hoped, if the man valued his reputation, that he wasn't going to back out. 'Er, yes,' he said, after an agonising second.

'Good.' Sally smiled and tried not to look too relieved. 'I'll open a nice red and let it breathe.'

'Sally, I won't be able to sta—' David started.

'Uh-oh, looks like rain's stopping play, my dears,' Eva said behind them.

'Oooh, shit,' Sally cursed. 'I've just straightened my bloody hai ... Ahem. Hey, ho, never mind though,' she brightened so much her halo practically pinged. 'Occupational hazard when you're the outdoorsy sort.'

Reaching the front door as the heavens opened with a vengeance, Andrea ducked from under the overcoat David was gallantly holding over them and scrambled into the hall.

All but falling in after her, David nudged the door closed behind them. 'On the bright side, the ground will be softer,' he said, attempting to inject a little levity into their very sodden situation. 'On the down side ...' He eyed his saturated coat unenthusiastically and then gave it a good shake.

'Ooh. Ouch!' Already out of her coat, Andrea shrieked as she was showered liberally with droplets of icy cold water. 'Ooh, you ...' Laughing, she turned around ready to admonish him, and found David's scrutinising gaze disturbingly on hers.

'Sorry,' he apologised, glancing down. Slowly down, his gaze coming to rest where the damp material of her shirt clung to her breasts.

'Um …' Feeling awkward as his gaze lingered, Andrea wrapped her arms about herself.

'Sorry,' David repeated, snapping his attention back to her face. 'I, er … You're drenched.' He indicated her definitely drenched state with a nod of his head, now looking hugely embarrassed.

Well, if she would stand there with her wares practically on display … And they were, Andrea realised, mortified. With her one and only bra swilled out and hanging on the airer, the wet material was doing nothing to hide her undeniably aroused state, which was more to do with the appreciative look she'd seen in David's eyes, she suspected, than the cold weather.

'Gosh, you don't say. And there was me wondering why I was dripping water all over your hall floor.' Andrea decided to make light of the situation. A situation she absolutely shouldn't be encouraging. She had responsibilities, for goodness sake. She was with someone. Where was bloody Jonathan anyway – again? Rolling her eyes theatrically, she turned away from David, whose close proximity was far too disturbing, attempting to tug her hair from the back of her collar as she did.

David laughed, a low deep chuckle, as she struggled with the damp tendrils. 'You look like a drowned rat,' he observed, stepping towards her. 'A very cute rat,' he added quickly, 'but definitely a drowned one. Here, let me.' One hand lightly on her shoulder, he smoothed her hair from her neck, and Andrea's skin prickled alarmingly from her head to her toes.

'Flattery will get you everywhere,' she said, trying very hard to keep her tone flippant.

'Will it?' he asked quietly, after a second.

Andrea closed her eyes, her heart fluttering manically as an undeniable tingle of sexual excitement shivered the entire length of her spine. 'David ...' Disorientated, she turned around to face him and, far from the awkward look of a moment ago, his eyes were now smouldering with an intensity that shook her.

Catching a breath, Andrea tore her gaze away. This was absurd. Dangerous. She had an almost irrepressible urge to reach out and hold him, be held by him. 'David,' she started falteringly again, 'I—'

'About bloody time!' Sophie's dulcet tones reached their ears from the landing. 'Where've you been?' Her tone was accusatory, and with very good reason.

Andrea felt herself blushing. 'Swimming,' she replied, stepping quickly away from David, 'obviously.'

'She's driving me mental,' Sophie imparted, clearly not happy as she thumped on down the stairs.

'Who?' Andrea asked, glancing worriedly past her truculent older daughter for signs of her younger daughter tumbling down after her.

'Granny-bloody-gaga, who'd y'think?'

'Sophie, language!' Andrea shot David an apologetic look. 'And your gran is not gaga. She just gets a bit confused, that's all. She's bound to be a bit upset when she's—'

'Under the bed,' Sophie cut in, her arms folded, her expression now total exasperation.

Andrea blinked at her, baffled. 'Well, what on earth is she doing under the bed?' she asked, feeling pretty exasperated herself as she made to bypass Miss Moody. A Sophie strop she could do without right now.

'I don't know, do I? I'm not under there, am I?' Sophie

marched on to the kitchen, her arms still belligerently folded, lest anyone doubt she was incredibly pee'd off and put upon. 'Probably the same as what she was doing in the wardrobe and the loo cistern.'

Andrea stopped on the stairs. 'Pardon?' She turned back, eyeing David now, completely baffled.

'The loo cistern,' David supplied, Sophie now otherwise engaged, whamming the volume up on the radio in the kitchen.

'But ...? What was she doing in the ...? Ooh hell!' Andrea skidded back down. 'Sophie.' She headed after her daughter. 'What's Gran been doing in the ... Sophie.'

'What?' Sophie asked, knowing very well what by the look on her face.

'Turn it down!' Andrea yelled over Bon Jovi at ear-splitting level.

'Rrright. Take it out on me, why don't you? Again.' Sophie huffily complied, snatching up the remote and zapping the volume down to enable hearing level.

Andrea shook her head despairingly. 'Sophie, I'm not taking anything out on you. I'm trying to talk to you. It's what adults do.'

'Maybe I should just leave home as well.' Sophie wasn't in the mood for talking, apparently. She stropped across the kitchen to flick the kettle on and crash a cup from cupboard to work surface. 'Then you'd have to find someone else to babysit the barmy old bat and blame everything on, wouldn't you?'

Andrea sighed. 'Sophie, I know you're having to deal with a lot right now, but—'

'And Chloe,' Sophie chuntered on over her, 'you'd have to find someone else to babysit her, too, while you go swimming ... with him.' She paused in her tea making efforts to sweep reproving eyes over David, who'd dared venture into the fray.

'Oh, *heck*, Chloe.' Realising she hadn't even considered where Chloe might be with Sophie downstairs, Andrea turned hastily back to the kitchen door.

'In with the boys,' Sophie informed her shortly. 'Nice you remembered you had at least one daughter.'

Realising Sophie was genuinely upset and feeling contrite, Andrea came back and walked across to her aggrieved older daughter, who obviously did feel 'put upon' and with good reason. Hadn't she lost all her worldly goods, too? And now she was having to share not just a room with her gran, but a bed. It was enough to drive anyone to despair, let alone a teenager who needed her space. 'Look, Sophie, I know it's difficult for you and I really do appreciate ...' Andrea stopped, Sophie's latest bluff to leave home suddenly ringing alarm bells. 'What do you mean, "leave home as well?"'

Sophie shrugged, her body language still sullen, but a slight flush to her cheeks.

'Sophie, as well as who?' Andrea asked, with supreme patience.

'Gran,' Sophie admitted, after a sugar spilling, water sloshing moment. 'She keeps saying she's going back to the cottage.'

Andrea's heart leapt into her mouth, images of her mum wandering along the riverbank springing to mind. 'She hasn't tried to, has she?' she asked worriedly.

'No, but ...' Sophie glanced at her from under inch-thick mascara, the one all-important accessory she did have, thanks to Sally. '... she keeps saying she's going to. I try to tell her she can't, but she's, "Oh, but I can. I'm not staying here." And then she's banging on about him doing away with her. And Eva, for Pete's sake.'

Her inept attempt at tea abandoned, Sophie turned to Andrea, looking now truly exasperated. 'She's lost the plot, Mum. I'm worried, you know?' She shrugged in the way teenagers do when admitting they care about something other than the content of their latest text message.

'I know. I know you are, sweetie.' Trying to assimilate, Andrea wrapped an arm around Sophie's shoulders and pulled her towards her. 'Of course you are. And I know you've probably been worrying about whether to tell me, yes?'

Sophie sniffed and nodded. 'She keeps trying to pack the holdall off the top of the wardrobe, and she's got nothing to pack in it apart from her teeth. Then she keeps trying to hide something in case he finds it and ... I dunno ... murders her or something. She's gone, Mum. Mind's officially left the building.'

'Sophie, in case who finds it?' Andrea eyed David, now very concerned. 'David?'

'No, not David. She's as smitten with him as you are.' Sophie shot David another reproachful glance, and then turned back to Andrea. 'Jonathan. She thinks Jonathan's turned into a mass murderer or something. That's what I mean. She's driving me mental.'

Andrea gulped back a hard lump in her throat and glanced again at David, who looked as thunderstruck as she felt. 'I'll check on the kids if you need some space to talk to your mother,' he offered shakily.

'Thanks, David.' Andrea summoned up a smile, though she wasn't sure she could summon up the energy to deal with another crisis.

'Sir Galahad rides to the rescue, again,' Sophie muttered behind them as they headed for the hall.

Andrea's shoulders sagged. She hesitated, torn between her needy daughter and her equally needy mother.

'Go on.' David smiled and nodded, indicating he was willing to risk death by killer look again.

Grateful but weary, Andrea mounted the stairs, and then

hesitated, curious as to how David might handle a truculent teenage girl. Also apprehensive as to how Sophie might react.

'There's Coke in the fridge, if you'd prefer,' she heard David offer politely.

'Got tea,' was Sophie's rude response.

'Right.' David paused. 'Well, if it tastes as disgusting as it looks, just help yourself.'

'Do you mind?' Sophie sounded affronted. Bad move, thought Andrea.

'Nope, not as long as I don't have to drink it,' David replied smartly.

Andrea could swear she heard Sophie's humph from the stairs.

'I thought we'd go and put some posters up,' David pushed on.

Silence.

'The boys and I,' he continued to chat to himself in the absence of comment from Sophie. 'Fancy joining us?'

More silence, then, 'What posters?' Sophie asked, making sure to keep her tone only vaguely interested.

'Missing dog posters, in the park, shops, anywhere else people might see them. What do you think?'

Yet more silence, then, 'I didn't think anyone gave a shit,' Sophie muttered, then promptly burst into tears.

Oh no. Andrea whirled around to dash back to the kitchen, but stopped herself short of the door when she heard David say, 'Hey, hey, it's okay to cry. If grown men can, I'm bloody sure young women can.'

Chapter Seventeen

Assuring her that his house wasn't about to burn down in her absence, David managed to convince Sophie it was okay to leave her family in his care and 'chillax for five' with her friend. Having checked which friend, where and what time she'd be back, he then headed upstairs in the hope of interesting Jake in helping with the dog hunt, musing the Dee dilemma as he went.

There was no doubt that what Sophie had recounted sounded like the ludicrous ravings of a demented old woman, but the fact was, Dee, as far as David could see, was at the early stages of Alzheimer's: confused sometimes, yes, but lucid a good part of the time. It wasn't his area of expertise, and it was a cruel disease, some people experiencing more rapid deterioration than others, but still, it just didn't add up in David's mind.

Hearing Dee as he passed the main bedroom insisting, 'He's trying to do away with me!' David was apprehensive. Very apprehensive.

'No, Mum,' he heard Andrea say as he detoured to the bathroom to check something out, 'Jonathan doesn't want to do away with you. He wants to ...' she trailed off then, *put you away* probably not sounding like a much less sinister option, David guessed.

Easing the lid off the cistern on the supposition that the old lady had actually been determined to hide something in there, he almost laughed. There atop the water floated a plastic beaker from the kitchen. Parking the cistern lid to the side, David fished the beaker out and unscrewed the top, half expecting to find Dee's wandering teeth inside.

Nope, definitely not teeth. Mystified, he extracted the piece of paper tucked inside the beaker, which had been quarter-folded and folded again, opened it and quickly scanned the contents, then, '*Bloody hell!*'

Well, well, Eden was right, after all. With age does come forgetfulness. Eva had quite clearly forgotten she'd misplaced her policy document – in David's toilet cistern. He had no idea what was going on, but one thing was becoming abundantly clear, personal dislike aside, Jonathan Eden's odd behaviour – his disappearing when his house had burned down, his ferreting around in Eva's house while she was lying unconscious on the doorstep – was becoming more and more questionable.

So, what did he do about it? Have a quiet word with Eden, threaten to break his neck if he caused Andrea any more grief? And he cheerfully would, David realised, which wouldn't do him any great favours in Andrea's eyes, if his instincts turned out to be wrong.

No, speaking to Eden, who wasn't likely to be very forthcoming, wasn't an option. David really didn't like the guy, probably because he didn't want to, he realised, but before he spoke to anyone, he needed to get to the bottom of what was going on. Eden had been searching for this document in Eva's house and Eva knew damn well he had. Question was, why? And why had Dee got it? More intriguingly, why was she hiding it?

It looked like the only way to shed any light on it was to speak to the insurance company direct. No doubt they'd have data protection protocol in place, but he'd got the investment details to hand, and Eva's personal details, date of birth, etc, would be on record at the surgery. David just hoped the floating document wasn't anything to do with fraudulent activity. Eva might appear as tough as nails, but the fact was she was old and possibly unwell.

Tucking the document into his pocket as he heard Andrea

emerge from the bedroom, David quickly replaced the cistern lid. He'd copy it downstairs on the printer, he decided, then make sure it was back before Dee noticed it was missing, which was bound to have her more agitated than she already was.

Which was clearly very agitated. 'I might be old, but I'm not demented,' David heard the old woman shout after Andrea.

Meeting him on the landing, Andrea sighed and eyed the ceiling.

'He's up to no good, you mark my words.' Dee's head appeared around the doorframe behind her. 'Just because Eva thinks the sun shines out of his bespoke-suited bottom, doesn't mean he isn't.'

'Ooh, Mum!' Andrea scrunched her eyes and her fists closed. 'You don't even like Eva,' she said, whirling around to face her.

'Yes, but it doesn't mean I want her dead, does it? If I wanted that, I'd have strangled the old lesbian myself years ago. What are you staring at?' The latter was addressed at a surprised David, before Dee twanged her head back and demonstratively closed the door.

Andrea's shoulders visibly slumped. 'I don't believe this,' she said quietly. 'I honestly don't think I can take any more.'

She blew out a sigh as she turned to face him – and David felt himself reel on his feet. She was crying, tears streaming down her cheeks, and though he'd expected the trauma to catch up with her at some point, David was taken completely by surprise. Instinctively, he stepped towards her and folded her into his arms.

'I'm sorry.' Andrea pressed her face into his shoulder. 'I just …'

'Shhhh,' David said as if quieting a child. 'Tears are allowed, remember? Therapeutic, so they say.'

Andrea emitted a muffled laugh – and then cried harder,

causing David's heart to constrict. She should cry. It would do her good to cry, but he couldn't bear to see her like this. Holding her close, he stroked her back, her shoulders, her hair. She smelled fantastic: clean, fresh air mingled with citrus shampoo – his, he guessed. It was better on her.

'Okay?' he asked, after a moment.

She nodded into his shoulder, lifted her head, and David's breath caught in his chest. Her dancing green eyes were glassy with tears, and up close they were remarkable. She was ... 'Remarkable,' he murmured as she moved in his arms, leaning into him, raising her face.

Feeling the soft brush of her lips against his, David was now utterly confounded. Knowing he shouldn't, telling himself he shouldn't, he pressed his mouth closer then, his heart paying no heed to his head, he pulled her tight, daring to take it further, gently parting her lips with his tongue, tasting her.

This was wrong. All wrong. He knew it was. So, why did it feel so damn right? Wrestling with his conscience, he groaned quietly inside as she slid her delicate tongue into his mouth, exploring, softly teasing. Breathing heavily, David eased back a little, needing confirmation. He searched her face, her eyes, saw what he needed to there, then, desire winning outright over caution, he locked his mouth back hard on hers. One hand tracing the soft curve of her back, one tangled in her mane of red and gold hair, he kissed her hungrily, allowing his lips to stray to her neck, her shoulders.

He wanted her; wanted to kiss her all over; every inch of her. To glide his hands ... *'Bugger!'* The sound of the boys' bedroom door opening was like a thunderclap, instantly forcing them apart.

'Er, we, er ... Your mum, she ... had something in her eye,' David offered by way of weak explanation to Ryan, who, having watched his mother shoot flustered into the bathroom, was now regarding him coolly.

'Rrright.' Ryan cocked his head to one side. 'Thus the mouth to mouth?' he enquired drolly.

'Er ...' David's heart sank. Lying to Ryan, he wasn't comfortable with. What had just happened with Andrea ...? David felt his emotions colliding, astonishment, euphoria, fear. It had felt right. It had felt one hundred per cent right, but ... In his wildest dream it could never be, with Jake not even beginning to come to terms with the loss of his mother. And what about Andrea's kids? Had he taken leave of his senses?

'Just don't take advantage.' Ryan shot him a warning glance as David sweated, wondering what the hell to say next. 'Comprendre?'

Getting the message, David nodded, thankful that Ryan hadn't pursued it with Jake able to overhear. 'I won't,' he promised earnestly.

Ryan regarded him a second longer and then, apparently satisfied, gave him a short nod back. 'Jake and me are getting some munchies, if that's okay?'

Snacks, David mentally translated. 'No problem,' he said as Ryan dragged his gaze away from him and drifted along the landing. 'If you fancy though, we could grab a burger while we're out.'

Ryan turned back. 'Out where?'

'Distributing leaflets,' David supplied, hoping that Ryan wouldn't think this was some feeble attempt to redeem himself in his eyes.

Ryan now looked definitely unimpressed.

'Missing dog leaflets,' David elaborated, guessing he probably did. 'I thought we might put some posters up, while we were at it.'

Still eyeing him suspiciously, Ryan considered. 'Good idea,' he eventually said, giving him a half-approving nod.

David dragged a hand through his hair, relieved. At least the kid hadn't told him where to stuff his leaflets.

'All right with you, Mum?' Ryan called.

Cringing on Andrea's behalf, David guessed Ryan's thinking was on a par with his, that his mother was hiding in there mortified, probably with her ear pressed to the door.

'Yes, wonderful idea,' was Andrea's rather high-pitched reply.

Coming back along the landing, Ryan gave him another one of his shrewd looks, reminding David that he might have a temporary reprieve but that he wasn't off the hook.

David nodded, indicating he'd got the drift, and then, 'Are you up for it, Jake?' he asked and mentally crossed his fingers.

'What?' Jake answered from his room. A short response, but at least it was a response.

'Distributing some leaflets in hopes someone might have spotted Ryan's dog. What do you think?'

'Yup,' Jake said immediately. 'I'm in.'

David watched Jake approach the door, not over-enthusiastically, but that, he guessed, was more to do with the Ryan style slope he was trying to emulate. 'We thought we'd get a burger while we're out, if you're hungry, that is?'

'Big Mac?' Jake eyed him curiously.

'Anything you fancy.'

'Minty,' Jake replied.

David closed his eyes and offered up a silent prayer of gratitude. Open adoration it might not be, but that was okay. He didn't need hero-worshipping. If his son could learn to like him again, even love him a little, it would be enough.

'Small problem,' Ryan pointed out, going back into Jake's room for his trainers. 'All the photos we had of Dougal are on the PC we don't have any more.'

'No problem,' Jake said, his feet already halfway into his trainers. 'He's a Yorkie, right? There'll be loads of Yorkie pics online. We can run some off on my PC.'

And now David was truly grateful. By some miracle, that miracle being Ryan, his son was actually conversing; talking openly. Jake might never be the carefree ten-year-old he should be, but this was the closest he'd come in a long time. David's attraction to Andrea was real. He felt it with every part of him. But could either of them really contemplate taking risks with their children's emotions?

Posters printed, fifteen minutes later, they hit the shops. All of the shops. And in all of those shops, hushed whispers and curious glances were swiftly followed by smiles of greeting. David smiled dutifully back, exchanged pleasantries about the weather, but comments about personal issues, his and Andrea's, he steered clear of.

Andrea, he imagined, wouldn't want him speculating with people as to what started the fire, when the insurance might pay up, when the enigmatic Jonathan had showed up, which the girl in the Tiny Tots shop openly had.

Human nature was to gossip, David knew that, and, yes, he had built a brick fortress around himself initially. The walls were coming down a fraction now though, thanks to Andrea, but still he didn't care to divulge more than he needed to, especially after what had happened between them.

'What's up?' Jake eyed him curiously as they walked from the car park into the park, Ryan off in front to 'check out suitable trees for posters' he'd said. To give Jake and him some space, he meant. David appreciated it.

'Nothing. Why?' he answered, puzzled. He hadn't spoken for the last couple of minutes, largely because his thoughts had drifted back to Andrea, the soft caress of her lips on his, her body pressed close to his.

'You're smiling,' Jake informed him as if it were as unlikely as catching him flying, which, after all, David supposed it was.

'Oh, right, sorry.' David arranged his face into a frown, which better suited thoughts about Eden, which followed hot on the heels of thoughts about Andrea. Whatever had happened, whatever might or might not happen between Andrea and him, as sure as God made little green apples, Eden was up to something. David could feel it in his bones.

Jake's eyes flicked back up to him. 'That's okay. It's allowed.' He shrugged awkwardly. 'I don't think Mum would have wanted us to be sad all the time.'

David swallowed. 'No, I, er …' He swallowed again and attempted to clear his throat. 'I don't think she would have done, Jake. She preferred to be around smiley people.'

Would she have wanted him to be happy, though? Find happiness again in a relationship? Somehow, knowing her as he did, that she genuinely did hate to see people miserable, David doubted Michelle would have condemned him to spend his life on his own.

Maybe he would find happiness again. One day.

'Dad?' Jake said, after a pause.

Dad? David closed his eyes. 'Yep?' he managed.

'Can we have a dog? We were going to have one, weren't we, before …' Jake trailed off, for reasons that were obvious to David.

'Depends,' he said, now struggling hard to keep his emotions in check.

'On?' Jake squinted up at him.

'On whether we find Dougal.' David nodded towards Ryan, who, having found a suitable tree, was now nailing a poster hard to it.

Jake followed his gaze. 'Oh, right.' He contemplated. 'And if we don't?'

David contemplated in turn, his mouth twitching into a smile. He had a distinct feeling he was being manipulated here. 'Give it a couple of weeks, hey, until Andrea and her family have got themselves sorted, and then we'll start looking around,' he relented. 'But only if you're prepared to do your share of the walk—'

'Yesss!' Jake whooped. 'And if we do find Dougal, my dog and Ryan's dog can be mates, can't they?' At which Jake set off at a run to help Ryan out, leaving David firmly grounded. Whatever he did, he realised, where Jake's future was concerned, mistakes were simply not an option.

Having fretted herself into a state of exhaustion, Dee now lay on the bed napping, her expression still one of pursed-lipped silence, which she'd adopted when Andrea had apparently 'taken Jonathan's side'. She was wearing one of David's jumpers, purloined because it would keep her warm, she'd said, until she'd got the Aga going. The Aga in her little river fronting cottage Andrea knew she meant, feeling emotionally drained and as confused as her poor mum must be. Gently, she covered her with the duvet and then gathered up an also sleepy Chloe. She'd pop her down on the sofa, Andrea decided, collecting 'new Igglepiggle' from the bottom of the bed and closing the door quietly behind her.

'CBeebies,' Chloe demanded, once tucked comfortably up with all of David's cushions, one determined little hand outstretched towards the TV and a thumb wedged in her mouth.

Andrea was tempted to ease her thumb away, but thought better of it. It obviously offered Chloe a little comfort at a time she sorely needed some. 'All right, darling,' she smiled, tucking yet another of David's sheets under her baby's chin, 'but quietly, hmm? Nana's sleeping.'

Popping the DVD in, Andrea was grateful for Ryan's foresight regarding essentials required to maintain some sort of normality. He might still be sloping about with his skinny jeans hip level, but he'd gone from monstrous teenage stage to mature young man almost overnight; in the absence of the man who should be in their lives, Jonathan, who was still missing more often than not, Andrea thought angrily.

Her anger, though, soon subsided, ousted by overwhelming guilt. She'd kissed David. It hadn't been a chaste peck on the cheek. It had been long and lingering, full on and passionate. Andrea's hand strayed to her mouth in the wake of David's lips hard against hers, his tongue, gently searching, sending shockwaves through her entire body and her emotions into complete chaos.

Leaving Chloe with her lush eyelashes tickling her cheeks, seeking to entice her to sleep, Andrea slipped silently from the room. Her arms wrapped about herself, she pulled her shirt tight. David's shirt. It smelled of him. Pulling the collar to her face, she inhaled the intoxicating smell of clean cotton suffused with the aftershave she knew to be his: a spicy oriental fragrance, with cinnamon and orange blossom undertones, which lingered in the fabric even after he'd washed it. It was nice, sensual, yet masculine – and comforting, somehow.

Was that what it was, her seeking some kind of solace in his arms? A weak moment of madness? No. Andrea's skin tingled and her pelvis dipped as she retraced the exquisite trail of his mouth soft on her throat, her shoulders. She'd wanted him. Wanted to feel his hands on her body, searching, touching, making love to her in the way she knew that he would. She could almost feel him inside her, making her feel whole again. Feel wanted and special.

Andrea swallowed, knowing now that Jonathan hadn't made her feel that way for a long time, preoccupied as he perpetually seemed to be; her fault, too, possibly, but wasn't that the core of the problem between them? That the intimacy had gone somehow. She couldn't remember when.

Was it more than a mad moment for David? she wondered, making a cup of tea for something to do. Had she compromised him? Was he even now regretting it?

Slowly, she stirred the tea, absent-mindedly watching the whirlpool that formed at the heart of it – and then almost knocking the cup over as the backdoor swung open behind her.

'Thought I'd slip in the back,' Jonathan said as she spun around to face him. 'Are the kids in?' He smiled, causing Andrea's guilt to multiply tenfold.

'No,' she said, a hand to her throat as if the evidence of David's kisses was scorched there. 'They're out … with David. The boys, that is. Sophie's at Hannah's and Chloe's asleep—' Andrea stopped, her eyes dropping from his face to the bump under Jonathan's overcoat, which seemed to be moving.

And yapping. Frenziedly.

'Dougal!' Andrea cried, overjoyed as his little blond-Beatle cut appeared over the top of the coat, followed by two sparkly chocolate button eyes. 'Oooh, Dougal!' Her tea abandoned, she flew across to pluck the now very frenzied dog from Jonathan's precarious grasp and hold him up high.

'So, do I get a kiss?' Jonathan asked hopefully as she cooed and made kissy faces at the dog. 'Or do I have to grow some fur and a tail first?'

Oblivious to the front door opening, Andrea laughed, then, pulling Dougal – plus manically lapping tongue – from her face, she leaned up to press a grateful kiss on Jonathan's cheek; but dropped quickly back down as joyous whoops from the boys alerted her to their presence behind her.

'Bloody hell!' Ryan gawked, eyes agog as he looked from Dougal to Andrea to Jonathan. 'Dougal!' he exclaimed ecstatically, then – laid-back Ryan nowhere in evidence – he moved like greased lightning across the kitchen to gather an equally ecstatic, scrambling Dougal to him.

'Come here, little guy. What have they been doing to you, hey, mate? Tell me all about it and I'll get them for you.' Bundling him in his arms like a baby, Ryan nuzzled the little dog close and serious face licking ensued.

'And me, I'll get 'em, Dougal,' Jake enthused, following Ryan across the kitchen to stroke the dog's wriggling, waggily rump.

Foregoing admonishments for snogging the dog, Andrea smiled delightedly, her gaze falling on David as she did. David's gaze faltered for a second, but when he looked back to her, he was smiling, albeit uncertainly.

Rightly or wrongly, Andrea felt a huge surge of relief. She'd been sure he'd feel so awkward he wouldn't know where to look.

'Can I hold him?' Jake asked, bouncing alongside Ryan. 'Can I, Ryan? Can I?'

His son's exuberance obviously evident, David's smile widened, reminding Andrea that whatever she felt, whatever David might feel, their children's emotions were absolutely paramount.

'Thanks, David,' she said, wishing she could convey how pleased for him she was that here, at last, was a glimpse of the uninhibited, carefree little boy Jake should be. 'David's been out putting up missing dog posters with the boys,' she filled Jonathan in. 'We're all really grateful, aren't we, guys?'

'Very,' Jonathan said, with a short smile. 'Pity it was such a waste of time,' he added, sounding not the least bit grateful and extremely sarcastic.

'Jonathan?' Andrea looked at him askew.

'Well, he's found now, isn't he, so ...' Jonathan shrugged, his gaze now fixed firmly on David, who, Andrea noticed, seemed as determined as Jonathan not to look away. Consumed with guilt now, Andrea glanced nervously between them.

'You can help me give him a bath,' Ryan's voice broke the discernible standoff. 'What d'y'reckon, little guy? Fancy a swim with me and Jake, hey?'

Relieved at the timely interruption, Andrea rolled her eyes about to make a witty comment about Ryan styling Dougal's fur afterwards, anything to dispel the uncomfortable atmosphere, when David spoke.

'Looks pretty good on it, doesn't he?' he asked, his eyes still on Jonathan. 'Where did you say you'd found him?'

'Park,' was Jonathan's short reply.

'Coincidence.' David furrowed his brow. 'We've just come from there.' He appeared to ponder then offered Jonathan a short smile. 'Well done on finding him anyway, though. The kids have missed him, particularly Sophie.'

No answer from Jonathan, Andrea noted, whose attention was now diverted to the dog's hairs on his coat. Trying hard not to judge him for being so uncaring, since Jonathan hadn't bothered to pick up David's cue and ask how Sophie was, Andrea turned to the door to see to Chloe, who was calling from the lounge.

'There's a clothes brush in the utility if you need one,' David said to Jonathan behind her, sounding not very impressed.

Concerned at Jonathan's peculiar behaviour, Andrea headed worriedly for the lounge, hearing Dee upstairs as she did, 'I see he hasn't done away with Dougal yet, then?' she said, presumably talking to Ryan.

'Yerwhat?' was Ryan's bemused reply from the bathroom.

'Nothing you need to concern yourself with, young man. You just concentrate on making sure the bath is free of dog's hairs when you've finished,' Dee instructed, most definitely not sounding too muddled now.

Plucking Chloe from her nest of pillows, Andrea glanced at David as he came into the lounge after her.

'Your mother sounds a little more lucid,' he said.

He'd obviously also heard Dee dishing out her orders then.

Andrea nodded. 'Yes,' she said, confused, and wary of her heart's sudden propensity to do a flamenco dance in her chest whenever David was near.

'How is she?' David asked nodding at Chloe, who was tearful, kneading her eyes with one hand, the thumb of her other still firmly wedged in her mouth.

'Tetchy,' Andrea supplied, planting a soft kiss on Chloe's baby-soft cheek.

'Bewildered, probably, by the strange surroundings when she woke up.'

'Bound to be.' Andrea hugged Chloe a little closer and then, wanting to dispel any uneasiness there might be between them, added, 'Thanks, David, for all your help, with Dougal, as well as everything else.'

David offered her an easy smile. 'No problem.'

'I am so glad he's been found safe and sound,' Andrea said, transferring Chloe to one arm and reaching for Igglepiggle.

David reached it first. 'Yep, definitely a small miracle,' he agreed, picking the toy up from the sofa and handing it to her. 'And he really doesn't look too bad on it, does he? Considering he escaped an inferno and then got lost in the park for nearly two days, I mean. You'd think he might be bedraggled enough to need that bath, wouldn't you?'

Andrea eyed him quizzically. 'Meaning?'

'Nothing, not really. It's just …' David shrugged awkwardly '… he looked a bit too well fed and groomed to have been wandering the streets, that's all.'

What? Andrea blinked at him. Were his feathers ruffled now? Because of damaged pride? She couldn't quite believe it. Narrowing her eyes, Andrea searched his face and realised they absolutely were. 'Oh, David … Not you, too? What's he supposed to have done now?' she hissed, lest Jonathan overhear. 'Plotted to murder the dog?' Shaking her head despairingly, Andrea pulled her gaze away and walked past David back to the kitchen.

Chapter Eighteen

David wasn't sure agreeing to go and see Sally had been a good idea, but him being out of the way would allow Andrea and her family some space, he supposed. He was pretty sure Andrea would prefer not to have to feel awkward in his company, which she would do after their kiss and now he'd hinted at his suspicions about Eden.

Sighing, David checked his watch and turned back to Sally's door to ring the bell again. Hearing noises inside, he waited a while longer, debated, and then peered through the opaque glass in the door. And then wished he hadn't.

'*Shit!*' he gulped, witnessing Sally tugging a silk kimono over ... not a lot ... as she clunked hurriedly downstairs in her high-heeled shoes.

Hell. She didn't think he'd come with anything other than talking in mind, did she? No, he'd caught her on the hop that was all. She was getting ready for bed. A bath. But ... hadn't she been expecting him?

'David!' Sally beamed, pulling the door wide.

'Sally.' David tugged in a breath and tried to avert his eyes as the kimono fluttered open, the apparel underneath definitely not designed for sleeping or bathing in.

'I'm so glad you're here,' Sally purred. 'Do come inside.'

David hesitated. 'Er ...' No, I won't, he was about to say, when he noticed a neighbour emerging from a house a few doors away. 'Thanks,' he said instead, stepping in as the neighbour walked her dog towards them. A scantily clad woman greeting him on her doorstep would definitely send the village drums into overdrive.

Sally closed the door behind him. 'I'm in the kitchen,' she

said, locking suggestive eyes with his as she squeezed past in the intimate space of the hall.

'Right.' David took another deep breath and then followed her as she sashayed toward the kitchen, trailing a heady aroma of perfume behind her.

'What do you fancy?' Sally paused at her work surface to glance over her shoulder. 'Red, white, tea, coffee?'

David hung back by the door. 'Er, something cold might be nice.' He ran his hand over his neck and wondered whether to stay and say what he'd come to, or make his excuses and leave.

'Perfect. I've just opened a chilled Sauvie B. It would be a terrible shame to waste it.' Sally picked up an open bottle and turned to fill a glass, already in position on the table.

Picking up the glass, she walked across to him, her eyes travelling over him, before resting purposefully on his. 'To a fulfilling future,' she said, offering him the glass and then holding on to it as he reached for it.

'That's what I wanted to talk about, Sally,' David started determinedly. 'I hoped we could talk and clear things ...' he trailed off, watching warily, as Sally ran the pink tip of her tongue slowly over her lips, tilting his glass towards her as she did.

'You're, er, spilling the, er ...' David stopped awkwardly again, as the wine bled through the thin fabric of her kimono, causing it to cling to her flesh.

'Oh, dear, clumsy me.' Sally sighed, a long expansive sigh, then eased the kimono from her shoulders to let it flutter to the floor.

'Would you like another?' she asked huskily, her eyes still on his. 'Or would you prefer ... something else?'

Transfixed, David watched the rise and fall of her breasts, firm and round, above the wispy lace of her basque, as Sally reached again for his glass, taking it easily from his dumbstruck hand.

He should go. Now. She was vulnerable, feeling hurt. She needed someone. Someone to make her feel wanted; to help ease the pain. She wouldn't find that in him. 'Sally, could we please just talk?'

'Later. We have plenty of time. We're practically living on top of one another now, after all.' Placing the glass on the surface next to him, Sally stepped towards him.

'Sally, I ...' David found his voice as Sally's hands sought to loosen his shirt. 'It's too soon ... for me. To get into a relationship, I mean. I should—'

'Then don't,' Sally said, holding his gaze as her fingers worked nimbly on shirt buttons. She leaned towards him, brushing his lips with more than a hint of a promise, before seeking the bare flesh of his chest, teasing his torso with her tongue, her mouth, her hands.

'Sally, I ... Damn it!' David reached for her, gripping her forearms to ease her away from him. 'Just stop. Please. You don't want to do this, not like this. I don't.'

Sally blinked, shock peppered with uncertainty flickering across her wide eyes.

'I'm sorry. I shouldn't have ...' Ashamed of himself, David fumbled for the right words. He shouldn't have pushed her away like that. Shouldn't be here. What the hell was he—?

Sally cut his thoughts short, her eyes on his now fiery and determined as she slid her hands provocatively over the silk bodice of her basque. David watched, perspiration tickling his forehead and his throat too tight as, slowly, silently, seductively, she eased down the top of the garment.

Stupefied, he watched on as she inserted her forefinger into her mouth, wetting it suggestively and then trailed it the slender length of her throat to her breasts, circled first one taut nipple, then the other.

'I think you do want to, Doctor Adams,' she murmured,

stepping towards him, pressing herself to him, her lips now hard against his, her tongue probing for his.

David pulled back sharply. 'Sally, I ...' Clamping his eyes shut, he faltered, then, 'I'm so sorry, Sally,' he said, on a long exhale of breath.

And Sally froze.

'For what?' she asked panic-struck as he stepped physically away from her, looking embarrassed, angry even.

'I just can't, Sally.' He glanced at her, hardly meeting her eyes. 'I'm sorry.'

'But why?' Sally asked, a tremor in her voice. 'Am I really that repulsive?' she asked tearfully.

'No,' David said adamantly. 'No,' he repeated, raking a hand through his hair, hastily re-buttoning his shirt. 'It's nothing to do with you and everything to do with me. I just ... can't.'

Sally eyed him narrowly. 'But you could before?' she asked quietly.

'Things have changed, Sally. I shouldn't have. Not then. Not now. I ... I have to go, Sally. Jake will be wondering where I am.'

David retrieved her kimono from the floor and handed it to her to cover her modesty.

'You're an attractive woman, Sally,' he mumbled, 'I—'

'Not attractive enough, obviously,' Sally said, clutching the kimono to her.

'Very attractive,' David insisted. 'It's just ...' He glanced towards the door desperate to be gone.

'You're not ready for a relationship,' Sally finished flatly.

David nodded slowly and dropped his gaze. 'I'm sorry, Sally, truly. You deserve much better than this.'

Sally notched her chin up. 'You're right, I do.'

'I'd better go.' David sighed heavily and turned to the door.

'You're all the same! Thinking you can walk away from your responsibilities,' Sally shouted furiously after him. 'Well, you can't, David Adams. I won't let you!'

Stepping out of her lingerie where she stood, Sally plucked the silly garments from the floor, then walked slowly across to plop them in the bin.

She was shocked. She felt as if she'd been physically punched. Pulling the kimono around her goose-pimpled body, she headed towards the door. Then back again for the remainder of the wine.

Wine bottle in one hand, glass in the other, she padded to her lounge and the warmth of the fire. She felt cold through to her bones, and hunched, and old. And cheap. And disgustingly unattractive, no matter what David had said. He'd been trying to let her down lightly, clearly having found some kind of moral code where before he'd had none. Swiping at a tear on her cheek, Sally unscrewed the bottle and filled the glass to the brim. How very noble of him.

A cushion clutched to her tummy, she seated herself on the edge of her sofa, and gulped back her wine, feeling as desolate and deserted as she had as a child, when her father hardly acknowledged she existed, when Nick had spurned her advances, no matter how hard she'd tried, finally to cruelly cast her aside. Most of all, she felt cold and lonely, just like she had when she'd walked away from the hospital without her baby. She didn't want to go there again, the dark black cloud descending, like a soft cloying blanket threatening to suffocate her.

Why had he turned her down? She was certain that what had passed between them previously hadn't been that bad. They'd done it every which way. In fact, if she'd let him, they'd have had sex before they got through the hotel room door. The man had almost been driven, passionate, exciting, and apologetic even, but driven somehow. And now Sally was single, and available, and so was he. It just didn't add up. If he'd been so ready and willing before, why would he be getting a guilt attack now? He had been widowed long before they met in the hotel so it wasn't because of a wife that was dead and buried, that was for sure. So it had to be because of someone current in his life. And the only person current in his life, permanently ensconced in his life, as far as Sally could see, was Andrea.

He might not have made a move on her yet, Sally contemplated as she refilled her glass, but he would. She was sure. Far from being put out by Andrea and her entourage camped in his home, David seemed to like having them there. The way he was with Chloe, like a father almost.

The way he looked at Andrea – with a smile in his eyes. Sally had seen it, the warmth and affection there. Yes, the more she thought about it, the more it made sense. Poor wounded hero, David Adams, was falling in love with Andrea, and sooner or later, he would do something about it.

Andrea might not know it, of course. Sally tried to quiet the green-eyed monster writhing inside her. Might not even encourage it, which was difficult to imagine, David being an eligible and extremely attractive man, but as sure as the sun rose in the East, he was being distracted by someone.

Sally had to stop it. Now.

'Oh, dear, I take it the exercise didn't help, then?' Andrea asked, reaching the hall from the stairs as David came through his front door.

'What?' Still contemplating his disastrous liaison with Sally, David looked up sharply.

Andrea eyed him curiously. 'The walk, to ease your headache,' she reminded him of the reason he'd said he was going out.

'Oh, right. No, it didn't much.' David stepped back to allow her to pass to the kitchen. 'Is everyone in?' he asked, looking her over as he followed her. She looked good. Still in his shirt, she looked … at home. Reminded that this wasn't her home and could never be, he sighed inwardly.

'He's in the lounge,' Andrea said quietly, meaning Eden David guessed. Then, casting him a brief guilt-ridden glance, she deposited Chloe's dish in the sink and turned to face him. 'He'll stay at his mother's again tonight. I hope we're okay to stay a little longer, just until I can sort something else out?'

'You're fine here,' David assured her, part of him wishing she could stay ad infinitum, however unfeasible it seemed. 'I actually meant Sophie, though,' he clarified. 'She was … Well, you know, a bit upset, earlier.'

Andrea stared at him for a moment, and then, looking towards the lounge where Eden and the boys were obviously into some space adventure film, she leaned towards him and brushed his cheek with a feather-light kiss. 'Sophie's back safe. She's upstairs with Dee and Chloe, and you're a lovely, caring person, David Adams,' she said, holding his gaze for a second, before she turned back to the sink.

David stifled another despondent sigh. He doubted she'd think that if she knew what had passed between him and her best friend.

'Nice aftershave,' Andrea commented. 'Is it new?'

David tried to quell a surge of panic, wondering whether she was referring to Sally's perfume. He was sure he must reek of the stuff.

'Er, no. Old stuff.' Flicking the kettle on – an excuse to move away – David tried to assimilate what Sally had said. Responsibilities? What responsibilities? They'd spent one night together. Their brief encounter she'd said then, intimating that that was all she'd wanted. A knot in the pit of his stomach, David scrambled through his brain, trying to think of anything he'd said that hinted he might have wanted more. The truth was, he couldn't remember half of what they'd talked about. He'd drunk too much. Away at a mind-numbing conference, he'd been anaesthetising himself that evening, as he had many a time since Michelle had died, craving at least a few hours' elusive sleep when no dark thoughts came in the night to haunt him.

Yes, he'd been willing. More than. No intimacy in his life since he'd idiotically destroyed what was left of Michelle's, the prospect of spending the night with a warm body up close was infinitely more inviting than spending it alone in a soulless hotel room.

As the thin light of dawn trickled through the blinds though, feeling not very proud of himself, it had occurred to him to consider the consequences – and there were none. How could there be? Michelle was gone. And when the sun pierced his addled brain, Sally had left. She'd scribbled a simple note – thanks for listening – and slipped silently out of his life. Or so he'd thought. They hadn't even swapped mobile numbers, so what the hell ...?

'You look terrible,' Andrea cut through his thoughts, looking him over as she stacked the dishwasher.

David ran a hand through his hair, feeling tired and utterly confused. 'I, er, think I'll go up and take a bath. Might help ease the headache.' A headache that was all too real since he'd left Sally's house, and which seemed to be exacerbated by the pungent perfume clinging to his shirt.

Andrea smiled sympathetically. 'Good idea. Chloe's already bathed. If you nip up sharpish, you might even be able to use your own bathroom before Sophie and her iPod take up residence in there. I'll make us all a hot drink when you come down. How does that sound?'

'Like a plan.' David smiled, wishing he could take her in his arms, but he couldn't, of course, particularly with her partner ensconced in his lounge as if he hadn't a care in the world. Had the guy really done anything about the insurance? He'd said the assessors were ringing him back, but surely if they'd already been in Andrea would have mentioned it. 'Andrea,' he started hesitantly, 'about the house insurance ...?'

Wrist-deep in water, Andrea gave him a sidelong curious glance.

'Have they given you any indication of when they might settle the claim?'

'No.' Andrea reached for the towel and turned to face him. 'Why?'

'I just wondered, now the assessors have been in, I mean, whether they're making any progress.'

Andrea looked at him warily now. 'The assessors haven't been in.'

'Oh, right.' David nodded contemplatively. 'Strange. Jonathan assured Eva they had.'

Andrea glanced down, looking troubled, and David hated himself for being the cause of it. Wasn't it better she was alerted to the fact that there might be something amiss, though ... if there was? David hoped he wasn't being overly paranoid here. He had good reason, after all, to want to discredit Eden in Andrea's eyes.

'She probably got muddled,' Andrea said, flustered now and on the defensive, which meant he'd be the accused, David supposed.

He hesitated, and then, 'Like Dee?' he asked pointedly.

'Yes.' Andrea shook her head. 'No. David, what's this all about?'

'I was there, Andrea, when Jonathan told Eva. I—'

'Well, he obviously forgot to tell me, then!' Andrea hissed. 'I don't understand this, David. I really don't. Two grown men in the house and they're acting more like children than the children are. What is the matter with you?' She tossed the towel angrily on the work surface and headed for the door.

David watched, deflated, as Andrea stuffed Chloe into her coat the next morning, refusing to meet his eyes, even when he passed her the frequently dropped Igglepiggle. She'd barely eaten any breakfast, hardly spoken to him.

'Where're you going?' Sophie asked, stifling a yawn mid-stairs in favour of eyeing her mum suspiciously.

'Out,' Andrea said shortly, glancing up at her. 'Can you keep an eye on Gran, please, Sophie? And put some clothes on, will you? I'm absolutely fed up with you walking around half-naked.'

'I've got some on,' Sophie protested, glancing down at the slightly longer T-shirt she'd obviously 'borrowed' from David's collection.

'And I don't need an eye keeping on.' Dee appeared in the kitchen doorway, a baked bean coated spatula in hand and wearing David's tennis sweater, he noticed, and wondered whether he might soon end up walking around half-naked himself. 'I'm perfectly capable of keeping an eye on myself,' Dee informed them and went back to the cooker, presumably to dish up more beans.

David wasn't sure he was partial to them being fried in bacon fat, but it was more than he dared to admit.

'Aw, Mum,' Sophie said, plodding on down the stairs. 'Can't I keep an eye on Chloe instead? At least then I'll look like any other normal teenager if I go out.'

Wincing at Sophie's wish to pass as a teen-mum, David caught Andrea's look of now utter despair. She rolled her eyes at him, which David saw as progress of sorts on the communication front, and then, 'No,' she addressed Sophie adamantly, turning to the front door.

'Typical. Give me all the dross jobs, why don't you?'

Sophie trailed past them to the kitchen. 'Morning, David,' she said over her shoulder, with a world-weary sigh.

'Morning, Sophie.' David looked at Andrea, his mouth curving into a smile, despite her stern glances. 'I see someone's talking to me, then?'

Andrea's answer to which was to huff, 'Yes, well, you've obviously won Sophie over, haven't you?'

She reached for the doorknob. 'Ryan, I'll be back shortly,' she shouted, out of necessity. The boys were hard at raucous tug-of-war in the lounge with Dougal – and one of David's socks.

'Need some company?' David asked, retrieving a once again abandoned Igglepiggle from the floor.

'No!' Andrea said quickly, and then, her shoulders slumping, she at last looked at him properly. 'I'm sorry, David.' She sighed down to her charity boots, which were actually too big, and which she'd filled out with woollen walking socks – his. 'I'm just ... confused.' She searched his face, and smiled, but it didn't quite reach her eyes.

You and me both, David thought, hands in pockets and his heart heavy as he watched her head purposefully towards her car. He didn't know where she was going. She hadn't said, and nor should she, he supposed. She was probably off to meet up with Jonathan, who he'd insisted on rubbishing in her eyes. At least that's how it must look.

He watched on as Andrea slowed at the end of the drive, looking towards the empty shell of her house with its boarded, soulless windows. Swiping at what David assumed was a tear on her cheek, she then turned the car towards the High Street and drove on, leaving David wishing he hadn't said anything about Eden. Hadn't kissed her, though every fibre of him had wanted to, wanted her. All he'd succeeded in doing was complicating her situation further. Hadn't she already had heartbreak enough?

* * *

Checking Jonathan's car wasn't there, Andrea parked in the car park and went around the front of the building to let herself into his office with the spare key on her ring. She seriously hoped Jonathan didn't suddenly decide to 'do a couple of extra hours at the office' today, as he often did at weekends, and find her there, rummaging through his things like some thief in the night.

'Two minutes, sweetie,' she said, leading Chloe in, who was quite content now she had learned that Ronald was no longer poorly and McDonald's was on the menu for lunch.

'Dougal!' Chloe exclaimed delightedly as Andrea turned to close the inner office door.

'No, sweetie,' Andrea whispered, alarmed at how Chloe's shrill tones seemed to resonate around the walls. 'Dougal's at home with ...' Andrea turned around and the words died in her throat. Astonished, she looked from the little dog's dish by the wall to the dog's bed parked next to Jonathan's filing cabinet. What on earth ...? He'd been keeping Dougal here? Why? And for how long? And where the bloody hell had he really found him?

Not the park, that was for sure. David had been right. Dougal hadn't looked at all bedraggled and, apart from the dog's hairs he'd been so fastidiously plucking from his coat, there hadn't been a hair out of place on Jonathan. Even his shoes had been clean, hadn't they? She tried to recall. The boys' trainers had been covered in mud, caked into the rubber soles and treading all over the kitchen floor. David's, too; he'd even apologised for the mess he'd made in his own house, for goodness' sake. She hadn't noticed Jonathan leaving a trail behind him.

Nipping worriedly on her lower lip, she turned back to Chloe. 'That's right, darling. That's Dougal's bed,' she said, in the best cheery tone she could muster.

'Dougal's bed,' Chloe repeated happily, and toddled over to tuck herself and Igglepiggle up in it.

Just in case she decided to go the whole hog and lap water from the dog's dish, Andrea retrieved Chloe's baby beaker from her bag and handed it to her, then headed for Jonathan's desk to rifle through papers, searching for anything that might resemble household insurance documents. Nothing jumped out at her. She wasn't even sure why she wanted them, other than to phone the insurance company and hear from the horse's mouth what the situation was regarding their claim, which actually she should know. David was right about that, too.

It was all surely just forgetfulness on Jonathan's part, though. Hadn't he been through a huge trauma, too? He was bound to be as stressed as she was. Did David take that into account when he was casting aspersions, for whatever reason?

Agitatedly puffing her fringe from her eyes, Andrea tried to stay loyal to Jonathan, though she couldn't possibly, she realised, guilt tugging again at her conscience, because she'd already been totally disloyal. And she hated herself for it. But she didn't, absolutely didn't hate David. Every nerve in her body had come alive at his touch, his kiss, which seemed to reach down into the very core of her. She felt safe in his arms, wanted, as she was: a sensual, sexual woman in her own skin, rather than tarted up in some breath-restricting, ridiculous bodycon dress.

She'd imagined him a cold-hearted, arrogant pig, but David was far from it. He'd shown himself to be sensitive, caring and completely understanding. Whereas Jonathan ... Andrea sighed. He'd been distracted and distant way before the fire, she reminded herself. She thought she'd known him. She'd thought she'd loved him. Had that love dwindled and died when she'd thought he'd deserted her on the night of the fire? Or had it faded before then, as Jonathan's love for her seemed to have done. Their lovemaking had been infrequent to non-existent. There was no passion in Jonathan's embrace, in his eyes, as there had been in David's.

Was she searching for reasons, though, to excuse her own unforgivable behaviour? No. David's kiss had ignited something inside her, but he wasn't the cause of her troubling thoughts about Jonathan, of that much Andrea was sure.

Swallowing back her guilt, she set about straightening the paperwork, attempting to leave it somewhere near how she'd found it, then stopped dead, her eyes falling on a Post-it note parked next to the phone. Assessors. Fri. 3.00 pm, she read. They'd been? But ... Jonathan hadn't said a single word.

Chapter Nineteen

Andrea felt a cold chill run through her as she stood outside the ruins of her home. A home the heart had been ripped out of. Her stomach twisting inside her, she surveyed the outside, having taken Chloe back to David's before coming across. The patio windows were intact. The paint on the metal frames blistered and bubbled. She traced the scorched surface with her fingertips, and then clamped her eyes shut on an image of what such heat might have done to baby-soft skin.

Surprised that the buckled back door yielded so easily, she held her breath and stepped inside. It smelled different now, like the forgotten ashes of the bonfire gone cold in the garden. Suppressing a shiver as the ghosts of her past gathered around her, she walked over to her restored farmhouse table, which had witnessed so many family mealtimes. It certainly appeared to have been in the wars now. It seemed skeletal, dead wood without a soul, as if the flesh had been torn away leaving only the bones. Broken, brittle bones. No magnets adorning the fridge. Hand paintings pinned haphazardly to walls now charred wisps of paper.

Careless of the acrid taste in the back of her throat, Andrea gulped back hard then, treading through glass and debris that crackled under her feet she made her way to the cooker, beyond which the wall was marked, as if flames like hot vipers' tongues had seared it darkest blood-black. The ceiling above it too.

Dee? Had she left a pan on? Andrea couldn't recall.

Listlessly, she trailed to the sink. The potato saucepan was still there, perched upside-down on the drainer, a sooty thick film on its base.

That would need some cleaning.

She hadn't left a pan on. They'd had potatoes that night.

Dragging a hand under her nose, trying and failing to make some sense of the chaos, Andrea glimpsed out of the window. The washing was still on the line, she almost laughed. She'd have to bring it in, she thought nonsensically, then tugged in a breath and held it until she thought her chest would explode – and her heart along with it.

It should have been Jonathan behind her, there for her, holding her. Andrea didn't care that it wasn't; that, once again, it was David who eventually pulled her into his arms, cradled her head against his shoulder and let her cry like a baby. She didn't stop him when he brushed her hair from her face, kissed away the hot tears from her cheeks, held her so close she could feel his heart beating.

'Okay?' he asked, after what might have been a minute or an hour.

Easing her head up, Andrea nodded, emitting a sigh that came from her soul. She didn't seem to have the energy to formulate actual words.

David cupped her face in his hands, gently tracing the tracks of her tears with his thumbs. 'Daft question really, isn't it?' He didn't wait for an answer. Dropping a soft kiss to her forehead, he held her impossibly closer for a second, and then, gently coaxing her, he steered her away from the broken remnants of her home and back towards his.

'Oh, yes, and where have you two been?' Sophie asked suspiciously, glancing up from her latest tea-making efforts as David steered Andrea into the kitchen.

'Just over the road,' David supplied.

'Rrrright, and Mum's suddenly so decrepit she needs help crossing back over it, I suppose?' Turning from the work surface, Sophie stopped, and blinked. 'Mum?' she said worriedly, her eyes pinging wide with unbridled surprise.

She glanced questioningly from her mum's sooty, tearstained face to David's.

'It's okay.' He gave her a reassuring smile as he guided Andrea towards a chair at the table. 'You might like to put an extra teabag in there, though,' he suggested nodding at the teapot, then turning to scoop up Chloe as she launched herself at her mother.

'And extra sugar?' Sophie asked, a tremulous edge to her voice now.

'Good idea,' David said, heaving Chloe higher in his arms, then glancing up sharply as there was a thunderous crash from upstairs and the ceiling threatened to cave in.

'I'd better go and see what they're up to.' David rolled his eyes heavenwards. 'Can you, er …?' He indicated Chloe who now had him in a neck hold and had obviously decided she adored him, judging by the sloppy wet kiss she slapped on his cheek.

''Course. I usually do, don't I?' Sophie said, maturity in her tone, rather than with her usual put upon groan. 'Come on, munchkin,' she said, easing Chloe away from him. 'Let's go and wash Mummy's face and make her some proper tea, shall we … while David strangles Ryan, with a bit of luck.'

'Choclat,' Chloe said, now deciding she adored her big sister, too, and not at all perturbed by the fact that big brother might be about to be strangled.

'Yeah, and choclat.' Sophie sighed good-naturedly, amazingly.

Catching Andrea's eye, David smiled, and felt his heart lift when she smiled back, albeit a bit shakily. 'Back in a minute,' he said, turning for the door.

'You look like a panda,' Sophie addressed Andrea behind him, pulling up a chair to park herself next to her mum.

'But a very cute one.' David gave Andrea a wink over his shoulder, which in retrospect he probably shouldn't have done.

Leaving Sophie gawking after him, David headed swiftly for the hall, taking the stairs two at a time to see what chaos the boys were creating.

Foregoing the 'knock before entering' rule, he squeaked Jake's door open to find Ryan and Jake sitting on the bed, faces the picture of innocence.

'It was Dougal,' Ryan said, nodding towards the midget sized dog sitting at his feet, tongue hanging out, and also looking the picture of innocence. Which begged the question, who, precisely, booted the football at the ceiling, dislodging light bulb, plus light fitting, plus half the plaster?

'Right.' David eyed the damage then the two angels perched on the bed despairingly. 'Well, you'd better help Dougal clean up the mess then, hadn't you?' He caught Jake's smirk and was hard pushed not to smile, which really wouldn't communicate assertive parent very well. The truth was, though, seeing Jake doing normal boy stuff made up for any amount of missing plaster.

'Now, Jake,' he instructed, wearing his best no-nonsense look.

'Come on, small-fry.' Ryan sighed theatrically and heaved himself off the bed. 'The old man's right. Better clear it up, before Dougal cuts his paws.'

Making sure to maintain his not overly-impressed expression, David gave Ryan a nod of thanks, made a mental note to call an electrician, and closed the door, unfortunately almost on Dougal.

'*Hell.*' Wincing as the dog yelped, David turned to follow Dougal's skitter along the landing – but was hindered somewhat by Dee cannoning into him from the bathroom.

'Have you been in my pot?' she asked, planting her hands on her hips and looking him distrustfully up and down.

David knitted his brow, clueless. 'Sorry?'

'My pot,' Dee repeated, now eyeing him with slit-eyed suspicion. David could see where Sophie got it from. 'Someone has. I put Sellotape on the cistern.'

'Right. Er ...?' Now totally confused, David glanced past her in hope of escape.

'And now it's broken,' Dee went on, with a determined little nod. 'So if you've been in there, Doctor Adams, you might as well own up.'

Ahhh. She was talking about Eva's floating policy document. David was getting the drift. He gauged Dee carefully, wondering whether the old lady wasn't half as muddled as she sometimes seemed to be. Her accusations about Eden might be extreme, but there had to be some foundation to them, at least in Dee's mind. Some reason she'd gone to such pains to hide that document.

'So you'll do something about it?' Dee gauged him equally as carefully.

David debated. He had no evidence anything underhand was going on, but if there was ...

'I fully intend to,' he assured her.

'Good,' Dee said, apparently satisfied as she about-faced to the main bedroom.

'But, Dee ...' David made to follow her. 'Why did you hide the—'

'Shhhh.' Dee turned back, gesturing him away from the boys' room. 'Because he knows I have it, and Eva doesn't,' she whispered.

'Er,' David shook his head, puzzled, 'not sure I'm following, Dee.'

Dee sighed expansively. 'Eva kept asking him about it,' she elaborated, 'out of earshot of Andrea, I might add. She insisted she'd given it to Jonathan for safekeeping, but he said it was missing, but it wasn't missing because it was in his pocket. But obviously it is missing now, because it's in my pot.'

'I see.' David nodded. 'I think I've lost the plot.'

'Doctor Adams, for an intelligent man, you can be very dense.' Dee gave him a withering glance.

David smiled flatly. 'Obviously.'

'Eva thought it was lost,' Dee enunciated slowly then paused, presumably to give his dense brain time to catch up, 'but it obviously wasn't because Jonathan had it.'

David followed, thus far. 'Okay, I've got that bit. And?'

'And now I suspect he knows I have it.' Dee poked herself in the chest. 'He's a worried man, Doctor Adams, you mark my words.'

So saying, Dee turned back to the bedroom leaving David with a prickle of apprehension running the length of his spine.

So Jonathan had been poking about in Eva's house trying to establish Eva hadn't retrieved the document somehow. Or got a copy of it, maybe? David mused as he went back down to suggest they go out for pizza for dinner. And he was poking about in her house, without her knowledge. Eva had been covering for him. There was no doubt of that in David's mind. But why had Eden held onto it in the first place? Assuming what Dee had told him was right, why did Eden want to hang on to it? Why not just give it back to Eva, unless … the document itself was evidence of something?

David sighed. He really had no clue what was going on, but gut instinct told him something was. There was no way Eden could have been unaware of Eva's fall. And, whatever cock and bull story he'd given Andrea about his whereabouts on the night of the fire, as far as David was concerned, it was just that. Bullshit. Concussed? The man would have to have been unconscious not to have had some inkling his bloody house had burned down. Even if he hadn't been able to get hold of Andrea, there was no way, in David's mind, he wouldn't have rung one of the kids on their mobiles, the neighbours, the local pub; anyone who might have been able to pass a message on to Andrea about why he was on the missing list.

Plus, there was no visible damage to his car, and David distinctly remembered him saying he'd been run into. Wouldn't he have said run over or knocked down if it wasn't a vehicle collision? It didn't add up. It was as simple as that. David was going to have to make some calls tomorrow. Assuming Eden had been taken to a local hospital and not one in the Outer Hebrides by flying pigs, David could soon check out that part of his story. As for the mystery of the policy document … if he couldn't bluff his way into getting information out of the investment company, at least he could alert them to the fact that something dodgy might be going on and prompt an investigation.

'Penny for them?' Andrea asked him as he walked into the kitchen.

David looked over to where she was perched on the chair, being titivated by Sophie with her coveted Armani cosmetics and a smile curved his mouth. She was looking better, more like her sunny self. That was good. 'Nothing exciting. I was thinking about pizza,' he said.

'Ooh, well, now that sounds quite—'

'Oh, Mu-um.' Sophie blew out a despairing sigh. 'Will you please stop moving your mouth.'

'Sorry,' Andrea said ventriloquist-like and dutifully pursed her lips for application of lipstick.

'Thought you might fancy going out for something cheap and cheerful for dinner,' David suggested, 'assuming Jonathan's not due to make an appearance, that is?' A very rare appearance, he didn't add.

Makeover complete, Andrea dropped her gaze, her buoyancy obviously deflating at the mention of Eden. 'I've no idea. He didn't say.' She shrugged, and then brightened. 'So, yes, as we're all dressed up, we'd love to go out for pizza, wouldn't we, girls?'

'Yeth,' said Chloe, looking up from her drawing endeavours, her rosy cheeks a shade rosier, David noted, and her eyelids blobbed with blue. 'Wiv chips,' she added, with a decisive nod.

'Your wish is my command, madam.' David dipped his head reverently. 'How could a man resist such a beautiful woman?'

'He could try taking his eyes off her for two seconds,' Sophie suggested, obviously noting David's gaze had now drifted towards Andrea. 'And I'm not coming unless I get veggie thin 'n crispy,' she said, walking between them, 'because there is no way I'm eating deep pan barbequed dead pig.'

'Right.' David raised an eyebrow as Sophie huffed on out the door, then felt his cheeks heat up as Sophie imparted, 'Mum quite likes you, too,' over her shoulder.

'That went well,' David commented casually as they all strolled back from The Leaning Tower of Pizza.

'Ye-es, if you discount Sophie's delightful little retching noises on sight of Ryan's Mighty Meaty pizza and her equally delightful comment afterwards.' Andrea peered despairingly over Chloe, who was nestled sleepily against her shoulder, to where her still-warring teenagers were now hotly debating the animal fat content of cheesy garlic bread, ergo how many dead animals Sophie had eaten. 'Honestly, I didn't know where to look. Jonathan would have had apoplexy.'

David laughed, recalling Sophie's rather inappropriate observation as Ryan had cut into his hotdog stuffed crust. 'Urrgh, 's totally disgusting.' She'd curled a lip in obvious repulsion. 'Looks like a penis.'

'It's a wonder the family on the adjoining table didn't

leave.' Andrea blew out a sigh, puffing up her fringe, and hoisted Chloe higher in her arms.

'Er, I think they actually did,' David pointed out, 'right about the time Jake decided to wear two pepperoni slices for eyes.' He glanced at his own reprobate son, who was also walking ahead all but super-glued to Ryan's side.

The kids had been a little over-exuberant – a lot, actually, but David had been more relieved than annoyed at Jake's behaviour. He'd smirked when he'd reprimanded him, but David had let it go, reminding himself that was what kids did. Backchat, cheek, teenage angst; normal childhood behaviour David felt he could cope with. Being cut dead by his son, as he had been up until recently; looked at by Jake as if he really did wish him dead, he honestly hadn't known how much longer he could have coped with.

Glancing sideways at Andrea, whose infinitely kissable lips were curved into a smile despite her annoyance, David wondered how he would cope with siblings at war on a permanent basis, but Eden apparently had. Must have, David supposed. He doubted Andrea would have stayed with him for more than two seconds otherwise, given how family orientated she was.

Deliberating a second longer, David took a breath then asked, 'They get on okay with Jonathan, though? Generally, I mean.'

Andrea thought about it. 'Yes,' she said, at length. 'At least they did until recently.' Furrowing her brow thoughtfully, she dropped a soft kiss on top of Chloe's head.

'Oh?' David tried to keep it casual lest it seem too obvious he was fishing for information.

'Ryan's not majorly impressed by the arguments we've had lately,' Andrea admitted, glancing at him cautiously. 'And Sophie's at her not majorly impressed with anything stage, as you may have gathered.'

They exchanged amused glances as, bang on cue, Sophie's familiar moody tones drifted back, 'Urgh, you two are so juvenile.' With which she folded her arms and stropped on ahead of her obviously embarrassing companions.

David shook his head, though he couldn't help but smile. 'They do get caught in the crossfire sometimes, don't they?'

'We weren't coming to blows or anything,' Andrea assured him, easing a now stirring Chloe higher in her arms.

'Here, let me,' David offered. 'She looks like a lead weight.'

'She is.' Andrea smiled gratefully and stopped to allow him to take her.

'Come on, little one.' David reached for the malleable toddler, who had her thumb still firmly planted in her mouth, the fingers of her other hand caught up in Andrea's hair, he realised, just in time.

Taking Chloe's weight, David carefully disentwined tresses and fingers, noticing again how, even in the fading evening light, Andrea's loose curls seemed to reflect a thousand iridescent flecks of red and gold. Did she have any inkling, he wondered, of how much he wanted to weave his own hands through her hair as she lay in his arms, in his bed; though preferably when Dee and the rest of her family had vacated it?

Couldn't happen, David reminded himself, soberly. Jake was his priority, and Andrea had priorities of her own. She didn't need, probably didn't want, him complicating her life further. Suppressing a wistful sigh nevertheless, he gathered Chloe securely in his arms. 'So, you were saying, no body blows?'

'No,' Andrea said, strolling beside him. 'Not even proper arguments really, just … differences of opinion, I suppose.'

'About?' As Andrea was confiding, David pushed it a little, hoping to glean more information about Eden's dealings with Eva. 'Financial issues, presumably?' He hedged a guess. 'It can't be easy with three children.'

'It's not, but no, not financial, not really. More to do with time, or lack of. You know, how to fit everything in around ceaseless family demands? Me wanting to fit a little me time into the equation.'

David nodded. 'You're talking about your business idea, I assume?'

'My pipedream, yes.' Andrea sighed despondently. 'I do wonder now, in light of all that's happened, whether I might have been a bit selfish, wanting to throw something else into the pot.'

David hesitated, then, 'And keep your mother at home,' he tacked on.

Andrea's step faltered. 'Sorry?'

David faced her. 'Tell me to mind my own business, Andrea, and I will, but … if there's one thing I've learned it's that being in a relationship with someone doesn't give you a right to stifle them or dictate what they do.'

Andrea studied him for a second, her head cocked to one side, her pretty green eyes troubled. 'It's also about compromise,' she said quietly, after a moment.

'True,' David agreed. 'But it's a two-way street, Andrea. Surely it needs both parties to compromise.'

Andrea nodded, her long eyelashes fluttering briefly over her eyes. 'I know,' she said. Then, smiling that smile that seemed to lift his spirits somehow, she reached out to brush first Chloe's cheek, and then his with her hand.

Sally's eyes almost fell out. What were they doing? She watched the intimate exchange through the slatted blinds at her window barely able to breathe. Outside her house! Right outside her bloody house! They might as well come in and copulate on her bloody Italian leather art deco sofa!

The absolute … total shit! He'd turned her down. She'd been naked, standing right in front of him, offering herself to him – all of herself, body and emotions laid bare, and he'd turned his back and walked away. And now she knew why. Not satisfied with one man in her life and three children – by different fathers, her green-eyed monster stopped hissing long enough to remind her – effortless beauty Andrea, with her bouncy hair and bubbly, totally bloody infuriating nature, had decided she was going to have two!

Had they gone beyond intimate touching? Had David already made love to Andrea in that same urgent, sensual, sweetly agonising way he had to her? A knot of panic settled in Sally's chest. She couldn't bear this. She really couldn't. She continued to watch as David and her best friend … hah! … peeled their lovey-dovey eyes away from each other and walked on.

Ambled on, more like, like lovers. Man and wife, with content toddler to complete the picture. This wasn't fair and it was not on. He was rubbing salt in her wounds and Sally was not about to stand by and let him. Let another man use and abuse her. She was going to do something about it. Right now! Just as soon as she'd checked her make-up and hair.

As for Andrea's feelings … Blow her. If the woman had any feelings, she wouldn't be two-timing Jonathan, confusing the hell out of her children by changing her men as often as her knickers, and sinking her talons into the man Sally had prior claim on. Andrea didn't know that, of course, Sally admitted as she headed for the stairs to make ready for her show-stopping performance. But she would know. Oh, yes, once Sally had shown him in his true colours, Andrea would have nothing to do with the not-so-good Doctor Adams ever again. She'd actually be doing the woman a huge favour. No doubt his only interest in Andrea was chalking her up as another notch on his bedpost. He wouldn't even have to go to the trouble of picking her up in a hotel bar either, would he, Andrea being readily available for whenever she took his fancy? Sally humphed furiously on up the stairs, conveniently forgetting who'd been picking who up that night in the hotel bar.

'I hope we weren't supposed to bring pizza back?' David nodded towards Eden's car parked on his drive.

'The wanderer returns.' Andrea glanced at David. 'Are you okay with him coming in?' she asked, no doubt apprehensive now David had made it known he was suspicious of the guy.

He nodded and smiled. Not a lot else he could do, he supposed. Eden was, after all, Andrea's … whatever he was.

Jonathan climbed out of his driver's door, looking not very happy, as they approached. 'Playing happy families again, I see,' he said pointedly.

'In your absence, yes,' Andrea replied, also pointedly.

At which Eden looked most definitely pissed, David noted.

'Why are you sitting outside, anyway?' Andrea asked, walking past Jonathan to the door. 'Didn't you knock?'

'Yes, obviously.' Jonathan shook his head despairingly as he followed her. 'Your mother decided she wasn't letting me in.'

Andrea glanced back at him, confused.

'Said she'd call the police if I didn't go away.' Jonathan rolled his eyes skywards. 'She really is confused, you know, Andy. You really ought to consider—'

'Making arrangements?' Andrea stopped to eye Jonathan angrily. 'Yes, Jonathan, you said. The answer is still no.'

Chloe still sleeping in his arms, David coughed, rather than barging between them. 'I'll just open up, shall I?' He indicated the door.

Eden sighed heavily, as David glanced at him, noting he did indeed look like a worried man. Reminding himself he would be, David tried very hard not to judge him. He was hardly wearing a shining halo himself, was he?

'I won't come in,' Jonathan said as Andrea stepped inside.
Andrea turned back. 'Oh?'

'I just wanted to check that you were okay. As you obviously are ...' Jonathan looked past Andrea to David '... I'll go and do a couple of extra hours at the office and leave you to it.'

On a scale of one to ten that look was definitely sub-zero. If Eden had an idea of how he felt about Andrea, David certainly couldn't blame him for that.

'Come on, you lot,' he urged the dawdling kids. 'Let's give your mum a little space, shall we?'

Jake glanced ruefully back at him as he walked inside behind Sophie and Ryan.

Oh, well done. You bloody idiot. David cursed his crassness. 'Jake,' he said, stepping towards him, 'I ...'

'It's okay.' Jake turned back. 'I'm good,' he said, mustering up a small smile.

'The best,' David assured him throatily, holding onto Chloe with one arm and wrapping his other around his son's shoulders.

'She's nice, isn't she, Andrea?' Jake said, after a second.

Which brought home sharply to David how careful he had to be. He'd love nothing more than for Jake to form an attachment to Andrea, if the circumstances and timing were different, and assuming Andrea might think there was a way forward. She hadn't hinted as much. Jake forming an attachment to another woman who might disappear from his life, though, David couldn't bear to imagine what detrimental effect that might have on his son.

'Very. That's why we're helping her out, Jake, until she can find a place of her own,' he said carefully.

Jake nodded thoughtfully. 'And Ryan, he's cool. We're going to stay mates when he moves.'

'Yep, most definitely,' David agreed, breathing a sigh

of relief. At least Jake hadn't got it into his head they'd be staying around, pity though it was. In moving in, Andrea and her family had given him his son back.

'And Sophie,' Sophie picked up with a roll of her eyes. 'She's, like, totally awesome.'

'Totally.' David laughed. 'Cheers.' He allowed awesome Sophie to relieve him of Chloe and went back to nudge the door closed to allow Andrea some privacy.

'Well, where else do you expect me to stay other than my mother's?' he heard Jonathan ask tersely as he did.

'I don't know, Jonathan,' Andrea replied, equally tersely. 'A hotel, with your family possibly?'

'Do you think there's any point?' was Jonathan's acerbic reply.

David hadn't reached the kitchen before Andrea followed him in, closing the front door firmly behind her.

'Has he gone?' Dee asked from the top of the stairs.

'He's gone. Again,' Andrea replied resignedly, walking past David to follow the children into the kitchen.

'Good.' Dee nodded satisfied and glanced down at David. 'I'm relying on you,' she said, giving him a meaningful glance, before turning back to the bedroom.

'Looks like we all are, for a while,' Andrea said, heaving out a sigh as David came in behind her. 'Thanks,' she said, dragging her hair from her face and giving him a grateful smile.

'No problem,' David assured her, reaching for a tendril she'd missed, then running his thumb and finger the length of it, before smoothing it behind her ear.

Chapter Twenty

Ten minutes later, Sophie, Ryan, Jake and Dee were parked in front of the TV all eyes on *Wreck-It Ralph*, an animated film guaranteed to please the whole family, according to Ryan. It seemed to be set in a video arcade, David noted, placing a cup of tea down on the coffee table for Dee, so it would score high with the boys. It might even keep the arguments at bay for a while.

'Wow! Pac-Man! Look!' Ryan enthused, while Jake gazed from the screen to Ryan and back, in obvious awe of the in-house gaming expert.

'Shhhh.' Sophie glanced at Ryan miffed from where she sat curled up in the armchair, Dougal tucked comfortably in her lap.

'And Blinky, Pinky and Inky,' Ryan went on. 'Cool!'

At which Sophie rolled her eyes. 'Boys and their toys.' She sighed.

'It's directed by Rich Moore,' Ryan ignored her in favour of talking to Jake. 'You know the guy who does *Futurama* and *The Simpsons*?'

'Would you just stop with the voiceover?' Sophie craned her neck to eyeball Ryan agitatedly now. 'You know, so we can hear it?'

'Chocolate digestives,' Dee said out of nowhere.

'Sorry?' David tried to keep up with the conversation.

'I prefer those with my tea. HobNobs get stuck in my teeth.'

'Oh, right.' David eyed the offending HobNob he'd perched on her saucer apologetically. 'We're all out of digestives. I'll—'

'Shhhhhh!'

'—get some in,' he finished on a whisper.

'Good.' Dee nodded. 'I'm relying on you, Doctor Adams.'

Sensing it wasn't restocking the biscuit barrel the old woman was relying on him to do, David gave her a firm nod back – and then made himself scarce as Sophie turned her agitated gaze his way.

Aware that Andrea was putting Chloe to bed, he went quietly upstairs, intending to check that the boys had in fact cleared up the mess caused by Dougal's well-aimed football, then ... Jesus! ... stopped dead on the landing. Gulping hard, David dragged his hand through his hair, debating whether to cough and make his presence known, or step back and risk squeaking floorboards, which would definitely make his dubious presence known.

Andrea was in the bathroom – half undressed in the bathroom. He should go. Turn around. Now. David's pulse kicked up a notch, his eyes disobeying his brain's instruction to do the decent thing and look away.

Oblivious, Andrea continued to pile her hair on top of her head, fiddling with it, trying to get it to stay there. She was wearing his shirt, little else underneath. Very little. David's eyes travelled the length of her, from the creamy fullness of her breasts, which were visible where the open shirt parted, down over the soft round of her tummy, finally coming to rest on the thin wisp of lace stretched across her hips, the tiny v in the middle of which only added to his uncomfortable predicament.

Pulling in a deep breath, David hardly dared breathe out. His heart ached, physically. His gut ached, his groin ached. He wanted her. There was no mistaking that. But he wanted all of her, he realised. Truculent teenagers, challenging mother, toddler; he wanted Andrea – and the whole frustrating, noisy, laughter-inducing, depression-lifting package that came with her. He wanted this woman permanently, in his home, in his life.

David knew it could never be, not in reality, but he couldn't help nurturing a tiny hope that it might. Somehow. Someday. Whatever the future held though, one thing was certain, there was no way he should be standing here spying on her like some sad, perverted peeping Tom.

Annoyed with himself, David averted his gaze, took a step back, and then snapped his attention back to the door as Andrea moved towards it. Clutching her shirt together, she reached to push the door closed – and locked wide, surprised eyes with his.

Shit! David scrunched his eyes closed.

'Oh,' she said, clutching the shirt tighter to her.

'Sorry,' he mumbled, wishing he could drop through the damn squeaky floorboards. 'I, er, came up to, er ...' He glanced hopelessly towards Jake's bedroom door, and then dropped his gaze guiltily to the floor.

'No, no, I am,' Andrea said quickly. 'I should have closed the, um ...'

David looked back at her, drinking in the natural beauty of her, her tousled hair, several tendrils of which had already escaped her efforts to tame it, her amazing green eyes, which communicated her every emotion, her lips, full and moist, and so agonisingly sweet against his. 'I'm glad you didn't,' he said hoarsely.

Andrea's eyes flicked down then back to his – and then, in the space of a single heartbeat, they were in each other's arms. David didn't know who'd moved first. Didn't care. Crushing his mouth hard against hers, he followed her back into the bathroom, nudging the door closed behind him. He wasn't sure who was leading. No hesitation this time, their tongues entwining greedily, she tugged urgently at his shirt, dragging it up over his shoulders, pulling at it, almost scalping him as she struggled to free him of it.

As frustrated as she, David yanked the restricting garment

over his head, then, breathing hard, he reached for her shirt, easing it over her shoulders, and down over her arms, his eyes following in its wake; roving over her, drinking in her exquisite nakedness. She was beautiful. David swallowed, his heart beating so fast, it was in danger of leaping right out of his chest.

Cupping her face in his hands, he kissed her gently, trailed his mouth down the slender length of her neck, softly caressing the satin-soft skin of her shoulders, the lush curve of her breasts. Slowly, wetting first one ripe nipple with his lips, then the other, he circled each with a thumb, his need escalating as a low moan escaped her.

Oh, how he wanted her.

David closed his eyes and found her mouth again with his tongue. With fumbling fingers, Andrea sought his waistband. Pausing again, out of necessity of breathing, fear and sweet anticipation running through him, David ran his hands longingly over her body, and then paused. 'You're beautiful, do you know that?' he whispered.

Gliding his hands over her hips, he continued to caress her with softly spoken words, with his hands tentatively exploring, easing fabric aside, then stroking, more sure and certain as she responded. 'I'm sorry,' he murmured. 'I shouldn't be rushi—'

Andrea cut him short, gasping out a breath as he slid a finger inside her.

'Perfect,' David murmured, circling her waist with one arm, pulling her close and lifting her to him. Making sure her back found the wall behind her, he held her tight, held her eyes. Then closed his own as her body arched the second he entered her. His own breathing ragged, his heart thrumming a steady drumbeat in his chest, David tried to pace himself, slow, measured thrusts, then, aware of where they were, how great his need was, he groaned and moved faster.

Moaning, Andrea caught his urgent rhythm, matching his

tempo, building to exquisite climax – at the precise second he whispered her name.

'Amazing,' David said huskily, kissing her forehead, her lips, then stopping, and listening; and panting out a different kind of groan as the bloody, bloody doorbell rang.

'Shit!' he growled, dropping his head to her shoulder. 'Who the hell can that be?'

'I'll get it,' Sophie called from downstairs, 'seeing as no one else is.'

'Sorry.' Easing away from her, David apologised. 'I, er ... No regrets?' He looked at her, concerned.

'No,' Andrea said quickly, moving hurriedly away from him to search for her clothes.

Dammit! Pulling on his own clothes and quietly cursing his impulsiveness, David turned to the door, as Andrea, clearly flustered, turned to make herself decent. Frustrated, furious with himself for rushing her, albeit slow sex wasn't an option, David headed down the stairs, praying they hadn't done something Andrea would regret, also hoping that they could find some space to talk soon. There was so much he needed to say, starting with how much he loved her. Why hadn't he bloody well said so just now? Instead, he says, No regrets? He really did despair of himself sometimes. Did she realise how he felt? Did she feel remotely the same? Damn! He should not have rushed her. How could she know what she was feeling with her emotions all over the place?

Sighing inwardly, determined to try to get Andrea on her own to establish how she did feel before creating more chaos in her life, David reached the hall, and his thoughts screeched to an abrupt halt. 'Sally?'

'David.' Sally gave him a tight smile. 'We need to talk.'

'About?' David eyed her warily.

'Can we go somewhere more private?' Sally asked.

David glanced uncomfortably towards the lounge, where

the film seemed to be in full swing. 'Can it wait?' He played for time, concerned at how confrontational the conversation might be, given how they'd parted. 'It's not really very convenient right now.'

Sally looked at him, then without a word, she turned to walk into the kitchen.

Perplexed, David followed, supposing he couldn't really do much else.

Pushing the door to, he turned to face her, eyeing her apprehensively.

Sally eyed him levelly. 'I'm pregnant.'

Steadying herself against the bedroom door, Andrea tried to compose herself. What had she been thinking? Her family only hearing distance away and she'd had sex with David!

Oh no. Burying her face in her hands, she tried to make some sense of her feelings, of her situation. There was none, she realised, wiping a hot tear from her face. Her heart had taken rein of her emotions. She hadn't had sex with David. She'd made love with him.

She was in love with him. That realisation finally dawning, Andrea pulled in a long breath. She loved him. And her family was actually minus one, she reminded herself: Jonathan, whose feelings for her these last few days, few months, appeared to amount to none.

Andrea nodded. So be it. She dragged her hair from her face and, peeling herself from the door, she went to check on Chloe and to search for her trackie bottoms.

She had no idea how David felt. No, that wasn't true. It was there, in his eyes. Far from cold and indifferent, distant and uncaring, as Jonathan's were, David's were full of concern, full of desire ... she caught a flutter in her tummy that spiralled downward to her pelvis and all the way up to her heart ... of undisguised longing, for her.

She doubted it was just lust. She was a mother of three, for goodness' sake, what was there to lust after? Did he feel the same way? Could his feelings ever be as strong as hers? What she felt for David was much more than sexual attraction. In a world where the sand seemed to be shifting under her feet and nothing was certain, Andrea was sure of that. She wanted to be with him. In time obviously; the children's feelings were paramount, but Ryan liked him. Sophie definitely did, she'd cried on his shoulder, even dropped the Miss Moody attitude for a while. Chloe adored him. Chloe ...

Jonathan's little girl.

But where was her father when she needed him?

And what about Jake? Andrea knew she could easily love the lonely little boy who seemed to have at last come out of his shell. Jake liked her, too, didn't he? He worshipped Ryan. Could it work, with careful handling? Had David even contemplated such a complicated future? Had he contemplated any kind of future together, or was she racing ahead of herself?

Only one way to find out. Tugging on her trackies, Andrea steeled herself to go down and ask him.

Hoping her cheeks didn't look as flushed as they felt, Andrea poked her head around the lounge door. 'Where's David?' she asked, ever-so-casually.

'Conservatory,' Sophie informed her, her eyes glued to the TV, as were Ryan's and Jake's. Dee was 'resting her eyes', puffing out little snores as she did. She looked content, for the first time in a long while. Andrea smiled, retracted her telltale face and turned for the kitchen. 'With Sally,' Sophie added behind her.

'Sally?' Oh? David hadn't said. But then, perhaps he'd been giving her time to get decently dressed. Feeling her cheeks flush afresh, Andrea had a quick drink of water from the kitchen sink then, no visible evidence of her illicit liaison evident – she hoped – she fixed a smile on her face and headed for the conservatory. Then stopped short of the doors.

Facing towards her, Sally looked upset. Her arms wrapped about herself, her eyes' downcast, her body language was tense and her face seemed to be bereft of make-up? But Sally wouldn't normally take in her milk without wearing her make-up. What on earth ...?

Andrea's attention was drawn to David. His back towards her, he seemed tense, too, agitated almost, dragging a hand through his hair, over his neck, taking a step towards Sally ... Shaking his head now and turning to drop heavily onto a conservatory chair.

Swallowing back a growing feeling of trepidation, Andrea reached for the sliding doors, both Sally's and David's attention snapping towards her as she stepped inside.

'Sally ...?' She looked her friend over worriedly.

Lowering her eyes again, Sally pulled in a shuddery breath, then, 'Andrea, I'm sorry,' she said, 'but I think you should know.' She notched up her chin as she looked back at her. 'I'm pregnant.'

Pregnant? Andrea stared at her, stunned for a second, then, 'But that's wonderful news!' She laughed, overjoyed for her friend. After all poor Sally had been through, this was just so amazing. Andrea couldn't quite believe it.

'I'm so pleased for you, sweetie,' she said, taking a step towards her, then stopping. Sally didn't look pleased. If anything, she looked utterly miserable. Andrea glanced towards David, who also looked troubled. Very troubled. Andrea's tummy flipped over. Sally had come to see him. David hadn't announced her arrival, because she'd come to see him.

Oh, no, not again. Surely this time, Sally could keep the child she so desperately wanted. 'Sally is there a problem?'

Andrea asked gently. 'Do you need to …' she trailed off as Sally lowered her gaze again, as if she couldn't quite meet her eyes.

Concern mounting inside her, Andrea glanced back to David. 'David?'

He wouldn't look at her either. His hands clasped between his knees, he glanced down, his shoulders visibly sinking.

Andrea's heart lurched. 'David?'

David said nothing. Instead, he pressed his thumbs against his forehead, then, finally, he glanced at her. Just a glance, but Andrea could see the answer to the question she absolutely didn't want to ask. It was there, in his oh-so-telling eyes. Where, a short while ago she thought she'd perceived love, his eyes were now a kaleidoscope of confused emotion: anguish, sorrow, puzzlement … shame.

Feeling as if the air had been sucked from her lungs, Andrea stood rooted to the spot. An hour-long second passed by, the palpable guilt-ridden silence punctuated only by the loud tick of the conservatory clock. It was his. The baby was his.

Nausea gripped her. The floor tilted off-kilter. Andrea backed towards the doors, stumbled on the doorjamb as she went, and then panic-struck at the thought of involving the children in the inevitable fallout, she yanked the back door open and fled.

The garden was overgrown, she thought numbly. There were far grander weeds fighting for space here than those on her patch of land in the playground. The old shed was dilapidated. A downpipe to the back of the house cracked and water dripped.

Why hadn't he tackled this, instead of magnanimously offering to help her at the school? Why indeed. She'd been such a fool. Her heart had ruled her head, because like a silly love-struck teenager, she'd allowed it to. Allowed him to …

No regrets. His words as they'd finished. He'd wanted sex. That was all. An illicit fuck just for the thrill of it. Could she ever have been more naïve? Swallowing back a sob, Andrea tightened her arms about herself, a shiver running through her that had nothing to do with the cold night air. She'd have plenty of time to tackle her school garden project now, wouldn't she? Her Second Chance Designer dream would have to go on the back burner, despite Eva's efforts to convince her otherwise. Her house had disappeared into the ether. She had no choice but to put her business plans on hold while she sorted her life out. And now her friendship with Sally had been destroyed too. Things could never be the same between them again. Why hadn't she told her? Why hadn't he told her? Damn David Adams! The bastard obviously hadn't got a heart.

What would she do? Where would she go? Jonathan's remark when she'd suggested they stay at a hotel together had summed up the state of their relationship. 'Do you think there's any point?' he'd said. Maybe that's what she'd wanted to hear.

Determined not to cry, to be strong for her family, Andrea looked to the stars, hoping for answers. There were none, of course, no magical fixes. It was up to her to pick up the pieces and find a way forward. And she would, because that's what she'd always done, for her children. Sophie and Ryan had been better off without their father in their lives, a violent aggressive man. They'd be better off without Jonathan, too, who seemed not to even care if they had a roof over their heads.

As for David Adams, who was obviously a weak, womanising liar, the sooner she was out from under his roof the better. Feeling chilled to the very core, Andrea waited a moment longer, trying to compose herself before going back in to her family, who absolutely did need her.

She'd have to find alternative accommodation, she realised. Now. Tonight. She'd book into a hotel short-term and then rent somewhere. She needn't offer explanations to Jonathan. She needed to talk to him, yes, but the arguments ... She'd had enough of those. As for David ...

'Andrea,' he said quietly behind her, causing her battered heart to leap into her throat.

Andrea closed her eyes. She didn't want to speak to him. Have anything to do with him, ever.

'You'll freeze to death out here.' David took a step closer. Andrea could feel him. She could smell him, the aftershave she seemed to be permanently bathed in, the musky male smell of him.

Destabilised, she didn't answer for a moment, then, 'Is that less painful, do you think, David, than dying from a broken heart?' she asked him, a solitary tear warming her cheek.

'Andrea ...' David spoke her name again, which hurt all over again. 'Please come inside. We need to talk.' He reached for her, placing a hand gently on her arm.

'Don't.' Andrea stiffened, a physical pain running through her at his touch. 'Please don't.'

David sighed heavily, but dropped his hand away.

'Is it yours?' Andrea asked, because she had to. There was no anger in her voice, no venom. She simply hadn't got the energy.

'Apparently, yes,' David said, after a pause.

Andrea turned to face him. 'Apparently?' She eyed him quizzically.

David glanced away. 'Sally seems to think so, yes.' He shrugged uncomfortably. 'I have no idea how—'

'No idea how?' Andrea almost laughed. Would have, if the comment wasn't so utterly absurd. 'I take it you struggled with the basic reproductive system in medical school, then?'

Emitting another sigh, David shoved his hands into his pockets and studied his shoes.

'Obviously you didn't struggle too much with female anatomy, though, did you?' He'd known where to touch her, how to touch her, setting fire to every nerve in her body, bringing her to such a sweet orgasm, she'd felt she might weep. No love there, though. No caring.

David glanced back at her, quiet pleading in his eyes. 'It was a mistake, Andrea. I—'

'A mistake?' Andrea stared at him, astounded. 'The same mistake you made when you slipped up and landed in bed with someone other than your wife, the woman who was carrying your child?' Now her words carried venom. Now she was angry. 'And then wondered why the neighbours gossiped? Well, welcome to the world, Doctor Adams. That's what people do around people who invite it!'

David met her eyes full on at last, a flash of anger in his own. 'No, not the same,' he said quietly. 'I was married then. I cheated on Michelle and hurt her as much as a man could hurt a woman. I know that, and I'll never forgive myself for it.'

Andrea's gaze faltered. She believed him, that bit at least. She could never trust him again, but she did believe that bit. 'Was it Sally?' she asked.

'What?' David looked at her, confused.

'Sally. Was she the someone you had an affair with while you were married?'

'No! There was no affair! I ... Christ, what a mess.' David ran his hand shakily through his hair. 'Sally and I met, once, in a hotel bar about two months back. I was at a conference. She was—'

'Spying on her husband,' Andrea finished, recalling what Sally had said about following Nick on his business trip.

'Yes.' David nodded wearily. 'She was lonely, needed someone to talk to. I was lonely ...'

'So you talked, and then went upstairs and had sex?'

David drew in a sharp breath. 'That's about the gist of it, yes.'

'But it's not, is it?' Andrea looked him over. 'There's a whole lot more to it. There's a baby, David!'

'I know.' Dragging his hand yet again over his neck, David glanced skywards. 'I know.' He looked back at her, his expression one of tired despair. 'I'm so sorry, Andrea. I had no idea.'

'Were you ever going to mention you'd slept with her, David?'

'Yes,' David said quickly. 'Of course, I was. I just ...'

'Wanted to choose the right moment?'

David exhaled slowly. 'I suppose.'

Andrea nodded thoughtfully. 'And that right moment was obviously going to be after you'd had sex with me, wasn't it, David?' She kept it clinical, purely physical. It hurt less that way.

'No!' David locked alarmed eyes with hers. 'I mean, I didn't think we ... Jesus, Andrea, what happened between us wasn't about sex. You must know how I feel.'

'I don't know how you feel, David, do I? I don't know you, other than what you've told me.'

David looked at her levelly. 'The truth.'

'The truth?' Andrea was really incredulous now. 'Apart from the one or two inconsequential little things you forgot to tell me? Or was it more than that, David? Three? Four? A hundred?'

'Two! Twice. Bloody hell, Andrea ...'

And that made it all right? She forced back the tears she desperately didn't want to cry in front of him, again. 'And I thought Jonathan was being devious. You take the biscuit, David, you really do.' Shaking her head, Andrea moved to walk past him.

'I'm nothing like Jonathan, Andrea,' David said quietly. 'I care about you.'

Andrea turned back. 'And Jonathan doesn't?' She knew in her heart that her relationship had been floundering long before the fire that had blown her world apart, before David ... She didn't believe Jonathan's tale about why he hadn't been able to contact her any more than his claim to have found Dougal in the park. He'd been piling lie on top of lie since that dreadful night, and she would tackle him. Right now, though, she was more interested in what lies this man might concoct to extract himself from his mess.

'Did he tell you the assessors had been?'

'I haven't had a chance to speak to him yet.' Andrea walked on.

'He's hiding something, Andrea,' David called after her. 'I'm not sure what, but the fire, his preoccupation with Dee's mental state, his story ... It just doesn't add up.'

Disbelieving, Andrea whirled around. 'You'll stop at nothing, will you? You paint yourself as a poor wounded hero, torn apart by grief and guilt and the havoc you created, and then you have the nerve to point out other people's failings? Why?'

'Andrea, I ... I don't know.' David shrugged hopelessly. 'I just want you to be careful, that's—'

'I mean, I'm no great catch, am I?' Andrea went on, her fury growing. 'Was what just happened between us another one of your mistakes, is that it?'

'No!' David fixed angry eyes on hers. 'Dammit, Andrea I do care about you. I—'

'I'm going.' Andrea turned away.

'Andrea, don't.' David caught her arm. 'Please. The kids ...'

'Don't you dare, David,' Andrea warned him angrily. 'Don't you dare try to manipulate me through my children!'

'They're getting ready for bed, Andrea. There's no point in upsetting them tonight.'

'Me upsetting them?' Andrea was flabbergasted.

'Jake ...' David swallowed. 'Give me a chance to speak to him, Andrea. Please, I'm begging you.'

Andrea felt her heart break inside her afresh, for Jake, for David, too, who was going to have to live with the devastating consequences of his actions; for Sally, who would surely need her friendship now, but which this man had made impossible. For herself.

'Stay,' David implored. 'Please? For tonight, at least.'

Andrea studied his face, saw the desperation in his eyes; eyes where so many conflicting emotions played out. How little did she really know him? She could have loved him. Did, still. Yet hated him.

'For Jake's sake,' she said, dropping her gaze to his hand still on her arm.

Relief flooding his face, David released his hold. 'Thank you,' he said, closing his eyes.

'One more thing,' Andrea said. 'Do you care about Sally?'

David looked confused. 'I ... Yes, I care about her,' he answered guardedly.

'I do, too. I'm not sure why she didn't tell me, but you should know she wants this baby, David. So, mistake or no, you have to decide what part you're going to play in your child's life, don't you?'

Walking back to the house, Andrea finally allowed the tears to fall. She did care about her friend, no matter what. She couldn't help that. Sally was desperate for this child. David had lost a child, along with his wife. Strange things happen. But perhaps this baby was meant to be.

Chapter Twenty-One

'Oh, dear, are you sure it's me who should be seeing the doctor? You look dreadful.' Eva looked David over with concern as she came into his office.

Gesturing her to a chair, David managed a half-hearted smile. 'That bad, huh?'

'Definitely,' Eva assured him, peering at him from under her gardening hat as she seated herself. 'You look as if you haven't slept for a week.'

'I'm fine, Eva,' David lied, rolling his aching shoulders in an attempt to ease the crick in his neck. He hadn't slept, not a wink. It was no more than he deserved, but after trying to get Jake off to school without alerting him to the fact that he'd messed up again, monumentally, followed by a hectic morning of patients presenting flu symptoms, two urinary tract infections and, more seriously, a toddler with pneumonia who needed hospitalising, he really did feel all out. Good thing Eva was his last patient.

Eva didn't look convinced. 'Doctor Adams,' she said, lacing her fingers on his desk and eyeing him steadily, 'you haven't shaved, you have dark circles under your eyes, your tie's askew and, quite frankly, you don't look at all the ticket. Have you been drinking?'

'What? No!' David sat up and straightened his tie. Rumours flying around that he was an alcoholic, as well as a womaniser and a complete bastard, was the last thing he needed. 'One,' he admitted, when Eva's dubious gaze didn't waver. 'A nightcap, that's all.'

'Hmm? Well, it obviously didn't help.' Eva dutifully pulled up her sleeve as he reached for his blood pressure meter.

'Eva, I don't have a drinking problem,' David assured her as he rolled the cuff around her arm. 'Scout's honour.'

'Yes, well, you obviously have a problem of some sort.' Eva waited while he placed his stethoscope over her brachial artery and measured her systolic and diastolic blood pressures, then asked, 'Would you like to share?'

'Slightly elevated,' David informed her, and noted the readings. 'I'd like to measure the other arm, if you don't mind?'

'Ho, ho.' Eva rolled up her other sleeve. 'I meant share your problem, Doctor Adams, as you very well know.'

David took the second reading.

'You obviously have one,' Eva continued to badger him.

'And some.' He exhaled heavily and jotted the latest measurements down.

'Well?' Eva, it seemed, wasn't going to give up.

'I'd like to take a measurement with you standing, Eva, if that's okay. Nothing to worry about. I just want to rule out orthostatic hypotension, since you've experienced light-headedness.'

'I'm more worried about you, young man,' Eva assured him, studying him intently as she got to her feet.

'You'll need to make another appointment,' David steered the conversation back to the business at hand, rather than his own. 'Can you make an appointment at reception for a follow up in, say, a —'

'However, if you feel you can't trust me ...' Eva went on, looking wounded.

David smiled, despite her insistence on giving him the third degree. 'I trust you, Eva,' he said, finishing up the blood pressure measurements.

'So?' Eva asked, finding her chair.

'So ...' David sat wearily in his. 'As I say, I'm not sure you have anything to worry about, but I'd like to keep an eye on you, just the same. Meanwhile, make sure you drink plenty of fluids, Eva, and—'

'A problem shared, Doctor Adams, is a problem halved,' Eva interrupted, again. 'Obviously, you don't feel you can confide, though, so I'll get back to my garden and leave you to your surgery. For the record, however, I can't abide gossip, either, so if ever you do need an ear, you know where to find me.'

So saying, she reached to collect her bag from the floor, now looking a bit crestfallen, David noted. And most definitely a bit giddy as she stood up.

'Eva,' David was on his feet supporting her in a flash, 'come on, sit.' Making sure she was comfortable, he fetched her some water, keeping an eye on her over his shoulder as he did.

He did trust her, he realised. The way she'd covered for Eden, David had no doubt that was for Andrea's sake, because she also suspected Eden of some wrongdoing. She obviously didn't revel in spreading unsubstantiated rumour, though. As far as David knew she hadn't mentioned her suspicions to Andrea or anyone else. Should he confide in her? he wondered. He wasn't sure he was ready to share his not-so-good news about Sally, but it might help solve the mystery of the floating policy document if he could get Eva to give him the go ahead to make some enquiries. And he needed to, more so now he had established that Eden's story about being hospitalised the night of the fire was absolute bullshit. The guy was piling lie on top of lie and, for Andrea's sake, David needed to know why.

'Eva, can I ask you something,' he said, turning to hand her the water, 'about your fall?'

'Oh, I'm as strong as an ox, Doctor Adams,' Eva insisted, taking the glass. 'There's no need for undue worry about me.'

'Yes, well, we'll see about that.' As stubborn as a mule, more like. David shook his head and waited until she'd taken a sip of water, then, 'Actually, I was talking about the events around the fall, Eva,' he clarified, 'about why Jonathan was poking about in your house uninvited?'

Eva studied the contents of her glass for a second, and then looked curiously up at him. 'You gathered he was there, then?'

'I did,' David nodded, 'searching for the missing policy document.'

Scanning his face, Eva seemed to debate, then, nodding decisively, she planted her glass on the table. 'I had no idea he was there, Doctor Adams. I certainly have no idea why he would be searching my house for a document he was already in possession of, which I'd also repeatedly asked him to return, and which he then purported was missing.'

David nodded slowly and sat back down in his chair. 'It isn't missing,' he said, after a moment. He really didn't want to say or do anything that might upset her, but his nagging doubt about Eden just wouldn't go away. Something serious was going on, David knew it; something that might possibly put people in danger – and very probably already had. David tightened his jaw and steeled his resolve.

'Dee had it,' he said, retrieving his copy of the document from his desk drawer and sliding it across the desk.

Eva knitted her brow, puzzled. 'Dee?'

'She heard you "repeatedly" asking Eden for it, apparently,' David supplied, watching Eva over steepled hands as she studied the document. 'She was concerned for you, it seems.'

Eva blinked at him and then raised her eyebrows so high they almost disappeared under her hat. 'Deirdre?' she asked, flabbergasted. 'Concerned for me?'

A long phone call later, Eva having given him authority to discuss her investments, David had all he needed to know.

The police wouldn't be called in until the investment company's investigations were complete and then, dependent on their findings, it might only go as far as the ombudsman. David hoped it would go further. It was as clear as daylight to him what Eden had been up to.

Gutted for the old lady, he looked over to Eva, who, though she'd obviously suspected something was amiss, was still shocked to the core. She managed a smile for the medical secretary, who'd brought her some tea, but was badly shaken and as white as a sheet.

Prison was too good for scum like Eden, David decided, fighting an urge to go and drag the little shit from wherever he was hiding and part him from his assets. Preying on a vulnerable old woman? The guy ought to have his legs broken, as far as David was concerned. As for what else Eden might have done to try to save his snivelling backside, he ought to have his neck broken, and, doctor or not, David just might be the man to do it.

The question was what, and when, to tell Andrea, who he'd left this morning on the phone to the bastard. She'd been calm, bar the look of disdain in her eyes aimed at him, rightly so. Given her contempt for him on a scale of one to ten was probably about eleven, David doubted she'd believe anything he had to say, not without absolute evidence. Why would she? He was the one she wanted out of her life. This thing with Eva aside, however badly Eden had treated Andrea, he was still Chloe's father, ergo would probably always play a part in her life.

Quashing his anger, for now, David turned his attention back to Eva. 'What will you do?' he asked her gently.

'I thought I'd fertilise my garden,' Eva said, clearly stoically trying to pull herself together. 'Bone meal's quite good, you know?'

David's mouth twitched into a smile. 'We'd make a great

team, Eva. I was just contemplating breaking a few bones myself.'

'Oh?' Eva met his gaze, the look in her eye telling David she'd very probably help hold Eden down while he did. 'Painfully, I hope.'

'Very,' David assured her.

'Poor Andrea,' Eva said, shaking her head sadly. 'As if she hasn't got enough on her plate. This will break her heart.'

David heaved out a sigh. He looked Eva over, then, on the basis she'd find out anyway, decided to put his pride in his pocket. Right now, Andrea's feelings were his priority. Eva obviously cared about her, and thanks to him adding spectacularly to her problems, Andrea might well need a shoulder.

'Unfortunately, I think I've already managed that, Eva,' he said quietly.

Eva looked back at him over her cup, a wary look now in her eyes.

'Sally and I, we, er ...'

'You're seeing Sally?' Astonished, Eva clanged her cup noisily into her saucer.

'Saw. It was just ... one night,' David clarified despondently.

Eva fixed him with a look which definitely wasn't too impressed. 'A one-night stand, you mean?' she said cuttingly.

David nodded, now feeling acutely embarrassed. 'I, er ... The thing is, she's ... Sally, she's—' he fumbled for a way to announce it outright.

'Pregnant?' Eva's jaw dropped. 'Oh, David, David ... What tangled webs we weave.'

David laughed wryly. 'Don't I just.'

'You know I'd hoped Andrea and you might—' Eva stopped, dropping her gaze as if she'd divulged too much.

'Not half as much as I did, Eva.' David drew in a breath. 'She's moving out,' he said, and then glanced quickly down feeling faintly ridiculous that he, a grown man, felt suddenly very close to tears. 'For obvious reasons.'

'But where will she go? The only property available to rent in the vicinity isn't fit to house little Dougal,' Eva pondered out loud, her brow crinkling worriedly. 'She could have rented the accommodation above the shop, of course, but Jonathan has probably put a stop to that, too, the horrible little worm.'

'How so?' David eyed her concerned, realising she was talking about the shop Andrea had set her heart on for her designer clothing idea.

Eva's shoulders sagged. 'I shall have to sell the property I think. I'd hoped to keep it for rental for income purposes, but now ... I think capital from the sale might be best, though invested rather more wisely, of course.'

Shit! Which meant Andrea really will have lost everything. Abruptly, David stood, dragged his hand through his hair, and paced to the door and back – then back again to the door, the small office not leaving him much space to work off his agitation.

'Maintenance costs on older buildings are so high, you see?' Eva went on as David tried to think on his feet. 'The living accommodation and the shop are almost up to spec, now the rewiring and plumbing works are completed, but the roof will soon need work and some of the brickwork will need repointing.'

'I'll buy it,' David said.

'Rental for income is fine if you have some money in the pot,' Eva sighed pensively. 'I do have other investments, so I shall hardly starve, but as the coffers are depleted somewhat, I ... Pardon?'

'I'll buy it. A cash transaction, all legal and above board. I have funds, Eva, and it will save you putting it on the market.'

'Yes, but what would you want with a three storey Victorian building on the High Street, Doctor Adams? It's hardly an investment in the current property climate, is it?'

'Rental for income,' David said, heading back to the door, to pluck his jacket from the coat-stand.

'Ye-es.' Eva gave him a wily look as he yanked the door open, unhooked his stethoscope, came back again, deposited the stethoscope on his desk then headed, once again, for the door. 'But you won't get much income if you're not charging rental, will you?'

'Nope.' David turned to give her a wink. 'And I'm relying on you to secure me a reliable tenant I won't be charging rental from – and to keep it under your gardening hat.'

Eva notched her chin up and her hat down. 'As I said, I can't abide tittle-tattle either, Doctor ...' Eva trailed off as he headed off down the corridor. 'Um, Doctor Adams ...?'

'Heck.' David about-turned back to his office. 'Sorry,' he said, offering his arm to assist his abandoned patient from her chair.

David was barely through his front door before Chloe had him in a leg-lock. 'Davie!' she cried delightedly, her arms wrapped around his shins. Narrowly avoiding falling over her, David hoisted her up into his arms.

'Hey, little one.' He smiled. 'How's Igglepiggle?'

'Gone,' Chloe said, splaying her hands and shrugging her little shoulders.

'Uh, oh.' David arranged his face into a frown. 'We'd better call the missing Igglepiggle squad. We'll put Detective Dougal on the case and crawl around and assist. What d'y'think?'

'Yeth!' Chloe clapped her hands gleefully, then transferred her leg-lock to a neck-hold and planted a kiss on his cheek.

Andrea watched the interchange from the lounge doorway,

her heart wrenching inside her as she fast-forwarded to where this scenario would be played over, another delighted child in his arms, a child that might not have been planned, but would most definitely be loved. Andrea had no doubt of that. She should hate him. Yet, she couldn't. Anger and grief seemed to be vying for attention inside her but not hate.

'I take it madam approves?' Chuckling at Chloe, David turned to the lounge, and then straightened his face fast as he met Andrea's eyes. In his eyes similar conflicting emotion to that she'd seen yesterday: sorrow, confusion, regret, all of those things – and also a quiet longing. The same longing that was burning inside her? she wondered. That somehow, in another world, another time, things could have been different?

'Hi,' he said uncertainly, a question in his eyes now as he noticed the packed holdall at her feet. 'You're going, then?' He looked back to her face, his expression one of tired resignation.

Andrea nodded. 'To a hotel.'

David nodded in turn, swallowed and dropped his gaze, then looked up sharply as Jonathan came down the stairs.

'All done,' Jonathan said, dropping a second bag on the hall floor containing most of their meagre belongings.

He glanced at David, a gloating look on his face, Andrea noticed. She had no idea why. One thing she did have to thank Sally for, she supposed, was opening her eyes to the fact that she, too, would rather live without a man than live a lie with one. Andrea wasn't sure she wanted to settle for less than a perfect love again either. She wasn't sure it even existed.

'I'll take her,' Jonathan addressed David shortly and reached to extract Chloe from his arms.

'Want Davie,' Chloe whimpered, holding on so tight David had to physically unhook her from his neck, which didn't endear him any further to Jonathan, judging by the peeved expression he now wore. Not that Andrea was too worried about Jonathan's feelings. Her only concern henceforth was to protect herself and her family from further emotional battering.

'I'll strap her in your car. Don't be long, darling,' Jonathan instructed as he walked past David to the front door, giving him a disdainful glance, which David reciprocated in his wake.

Andrea felt mildly amused. She should be flattered that two grown men looked daggers at each other over her, she supposed, were it not for the fact that the man she was supposed to be with couldn't be bothered to make an effort to keep her, and the man she wanted to be with ... Well, David had made his bed elsewhere, hadn't he? Many places elsewhere, for all Andrea knew. He was obviously very accident-prone. He might well have mistakenly fallen into bed with women the length and breadth of the country.

'Come on, baby. Daddy will get you some sweeties on the way,' Jonathan's voice trailed after him as he headed for the car. 'How does that sound?'

'Thweeties,' Chloe repeated, sounding reasonably placated, which was at least one blessing.

Andrea looked back to David, who looked utterly exhausted.

David plunged his hands in his overcoat pockets and glanced at the ceiling. 'Are you ...? Is he ...?' Tugging in a breath, he blew it out and looked back to her.

'I'm not sure. I obviously need to rent somewhere as soon as possible. That's why I rang Jonathan,' she didn't elaborate. The man owed her that much, she'd decided, helping her provide a roof over his child's head if nothing else. 'I'm living pretty much day-to-day at the moment, so ...' Andrea shrugged, and managed a smile. 'I'll see what tomorrow brings.'

'The kids?' David asked. 'Are they ...?'

'They're fine,' Andrea assured him. 'Ryan collected Jake from school, as promised. He had a good day, apparently. Ryan's up with him now.'

David nodded again, obviously immensely relieved, obviously apprehensive, too. As he would be. Jake had come on leaps and bounds with Ryan and Dougal around. However Andrea felt about David's ... liaisons, she wouldn't wish Jake's relationship with his father to go backwards. The children's welfare was her overriding consideration, Jake's very much included, which is why Ryan had selflessly offered to stay 'mates' with him, taking him to and from school, bless his understanding socks. If there was one good thing to have emerged from the ashes, it was that her monstrous teenagers seemed to have matured into caring young adults.

'Jonathan will be waiting,' Andrea said, filling the sudden uneasy silence. 'I'd better go.'

She moved past David, the nearness of him reminding her painfully of how close they'd been just a short while ago. She could still taste him. Smell him. She swallowed, feeling his gaze on her, seeming to burn right through her clothes to her skin.

Closing her eyes, Andrea found her voice and called up the stairs. 'Sophie.'

'On our way,' Sophie called back from the landing. 'No, Gran, that's David's,' she said over her shoulder. 'Put it back.'

'But he'll never miss it,' Dee's voice carried from the bedroom.

'Gran ...' Sophie's footsteps could be heard stomping back. '... it's his bloody alarm clock! He might miss it when he doesn't wake up in the morning, don't y'think?'

Oh no, her mum had turned into a kleptomaniac. Andrea had already extracted his tennis sweater and four pairs of his socks from Dee's carrier bag. 'Sorry.' She glanced back at David, shrugging helplessly as she did.

David smiled. 'Don't worry about it. It's useless anyway. I usually set the alarm on my mobile,' he said, dragging his hand over his neck in that way he did. He really did look bone-tired. Andrea wished she could go to him, pull his hand away, pull him into her arms and make it all go away.

She couldn't, of course. He'd probably never wanted more than one passionate bout of hot sex anyway, she reminded herself, stepping back to allow Sophie and Dee to pass, Sophie shooting David a disparaging glance as she did.

'I knew you were too nice to be true,' she said, causing David to lose the smile once again.

'Is it yours?' Dee asked, stopping smack bang in front of him.

'I, er ...' David looked at Andrea uncomfortably. 'Yes, I believe so.'

'Could have sworn it was mine.' Dee tottered on, leaving David gazing perplexedly after her.

'The clock,' Andrea clarified. 'They do know, though,' she thought she ought to warn him, 'Sophie and Ryan, about the, um ... You and Sally.'

'Right.' David now looked gutted and Andrea reminded herself again that whatever mess he was in, he'd brought it on himself. In any case, it might not be quite such a mess as it seemed. Sally and he might get it together and be very happy ... together.

That thought slicing like a knife through her chest, Andrea quickly picked up her bag. 'They heard, by the way,' she informed him, should he be making wrong assumptions, 'you and me ... talking ... last night, just in case you think I've been fuelling neighbourhood gossip.'

'I think I've managed that pretty much by myself.' David smiled wryly. 'Stay safe, Andrea,' he said, holding her gaze, 'that's all I ask.'

Andrea nodded. What did she do now? Shake his hand?

'Could you let Ryan know we're outside when he's ready,' she said calmly instead, then left before she was tempted to shake him.

Chatting animatedly, Ryan and Jake were coming along the landing as David reached it. Ryan had obviously taken Jake under his wing, again, after realising his idiot father seemed to be going all out to screw up his life. That was why he'd volunteered to take Jake to school, David realised now, knowing it was one way of injecting some enthusiasm into Jake and actually getting him there. Knowing, too, that school was probably the best place Jake could be while Andrea worked out what to do with the remnants of her life, which David must also appear to have been hell-bent on screwing up.

Holding his breath as the boys approached, David hardly dared imagine what might be going through Jake's mind. Did he know?

Ryan cast him a look as he slowed in front of him, respect therein nil, which was pretty much what he deserved.

Jake appeared not to have even noticed him, his attention distracted by Ryan and Dougal, who, well-positioned in Jake's arms, was intent on washing his face.

'So, we'll go every evening?' he asked Ryan enthusiastically.

'Yep,' Ryan answered, 'if you're up for it. And now your dad's getting you that dog you wanted …'

He was? Noting the meaningful glance Ryan slid in his direction, David guessed he probably was.

'… we'll probably have to go a couple of times at weekends to train it and stuff,' Ryan went on obviously satisfied David had got the gist. 'Dougal can show him the ropes.'

'Cool,' Jake said. 'I bet my Labrador will be a lot faster than Dougal, though.'

Labrador? David blanched, thoughts of chewed carpets, table legs, puddles on the floor and general pandemonium in mind.

'Not a chance, mate. Dougal'll run rings round him.'

'Yeah, right.' Jake laughed. 'He's only got two-inch legs.'

'Yeah, but size doesn't count, does it?' Ryan replied smartly, causing David to wonder what mind-boggling conversation they'd had around that. 'Do you want to go and say goodbye to Mum and Sophie?' Ryan prompted Jake on as they neared the stairs. 'You can make sure Dougal's safe in the car, while you're at it.'

'No problem,' Jake said, heading happily down. 'Come on, Dougal,' he said in the dog's ear as he went, 'you need to save your two-inch legs for when you race Homer.'

Ryan waited until Jake had disappeared out of the front door, then, 'A black one,' he informed David shortly, fixing him now with a look of pure ice cool contempt.

'Right.' David nodded, assuming they were talking about the dog.

'He's got his heart set on it. Don't want to let him down, do you ... again?'

David got that pointed message, loud and clear. 'I'll sort it,' he assured him.

'Good,' Ryan said and headed onwards.

'Ryan ...' David fumbled for a way to ask. 'Jake, does he know?'

Ryan looked back at him. 'What? That you're a prat?' he said, point blank.

'And some.' David glanced down under Ryan's unflinching gaze.

'As far as I know, no,' Ryan put him out of his misery. 'Sophie heard you and mum talking. She texted me, so ... Don't worry, we won't rubbish you in Jake's eyes. You seem to be doing a great job of that all by yourself. The kid can't help it if his dad's a dipstick, can he?'

'Thanks,' David said, relief flooding through him. Obviously Jake would have to know, but not right now, and not second-hand. David wasn't sure he ought to be thanking Ryan for the insults, but then, he'd called himself pretty much all of that and more since last night.

'We'll go along with what you tell him. Mum likes Jake. She knows he needs all the help he can get.' With that, Ryan dragged his unimpressed gaze away and turned back to the stairs.

David sighed and plunged his hands in his pockets. 'I'm sorry,' he said uselessly behind him, not knowing what else he could say.

Ryan glanced back. 'Yeah, right. Doesn't help anyone very much though, does it?'

What the hell? Jolted from a fitful sleep, David blinked a bead of sweat from his brow and tried to focus on the pale figure standing at the side of his bed.

'Can I come in with you?' Jake asked, dragging a hand under his nose and shivering from head to toe, David noticed.

'What's up, small-fry?' he asked, throwing back the duvet.

'I keep hearing things in my dreams,' Jake said, immediately scrambling under it.

'It's just the pipes rattling, Jake. Nothing ominous,' David assured him, trying hard to still a recollection of the haunting things he'd heard in his dreams, the urgent cry of a baby, the soft tears of a woman. He hadn't been able to make out her face. Her form had been ethereal and surreal. The dream had been telling, prophetic and all too real.

Making room for him in the crook of his arm, he tucked the duvet up to Jake's chin, and then lay awake, waiting until he was safely off to sleep. Hearing the steady rhythm of his breathing after a while, feeling the rise and fall of his chest as Jake drifted into settled slumber, David swallowed and eased his son a fraction closer. He wouldn't know what to do without him. Jake had been his reason for living when the nightmares had been too many and the nights were too dark. He loved him. Simply wouldn't know how to be without him.

And now there was another child. A child who would need him to be there, as he should have been for his unborn baby girl, and for Jake, consistent, caring, helping to show him ... or her ... the way in a world that seemed too big and overwhelming sometimes.

David had no idea what Sally might want, what kind of compromise they might come up with to provide a stable environment for that child.

He liked her, of course he did, but he didn't love her, not in the way a person should love someone: enough to embark on parenting a child together as a couple. And, heartless though it might seem, he doubted he'd ever learn to love her. He would love his child though. He wouldn't need to learn how to do that.

He wouldn't use the word 'mistake' again either. No child should ever start life as that. It was a mess. There was no escaping that fact. A baby by a woman he didn't have the right feelings for wasn't something he'd planned on. But then, nor was losing the woman he'd loved, twice.

It had happened, though. He squeezed his eyes tight as images of Andrea, her lips soft on his, her body entwined with his, once again tormented his thoughts. He couldn't change it, although he wished he could. And whatever Sally needed of him, whatever their child needed of him, he'd just have to make damn sure to provide it. Because one thing he was certain of: he wouldn't neglect his responsibilities as a father ever again.

He'd get that dog, too, he decided, as his mind slowed, enticing him back to much-needed sleep, tomorrow, after morning surgery. A great lolloping black Labrador, chewed furniture, puddles on floors and all, because, right now, that's what Jake needed to make his world safe.

Chapter Twenty-Two

David wasn't sure he wasn't going to regret it, however. Having already had to crawl around on his hands and knees trying to entice a quaking Homer from under the sofa, he now watched forlornly as it peed all over the shop floor.

'Whoops-a-daisy.' Eva rested her roller on her paint tray and whipped out a cloth. 'Looks like you're going to have your hands full, Doctor Adams,' she said, bending to mop up the puddle.

'And some,' David despondently agreed, trying to get his head around how he was going to juggle puppies and babies and house decorating in duplicate, as well as his job and Jake, and then berated himself for allowing Eva to clean up the dog's mess.

'Eva, I'll do it,' he said, going over to assist her as she straightened up and obviously had another dizzy spell in the process. 'You know you shouldn't be overexerting yourself. On which subject, what the hell are you doing here?'

'Decorating, dear boy,' Eva informed him as he helped her across to a chair. 'I'd have thought that was obvious.'

'But I thought you said the decorators were in, Eva. I didn't think you meant you were ... *Oh hell*,' David's attention was diverted by the dog, who'd now decided on a thorough investigation of the premises.

'They are,' Eva said as David went back across the shop to extract Homer from the paint tray. 'He's just outside having a tea break. He's a local man, very reliable and ... Ah, here he is now.'

A cigarette break, David deduced she meant, as a man, who looked about as likely to climb up a ladder as fly, hobbled in through the back entrance – one dodgy knee obvious and wheezing like an asthmatic.

'This is Bob, Hibberton's local DIY man,' Eva introduced him, at which Bob coughed heartily, and then limped over to pick up the cuppa he'd obviously forgotten to take out on his 'tea' break from the floor.

Unfortunately, the dog got to it first. 'Homer ... Sorry,' David apologised for his recalcitrant charge and plucked up the dog before it could do any more damage.

'Not to worry, doctor. We've got plenty of teabags, haven't we, Eva?' Giving David a smile and Eva a wink, Bob limped over to flick the kettle on, signalling another imminent tea break. 'Lifeblood,' he said, over another lung-rattling wheeze.

Yes, and you might need some, David thought despairingly, if you keep sucking on those things.

'Right, better get on.' Bob wandered painfully over to a pot of paint. 'We'll soon have this place fixed up, hey, Eva?'

David watched as the man struggled to lever the lid from the tin with a screwdriver and doubted very much whether Bob would be fixing anything up any time soon.

'You're a one man band then, Bob, are you?' he ventured to ask, whilst trying to hang on to a wriggling Homer, who was probably very likely to pee all over him.

'He has an assistant,' Eva supplied, while Bob caught his breath, and then tried again with the lid. 'Darren's not with him today, though, is he, Bob?'

'Sorry, Eva?' Bob's attention was still on his pot.

'Young Darren, I said he's not with you today,' Eva shouted as Bob plucked up his hammer to give the screwdriver a good thwack.

'No, not today, Eva.' Bob gave the screwdriver another blow, and then looked mightily pleased with himself as the lid finally popped off. 'Missus is poorly again, apparently. She's expecting twins,' he addressed David. 'I expect you've had the pleasure?'

'Er ...?'

Ignoring what could conceivably be a double entendre, David tried to recall seeing a mum expectant with twins, then almost choked when Eva said drolly, 'Not yet, no.'

'Sorry?' Bob cocked an ear.

'Nothing.' Eva gave David an arch look. 'I was just saying, I don't think the doctor has got around to all his female patients yet.'

Cheers, Eva. David sighed and eyed the ceiling, which was also in need of painting.

'Right, well, sitting around here all day won't get the job done.' Eva eased herself to her feet, and gave David a vigorous pat on the cheek. 'Don't look so worried, Doctor Adams, I know your heart's in the right place,' she said, going back to her roller, 'even if certain other parts of your anatomy tend to go wandering.'

'Eva ...' David sighed in earnest. It was no more than he deserved, he knew, but he'd really hoped Eva wasn't a gossipmonger. He'd been counting on her to keep his involvement in the property purchase to herself, at least for now. Buying his way into Andrea's affections wasn't on his agenda. He doubted Andrea would be very impressed if she thought he might be. Making sure she and the kids had a decent roof over their heads, in absence of Eden doing anything practical, was.

Eva came back across the shop, roller and tray in hand and a wily look in her eye. 'He's hard of hearing,' she told David.

David glanced at Bob, who with his back towards them seemed oblivious to the conversation, then back to Eva, relieved.

'Deaf as a post half the time,' Eva assured him. 'I stay true to my word, Doctor Adams, worry not.'

David shook his head. How Eden got one over on this woman he had absolutely no idea, though he intended to find out. 'Eva, it's you I'm worried about,' he said, quickly scanning the room for other dog enticing items, before allowing Homer loose on the floor again. 'You really shouldn't be doing this. Come on, let me have a go.'

Eva looked down at her roller, then dubiously back to David.

'I'm a dab hand at DIY,' David assured her, figuring if he wanted the job done sooner, rather than later, he'd better do it himself.

'Well, as you're already covered in paint, I suppose you might as well get stuck in. Here you go.' Eva smiled and handed him her decorating paraphernalia. 'We could certainly use another pair of hands.' Tray in one hand, roller in the other, David glanced down at his blue business suit, which now sported several Homer-sized magnolia paw prints. For Jake's sake, he counted silently to five and reminded himself why he'd bought into yet another bundle of trouble.

Stepping down from the ladder, David narrowly missed the paint tray but unfortunately found the dog. 'Damn! Homer, here, boy.' Righting himself on his feet, he turned for the door and the direction the yelping puppy had skidded in – to see two unimpressed teenagers regarding him coolly.

'I see you managed to mess up again,' Ryan commented, bending down to Homer, who, abuse now clearly forgotten, was sniffing excitedly at his trainers.

'Sorry?' Furrowing his brow, David surveyed his handiwork, which he didn't think was that bad, even though he was actually rubbish at DIY.

'He's supposed to be black not white,' Ryan remarked, the tiniest of smirks twitching at his mouth as he pointed the scrambling, paint-covered puppy in Sophie's direction.

'Magnolia,' David corrected him, risking a small smile back. 'We thought the, er, tenant might prefer neutral, until she decides on a colour scheme.'

'She?' Ryan's expression went quickly back to unimpressed.

'Aw, he's gorgeous, aren't you, hey?' Sophie picked the puppy up. 'What's his name?'

'Homer,' David supplied, glancing from Ryan to Sophie then back to Ryan. He wasn't sure why they were here, but he doubted it was to tell him all was forgiven in their eyes.

'Hellooo, Homer Adams,' Sophie cooed, nuzzling the dog and taking a step in. 'Jake's just going to love him, isn't he, baby?' Smiling, she looked from Homer to David, Miss Moody nowhere in evidence.

'I hope so.' David smiled back. 'You're still talking to me, then?' he asked hopefully.

Miss Moody was back in a flash. 'No,' Sophie informed him, nose in the air over the dog's head as she took another step in.

Ryan stayed where he was. 'Thought this was the shop Mum was interested in.' His gaze was now two degrees below zero.

David took a breath. 'That's right.'

'But you've already got a tenant in?'

'Er, yes.' David realised he was digging a hole and was about to drop himself in it. 'That is ...' He glanced at his paint-spattered shoes, looking for inspiration.

It came, in the form of Eva. 'I have,' she said authoritatively, coming through from the washroom at the side of the shop. 'Your mother,' she went on, wiping her hands robustly on a paint cloth and handing it to David.

'I'd already decided to offer her the shop plus accommodation before circumstances meant I had to sell. And, as Doctor Adams isn't officially the landlord until the sale is complete, he didn't have a lot of choice, did you?'

'Not a lot, no.' David sighed and did his best to look compromised.

'Right.' Ryan's look went from ice cool to reasonably tepid. 'You're buying it, then?'

'He is,' Eva answered on David's behalf, fetching her coat and handing it to him.

'Which is why you'd be decorating it?' Ryan went on.

'That's right. I'm the new decorator's assistant.' Glad of an excuse to extract himself from Ryan's scrutinising gaze, David turned to help Eva into her coat.

'In magnolia.'

'Yep,' David said, giving Eva a grateful smile as he escorted her to the door.

'Rubbish choice,' Ryan observed, stepping in as Eva left and glancing around. 'I'll ask Mum what colour scheme she wants, seeing as you're only halfway through, shall I?'

'No!' David said quickly. 'That is. Not yet. It's just ...'

'You'd rather wait until Eva has actually offered it to her,' Ryan finished shrewdly.

'I, er ... Ahem.' Noting the knowing glances exchanged by siblings who'd obviously called a temporary truce in order to call his bluff, David raked his hand helplessly through his hair.

'So are you going to show us around, then?' Ryan strolled further in. 'Before you go and pick Jake up from school?' He nodded towards the dog still in Sophie's arms, which actually David couldn't wait to show Jake.

'Er, yes. No problem.' David shook his head, baffled. What just happened there? he wondered. Shouldn't they be telling him where to stuff his magnolia? Kicking his ladder over, preferably while he was on it? Perhaps they were planning on pushing him out of one of the upstairs windows. Giving them each a curious glance, at which Ryan and Sophie exchanged more knowing glances, he dutifully led the way to the stairs.

'There's two storeys, four bedrooms, one of which would easily convert into two, two bathrooms, and a yard out back for Dougal. The fence needs some work, and it could do with a grassed area and a swing, maybe, but it's pretty ideal overall, I'd say.'

'Cool,' Sophie said, dumping Homer back into David's

arms and scooting on up before them and then calling down, 'Mine's the attic room.'

'And the price is right?' Ryan paused before going up. 'As in Mum will be able to afford it?' he asked, the emphasis on Mum, David noted.

'Dead right,' he assured him, then spat out Homer's tongue. 'Minty.' Ryan nodded and went on up.

Did that mean he'd got some kind of tacit approval? David wondered, dog in arms as he followed him.

'Oh, by the way, Mum's in school today. Just so you know,' Ryan said, hands casually in pockets, which were about thigh level, 'if you're out to try and impress her, your dog just pissed all over your shirt.'

'Are you okay?' Andrea tried again to have a quick word with Sally, before she went home. The woman had avoided her all day like the plague. Whatever had happened between David and her, a moment of total insanity on Andrea's part, it was over. And Sally couldn't possibly know anything had actually happened. As far as Sally knew, she'd stayed with the man, that was all. She'd had no designs on David when she'd been forced to move in with him, Sally must realise that. Surely, for the sake of their friendship, they could get past this and move on.

Sally continued to tug on her coat. 'Yes, fine,' she said shortly, without even glancing at Andrea.

'Sally ...' Andrea walked over to lend her a hand. With the coat sleeve inside out, Sally would be hard pushed to stuff her arm furiously in it, which she seemed intent on doing. 'Can't we at least talk?' she asked, fishing the sleeve from inside the coat, before Sally tied herself in a knot.

Sally didn't answer for a moment, then, 'I assumed you didn't want to speak to me,' she said, at last meeting Andrea's eyes. Hers weren't over friendly, Andrea noticed.

'But why?' Andrea scanned Sally's face, puzzled. 'I stayed

with David for a few days, Sally. That's all,' she lied, not sure why she was on the defensive. Guilt, she supposed. She was still struggling to say his name without a pang of that, along with a good dollop of heartache. 'It's not like we were living together.'

Sally humphed, audibly.

Andrea chose to ignore it. 'Look, Sally, this thing with David and you, the fact that you and he ... Well, I wish I'd known, I wish you felt you could have confided in me, but, whatever, I'm perfectly fine with it.'

'Very magnanimous, I'm sure,' Sally huffed, and turned to unhook her scarf from the stand.

Andrea shook her head, not sure she was getting the subliminal message. 'Sally, why wouldn't I be?'

Sally turned back, glancing past her to check there were no ears flapping in the staff room, presumably. 'Why indeed,' she said accusatorily.

Andrea decided she must be having a very dense day, possibly because of the lumpy Travelodge mattress, being woken in the night by a fretful Chloe and Dee's incessant snoring, but she really wasn't getting it at all. 'You're going to have to help me along here, Sally.' Andrea parked herself wearily on the edge of a chair. 'Because I'm really not sure what I'm supposed to have done.'

'Hah!' Sally threw the end of her scarf over her shoulder. 'Obviously nothing,' she said, so facetiously Andrea felt her cheeks blush.

'That's right, nothing,' she stated emphatically, whilst trying very hard to maintain eye contact.

'Oh yes, of course.' Sally folded her arms. 'So why did you look so bloody shocked then, Andrea, when you found out the baby was David's?'

Andrea gulped back another stab of pain. 'Because I was shocked, Sally. You hadn't told me. David hadn't said a word. You caught me unaware—'

'And why pack up and leave immediately you did find out?'

'Because ...' Andrea fumbled for a way to explain what obviously was a very sudden departure, particularly as she'd had nowhere to depart to '... with a baby on the way I thought David and you might need some space. Three's a crowd, after all, isn't—'

'Precisely!' Sally spat, her tone now almost venomous. 'I saw the way he was looking ... You were looking at him. I saw the furtive glances and the lovey-dovey, touchy-feely body language between you two, Andrea. I'm not stupid.'

Andrea stared at her, bewildered, and then glanced down. 'I never thought you were.'

'You've already got a man,' Sally went on angrily. 'You have three children, Andrea! And then you move in on David before I've even had a chance to talk to him.'

'I didn't know,' Andrea tucked her hands under her thighs. 'You didn't tell me.'

'I wasn't here! I didn't know David was here. And when I did, I couldn't get a look in!'

Silence then, very profound silence.

'I wasn't moving in on him, Sally. What you thought you saw ...' Andrea glanced up, needing Sally to believe she wouldn't deliberately do anything to hurt her. She'd leave the county if it meant that Sally could have her baby happily and safely. But she'd much rather stay and be here for her. 'It wasn't what you thought. There's nothing between David and me.'

Sally breathed deeply. 'No?'

'No.' Andrea held her gaze. Her heart felt like it might break, but that was her cross to bear. She made a mental promise to herself. She wouldn't do anything that might cause Sally further pain. 'Can we stay friends?'

Sally's gaze faltered, and then she glanced away. 'I've got

to go,' she said, her eyes flicking briefly back to Andrea's, before she turned for the door. 'I have to go to the shops. David's coming over later.'

'Right.' Andrea tucked her hands further under her thighs as Sally closed the door without saying goodbye. She had her answer, she supposed. Sitting in the staffroom crying like a schoolgirl wouldn't do though, would it? She wiped the stubborn tears away.

Well, she'd tried, but it was obvious her friendship with Sally had cooled to the point of non-existent, all thanks to the enigmatic Doctor Adams who was currently once again attracting the attention of every female in the playground and had probably charmed the birds from the trees on his way there.

Andrea couldn't help but smile, though, as a jubilant, whooping Jake finally stood still long enough for David to pour the puppy into his arms. It really was a sight to melt hearts. The look on David's face certainly was as he watched his son laughing and giggling as a ten-year-old should. Getting Jake a dog had been exactly the right thing to do. David had finally managed to impress his son, Andrea had to concede, even if he hadn't managed to do the same regarding the women in his life.

Andrea just hoped he'd do the right thing by Sally and the child she was carrying. His child. Swallowing back the hurt that settled like a stone in her chest, Andrea decided she should go and speak to him, for Jake's sake. Whatever the circumstances between them, Jake had suffered enough loss in his life. He'd be bewildered if the new friends he'd found suddenly abandoned him – and Andrea counted herself as one of those friends.

David looked tired, she noted as she neared him, but still breathtakingly handsome. That hint of stubble evident on his chin, which definitely looked sexy on him, his black overcoat complementing his broody looks and dark colouring. Paint in his hair, she noticed, and on his shoes, lending him a dishevelled appearance which would have a woman's nurturing instinct caving in in an instant. Andrea wished she'd never set eyes on him. That she'd never come to know the person behind the aloofness she'd first encountered; never fallen in love with him.

'Man done good,' she said lightly, nodding approvingly at Jake as she walked towards him, who was now excitedly showing his new puppy off to his classmates.

His attention on Jake, David looked startled as she spoke. He glanced at her anxiously for a second, and then smiled uncertainly. 'Hi,' he said.

'Hi,' Andrea said, at the exact same time. 'Sorry,' they both said together.

'So, how are you?' he asked, after an awkward pause.

'Ooh, you know, wonderful,' Andrea lied blatantly, which had what she supposed was the desired effect. David dropped his gaze immediately. 'Better for seeing Jake so obviously thrilled, though. Really. Well done, David.' Andrea softened the sarcasm. After all, what good would it do?

David glanced back up and smiled. 'Ryan's idea,' he admitted, with a self-effacing shrug. 'I didn't have a lot of choice really, between the two of them.'

Andrea laughed. 'No,' she said. 'They have a way of getting their own way, don't they?'

'And some.' David smiled, a little more easily this time.

'So, how are things?' Andrea asked, wondering how on earth they could ever have a conversation again without the obvious subject coming up.

'Good,' he said. 'Well, you know.' An awkward shrug this time. 'As well as it can be.'

'Good,' she said. 'Shouldn't you be at the surgery?' she asked him, for the want of something else to say.

'I mentioned I might need some flexibility the first few weeks, just in case of emergencies, you know. I, er, figured under the circumstances getting Jake his dog qualified as one.' David glanced down again, then back.

'Good idea.' Andrea nodded – and then decided that the stilted conversation around the obvious elephant in the room was not only ridiculous, but far too painful. They'd been laughing together a short while ago. Couldn't they at least talk?

Steeling herself she tugged in a breath, then, 'How's things with Sally?' she asked, trying for casual – and failing.

David ran a hand over his neck. 'I haven't spoken to her yet,' he said, now not quite able to meet her gaze. 'I'm seeing her shortly, while Ryan's, er ...' he trailed off obviously embarrassed by the realisation that her child would be looking after his child while he discussed his yet to be born child with Sally.

Andrea nodded, and forced a smile. 'You should,' she said quietly.

'And Jonathan? How's he?' David asked. 'Busy, I imagine.'

Andrea looked at him and debated. Should she confide? She could say he was fine. Should, probably, but then David already knew everything was far from fine between them. 'Truthfully, I don't know,' she admitted. 'We haven't really talked yet either.'

'Look, Andrea, can we talk?' David glanced towards Jake, still revelling in the midst of all the enthusiastic attention. 'Please?' he added, when Andrea looked doubtful.

Andrea studied him for a second and then relented. It would probably be the last private conversation they had. But not in the staffroom, behind closed doors where it might be construed as some sort of secret liaison. In relative public she thought might be best. She nodded and turned towards the main entrance, where everyone had mostly vacated the building. 'We can keep an eye on Jake from here,' she said, swinging the door open to allow David inside.

'Well?' She turned to face him, and waited.

David raked his hand through his hair, indicating he was nervous, or tense, frustrated or angry, possibly all of those things. She'd learned to read the signs. 'You do need to talk to Jonathan, Andrea,' he started, 'and soon.' His tone was firm, almost as if he was issuing an instruction. Andrea blinked at him, confused, and then just the tiniest bit miffed. No, a lot miffed actually.

'I am,' she said, gauging him carefully. 'We're meeting, tonight, as it happens, but I'm not sure that's any of your business, David. Not any more.'

David nodded, and shrugged, and then obviously decided it was his business. 'Something's not right, Andrea. Seriously not right. You need to ask him some questions, trust me. This thing with Dee—'

'Oh, not again.' Andrea sighed despairingly. 'David, this really is none of your concern. I'm not sure it ever was.'

'Andrea, there are things you need to know. Things he's not telling you. Please hear me—'

'Things he's not telling me?' Andrea stared at him, astounded. 'David, I have no idea what this is all about, but whatever it is, I've heard enough. Don't you think you should be concentrating on your relationship with Sally, rather than trying to find reasons to interfere in other peoples' lives?'

Things Jonathan wasn't telling her? Well, that just really did take the biscuit, didn't it? What on earth was wrong with the man? Shaking her head, Andrea turned to huff off, leaving David raking that hand through his hair, frustrated, obviously, that he hadn't succeeded in totally rubbishing Jonathan in her eyes. Perhaps she should let David know that he didn't need to expend quite so much energy on his efforts. Jonathan was already doing a perfectly good job of that for himself.

Chapter Twenty-Three

Finding Sally's door on the latch, David knocked lightly and then, with some trepidation, went on in. Sally had said she was about to take a shower when he'd rung, so to make himself at home. Thinking that saying he'd rather not might be a little pointed, David had wasted some time doing a few household jobs and then came over. He just hoped she didn't come downstairs dressed in the silk kimono affair.

He didn't dare let his mind linger too long on the last time he'd been here, and the fact that Sally had evidently assumed they'd pick up where they'd left off. She'd been crushed when he'd pushed her away. Shame washed over David afresh as he recalled the look on her face, how much he must have hurt her. Small wonder, when he'd been so willing that first time, leaving Sally ...

Pregnant. *Unbelievable*. David still couldn't quite get his head around it, much less how. Contrary to Andrea's barbed, but understandable comment, he was all too familiar with the reproductive system and the consequences of not being careful. They had been, but obviously not careful enough. The result: he'd successfully ruined another woman's life. Way to go, David.

Despairing of himself, he headed for the lounge to wait. He'd stand by Sally, by his child. He was determined to do that, assuming she wanted him to. She really did deserve better, though, than someone who'd treated her so ...

David's thoughts were cut short as he neared the lounge door. 'Oh, Mum, stop worrying, I'm fine,' he heard Sally say into the phone. 'It's just stomach cramps.'

David shook his head then, feeling more than the slightest bit confused, and waited for Sally to end the call.

'Oh, he's perfect,' Sally went on dreamily. 'Yes, a doctor, quite a catch. Uh, oh, talking of whom, I'd better go. He's due here any second.'

Saying her goodbyes, Sally plopped the phone down and then, humming happily to herself, turned around and with an 'Oh my!', stopped dead. 'You almost gave me a heart attack!'

'Sorry, I, er ...' David squinted at her, perplexed.

'You really shouldn't creep up on people, David, you know?'

'No. I know. Sorry.' He looked her over. She wasn't wearing the seductive silk attire, he noted. She was wearing a loose fitting top that didn't give anything away. His eyes strayed to her midriff. It would be too early for her to show yet anyway, he supposed, but ... 'Stomach cramps?' He glanced at her quizzically.

'Morning sickness.' Sally lost the annoyed look and smiled stoically.

David furrowed his brow. 'Oh.'

'I know, it's awful, isn't it? Having to lie to your own mother, but she was so upset after I lost little Lucas.' Sally glanced down, pressing the palm of her hand lightly to her tummy.

And now David was shocked. 'You lost a child?' he asked, concerned – for Sally and for himself. Was he really that much of an unfeeling bastard, he'd only considered what effect this pregnancy might have on his own future? Had he even thought about Sally's feelings in all of this?

Sally nodded sadly. 'Five months.'

'Blimey.' David closed his eyes, empathising more than she could know. 'I'm sorry, Sally. That must have been hard.'

'It was.' Sally blinked back a tear, and David felt even worse. 'Mum had to pick up the pieces; then again when Nick buggered off with his anorexic stick insect. She'd be round here in a flash if she thought I was pregnant again. I'd rather wait before I tell her, you know.'

David studied her for a second longer, then nodded, understanding. 'I'll arrange for you to have a scan.' He offered her a reassuring smile. 'Best keep a close eye on things.'

'Oh. I, um …' Sally's eyes flickered nervously down again. 'I'm seeing someone else at the surgery,' she said quickly, looking back at him. 'Doctor Paton.'

She was? David was now very confused. She was on his list. He'd checked.

'I wasn't sure you'd be very pleased at the news,' Sally explained, before he could ask why. She walked over to perch herself on the sofa, where she plucked up a cushion and clutched it to her. 'I thought it might make it less awkward for you.'

Which summed up how badly he had treated her. Running a hand over his neck, David sighed at his ineptitude in handling any kind of emotional situation. 'I am pleased,' he said, going over to her.

'You are?' Sally looked up at him hopefully.

'Well, it wasn't planned, obviously, but …' David shrugged and smiled '… I'm getting used to the idea.'

Sally smiled tremulously back. 'So you'll support me, then?'

David sat down beside her. 'Of course I will.' He nodded, then, reluctant to take her hand, lest she think he might be about to, he patted her cushion instead. 'That's some bump. Eight months, I'd say. You'd better get on and get that scan organised.'

'Idiot.' Sally laughed, but her smile froze on her lips as a Homer-shaped missile shot from the hall, clearing the lounge floor in two seconds flat, to attempt to scramble onto David's lap.

'Eeeargh!' Sally shot to her feet. 'Get down!' she screeched. 'Get … down!' she said again, thwacking the dog with the cushion before David had a chance to get a hold of him.

'What?' Shooting across the room after him, David finally managed to pick the bewildered puppy up. 'Do you have a problem?' he asked, thinking she must be allergic to dogs, scared of them. Something.

'Yes!' Sally looked in boggle-eyed disbelief from him to the sofa. 'It's Italian leather art deco! A Jean Renoir with contrast leather piping! I don't want animals jumping all over it with muddy paws.'

'Ah, right.' David plucked up one of Homer's paws and peered at it, seeing no evidence of mud thereon. What about children jumping all over it though, he couldn't help wondering, with sticky hands? He'd spent ten minutes trying to clean the evidence of Jake's chocolate smoothie from one of his own armchairs before he'd given up, figuring in the great scheme of things, it didn't really matter. If Sally was that particular, she was going to struggle with a toddler's fingers on everything. David couldn't help thinking about Chloe, and Andrea's remark about how the mess her children would make of Sally's elegant furnishings and décor would drive Sally to move out. Jake and Sally would most definitely not hit it off, that was for sure.

'I'll take him home,' David said. Before he pees on the oriental rug, he thought, bemused, as Sally dove into her cupboard for a cloth and polish, obviously kept handy for just such emergencies.

'See you later,' he called, rolling his eyes as Sally set to buffing her Italian leather art deco sofa with vigour. 'Better not pee on that, Homer,' he whispered in the dog's ear as he headed to the front door – to find Ryan and Dougal on the other side of it, a sheepish looking Jake peering out from behind Ryan.

'Sorry, Dad. He slipped his lead,' Jake said, not looking all that apologetic as he dangled the evidence, one dog-free collar. 'Homer hasn't upset the neighbours, has he?'

Not half as much as I have, David thought ruefully. 'A bit,' he said, wanting to reinforce that with dog ownership came responsibility. 'Tighten the collar a notch, hey, Jake?'

'Will do,' Jake said, dragging a hand under his runny nose. David didn't dare imagine what Sally's reaction to that on her contrast piping might be. 'Ryan's got to go. We came to tell you.'

'Oh, right. Okay, take Homer inside.' David handed him over. 'And make sure he has some water in his dish, Jake, yes?'

'Yep,' Jake said, heading for the house, puppy in arms.

'Look, Jake! Left and right,' David shouted, stopping him short of the road.

'Oops,' Jake said over his shoulder, dutifully obliged, then scooted happily on.

'Cheers, Ryan.' David smiled as Jake headed up the drive. 'In case I forget to mention it, you're all right.'

'Yeah, I know.' Ryan shrugged modestly. 'Pity the girls don't think so.'

'Oh.' David sensed he might be confiding, but also sensed he probably didn't want to go too far down that road. 'No luck yet, then?'

'Not with your kid in tow, no,' Ryan said bluntly.

'Ah, right.' David nodded. Ryan had been a real godsend. David wasn't sure he would have been able to cope without him taking Jake under his wing. Looked like he would have to learn how to now. 'Look, Ryan, you've been brilliant. I'm really grateful for your help with Jake, but if you need some space …'

''S'okay,' Ryan said, with another casual shrug. 'I like him. If I get an offer from a fit female, I'll let you know.'

'Do that.' David laughed, relieved. 'I might have to ask you for a few parenting tips, though.'

Ryan nodded, only a hint of a smile on his face, lest

he show too much emotion for an emotionally charged punk rocker, David guessed. 'You're doing all right,' he commented.

'I'm trying.' David bent to give Dougal a pat and then stepped past Ryan towards his house, while he still had one. No doubt Homer would be doing a wall-of-death around the lounge by now, Jake whooping and cheering him on.

'I meant on the girlfriend front,' Ryan said drolly behind him.

Ouch! David winced. Well, he definitely deserved that, he supposed. 'Not with the one I'd like to be, Ryan,' he admitted, turning back.

Ryan regarded him thoughtfully. 'Gotta go,' he said, after a second. 'Eva's looking after Dougal while we're at the hotel. I have to take him back and Mum's waiting to go and get dinner.'

'Give her my regards,' David said as Ryan headed off, skinny jeans still hanging in there and laces trailing flatly behind him.

'Will do. Oh, she has a new mobile, by the way,' Ryan said, over his shoulder. 'I'll let you have the number. You'll probably need it to discuss the flat Eva's offered her so the landlord can stay incognito. Catch you lata.'

David couldn't help but smile. Weren't all adolescents supposed to be uncommunicative and moody? Ryan might not say a lot and his mood was generally 'chillaxed', in keeping with his image, but he was caring, and what little he did say communicated volumes.

'Cheers,' David called after him, smiling again as Ryan plucked Dougal up to carry him, 'cos you've only got short legs, haven't you, hey, little guy?'

Home not-so-sweet home, Andrea sighed, heading back from the café to the Travelodge. It might not be home, but at least the kids seemed reasonably happy now they dined on food to suit their palate: banana leaf thai curry for Sophie, Tower Burger for Ryan, which he delighted in graphically describing the meaty ingredients of to his sister. Dee had a traditional steak and ale pie, with a beer on the side, and Chloe and she had shared a platter with essential chips. All were replete. At this rate, though, they'd soon be sharing one platter between them in their room, singular, as opposed to the family room plus a room for Ryan she was currently splashing out for.

'Sleepy, munchkin?' Andrea asked Chloe, peering down at her bleary-eyed toddler as she carried her back to the family room.

'Hodilay,' Chloe mumbled around the thumb she was sucking on, and nestled further into her shoulder.

'That's right, sweetie, holiday.' Andrea kissed the top of her baby's head and silently thanked God for her. At least, in her innocence, Chloe thought it was all one big adventure, excited at tucking up in the pull-out bed with her sister, while Dee and she shared the double bed. Sophie had cheered up immensely this evening, though, having apparently already viewed the accommodation over the shop Eva had offered them.

Eva had mentioned the premises when Andrea had dropped Dougal off at her house earlier, Eva having volunteered to dog-sit while Andrea searched for somewhere else to stay that was more dog-friendly, bless her helpful heart. Not sure how practical an apartment would be; Andrea said she'd think about it, but then, when Sophie had arrived back at the hotel bursting with news of the 'cool' attic room she'd bagsied and Ryan apparently being 'cool' about it, too, Andrea had made up her mind to accept Eva's offer. She wasn't so sure about accepting her offer of rent-free for a few months until she got back on her feet, though.

She'd need to speak to Eva more about that, about the

shop aspect of things, too. She couldn't realistically pursue her Second Chance Designer idea now, with the future so uncertain. Ah, well, at least they were all here and healthy. The future could have been a lot bleaker, she reminded herself, reaching into her pocket for her key, and then waiting while her straggly entourage caught up.

'It was probably horse meat,' she heard Sophie say as she dawdled along the corridor, obviously on the offensive after Ryan tormented her with tales of the contents of his bun.

'Was it?' Dee stopped, for at least the third time in the space of twenty yards.

'Nah, it was a hundred per cent dead cow, Gran,' Ryan said, true to form.

'Oh, good.' Dee nodded satisfied, and trotted on.

'Yeah, right,' Sophie scoffed. 'More like forty per cent with muscle and connective tissue thrown in, and soya and beef fat ... and minced up eyeballs.' She smirked as she waltzed past Ryan.

'Mmmm, delish,' Ryan responded, rubbing his tummy, but quietly curling a lip, Andrea noticed, amused.

Dee stopped, again. 'I thought mine was a bit chewy,' she pondered. 'I hope I haven't got bits of eyeball stuck in my teeth.' With which, she promptly reached to extract said teeth as an alarmed looking occupant emerged from a room alongside.

'Mum!' Andrea skidded hastily back towards her. 'Sorry,' she said, beaming the young woman a slightly imbecilic smile. 'She's quite harmless,' she assured her, urging Dee on, 'as long as you don't mind being driven batty along with her.'

'I'm not batty,' Dee objected, still attempting to remove her teeth.

'Nah, Gran, just eccentric.' Ryan smirked. 'We love you, don't we, Sophe?'

Mortified 'Sophe', however, Andrea noted, had

disappeared into the room, possibly faster than she'd ever moved in her life.

'That's heart-warming, Ryan. Truly gratifying,' Andrea said, her smile now a bit on the tight side. 'Here you go.' She passed big brother his little sister. 'Tuck her in for me, please, and since you love your gran so much, you can make sure she's tucked up, too.'

'Yer what?' Ryan gawked over Chloe. 'But I was going to watch telly.'

Andrea pointed him onward. 'In there,' she instructed. 'I need the use of your room.'

'Oh, yes?' Ryan arched a curious eyebrow.

'To talk, Ryan,' Andrea clarified, lest he think she was entertaining men to keep him in Tower Burgers.

'Right.' Ryan nodded. 'To who?'

'Jonathan. Who did you think?'

'Oh, right. Probably best if we keep a low profile, then.' Ryan sloped on into the family room, not looking overly thrilled.

Low profile? Andrea frowned after him. They hadn't really reached the stage in their relationship where her children stayed out of the way, had they?

At least she hadn't had to concern herself with titivating and pouring herself into ridiculous breath-defying dresses this time. Andrea tried not to dwell on their last arranged meeting and the disastrous events of that evening, but her mind kept drifting back to it anyway, images of her home and everything in it being voraciously devoured by fire.

Stop! She told herself firmly, clamping her eyes shut on hot, hungry flames licking at the bars of her stairs, smoke creeping along her landing to curl under the doors of bedrooms with her sleeping children therein.

Television, she instructed herself, flicking the remote to

watch whatever rubbish might be on, and checking her watch for the tenth time. She couldn't believe he was late. Hadn't she said when she'd phoned him that they needed to talk about their future plans? Surely Jonathan must have realised she meant whether they actually had a future together worth planning for?

He'd suggested they meet at 'their' restaurant. Yes, that had worked out really well last time, hadn't it? she'd pointed out, with more than a hint of sarcasm. She'd be sitting there now just the same, waiting, worrying, but with one slight difference, she supposed. This time she hadn't got a house to bloody well burn down while she did.

Very annoyed now, Andrea stood up to flick the TV off and allow Ryan the use of his room back. Jonathan wasn't going to come, was he? She should have known. He'd said he'd been taken to the hospital that dreadful night, when he hadn't shown. She'd accepted his explanation. She'd wanted to believe it, but she didn't, not deep down. And now, with their whole world torn apart, her children's security ripped from underneath them, here was Jonathan obvious by his absence, again. Did he care, at all? He certainly hadn't shown any evidence he did lately. Had he ever?

Pulling in a shuddery breath, Andrea headed for the door, her mind racing ahead to what she should do next, pursuing the insurance claim being number one on her list. There had to be a way to get details, through the mortgage provider possibly? Pondering, she almost parted company with her skin when the door knocked as she reached it. Jonathan?

Torn between relieved and furious, Andrea spied through the peephole, then pulled the door open, determined not to let his tardiness cloud the issues they had to discuss.

'My, you're keen, aren't you?' Jonathan smiled. 'I bought you these,' he said before Andrea could speak, producing a bunch of red roses from behind his back.

'Oh.' Taken aback, Andrea blinked at the roses and then him, bemused.

'Well, don't look so surprised,' Jonathan said, looking crestfallen. 'Men do buy flowers for the women they love, you know.'

'How thoughtful,' Andrea said, stepping back to allow him access. 'Pity you didn't think to bring something to put them in.'

'Ahhh.' Jonathan smiled awkwardly, obviously having forgotten the trifling fact that her house had burned down, meaning she hadn't got a stick to her name, let alone a vase.

'So why the sudden gesture?' she asked, suspicious of his motives. Whatever his reasons for this rare display of affection, he should know it would need a hell of a lot more than a bunch of flowers to set things right. 'I mean, you don't buy me flowers, do you? Not often anyway?'

'No, I don't, do I?' Jonathan turned to face her. He looked exhausted, haggard almost. Bags under his eyes she could pack her luggage in, if she had any.

'I should have.' He shrugged, looking as disconsolate as Andrea felt. 'A beautiful woman deserves flowers. Sorry I was late, by the way,' he said, removing his jacket and seating himself tiredly on the bed.

'So, why were you?'

'Hectic, as usual. Phone's been going non-stop. Haven't had a minute all day, I swear. Come, sit,' he said, loosening his tie with one hand and patting the space next to him with the other.

'And was one of those calls from the assessors, Jonathan?' Andrea asked, preferring to stand while she got straight to the point. 'It's just, as they have actually been to the house ...' she paused pointedly '... I'd assumed they were processing the claim.'

A little furrow forming in the middle of his brow, Jonathan glanced down. 'Yes.' He nodded thoughtfully. 'Yes, they are.'

'So they'll be releasing an emergency fund soon, then?' she asked, gauging him carefully as he proceeded to pluck bits of fluff from his trousers.

'I imagine so, yes.' Jonathan looked back at her. 'Come and sit down, Andy,' he said, breaking eye contact, after a second. 'You're making me uneasy, standing over me like that. Can't we just relax and talk?'

'Why would you be uneasy?' Andrea turned to place the flowers on the dressing table. She really didn't feel like sitting, and relaxing was certainly something she wouldn't be doing a lot of in the foreseeable future.

'Because …' Jonathan hesitated '… things haven't exactly been good between us, have they, Andrea?'

'No.' Andrea braced herself and turned to face him. 'Do you want them to be?'

Jonathan got to his feet with a sigh. 'Of course I do. You know I do, it's just …'

Andrea waited while he paced, wondering what he was going to cite as the reason. Her mum? Her insistence on trying to steal some time for herself with her Second Chance Designer 'hare-brained' idea, which was probably dead in the water anyway? Her children? Her?

'… I don't think I stand a chance with Doctor Adams and his bleeding heart moving in on you, do I?' Jonathan stopped pacing and faced her.

Oh no. Andrea closed her eyes. 'I moved in with him, Jonathan,' she reminded him, drawing in a breath. Her cheeks were burning, her guilt was choking her, but what had happened between David and her wasn't the reason their relationship was floundering. The problems between Jonathan and her had started when David was no more than a stranger. Before he'd even come to the village. Jonathan knew it as well as she did and she would not have him manipulate the conversation away from the real issues.

'So I noticed,' Jonathan almost sneered, his eyes on hers, burning with accusation.

Andrea looked him over, noting the tight set of his jaw and trying hard to work out where this was leading. What was it he was accusing her of? Did he really think, as she'd watched her house burn to the ground, not even knowing whether her family was safe, she'd been formulating some plan to move in with another man?

'I didn't have much choice, Jonathan, did I?' she pointed out quietly.

'Oh, come on, Andrea, you had plenty of choice.' Jonathan dragged derisory eyes away from hers and resumed pacing. 'You could have gone to any one of the neighbours. Eva, Sally, the pub. Here.'

'My house had just burned down, Jonathan. The children were already in David's house, being comforted by David, having been bloody well rescued by him! They were traumatised. Chloe was! Do you honestly think it would have been in their interest to drag them out past their burning house all over again?'

Jonathan's step faltered. 'No. Of course not. I—'

'They hadn't got a stitch to their name, and you were missing!' Andrea pointed out angrily. 'At the hospital, or so you said!'

Jonathan stopped, and turned, his expression livid. 'Which means what exactly?'

He took a step towards her. Andrea stepped back, into the table. 'You could have rung any one of the neighbours, Jonathan. Couldn't you? The school? The pub?'

'I don't believe this,' Jonathan growled, his breathing heavy, his face tight. 'I really don't. Thanks for your concern, Andrea. Thanks a lot!'

Eyeballing her furiously, Jonathan yanked off his tie. Andrea's hand went to her throat.

'I could have been dying! And your only concern is that

I didn't ring?' Jonathan shook his head, incredulously. 'I couldn't get to a phone, Andrea, did that occur to you? Did it occur to you to ring around the hospitals?'

'No, I …' Andrea faltered, trying to think back. He hadn't come to the restaurant. She'd spoken to him on the phone. She'd no reason to think—

'No,' Jonathan seethed, an inch from her face, 'because you were too busy getting acquainted with our new neighbour. Don't throw stones, Andrea, not when you're on shaky ground.'

She watched him walk to the bed. Heard David's voice in her head: 'Something's not right, Andrea.' Then Dee: 'He's trying to do away with me.'

'Where was Dougal,' she asked, keeping her eyes on him as she moved away from the table, 'when you found him?'

Jonathan looked sharply back at her. 'In the park, I told you. Why?'

'No reason,' Andrea took a step towards the door. 'It's just he didn't look very bedraggled for a dog who'd been wandering around lost. He wasn't very hungry either. I just wondered, that's all.'

'Right, I see,' Jonathan said, with a long exasperated sigh. 'You're right, obviously. He wasn't in the park. I kidnapped him so I could claim the ransom. Of course I did.' He locked eyes with hers, his now blazing with anger. 'And while I was at it, I set fire to the house so I could claim the insurance. I mean, why not go the whole fucking hog, hey?'

Andrea nipped worriedly at her bottom lip. The dog flap, she tried to think rationally, though her mind was reeling. Dougal had escaped through the dog flap. Sensing danger, he'd beat a hasty retreat, that's what Dougal would do. So, how did he get out of the garden? A garden they'd made absolutely sure was secure? Unless … Someone helped him out? During the fire? After? Before?

'Bloody hell, what is this, Andrea?' Jonathan shouted, startling her thoughts from her blackened kitchen, where it appeared the fire had started. 'Where do you think he was, if he—'

'In your office!' Andrea blurted. 'I saw the bed. I saw the dish. He was in your office, Jonathan! Why won't you tell me the truth? When did you find him?'

Jonathan didn't say anything, just looked at her, his expression thunderous. 'You've been in my office?' he said quietly, after a moment.

'I have a key. Your spare. You gave it to me, just in case ...' His fury now palpable, Andrea tailed off.

He moved towards her. Andrea took another step to the door.

'Spying on me?' Jonathan took two swift strides, and was on her. 'That's rich, Andrea,' he said, catching hold of her arm. His face was close to hers, one hand pressed against the door, right next to her.

'I wasn't spying. I—'

'Really fucking rich. You're shacked up with some bloke you hardly know, shagging him for all I know, and *you're* spying on me?'

'Jonathan! You're scaring me!' Frantically, Andrea searched his eyes, which had changed, from tumultuous to ... murderous? Nowhere to go, Andrea was terrified.

She held her breath. Jonathan inhaled deeply, breathed out raggedly, then, 'Fuck!' slammed his hand against the door, bare millimetres from her head.

'Fuck,' he said again, dragging his hands over his face. 'I don't believe this. I ...' He blinked hard, then ground the heels of his hands against his eyes and finally looked at the ceiling. 'What happened to us, Andrea?' he asked, looking back at her, looking wretched. 'Why are you doing this?'

Andrea couldn't speak, couldn't breathe. She stared at

him, bewildered. The door handle rattled beside her. 'Mum?' Ryan's voice came from outside.

'I'm coming. I'm fine.' Andrea turned and grabbed for the handle, attempting to open the door. At which Jonathan muscled in beside her and leant his full weight against it.

'Don't, Andrea,' he said, his tone now scared, but most definitely holding a warning. 'We need to talk. We—'

'Get *out* of my way!' Her heart palpitating manically inside her, Andrea grappled with the handle, tugged hard at it. 'Jonathan, I need to go.'

'For God's sake, Andrea, stop!' Jonathan clamped a hand over hers, wove an arm around her, attempting to force her bodily away from the door.

Desperately trying to prise his grip from her waist, Andrea struggled, kicking out behind her. They were nothing but useless flails meeting with fresh air. He was bigger than her, much stronger than her. She was powerless to prevent him whirling her around and leaning his back heavily against the door.

'Mum!' Ryan, urgently now.

'Ryan! Call the—' Andrea stopped, gagged by the hand that Jonathan now had clutched to her face.

'Just stop,' he hissed in her ear. 'Calm down, for— *Fuck!*'

Wincing as Andrea's fingernails gouged his flesh, he loosened his hold.

And Andrea grabbed her chance. Summoning her strength, she wriggled out of his grasp, lurching forwards, away from him, only to stumble. The light was white, blinding, as her cheekbone cracked against the sharp wooden edge of the dressing table.

'Andrea?' Jonathan's tone was now one of horror. 'Oh God, Andrea ...' He moved towards her as she blinked against the searing pain and attempted to right herself.

Crouching, he caught hold of her forearms. 'You're hurt,'

he said, his voice hoarse as he eased her to her feet, his touch gentle as he reached out to brush the tender bruise already forming under her eye.

'Mum?' Sophie said, shocked and tearful behind him.

'What the fuck's happening?' Ryan demanded, his keycard in his hand, his expression more furious than Andrea had ever seen him.

'Don't, Ryan!' Andrea stopped him as he stormed towards Jonathan. Ryan would stand no chance against a man a head taller than he was. 'Leave it. Please, Ryan,' she asked, seeing her boy was now trembling with ill-suppressed rage. 'He's going.'

She turned coldly towards Jonathan, who closed his eyes, looking haggard, a hundred years older. His anger visibly dissipating, he looked back at her. 'I'm so sorry, Andrea,' he said, his voice catching. 'I love you. I never meant to hurt you, I swear.'

Andrea fixed him with a contemptuous gaze. 'I've heard enough, Jonathan,' she assured him, working hard to control her own temper. 'And my children have seen enough. You have thirty seconds to leave.' With which Andrea drew in a breath and turned away.

'Right.' Jonathan sighed heavily behind her. 'Can I at least use the bathroom before I go?'

What? Andrea's step faltered. She was contemplating calling the police and he wanted to avail himself of the facilities?

'The bathroom,' Jonathan repeated as she shot him an incredulous look over her shoulder. 'I, er, need a moment.'

'Thirty seconds,' Andrea reiterated, ushering Ryan and Sophie ahead of her out of the room.

'Bastard,' Ryan threw after him as Jonathan headed towards the bathroom, presumably to compose himself. 'You should report him.'

'Leave it, Ryan,' Andrea asked him, pulling the door half to and then reaching gently to prevent Ryan pressing the digits on his mobile he obviously wanted to. 'For now,' she said, locking eyes with his. 'He's Chloe's father. I'm not making excuses, I promise. I need time to think. Meanwhile, I want him gone.'

Pulling in a deep breath, Ryan held her gaze, tangible anger in his own, and then reluctantly, he nodded.

Grateful, Andrea squeezed his arm and turned her attention to Sophie. 'All right, sweetie?'

Sniffling, Sophie ran an arm under her nose. 'Uh-huh,' she said. 'You?'

'I've been better,' Andrea answered honestly.

'Ryan's right. He is a bastard,' Sophie agreed with her brother, unusually.

Andrea might have smiled, but for the circumstances. 'Where's Gran?'

'Soaking her feet,' Sophie assured her. 'Just as well she is. We'd have been hard pushed to stop her trying to give that wanker a taste of his own.'

'Exactly.' Andrea reached to fluff up Sophie's drooping spikes. 'I don't want her to hear, kids. Understand? Or Chloe.' She glanced meaningfully at them both in turn and then thanked God for them both as they nodded simultaneously back.

Relieved, Andrea turned back to the door to see Jonathan warily emerging. 'So ... How are you two?' he asked awkwardly, glancing between Sophie and Ryan.

Neither of the children answered.

'How's Chloe?' Jonathan tried.

Silence.

'I thought I'd just pop in and say hello to her.' Jonathan took a step towards the door to the family room.

'Uh, uh.' Ryan shook his head and sidestepped, bodily blocking the doorway.

Sophie folded her arms and closed ranks with her brother. 'She's sleeping,' she informed him.

'Right.' Jonathan nodded, glancing apprehensively at Andrea. 'How's Dee?' he asked, forcing a smile.

'Still alive,' obviously having finished attending her feet, Dee piped up from inside, 'despite your best efforts.'

Jonathan shook his head, a wry smile on his face. 'She's still not confused then, I see.'

'Not half as confused as you seem to think I am, young man.'

'I'd like you to go now,' Andrea said as Jonathan loitered, looking uncertain. 'I don't want Chloe woken. She's been through enough. We all have.'

Jonathan shrugged. 'Okay,' he said, after a long intake of breath. 'I'll call you tomorrow.'

'Don't be surprised if she doesn't come running,' Ryan muttered, looking Jonathan over disdainfully.

'Sense of humour still intact, I see, Ryan.' Jonathan smiled shortly, and turned to Andrea. 'We'll need to chat further ...'

Chat? Andrea's hand went to her face, which was badly bruised and which she guessed bore a cut where the corner of the table had broken the flesh. It was all she could do to stop her eyes boggling in her head.

'About what happens next,' Jonathan went on, apparently oblivious to the considerable stress he'd just caused.

'What happens next is you leave,' Ryan suggested. 'The exit's that way.'

'Okay, fine, I can see where I'm not wanted. I'll catch up with you later.' Jonathan gave Andrea a nod and headed down the corridor. 'Oh, just so you know, though.' He turned back. 'Chloe is my daughter, Andrea. Whatever happens, I will want to see her.'

'Prat,' Ryan imparted his thoughts on the subject as Jonathan walked on.

Chapter Twenty-Four

'What do you think?' David asked Jake, dragging an arm across his forehead as he stood back to appraise their evening's handiwork repainting the walls orchid white, Andrea's colour of choice, as reliably informed by Ryan. Unfortunately, the information had come a little late. It had taken him a week, working late into the night, to paint the entire property the first time round. Now, with the furnishings arriving this coming Saturday, which David really wanted in situ before Andrea moved in on Sunday, he had only three evenings left to repaint it.

Sally hadn't been impressed with his continued excuses for not dropping by to 'cosy up on the sofa' and share an evening together. David was actually beginning to wonder if he dared to even sit on the sofa. The last time he'd dropped by, she'd asked him would he very much mind leaving his shoes at the door and then fluffed up the cushions on the Italian leather almost before he'd left his seat. David didn't mind, not really. He was more concerned at Sally's tendencies to OCD and how she'd cope when the baby came. It could well be something to do with the loss of her previous child, David thought, anxiety exacerbated by post-natal depression, possibly? He was worried for her.

Jake looked up from where he was kneeling, painting the patch of wall David had allocated him. 'It looks better on the walls.' He smirked, indicating David's arm, which was also orchid white, as was his forehead now, he gleaned, along with pretty much every other part of his visible anatomy.

Jake looked as if he'd been dipped in the stuff too, but the boy painted on, unperturbed, and quietly pleased that he'd been entrusted with a paintbrush, David reckoned. Pretty enthusiastic, too, since it was Ryan's 'pad' he was helping redecorate. Watching him, David smiled, his heart swelling with pride for his son; his son more as he should be. Yes, he was still moody sometimes, a bit loose with the backchat; introverted occasionally when, perhaps prompted by some reminder, his thoughts drifted to his mother. He'd yet to look at him with adoration in his eyes, like Dad was his hero, but he was more the boy he used to be. That would do for now. David just hoped he could find a way to tell him the news about Sally without breaking the kid's heart all over again, which he'd have to do soon, before Sally did start announcing the pregnancy and it reached Jake via the village grapevine.

'How long do we have now?' Jake asked, his tongue protruding as he concentrated on getting a straight line at the skirting board. His endeavours weren't bad, actually, David noted.

'You're a natural,' he said, nodding towards the wall. 'You obviously take after your mum.'

Jake stopped, cocked his head to one side to examine his efforts, then, 'Yeah,' he said, with a satisfied nod. 'She was ace with a paintbrush. I must take after her, not you.'

'Yes. Cheers, Jake.' David glanced at his own work, ceiling lines passable but not perfect. 'The artistic gene obviously passed me by.'

'Yeah.' Jake smirked, his attention now back on his patch of wall. 'Do you think Andrea would like some of Mum's paintings?' he asked, catching David off guard.

He sucked in a breath. He hadn't thought much about Michelle's paintings. It still pained him to think about her working on them in their spare room. That's where she'd told him the good news, that she was pregnant. That was another time he got covered in paint. Body art, Michelle had called it, squirting a cold blob of yellow ochre – so she'd informed him – onto his chest and rubbing it in liberally.

David closed his eyes as he remembered; that was not long before the bad news arrived – and the paintings had turned dark.

'I don't know, Jake,' he said, imagining that Andrea, under the circumstances, wouldn't appreciate having his lost wife's paintings adorning her walls. 'I'll ask her, once she's moved in.'

'Okay.' Jake nodded happily. 'So?'

'So … What?' David glanced down, now at work on the wall above Jake.

'So how long do we have?' Jake repeated the question he'd asked before David got lost in his thoughts.

'Oh, right.' David checked his watch. 'Two hours and counting.' And that would be pushing it. Jake had already had one late bedtime this week. 'What we need if we're going to get this done in time for Andrea to move in …' David stretched to reach a bit he'd missed.

'Oi,' Jake said from below as a drip rained down on him.

'Sorry. It'll match the rest though,' David suggested helpfully.

'Yeah, cheers, Dad.' Jake shook his head.

'We need …' David went on, surveying the shop walls, which he'd left until last and were nowhere near finished, '… a bloody miracle.'

'Language,' Jake admonished him.

'You have one,' Eva said behind him, causing David to drip another fat splat on Jake's head.

'Crap!' Man and boy exchanged worried glances, then both looked over their shoulders as Eva bustled on in, followed by Thea and Nita, Ryan helping guide her chair through the door, only to be told, 'I have arms, you know. I can do it myself,' by the unimpressed occupant of the chair.

'Ryan said he was coming over to lend you a hand,' Eva said, glancing around the room with a critical eye; 'so we thought we'd join him. Show a bit of community spirit and whatnot. Soon have the job done. You've missed a bit, by the way.'

'Right. Thanks, I think.' David swapped amused glances with Jake as Ryan, unruffled by Nita's chastisements, continued to steer the chair – over the paint tray.

'If you insist on handling my daughter, dear boy,' Thea said haughtily, removing her faux fur coat to reveal diamante-belted overalls underneath, 'do you mind doing it gently?'

'Ooh, Mum!' Nita scowled as Ryan blushed, glancing embarrassedly at David.

'Think you might have scored.' Jake giggled.

'Yeah,' Ryan eyed the ceiling and walked over for a cloth, 'unfortunately not with the old trout of a mother.'

'I heard that,' Thea boomed indignantly, behind him.

David winced. 'Nope, definitely not impressed.' He gave Ryan a shrug of commiseration and handed him the roller.

'Cheers,' Ryan said, looking at it as if he wasn't quite sure what to do with it. 'Do you have your phone?'

'Yes,' David eyed him curiously, 'why?'

Ryan reached into his jeans pocket for his mobile. 'Texting you Mum's number,' he said, 'just in case. You'll know who it is then, if she needs to contact you at short notice.'

'Oh, right. Cheers, Ryan.' David regarded him evermore curiously as his own phone beeped incoming text. Just in case of what? he wondered warily.

Andrea noted the last caller on her mobile and debated the wisdom of letting Jonathan have the number. But then, his calls on the hotel phone had become nuisance calls, always arriving when Chloe had just closed her eyes. And she certainly didn't want him ringing Ryan or Sophie to arrange when he might drop by to see Chloe.

He could see her, of course, but bearing in mind the

last time Andrea had seen him, she'd prefer it to be in her company and in public, at least until they'd talked civilly about where they went from here.

Wherever it was, it wouldn't be together, that much Andrea was sure of, which meant she'd have to go through the custody thing all over again, she supposed. Shaking off a shudder of déjà vu, she turned to gather Chloe up, who was busy putting Igglepiggle to bed in a shoebox. Clearly this little madam didn't think losing all her worldly goods was a major catastrophe. Maybe going back to basics would be no bad thing – and basic it would be with hardly a stick of furniture to furnish their new home with.

At least they'd have beds to sleep in, though, thanks to Eva generously donating her spare single and Beki at the Tiny Tots shop supplying Chloe with a bed, bless her. Even Thea had come up trumps, also offering a single and two sleeping bags – and a man with a van to deliver it all while Andrea was at school. Such were the benefits of living in a small community. Yes, news travelled fast, to the chagrin of people like David Adams who seemed intent on making headlines, but that was no bad thing if you needed help in a hurry. Andrea's own situation was proof of that.

How fast would David and Sally's news travel, once Sally had announced her impending happy event? Strange that she hadn't yet. How was she? Andrea wondered. She'd looked a bit peaky when she'd last seen her, no surprise there, she supposed, given her condition, but Andrea hadn't been able to ask her. They'd barely spoken other than a passing acknowledgement in the school corridors. She'd have to go and see her, she decided. Try to make Sally see that her relationship with David was platonic, assuming David and she were speaking, of course, after their last chat, which hadn't been very civil either. She'd avoided him since, other than a cordial wave across the playground, though that was possibly more because she'd prefer the bruise to have faded on her cheek before coming face to face with him. She would go and see Sally. Andrea made her decision. Later though. First of all, she needed to get her family and what few belongings they had into their new home.

'Ready guys?' she asked, glancing over to Sophie who was idly skimming the channels on the TV from her seat on the bed settee.

'More than,' Sophie assured her, tossing the remote and moving with more enthusiasm than she had possibly ever.

'Can't find my teeth,' Dee called from the bathroom.

'In your mouth, Gran,' Sophie supplied, with a roll of her eyes.

'Mothers.' Andrea sighed good-naturedly.

'Who'd have 'em?' Sophie did likewise, her mouth twitching into an actual smile as she linked arms with her mum.

'You, obviously,' Andrea suggested wryly, 'even if it is a rubbish one.'

She still couldn't quite believe she made such abysmal choices regarding the men in her life. First Sophie and Ryan's father, who most definitely had aggressive tendencies – but then, she wouldn't have Sophie and Ryan without him. Then Jonathan. She wouldn't have had Chloe either though, without him, she reminded herself. And the bruise to her face, which had now faded to a lovely shade of mottled yellow, hadn't been physically inflicted by him. Indirectly, though ...? Could she really risk putting her children in that situation again?

'Nah, you'll do,' Sophie said, with a nonchalant shrug.

'Thank you.' Andrea accepted the closest she was likely to get to a compliment gracefully. 'Right, come on then, troops,' she hoisted Chloe higher, 'let's go and collect Ryan, before he morphs with the TV.'

* * *

'I still think the dining suite looked better in the window.' Eva glanced around the lounge of the flat thoughtfully.

'You think so?' David ran his hand through his hair and looked to where he'd just dragged the corner sofa. Eva was right, he decided. In front of the low bay window, the sofa blocked out the light and didn't do the space justice. The solid wood dining table and chairs made the window more a feature and Andrea might prefer the view, people-watching over breakfast. Dee, too.

'Right.' He nodded, and set about heaving the heavy furniture about for the third time that morning.

Dining table and sofa finally in position, and every bone in his body aching, David was finally satisfied.

'What do you reckon?' he asked Eva, glancing over his shoulder as she came back in with tea. 'Think she'll like it?'

'Ooh, I should think she'll love it.' Eva bustled over to deposit the tray on the dining table. 'Why don't you ask her?' She turned back, nodding past him to the door.

With some trepidation, given they hadn't exactly parted friends last time they'd met, David turned around to see Andrea behind him, her pretty green eyes wide with surprise.

Pleasant surprise, David hoped. 'Well?' he tugged in a breath and held it, while Andrea gazed around, taking in the orchid white walls, the dining table – now looking spot on in the bay window with the retro print blinds as a backdrop – the mahogany fireplace, much like the one in David's house, restored and resplendent against the paintwork, the wooden floors, which he'd overlaid as the original wasn't up to much. She glanced from the four wrought iron candle holders he'd placed on the mantel, to the contemporary cast iron wall designs he'd positioned above, to the wrought iron chandelier he'd picked up from the second-hand shop, and then back to him, astonished.

'I …' she started.

'Wow! Mum!' came a delighted whoop from the attic room above. 'You just have to come and see this; it's totally wicked!'

'I love it.' Andrea laughed out loud.

Yesss! David thought, on the verge of an unseemly whoop himself. He'd managed to get something right in her eyes at long last.

'But why would you—?' Andrea looked at him quizzically.

'Boy done good, hasn't he?' Eva interrupted.

'Extremely good.' Andrea looked from Eva to David, still smiling but obviously perplexed. 'But I don't understand why he's done all—'

'I don't know what I'd have done without Doctor Adams offering to help out, what with young Darren about to give birth and Bob having to take time off with his asthma. If it wasn't for David—'

'Ooh, a proper bath!' Dee's delighted tones drifted down the hall. 'I'll look forward to soaking my bunions in that.'

Andrea winced. David smiled. 'Roll top cast iron I found on eBay,' he supplied. 'I thought it would go with the general décor.'

'But why would you do all this?' Andrea finally managed.

David shrugged evasively. 'Practice.'

Andrea didn't look convinced.

'Well, Eva couldn't do it all,' David pointed out.

'Not with him insisting I keep my legs in the air,' Eva added, with a mischievous wink.

'And, as Eva says, the decorators are out of commission, so ...'

'We called in the cavalry,' Eva said, giving David's cheek an affectionate pat.

Andrea was still staring at him awestruck, which felt pretty good. 'You did all this, on your own?'

'Ah, well, no, not quite. I had a little help,' David admitted, nodding towards Jake, who came in with Ryan, both boys smirking from ear to ear. 'They've got the job, by the way.'

Andrea looked him over, a definite twinkle back in her eye. 'I'm overwhelmed,' she said stepping forward to plant a soft kiss on his cheek. 'Thank you.'

'My pleasure,' David said, noting she was wearing make-up. 'So,' he said, drawing in a tight breath as he scanned her face more closely, 'you're good with it, then.'

'I'm ecstatic,' Andrea assured him, gazing around. 'I really do love it, David. I couldn't have chosen better myself. Actually, I couldn't have chosen at all, until the insurance people pay ...' she trailed off.

'Great. I'm glad.' David smiled. 'Ryan, do you fancy nipping to the shops to get some Pepsi? I should think you both need a drink, yes?'

'Nah, I'm—' Ryan stopped as he met David's meaningful gaze. 'Minty,' he said twirling around. 'Come on, Jake.'

David's gaze shifted to Eva, who noted the slight incline of his head towards the door and decided, 'You'll need some general supplies, Andrea. I'll pop to the village shop with the boys. Oh, Deirdre,' she called, heading for the hall.

'She's not here,' Dee informed her from the loo.

'I thought we'd pop to the store for some groceries,' Eva suggested sweetly. 'What do you think, my dear?'

A pause, then, 'I think I'm hallucinating. Must be the paint fumes.'

'We could dig up some edibles from my garden on the way,' Eva's voice floated back as Dee shuffled, muttering, from bathroom to hall.

'Might have known there'd be a blooming catch,' was Dee's unenthusiastic response.

Andrea laughed as the two women made precarious progress onwards, Eva all sweetness and light, Dee her usual rude self. 'Honestly, what would you do with them?'

'Well, maybe not put them out to grass, just yet,' David suggested, not very diplomatically probably, but he couldn't help himself.

'No.' Obviously getting his meaning, Andrea glanced away. 'I adore the furnishings,' she said, walking across to trail her hand over the back of the sofa. 'And the décor. I can't think how you knew I was about to decorate my lounge in this colour, before the fire, obviously.'

'Ryan, he put me right on a few things,' David said. 'Andrea?'

'Hmm?' Andrea was now admiring the blinds.

'Where did the bruise come from?'

David watched, keeping a tight rein on his anger, as Andrea glanced immediately down, visibly debating whether to drop that bastard Eden in it.

'I ... fell,' she eventually mumbled, her shoulders deflating.

'Right.' David nodded slowly. 'And was Jonathan in the vicinity when you fell, by any chance?'

'No, I ... Yes. It ...' Andrea turned around and leant wearily against the edge of the dining table. 'It wasn't what you're thinking, David. It was an accident.'

'I see.' David nodded again and counted silently to five. 'Andrea,' he glanced at the ceiling, 'if you knew how many times I'd heard that.'

'David, it wasn't ... He didn't—'

'How many times I've had people, women mostly, come into my surgery with bruises, broken bones, smashed in faces—'

'David, don't!' Andrea pushed herself away from the table.

'They all trip or fall, Andrea! Or walk into doors. I've heard every conceivable excuse there is for a bruise that was more probably caused by a fist!'

'It was not!' Andrea stood her ground adamantly, but glanced away again under his questioning gaze.

David closed his eyes, furious inside. He didn't want to upset her. He didn't want to frighten her, and he possibly was, but he most definitely wanted the truth. 'Did you argue?' he asked more quietly.

Andrea deliberated. David waited.

She nodded, finally. 'The bruise was an accident, but, yes, we did argue.'

And that, as far as David was concerned, was enough. An argument that resulted in a person sustaining physical injury meant it was a violent one. 'And did you resolve anything?' he asked, his throat tight. As in, did Eden admit he was a thieving piece of scum?

Andrea shook her head. 'Not really.'

No, David thought not. 'There are some things I need to tell you, Andrea.' He made up his mind. For her own sake, she needed to know. 'About Jonathan's business dealings.'

'I'm not sure I want to hear them, David. You didn't exactly warm to him, after all, did you?'

For personal reasons, David knew she meant, and wasn't sure how to answer.

'I need to get some things from the car.' Andrea made to walk past him.

'Andrea, hear me out, please?' David caught her arm. 'It's important.'

Andrea scanned his eyes, nodded slowly, then glanced down to his hold on her arm.

Which was wholly inappropriate this time, David realised, dropping his hand away. 'Jonathan was hiding something,' he went on, 'a policy document. Dee got wind of it and—'

'Don't be ridiculous! Why would Jonathan be hiding the insurance documents? The assessors have already been. He—'

'Not the household insurance documents, Andrea, investment documents.'

Andrea looked at him as if he'd taken leave of his senses. 'Right,' she nodded, obviously unconvinced. 'Whose? And why?'

David hesitated. 'I'm not at liberty to say whose. As for why, because they're forged,' he said bluntly.

Andrea's mouth dropped open. 'What?'

'They're forged, Andrea. He never invested the money. The document proves he never made the investment.'

'You're mad.' Andrea laughed, disbelieving.

David dragged his hand over his neck. 'It's the truth, Andrea, I swear.'

'This is unbelievable.' Andrea shook her head incredulously. 'It really is. The clients take income from their investments, Doctor Einstein! Withdrawals! How could they do that if there was never any investment in the first place?'

'He's been paying income from other investments coming in, Andrea,' David persisted. 'That's why the client never suspects—'

Andrea walked past him to the door. 'You're talking absolute rubbish,' she snapped angrily.

David skirted around her. 'Andrea, I'm not. He's running a fraudulent operation. He was never going to tell you and you bloody well need to know!'

Andrea stared at him, the look on her face still one of absolute incredulity.

'It's known as a Ponzi scheme,' David pushed on, forcing the point painfully home, and hating himself for it. 'It's an operation that pays returns to its investors from their own money or money paid by subsequent investors. The company running the scheme entices new investors by offering higher returns than other investments.'

David stopped, feeling like a total shit. If she was hurt before, this time she'd be devastated. What choice did he have, though? He really needed to open her eyes to the fact that Jonathan Eden was bad news. Back to the wall, he was dangerous; David truly believed that. And seeing that bruise on Andrea's face scared him.

'And you have evidence of all this, do you?' Andrea asked, her cheeks ablaze and her wide green eyes wild with fury.

David's heart plummeted. She didn't believe him. Why would she? Now what did he do? 'He's under investigation, but it doesn't look good,' was all he could offer, because, for now, that's all he had.

'You are mad,' Andrea said, her expression now one of utter astonishment. 'And very sad, David Adams,' she added, her meaning implicit. 'What is it with you? Are you hell-bent on ruining women's lives? If you can't fuck them you just have to fuck them up, is that it, David?'

That hit home. David felt as if he'd been physically winded. 'He's desperate, Andrea,' he said quietly. 'The last thing I want is to ruin your life. I just want you to be careful, that's—'

'You're doing a damn good job of it, David!'

Well, if she didn't hate him before, she hated him now. David swallowed a tight lump in his throat as he watched Andrea storm from the room. That was okay. He didn't need her to like him. He needed her to be alerted to the fact that Eden was a manipulative, desperate man, who had not got her interests at heart.

Eden's interests lay in getting his hands on the payout from the household insurance. David would bet his life on it. With which, he suspected Eden had been intending to replace the investment monies he'd stolen from Eva – hopefully before Eva found out they weren't there. Which begged the question, if the house hadn't burnt to the ground, where had Eden been intending to get those funds from? It struck David that it was far too convenient that his house just happened to catch fire, almost killing his family in the process. Add to that Eden's disappearing act, which had nothing to do with him being hospitalised, his digging around the burned out house when he finally did show up – hoping to locate the forged document in Dee's belongings, David guessed; his general evasiveness ...

Now it was beginning to add up.

And there was no convenience about it. David raked his hand angrily through his hair. That fire was fucking well planned and Andrea needed to know, at least enough to want to get well away from the bastard. If she despised him because he'd told her what she didn't want to hear, then he'd just have to learn to live with it.

Chapter Twenty-Five

David waited for a lull in the surgery then tapped on Doctor Paton's door and poked his head around it. 'Have you got a sec?' he asked.

'Hi, David.' She smiled and beckoned him in. 'How's it going?'

'Hectic. Five people with flu symptoms already this evening.'

'Ah, that'll be the flu symptoms they've been told to stay at home with. If you thought working here was going to be a holiday, David, you've been sadly misinformed.'

David smiled. 'I didn't, though I didn't think it would be quite so busy, I must admit.'

'Manic Monday.' Doctor Paton nodded knowledgeably. 'People tend to get sicker on Mondays than they do on Fridays.'

'Tell me about it.' David parked himself tiredly in her visitor's chair.

'You might do better for a good night's sleep,' she suggested, peering at him over her glasses.

David laughed ruefully. 'And that.' Between rattling pipes, nightmares, worrying about Jake, Andrea, Sally and imminent babies, he doubted he'd get another decent night's sleep ever again.

'So what can I do for you?' Doctor Paton twirled away from her monitor to give him her full attention.

'Sally Anderson,' David got straight to the point, 'I believe she's recently swapped to your list.'

'Oh, dear, she's not enamoured of your considerable charms, then?'

'Er, no, obviously not. I just wondered—'

'I hope you're not about to ask me to break patient confidentiality, Doctor Adams?'

'No.' David did his best to look the picture of innocence. 'Well, bend it a little maybe,' he admitted, with his best winning smile.

Doctor Paton arched an eyebrow.

'I saw her socially, at a dinner party,' he lied, but more out of concern for Sally than himself. As far as he knew she hadn't done anything about that scan yet and, given her history, David thought she should, sooner rather than later. 'She had to leave early, stomach pains, and I thought as she's pregnant, I'd mention—'

'Pregnant?' Doctor Paton now looked surprised at him over her glasses. 'Really?' She furrowed her brow. 'Well, obviously I can't divulge information, but … Are you all right, David? You've gone quite pale.'

David was too stunned to speak for a second. She'd seen Doctor Paton. Had the bloody pregnancy confirmed by her, she'd said. And Doctor Paton didn't *know* she was pregnant?

'David?'

'What? Oh, yes.' He forced another smile and shakily got to his feet. 'I, er … Jake. I just remembered I was supposed to pick him up.'

'Uh, oh.' Doctor Paton chuckled, turning back her monitor. 'Someone's not going to be very happy.'

No, David thought heading swiftly for the door, someone is most definitely not.

With Ryan out with Jake and her gran having a snooze, Sophie chose her moment to tackle her mum about what she'd overheard David and her arguing about. She didn't know what to make of him with everything that had gone on, but after also seeing the argument between Jonathan and her mum, and her gran acting nuttier than a fruitcake, Sophie wanted answers. 'Mum?'

'Hmm?' Andrea basted the roast chicken they were having as a celebratory dinner – now they'd actually got an oven to cook one in – and fed it back into the oven.

'Can I ask you something?' Sophie continued peeling her potato, determined to do the whole thing and get one long spiral.

'Ask away,' Andrea said, checking Sophie's nut roast, and then turning to the fridge, which was well stocked with loads of Eva's vegetables.

'About David.'

'Oh.'

Sophie could feel the vibes across the room. Her mum might make out she wasn't interested in him, but it didn't take a genius to work that out. 'He's kind of all right, isn't he?'

'He's been absolutely wonderful, Sophie.' Andrea clanged the fridge door closed. 'But I'm not sure I know him well enough to say whether he's all right, or not.'

Yeah, right. 'I mean he's obviously a total idiot, getting someone pregnant when he's a doctor – like, hello, condoms.'

'Sophie!'

'What? It's not like I haven't heard of them, you'll be relieved to know.'

'What do you mean, relieved?' Andrea asked, apprehensively.

Sophie glanced behind her, noted her mum wide-eyed with alarm and rolled her own eyes ceilingwards. 'I mean, I won't make the same mistake Sally made, if I ever go near a boy that is, which I won't 'cos they're totally gross.'

'Oh, good,' Andrea said shakily.

Sophie rolled her eyes again and then – pants – broke her spiral. 'He is kind of okay, though, isn't he?' She plucked up another potato and started afresh.

'I suppose so, yes.' Andrea peered over her shoulder into the bowl. 'You're supposed to peel the whole potato, Sophie, not half of it.'

'I am. I'm just doing it my way instead of the boring way. So, what were you two arguing about?' Sophie went back to her spiralling endeavours. 'You and David, I mean.'

'We weren't arguing, Sophie, we were talking.'

'Okay, talking about then?' Sophie shrugged. 'It's just, I heard some of it, and what with Jonathan acting really weird and Gran driving me mental, hiding things in wardrobes and banging on about him doing away with her, I just wondered ...' Sophie sighed as the doorbell rang and her latest spiral plopped into the sink '... if David might be right? About Jonathan's business dealings, I mean.'

No answer from her mum, Sophie turned around. 'Typical,' she muttered, realising she was talking to herself. 'Just ignore me, why don't you?'

Andrea sighed as she headed for the door. It seemed David really did charm everyone he came into contact with, including her own daughter, who, in Andrea's estimation had been right in her previous opinion of him. He really was too nice to be true. Far too nice. If ever anyone was a manipulator and a con artist, it was David-oh-so-charismatic-Adams. The man was some kind of delusional sociopath, pretending to be caring and loving, when he was blatantly promiscuous and probably incapable of love; determined to control women in some twisted way. Why else would he go to the trouble of decorating three floors of an apartment, if not to keep tabs on her, for reasons she simply couldn't fathom. It wasn't as if he had time on his hands, and it certainly wasn't as if he couldn't attract the attention of many a not-so-dim young thing, women far sexier and prettier than she.

He already had. Sally for one, who might not be much

younger, but was certainly prettier, and who Andrea absolutely didn't believe he'd only ever met once. It was just too preposterous that he, a doctor, would make the kind of 'mistake' he had. The man was a liar. The worst part was, she'd been fool enough to fall for his lies, for him – at least until he'd spouted that last load of outrageous twaddle. She didn't believe it. Not any of it.

Well, God help Sally, that's all Andrea could think. They'd both obviously been taken in, Sally and she, along with probably a multitude of other unsuspecting women, but at least she could walk away reasonably unscathed. Poor Sally was having the man's baby.

They were here though. And the apartment, Andrea had to admit, was lovely. So, for her family's sake, this is where they would stay, until they chose to do otherwise. There was no doubt that Jonathan had some explaining to do. Andrea reached for the door. And explain he would, once ...

'Jonathan?'

'I'm hoping you won't slam that in my face.' Jonathan nodded at the door. 'I wouldn't blame you if you did. There's no point saying I'm sorry, I know, but can we at least talk, Andrea?' He shrugged sadly. 'For Chloe's sake?'

'We need to talk,' David addressed Sally shortly, his temper on a short fuse after knocking repeatedly. Having glimpsed her through the window, he'd known damn well she was in.

Sally peered at him through the half open door. 'David, I can't. I'm not feeling very ... sociable. Can you ...?' Sally stopped, no doubt noting David wasn't actually feeling very bloody sociable either. Far from it. Never mind him, did she realise what kind of trauma she might have put Jake through? Yes, David would have had to deal with it, if it were true, but ... did this woman have any bloody idea?

'Can you call back later, David? Or ring me—'

'Now, Sally,' David insisted, pressing the flat of his hand against the door. There was no way he was going anywhere until he had some answers. No way.

Sally's eyes flicked down and back to his face. Then, obviously noting his thunderous expression, she nodded and pulled the door open.

'Would you like to tell me what's going on?' David asked as calmly as he could, once inside the hall.

Taking her time, Sally closed the door and turned to look at him quizzically. 'Sorry?' she said as if she didn't have the slightest idea what he was talking about.

'Not half as sorry as I am,' David grated.

Sally shook her head. 'David, I don't …'

'What the bloody hell have you been playing at, Sally?' David demanded, now very close to losing it.

Clearly shaken, Sally stepped back. One hand on her stomach, one hand on the wall, she looked at him convincingly wide-eyed and shocked.

Oh, very good. David shook his head. Did she really intend to keep up this insane charade? Had he got idiot stamped on his head, or what? Obviously, he must have. David was torn between applauding her performance and telling her exactly what he thought of her.

'I think you owe me an explanation, Sally, don't you?' he said instead, attempting to keep his tone somewhere near civil.

'David, I don't u … Ugh.' Sally gripped her stomach more tightly.

Oh, for … David sighed and dragged a hand through his hair. 'Sally,' he started, in no mood for more games, 'just drop the bloody theatricals and tell me what the fu—' David stopped, looking at her more closely as Sally panted out a breath and leaned against the wall for support.

She looked pale. Very pale. He noted the bead of sweat

above her upper lip, the positioning of her hand. Her eyes squeezed closed now, two hands against her stomach, the woman was most definitely in pain.

'Sally …?' David caught her as her legs gave way. Scooping her into his arms, he carried her to the lounge and placed her gently on the sofa. 'Where's the pain, Sally? Can you show me?'

'Mmmmf,' was all Sally could muffle, placing her hand to the right of her abdomen.

'Let me take a look.' David reached to ease her hand away but Sally recoiled. 'Sally, I need to examine you,' he said, careful to keep his tone professional now – and considerably softer than it had been.

'No!' Sally tried to scramble away, now looking terrified. 'I don't want you … Oooh, God!'

'Sally, just lie still.' Even doubling up, the woman wouldn't let him near her, though it was obvious she really was in severe discomfort. Exasperated, and growing very concerned, David tried again. 'Sally, I won't hurt you. I just need to—'

'No,' Sally whimpered. 'I—'

'Sally …' David raked his hand though his hair as she attempted to lever herself from the sofa, and failed. 'For Pete's sake, Sally, I know you're not pregnant!'

Or was she? David tried to still a sudden panic as he realised there was a possibility she might be. That she might be miscarrying. Or worse, that it could even be an ectopic pregnancy, in which case …

'Sally, please,' he tried. 'I'm not angry. I'm concerned, that's all. Please let me examine you. It could be serious.'

Catching a sob in her throat, Sally looked at him tearfully and, finally relented.

David sighed with relief and pressed a hand softly on her stomach. The uterus definitely wasn't raised above the pelvic bones he established quickly, ergo no physical sign of pregnancy. 'Show me where it hurts, Sally. Can you do that?'

David cursed his initial abruptness and made sure to be as gentle as he could.

Sally's hand strayed again to the right side of her abdomen.

'Here?' David checked for rebound tenderness, pressing lightly over the area.

'Yes!' she winced, obviously experiencing more tenderness as he released the pressure. The muscles were tensing in response to touch, too. 'Is it constant?' he asked, searching her face, feeling her forehead. Her temperature was probably through the roof.

She nodded. 'Yes. It wasn't, but it is now.'

'Right.' Cautiously, not wanting to upset her any more than he already had, David quickly tested for pain on flexion of the hip, pain on the right side.

'Any sickness?'

Sally nodded again, her breathing definitely indicating acute pain.

'Loss of appetite?'

Getting an affirmative on the latter, too, David didn't waste any more time. 'I think it could be appendicitis. We have to get you to the hospital.' Which, calculating the time it would take an ambulance to arrive, would probably be quicker by car, he decided.

Once again, Sally seemed reluctant to let him help her. No surprise there, David supposed, given how he'd barged in … and why.

'Sally, it might burst, in which case it will release bacteria and cause severe infection. Come on, please. You can trust me, I'm a doctor.' David tried a smile.

Sally looked at him guardedly then, but acquiesced, allowing him to ease her from the sofa into his arms.

'We'll straighten the cushions later.' David gave her another reassuring smile and headed as fast as he could to the hall.

Sally managed a weak smile back. 'I bet you hate me, don't you?' she said as he manoeuvred her out through the front door.

'I don't hate you, Sally,' David assured her, carrying her across the road, to the surprise of one or two onlookers.

Sally grimaced and rested her head on his shoulder. 'But you don't love me?'

David hesitated. 'You're a beautiful woman, Sally. I like you but, no, I'm not in love with you.'

'Did you love your wife?' she asked weakly.

'Very much,' David said adamantly.

'Do you love Andrea?'

David debated, then, 'Yes, I believe I do,' he admitted.

'Tell her I love her, too. Will you do that?'

'I will.' David nodded. 'But you can tell her yourself.' At least she could if he could get her into the bloody car and to the hospital asap. Dammit, where were his ...

'Sweeping women off their feet, I see. Again,' Ryan observed, arriving most definitely like the cavalry, just in time.

'Keys,' David instructed shortly. 'Left jacket pocket.'

'What's up, Dad?' Jake asked, standing off with Homer and Dougal as Ryan, obviously sensing the emergency, dutifully obliged and unlocked the car.

'Appendicitis, I think,' David called, lowering Sally gently inside. 'Ryan could you ...?' He nodded towards Jake and ran around to the driver's side.

'No probs.' Ryan nodded maturely and nodded David on.

'So the insurers are definitely going to pay up?' Andrea held Jonathan's gaze, looking for signs he might still be spinning her a web of lies.

'I can't know that for certain, but I've had confirmation and I'll keep chasing it, obviously,' Jonathan promised. 'I am sorry, truly, Andrea, for everything. I know there are no excuses for raising my voice the way I did. I ...' Jonathan trailed off, glancing down under Andrea's astounded gaze.

Raising his voice? Andrea stared hard at him. Had he any idea how much he'd terrified her? How upset the children had been?

'I was stressed, Andy.' Jonathan walked towards the window, having refused the offer of a seat.

'You were stressed?' Andrea said incredulously behind him.

Jonathan sighed. Plunging his hands in his pockets, he looked pensively out at the night sky. 'We all are, I know. I'm not trying to lay blame here, Andrea. It was my fault, no one else's. I lost it. What can I say?'

'Not a lot.'

Jonathan sighed again, and nodded. 'So,' he said turning back with a shrug, 'there's nothing I can do to put things right, then?'

Andrea looked him over. He looked terrible. His eyes were bloodshot. He'd lost weight. He seemed genuinely remorseful, but ... even if he had a magic wand to wave, even if he could make their house rise from the ashes, make the hurt go away, the fear and the uncertainty, having shown his dark side, he couldn't rekindle her love for him. She breathed in, bracing herself to say what needed to be said, possibly should have been said, before fate had so cruelly intervened. 'I'm not sure there is, Jonathan. I think I need to be on my own, for now at least.'

Jonathan nodded slowly again and looked at her, a long searching look. 'Do you love him?' he asked quietly.

Andrea glanced down.

'It's not rocket science, Andrea!' Jonathan shouted then, causing her to almost jump out of her skin. 'It's a yes or no answer. I said, do you—' Jonathan stopped as the lounge door opened.

'What's he doing here?' Sophie demanded, looking Jonathan up and down, an angry flush to her cheeks.

Jonathan shook his head. 'Nice to see you, too, Sophie,' he said, smiling sardonically.

Sophie ignored him. 'Mum?'

'We're just talking, sweetie,' Andrea assured her. 'He won't be here long.'

Sophie shot her an admonishing glance. 'Yeah, right, I've heard that one before.'

'Sophie, he—'

'I came to say goodbye,' Jonathan interrupted. 'Don't worry, Sophie, I'll soon be out of your hair.'

Glancing at him quizzically, Andrea turned back to Sophie. 'We won't be long, I promise. Go on, go and keep an eye on your gran for me. I'll be with you in a minute.'

'Someone needs to keep an eye on her, that's for sure,' Jonathan muttered.

Andrea's jaw tightened, along with her resolve. She shouldn't have let him in. No matter how plausible his apologies, no matter how puppy-dog-eyed and dishevelled he'd looked, once he'd relayed that the household insurers were finally going to pay up, she should have told him to leave. 'And, Sophie,' she stopped her daughter short as she backed out of the room, 'don't hesitate to dial 999 if you feel you need to.'

Jonathan gawked at her, astounded. 'Bloody, hell, Andrea?'

Andrea folded her arms and said nothing.

'That bad, hey?' Jonathan smiled sadly.

'That bad, Jonathan.' Andrea's gaze didn't falter. 'So, you're leaving the area?' She picked up on what he'd just said about saying his goodbyes, though she was only interested in what he did and where he went for the sake of his daughter.

'Not a lot of point staying, is there?' Jonathan shrugged. 'I'm going tonight, so you can tell our charitable neighbour the coast is clear now, can't you?'

Andrea didn't rise to the bait. 'Where are you going?'

'London.' Jonathan leant against the edge of the dining table, his attention now on whatever speck of dust he insisted on plucking from his clothing. 'Just for a while, until I can sort myself out.'

'What about your business?'

Jonathan straightened up and turned to walk back over to the window. 'Doesn't much matter about the business any more, does it?' He shrugged again, indifferently this time.

If you say so, no. Andrea did likewise. 'I need to get on,' she said, not really wanting to listen if he was about to play the sympathy card.

'I'm in a mess,' Jonathan said as she turned to the door. 'Financially,' he went on as Andrea turned back. 'Nothing major, just ... a mess.'

'Since when?' Andrea furrowed her brow. Was that why he'd been so dead set against her doing something different? Oh no! Her eyes shot wide. Had David been right?

'A while,' Jonathan admitted. 'That's why I didn't want you to give up your job. We might have managed on one salary, but ... Anyway, it doesn't matter now, does it?' He faced her, smiling stoically. 'I might be able to raise a bit of cash from my client portfolio. I'll just sell up what business assets I have to another adviser and move on, as they say.'

'But ...' Andrea looked at him, appalled, but more with herself than with him. Why hadn't she realised? 'Why on earth didn't you say something?'

'Would it have made a difference to where we are now?'

'Yes! I ... 'Andrea stopped, because the truth was, she didn't know. If Jonathan hadn't been so distracted, so seemingly disinterested, would her head still have been turned by the obvious charms of David? Andrea nipped on her bottom lip, feeling guiltier by the second. Had she been the distracted and disinterested one?

'Pride, I suppose. I didn't want to lose face.' Jonathan glanced down and then back. 'I didn't want to lose you, Andrea, but I think I've succeeded on both counts now, haven't I?'

'Jonathan, I ...' Andrea shook her head. She didn't know what to say.

'Thought so. Right, well, I'll just piss off out of the way, then.' Jonathan smiled tightly, a flash of fury in his eyes. 'Wouldn't want to cramp Doctor Bleeding Heart's style, after all, would I? I take it you've no objections this time to my seeing Chloe, before I go?'

'She's in bed, Jonathan.' Andrea moved to block his way. With his tone back to aggressive, there was no way he was going anywhere but out of the front door. 'I don't want to wake her.'

'She is my daughter, Andrea. I mean, I've gathered I'm surplus to requirements where you're concerned, but I think I'm entitled to see my own child, don't you?'

Sophie turned from where she'd been listening outside the lounge door to tiptoe to the bedrooms. She had no idea what was going on, but she had a really bad feeling. Her gran might've sounded gaga, but the more she saw of Jonathan lately, the more she was wondering whether it was him who was mental. Whatever, she wanted Gran on her toes.

'Gran,' she whispered, going into the room her gran was sharing with her mum until they'd sorted out who was sleeping where. 'Gran, are you awa— Gran?' Pants.

'Gran?' Quickly, Sophie checked the bathroom, and then went back to the kitchen, where she noted the chicken and nut roast had been taken out of the oven, which meant her gran was up and about. God, silly old bat, where was she?

Twirling around, Sophie checked the other rooms downstairs, then climbed over the baby gate and nipped deftly upstairs. No Gran in the upstairs bathroom, she checked her own room, the wardrobe, under her bed, then heaved herself up to strop back across the room.

'Gran, you ought to know I'm getting seriously peed ...' Sophie stopped as she passed Chloe's bed, and stepped back. 'Oh, crap! Mum ...?'

'Mum!' Her tummy doing a somersault inside her, Sophie thundered downstairs, almost falling over the gate, before bursting into the lounge.

'Mum?'

'I just want to say goodbye to her,' Jonathan was droning on. 'I'll be two minutes.'

'Mum!'

'Sophie, just wait a minute, will you?' Jonathan snapped. 'Your mum and I—'

'She's gone!' Sophie's screamed over him. 'Gran, Chloe! They've gone!'

Chapter Twenty-Six

'Do I look dreadful?' Sally asked, still groggy from the anaesthetic.

'Yep, but beautiful nonetheless,' David assured her.

Sally's mouth curved into the tiniest of smiles. 'Flatterer,' she mumbled.

David smiled back, and squeezed her hand. He watched as Sally's eyelids grew heavy. She'd drift in and out for a while, he guessed. The painkillers were obviously doing their job. She'd be sore, but she was alive, fortunately. The appendix had been gangrenous, dangerously close to bursting. Why she hadn't called an ambulance before, he couldn't fathom. Yes, he could, he realised, instinctively checking the drip before he left.

Because she hadn't wanted an ambulance pulling up to alert him to the fact that he wasn't an expectant father, after all.

David felt a pang of regret. Having again been reminded that life was too short, far from being furious with Sally, he now felt sorry for her. Sorry that he'd used her. Yes, it might have been mutual, but ... Did he really imagine he was the only one in need of solace? That only he wanted someone to help him release the pent-up frustration that comes with loss of love, faith, life? Detached sex didn't work, he'd learned that now. There was always baggage around it. Always consequences. She'd obviously been depressed, very, if she'd been on anti-depressants, which she'd admitted she had before she'd gone down for surgery. The consequences, he now realised, could actually have been a lot worse.

'I'll be back,' he promised, leaving her to get some sleep. He'd collect some stuff for her, he decided, a nightdress, toiletries, etc. He hadn't really got a clue what she might need, though. Andrea would be the best person to ask, he supposed, assuming she'd give him the time of day, which he very much doubted after his revelations about Eden. David fervently wished he'd kept his mouth shut. Andrea would have found out eventually just what kind of snake in the grass the guy was. But then, David's concern had been about what might happen in the interim.

Sighing, he headed off down the corridor, remembering he'd had a text alert as he did. Pulling his mobile from his pocket, he checked it as he walked and noted he'd actually had several texts, plus two missed calls – all from Ryan. Jake? Speed dialling Ryan back as he broke into a run, David banged through the exit doors and stopped dead.

'Missing?' He tried to make sense of what Ryan was saying. 'What, Dee and Chloe? Shit! I'm on my way.'

'Sophie, where are you going?' Andrea shouted, berated herself for shouting, then tried to breathe past the tight knot in her chest.

'To meet Ryan!' Sophie shouted back, already half out of the door. 'To look for them, Mum. Where d'y'think? There's no point in us all standing around here.'

Andrea closed her eyes. 'Go.' She nodded, trying to stay calm, to think rationally when all rational thought seemed to have deserted her. 'But be careful!'

'I will.' Sophie headed off, down through the shop.

'Phone me if you hear anything,' Andrea called after her. 'And keep your mobile switched on.'

'It's on,' Sophie called back, and then she, too, was gone – into the dark night, and Andrea didn't think she could bear to do this, not all over again. 'Where *are* they?' She turned back to Jonathan, panic gripping her stomach like a vice.

'I don't know,' Jonathan said, looking as shocked as she felt. 'I …'

'The police?' Andrea turned towards him, dragging her

hands over her face, through her hair. 'You said they were coming. They should be here by now, surely? Where are they?'

'Andrea, I don't know.' Jonathan shrugged helplessly. 'On their way probably.'

'But why are they taking so long?' Andrea checked her watch, where the last ten minutes had ticked heavily by like ten hours and two lifetimes. 'We need to ring them again,' she said, searching fruitlessly for her own mobile. 'They shouldn't be taking—'

'I have, Andrea! I've rung them twice. They'll be here soon.' Jonathan came towards her, tried to wrap his arms around her.

Andrea pulled away. 'I have to go,' she said.

'Go … where?'

'Sophie's right. We have to look. Scour the streets. There's no point—'

'Andrea, wait,' Jonathan said as she flew to the door. 'I'm coming with you.'

'No, you need to stay here. Someone needs to be here.'

'She's my daughter, Andrea.' Jonathan caught up with her. 'If anything's happened to her because of that demented, old …'

Andrea turned back, blind fury bubbling up in her chest. 'She's my daughter, too! And that's my mother you're talking about!' She flailed a hand at him, uselessly. She had no strength. Nothing left. She couldn't do this. Couldn't.

Jonathan caught her wrists. 'Stop,' he said firmly. 'Breathe, Andrea. Come on. It'll be all right. We'll find them. The lights were still on at Tiny Tots. We'll ask Beki to keep an eye on things here. Okay?'

Andrea nodded and shook her head all at once, then hurried off ahead of him, impatient to go, to be doing something; anything.

'We'll go together. My car's out front,' Jonathan said behind her as Andrea hit the street. 'You keep a lookout, I'll drive.'

Andrea caught the keys he tossed to her and climbed in the passenger side. She didn't want to discuss it, didn't want to talk. She just wanted to go. 'Come on,' she urged him as Jonathan tried to attract Beki's attention through her shop window. She was obviously stocktaking, probably out back. 'Hurry up. Please.'

Where were they? Andrea gulped back another nauseating wave of panic as she waited. Where would her mother take Chloe at this time of night? It would be pitch black out of the village. There wasn't even a moon. Where could she have ...?

Oh no, no ... 'She's gone home,' she said numbly as Jonathan climbed in the driver's side. Fear settling like ice in her chest, Andrea pictured the little riverside cottage at the dead of night. It was under renovation; she recalled with sinking dread, building works beyond it – and two huge river locks only yards in front of it.

Humping the car half on the pavement in his haste to park it, David banged out of the driver's side. 'Any news?' he shouted to the group now gathered outside the shop.

'Nothing,' the girl from the Tiny Tots shop said. 'They're all out,' she added as David ran towards the entrance to Andrea's flat.

'Searching,' Eva said anxiously. 'We were just organising a search group ourselves.'

'Has someone notified the police?' David asked, never more relieved to see a group of gossiping neighbours. Please, someone find them, and soon. Andrea would be insane with worry. What on earth had possessed the old woman to ...?

'Jonathan,' the girl supplied. 'He said he'd phoned them twice and asked me to wait here in case they came.'

Eden? Cold foreboding washed over David. 'Right,' he said tightly, exchanging concerned glances with Eva.

Dammit, what had he been thinking? He should have

informed the police the old woman was living in fear of her life, instead of waiting around for the investment company to complete its bloody investigations; for the household insurers to pay out, which David had truly hoped they would, as it would have meant there were no suspicious circumstances around the cause of the fire. His gut told him differently but David would much prefer Eden had played no part in it, for Andrea's sake. Maybe he hadn't. Maybe he'd never intended his family any harm, possibly didn't intend Dee any harm, but she had been worried about what lengths he might go to in trying to retrieve that document, that evidence of his fraudulence. That's why she'd taken off into the damp, dark night when Eden showed up. Why she'd taken Chloe though, David couldn't understand.

Unless ... Had she thought Eden might take her? It was possible, absconding with his daughter seeming a better option than fighting for custody through the courts, particularly if his character turned out to be questionable.

So what the hell did he do now? Search, David supposed, though with no streetlights beyond the village, it would be like searching for the proverbial needle in a haystack. At least he'd got Ryan with him, which might help in terms of possible locations. Jake was with them too. David would prefer he wasn't, but he'd had no choices there. At least he'd be another set of eyes.

'We'll drive around,' he said, offering Eva a reassuring smile. She looked worried to death, too. Her face was ashen. Whatever he was up to, that bastard Eden had got one hell of a lot to answer for. David swallowed back his anger as he turned back to his car.

'Anything from Sophie yet?' he asked Ryan, climbing inside.

'Nothing,' Ryan said, thumbing another text urgently into his phone.

'Your mum?'

'Nope.' Ryan sighed.

'She might have left her mobile upstairs,' Jake suggested, nodding towards the shop. 'If she was worried, I mean. She could've come out without it.'

'Good thinking, Jake.' David climbed out again. 'I'll be two minutes.'

'I'll try Jonathan,' Ryan said behind him.

It actually took David one minute to locate the missing phone. Ringing it as he let himself in with his spare set of keys, he'd walked straight over to where it had apparently fallen – into Jonathan's overcoat pocket?

Sophie hadn't been sure what she was going to ask if there was anyone around. 'Helloo, you haven't seen a barmy old bat tripping along the towpath in her nightie, have you?' she fancied might make her sound as loopy as her gran.

The place was deserted though. Not a soul about, making it dead creepy. The old British Waterways cottage looked like it was empty, too. Apprehensively, Sophie tucked her mobile in her pocket and ducked under the scaffolding to try the front door. Locked. Pants.

Now what did she do? Stepping back, she glanced at the windows upstairs and down, all dark, like blind eyes watching her. Sophie shuddered as a cold shiver ran the length of her spine. She'd thought her gran might be in there. Obviously, she wasn't. She had a listen. Not a sound, bar the plop-plopping she kept hearing from the water, which was totally spooking her. The wind whipping the trees were giving her the collywobbles, too.

And the crunches on the gravel she could swear she could hear behind ... 'Crap!' Sophie nearly shot out of her trainers as some prehistoric looking bird with a wingspan of yards took off in the distance to swoop low over the weir.

She didn't like it here. Growing more apprehensive as she

stood alone in the unfriendly night, Sophie looked sharply over her shoulder, definitely hearing something behind her now, a scuffling and shuffling, like a ... 'Oooh, God,' ... if it was a water rat, she was gone. Outta there.

She didn't fancy going back the way she'd come, though. Nervously, she peered back across the locks to where the taxi had dropped her off, and then blinked, then blinked again, then swallowed.

Oh no. Oh no. She took a step back, away from the pale apparition floating petrifyingly along the footbridge. Oh, G— 'Gran!' Sophie scowled and planted her hands on her hips as Dee came into view. 'What the bloody hell are you doin', Gran? You almost gave me a heart attack.'

'Going home,' Dee said, bypassing her to head for the front door, Chloe in her arms.

'I gathered,' Sophie said, reaching for Chloe, who at least had her denim jacket on over her jim-jams. Her gran too had a coat on over her nightie, which Sophie supposed was slightly less embarrassing than it might have been.

'But how did you get here?' she asked as Dee ferreted in her coat pockets.

'By taxi, obviously,' Dee informed her. 'I haven't sprouted wings yet, much to Jonathan's disappointment.'

'Right.' Sophie rolled her eyes. 'Um, Gran, how're you going to get in?'

'Key,' Dee announced, producing said key from her coat, bobbing under the scaffolding and letting herself in.

'Right.' Sophie nodded resignedly as Chloe jiggled and said, 'Sophie, wanna wee-wee.'

'Hurry up then, Sophie,' Dee gestured her on in, 'before the child wets her knickers.'

'I think I already did.' Sophie sighed, ducked, and shuffled inside.

* * *

Assuming the High Street had already been checked, David double-checked it anyway, hoping that Dee had realised it was way too late and cold to be wandering around with Chloe and decided to come back home. Waiting in a doorway, possibly, making sure Jonathan's car wasn't around?

David slowed at all likely doorways, then cruised to a stop as he noted a parked police patrol car, also noting the premises it was parked outside of – Jonathan Eden Investment Management Services, no less. Strange they should be calling here when the shop Andrea's apartment was over, and presumably the address Eden would have given when he'd called, was the other end of the High Street.

'I'll just have a quick word. See if they have any news,' David said to Ryan, whose complexion had drained of all colour, he noticed. Yes, Eden most definitely had a lot to answer for. And answer he would if David got hold of him.

It didn't take long for him to establish the police were not looking for Dee and Chloe. David had wondered about the police being so keen to attend a callout regarding a grandmother gone missing with her own grandchild when they'd only been missing for … what, a couple of hours? It didn't add up to David. This did though. Apparently, it was Eden they were looking for. In regard to a certain other premises, David pondered, one that had conveniently caught fire? Eden hadn't called them. That much was clear. There was no way he would want the police sniffing around now, which is why Andrea's phone had got lost in his bloody pocket.

Yes, the man most definitely had some questions to answer, and David would like no better pleasure than to put those questions to him, preferably in some secluded location. 'No news,' he said, offering Ryan a small smile as he climbed back in the car.

Ryan nodded, holding eye contact with David briefly, before looking away. 'Just don't tell me no news is good news,' he said, gazing out of the passenger window, composing himself, David guessed.

'We'll find 'em, Ryan, don't worry,' Jake said, placing a hand on Ryan's shoulder. 'We won't give up until we do. Will we, Dad?'

'We won't, Jake,' David assured his serious-faced son.

'That's what mates are for, right, Jake?' Ryan said, even now trying to look out for Jake, David realised. He didn't know who Ryan's father was or where he was, but he'd missed out big time.

Determined to do all he could, in the absence of any kind of a father, David started the engine, took a right, and a left, all eyes on pavements and passers-by as they went. No sign of the old lady.

Sighing, he took another road, then, 'Got a text!' Ryan said as David paused at a T-junction. 'It's Sophe.'

'And?' David waited, holding his breath.

'Weak signal. At the cottage. G&C safe,' Ryan read. 'She means Gran's cottage! Take a right.'

Relieved, David exhaled, and did as bid, taking a right heading for the main Worcester Road.

'It's by Diglis Locks, on the River Severn. You can park opposite, and then we approach it on foot over the locks.'

'The locks?' David wasn't sure he liked the idea of Dee climbing over lock gates with a toddler.

'It's an old British Waterways cottage,' Ryan explained. 'Only accessible via the towpath, at least until they've finished the renovations. David,' he hesitated, 'do you think Jonathan was right, about Gran needing to go away, I mean?'

David tensed his grip on the wheel and glanced sideways at Ryan, debating. Should he tell him? Some, he decided, but not all of it. The fire and probable cause of it, he'd leave out. He couldn't justify dropping that kind of bombshell without being sure that's why the police wanted to 'have a word' with

Eden. The rest? If Andrea wanted nothing to do with him again, so be it. But she'd need someone to look out for her. David reckoned Ryan might be man enough to do that.

'Truthfully ...' David tugged in a breath. '... no, Ryan, I don't. I think it was Dee who was right thinking she needed to get away from Jonathan.'

Sophie read the document Dee handed to her, then re-read it and blinked at her gran, puzzled. 'I don't get it. What's it supposed to prove?'

'It's a forgery,' Dee said, her chin jutting determinedly. 'Jonathan never invested Eva's money. This ...' She jabbed a finger at the evidence. '... proves he intended to defraud the old bat out of her cash. He knows I have it and he wants it back. But I'm ...' She jabbed her finger at her chest. '... not about to let him have it.'

'Sophie, want upsies,' Chloe demanded, hanging onto Sophie's jumper.

'Inaminit munchkin.' Sophie looked from the piece of paper to her gran and back worriedly. The document didn't look like a fake, but then what did a fake look like? If it was genuine though, it must mean Jonathan had stolen the money, she supposed. 'Is that why you thought he was trying to do away with you, Gran?' She eyed Dee, concerned.

'He'd do anything to get that back, Sophie, you mark my words.' Dee wagged a finger at her. 'And then, if he couldn't bump me off, he wanted me shipped off to some old fogies home where everyone would think I was totally gaga. Well, I'm not, so there!'

Dee stopped jabbing and wagging fingers to fold her arms, defiantly.

'I know you're not, Gran.' Sophie felt her cheeks flush up to her emo anime hairdo.

'He's not taking Chloe either,' Dee said, somewhat

328

placated but still adamant. 'Thought he'd "say hello to her", wants to "say goodbye to her", my eye. Do I look like I was born yesterday?'

Sophie looked her gran over, more worried than ever now. Jonathan had said he was going away, but … he wouldn't take Chloe. Would he?

'No, Gran, you don't,' she assured her. 'Come on,' she said, giving her a firm hug, 'let's find somewhere we can all sit and cuddle up together until Ryan gets here.'

The document still in her hand, Sophie reached to pick up a jiggling Chloe, and then froze as a torch beam illuminated a thousand dust motes through the window.

'Crap!' Sophie gulped back her racing heart. 'That'll be Ryan.' She looked towards the front door, relieved for the first time since forever to be setting eyes on her annoying brother.

'But it might not,' Dee whispered, clutching her arm as the torch beam swept the walls. 'It might be him.' At which she turned to flee to the kitchen.

'Gran, wait!' Sophie hissed, struggling to get hold of Chloe, who'd given up on the jiggling and was gearing up for a tantrum. Oooh, Gran! 'Come on, Chloe, let's go find Granny, shall we?'

'No want to,' Chloe whined and dug her heels in.

'Chloe, come on munchkin,' Sophie tried to lift her, eyeing the door in panic as the door handle rattled.

'Nooo want to,' Chloe wailed.

'Chloe?' Jonathan's voice came from outside.

'Want Dad-dee,' Chloe wriggled, and …

'Crap!' Sophie lost her grip on her as the front door banged wide.

'What the bloody hell's going on?' Jonathan demanded. 'Come here, baby.' He swept a snotty-nosed Chloe up into his arms and glared at Sophie furiously.

'Nothing. I ...' Sophie stuttered, torn between turning tail after her gran and nipping past him through the front door. 'We—'

'Sophie?' Andrea came in behind Jonathan, eyeing her accusingly. Far from being relieved, Sophie felt as if she'd been tried, judged and was about to be executed. Hello, not guilty, she wanted to point out, but guessed by the look on both their faces they weren't about to start listening.

'Gran,' she waved an arm behind her, 'she—'

'Silly, senile old fool, ought to be bloody well locked up,' Jonathan seethed, taking a step forward.

'She's not senile. She's ...' Sophie stopped, her eyes falling on the document Dee had gone to such pains to keep secret lying barely six inches from Jonathan's feet. Oh, way to go, Sophe. She closed her eyes as, following her gaze, Jonathan bent to sweep the document up before she could make any attempt to try to reach it.

Straightening up, Jonathan locked eyes with hers, a question in his, Sophie noticed. He wasn't sure whether she'd seen it! 'She's worried that's all, about why she keeps forgetting things,' she went on, deciding playing ignorant was definitely her best option. 'Like she could forget she'd got Chloe in her arms when she walked out the door, barmy old bat. She's driving me mental, I swear.'

Sighing audibly, Sophie puffed up her purple fringe, rolled her eyes sky-high and turned for the kitchen.

'Why didn't you ring us, Sophie?' Andrea said behind her. 'I've been out of my mind with worry. I told you to—'

'Oh, right.' Sophie turned back, arms folded demonstratively. 'Like, have a go at me, why don't you? I only flipping found her, didn't I? There's no signal, is there, obviously.'

With which Sophie shook her head and turned to strop on to the kitchen. 'Act like normal,' she whispered in her gran's ear.

Chapter Twenty-Seven

'Jonathan's.' Ryan indicated the car, already parked on the opposite side of the lock to the cottage.

'I gathered.' David pulled up alongside it, trying to work out what the best course of action might be. The man might be guilty of no more than fraud, as if that wasn't bad enough. Was he really desperate enough to want to silence an old woman, though? Yes. David reminded himself of another old woman Eden had left lying on her doorstep. How desperate would he be now the police were involved was the worrying question.

Tugging in a breath, David looked towards the dark expanse of murky, green water in the locks. Wide-beam locks, allowing access to the River Severn. David wasn't much into boating but he was au fait enough with the area to remember these were two of the deepest locks in the country, twenty feet or so wide, ninety odd feet long and at least eighteen feet deep. Beyond them, the river. In flood, fast-flowing and deadly.

Perfect conditions for Eden to claim some kind of tragic accident, David realised, trepidation growing inside him. 'Let's go and make sure they get back across safely, hey?' Giving Ryan an encouraging smile, he reached to grab his torch from the glove compartment, indicating Jake with an incline of his head as he did.

Ryan got the drift. 'Jake,' he said, twisting to face him, 'you need to be our lookout.'

'Aw,' Jake was already half out his door, 'but I want to come.'

'Seriously, Jake,' Ryan locked eyes on his, 'we need someone to stay here, in case they come back. If they do, you need to text us, like, immediately, particularly if anyone is looking stressed or upset. You with me?'

'Ah, right. Got you.' Jake nodded and settled back in his seat.

Thankfully, thought David. His son near the water in these conditions was the last thing he wanted.

'And keep the doors locked, Jake, okay?' David instructed him as he and Ryan climbed out.

'Yup,' Jake nodded, dropping the central locking as David closed the door.

'Cheers, Ryan,' David said as they headed for the footbridge, one of those white, metallic things that moved underfoot, and which he wasn't really comfortable with, but at least it was better than walking over the actual lock gates. Heights, he thought it better not to mention to Ryan, were never really his thing.

'No probs,' Ryan said, over his shoulder. 'Oh, and in case I forget to mention it, you're all right, too. Looking out for my mum and stuff,' he added, with a nonchalant shrug.

'My pleasure,' David assured him, his eyes on his feet as the bridge bounced underneath him.

'Do you like her?' Ryan asked out of the blue as they hit the path.

David dragged his hand through his hair. 'And some,' he admitted, realising it must have been pretty obvious to everyone, Sally included, probably even before he knew it himself.

'Okay. Well, just so you know, I'm cool with it,' Ryan said, blowing out a steamy breath and nodding them on.

David wasn't sure Andrea was actually cool with it. 'Cheers, Ryan,' he said with a smile, assuming that was definitely some kind of approval.

'Wait.' David caught Ryan's arm a yard or so on. Ryan

followed his gaze, his relief palpable, as he, too, spotted the yellow beam of an oncoming torchlight.

'Is it them, do you think?' David asked.

'Not sure,' Ryan squinted into the darkness, and then laughed as Sophie's unmistakeable tones drifted towards them.

'Yeah, right. Cheers, Sophe,' she grumbled loudly to herself, 'we're really, really grateful. Of course we'll buy you some new trainers to replace the ones you've totally ruined looking out for your little sister and your gran.'

'Sophie, I'm grateful. We both are,' Andrea assured her. 'I'll buy you two pairs of—'

'I don't need looking out for,' Dee's voice cut across her. 'It's him you should be looking out for.'

'Do you think we could have a little less chat and concentrate on getting back?' Jonathan asked irritably.

Ryan shook his head. 'Yep, definitely them, I'd say.'

And from the fairly normal tone of the conversation it seemed that everybody, including Chloe, was accounted for. David breathed a sigh of relief. He would have a word with the guy. He'd already decided to do that, when he could get him on his own out of earshot of Andrea — and anyone else, a forceful word being what David had in mind. For now though, he just wanted to make sure Andrea and her family got back home safely.

'Having a strop again, I see, Sophe,' Ryan said as the group approached, Sophie heading it. 'What's up? The damp weather wilted your spikes?'

'Oh, ha-di-ha-ha. Shut it, dipstick,' Sophie imparted. 'And stop shining that bloody light in my face. Mum, tell him.'

Ryan squinted at her askew, then down to his torch, which was aimed at the ground.

'Act normal,' Sophie whispered as he glanced back at her. 'Don't let Jonathan take her,' she added quickly.

'Shit.' Ryan exchanged meaningful glances with David.

Worriedly, David looked past Sophie to where Dee, followed by Andrea and Jonathan, approached, Jonathan holding onto Chloe, he noted. Surely he wouldn't try anything here, though, would he? Was he seriously thinking of absconding with his own daughter?

'David?' Andrea paused in front of him.

'Hi.' David smiled, his gaze on Jonathan, who, as David suspected he might be, seemed reluctant to stop. 'Ryan needed a lift, so I thought I'd help.'

'Excuse us,' Jonathan said, skirting around them. 'I think my daughter's had enough fresh air for one night.'

'Davie,' Chloe said, stretching her arms out to him as they passed. 'Want Davie.' She flexed her little fingers, determinedly.

'You can't, baby. Mummy's got him,' Jonathan said, pointedly. 'Let's get in Daddy's car, shall we, where it's nice and warm.'

David twirled around, watching his progress, noting Sophie and Ryan already on the bridge ahead of him.

'I'll take her,' Ryan said, taking a step towards Jonathan. 'I've got a new app on my phone I want to show her.'

'You can show her later. She's tired.' Jonathan held Chloe just that little bit tighter.

He was, David realised, half-disbelieving. The bastard really was going to ... Uh, uh. 'Eden!' he shouted, causing Jonathan's step to falter.

David moved towards him. 'Let Ryan have Chloe, okay?'

Jonathan turned back. 'Or what?' he asked, eyeing him narrowly.

'Or so help me—' David dragged his hand through his hair.

'David?' Andrea caught his arm. 'What on earth ...?'

David glanced at her, taking his gaze off Jonathan for a second, and Jonathan took his chance.

'Shit!' David started after him as Jonathan pushed past Ryan, and then shoved Sophie aside, hard.

'Bastard,' David uttered, slowing as Sophie hit the ground, winded.

'Go!' Sophie gasped as he instinctively stopped to check on her. 'David, go!'

'Sophie!' Andrea was close behind him.

David locked eyes with her for an instant as she crouched down to Sophie, then, noting the fear in hers, he straightened up and bolted after Eden, only to grind to a halt the other side of the bridge. Standing by Jonathan's driver's side door, his arms folded and a defiant look on his face was Jake; by the passenger door stood an equally determined Dee.

It looked like the only way Eden was going to gain access to that car, was through them, and if he laid even one finger on his son ... David's jaw tensed.

'Don't do it, Jonathan,' he grated, taking a cautious step towards him.

Breathing deeply, Jonathan dragged a hand shakily across his mouth. 'Come on, baby,' he said to Chloe, still firm in his hold, but tearful, David could see, kneading her eyes, probably wondering what the hell was going on.

'Want Mummy,' Chloe whimpered.

'It's okay, baby,' Jonathan tried to reassure her. 'We'll go and get some sweeties and then we'll go somewhere fun, okay?'

'Home,' Chloe said, looking at him uncertainly.

'Home, it is,' Jonathan said tightly, turning to set off on foot, only to find Ryan blocking his way.

'Jonathan ...' David took another step towards him.

'Oh, Jonathan is it now?' Jonathan sneered, turning back.

'Look, Jonathan, you don't really want to do this, do you?'

'What? Put my own daughter in my own car. As it happens, I do. Now why don't you do us all a favour and fuck off and mind your own business, *David*.'

'David? What's going on?' Andrea said worriedly behind him.

Keeping his eyes on Jonathan, David extended an arm, gesturing her to stay back.

'*David? What's going on?*' Jonathan mimicked in soppy tones. 'You really do think he's something special, don't you?' Looking David over, he shook his head disdainfully. 'Good with his hands, is he, Andrea, our family GP? Thorough, I bet, hey, Andrea? Is that what the attraction is?'

'Jonathan, stop!' Andrea moved towards him, only to be blocked again by David.

'You know something, Andrea.' Jonathan's gaze travelled contemptuously over her. 'I thought I cared that you were ready to drop your knickers the minute he clicked his fingers, but I don't. If you're so impressed by his credentials you want to shack up with him, you're welcome, but there is no way you're moving my daughter in with another man. Got it? Now, get out of my way. All of you.'

'Mum-meee!' Chloe cried in earnest now, squirming in his arms, making Jonathan's hold on her precarious.

'She doesn't want to go with you, Jonathan!' David shouted, frustrated and terrified, because Chloe was terrified, and he had no idea what to do. 'You're yards away from that water. Do you really want to take another risk with your daughter's life?'

Jonathan debated – for a millisecond – then, apparently willing to take that risk, he walked on, to the side of David, towards the lock gates.

Shit. David's heart skidded to a stop in his chest. He was going across. 'Eden, don't!' Instinctively, David lunged towards him.

'Back off!' Jonathan spat, spinning around to face him. 'You've got my wife. You're not having my daughter, Adams, so just back off. Now!'

David stopped dead, his fear escalating. *Wife?* The man was bloody well losing it.

'If you don't …' Jonathan said, his breathing erratic, his face taut and white. He took another step sideways, another step towards the lock, and nodded meaningfully … towards the water.

What? Fuck, no! David dragged his hand over his face. 'Okay. Okay,' he said, pulling in a tight breath. 'If you want to cross, go. I won't stand in your way. But take the bridge, not the gates.'

Jonathan looked at him, looked past him to the bridge. He'd have to go around him, past Andrea. David could see the deliberation in the guy's eyes. He wasn't going to go for it. 'We'll back off, I promise,' he tried, desperately trying to keep him engaged. Keep him talking. 'Andrea?' he said behind him, hoping she'd realise they had no choice but to give him some space.

Jonathan looked at him again, a mixture of panic and pure loathing, and then he moved. Sideways. Fast. In two strides he was on the gate, endless depths of muddy lock water behind him, icy river water swirling treacherously in front of him: the twenty foot drop in between having any number of fall-breaking, bone-crushing obstructions.

Dear God, don't let him do this. David's gut twisted inside him.

Chloe was screaming.

'Chloe!' Andrea screamed behind him.

His gaze flicking towards Ryan, who was shouting into his phone, David didn't debate.

Jonathan was two, three yards along the gate, every faltering step taking that child towards possible death. Attempting to quell his rapidly rising panic, David stepped cautiously up after him. 'Grab hold of the rail, Jonathan,' he said quietly, seeing the man stumble forward another step and then seem to freeze where he stood. 'Loose one hand away from her and take hold of the rail,' he repeated it as Jonathan swayed, visibly. 'Chloe, hold tight onto Daddy's neck, baby. Can you do that?'

Jonathan held Chloe tighter. He didn't take hold of the rail. His eyes fixed on the water, he didn't look up.

'You're not taking her home, are you, Jonathan?' David asked, working to keep his tone calm.

Jonathan dragged in a deep breath. He didn't move.

David closed his eyes. 'She's cold,' he said, after a second. She was. Shivering, violently, and hiccupping now, rather than sobbing, her little body jolting in his arms with each cough. David edged carefully closer. 'Pass her to me, why don't you?'

That got his attention. Jonathan snapped his gaze up.

'She trusts you, Jonathan. You're her dad. Don't let her down.'

He was wavering; and still swaying. David swallowed back a sick taste in his throat. 'Pass her back to me, hey? You need to go, but you won't get far with a toddler in tow, Jonathan. She'll need feeding, changing. She'll need her mother.'

'She's my daughter,' lowering his face towards Chloe, Jonathan finally spoke. '*My* daughter.' He looked back to David, his distress palpable, petrifying.

'I know she is. I know you love her.' David risked another step towards him.

Shit! He cursed silently as Jonathan dropped his gaze back to the water. 'I know you didn't mean her any harm, Jonathan. But you'll bloody well harm her now if you do this. She wouldn't stand a chance, Jonathan. You *know* she wouldn't.'

'Jonathan, *please*,' Andrea begged wretchedly from the bank.

'I thought they were out.' Jonathan brought his gaze sharply back up, looking towards her. 'You said they'd all be out! I would never have hurt them. Never!' He looked between Andrea and David, his voice frantic. 'It wasn't supposed to take hold. The damage was supposed to be minor. I didn't mean for anyone to be trapped. I just needed some breathing space. Some time, that's all. An injection of cash to pay back Eva's money.'

'Told you so, didn't I?' Dee said, a triumphant edge to her tone.

'It got out of hand. I tried to … I didn't mean …' Clutching Chloe closer to him, Jonathan trailed off on a sob.

'They know, Jonathan,' David tried, desperation in his own voice. 'They know you wouldn't deliberately hurt them.'

'I saw them,' Jonathan admitted, turning back to Andrea.

'Saw who?' Andrea pleaded. 'Jonathan, you're—'

'I was *there*. I saw them. I saw him …' He nodded towards David. '… bringing the kids out. Carrying *my* baby into his house.'

Jonathan stopped, the rush of the water seeming to grow louder against the silence punctuated by the frightened whimpers of a child. 'I can understand what you see in him,' Jonathan went on, with a short, throaty laugh.

'You're scaring Chloe,' Andrea tried tremulously. 'Please, Jonathan, don't—'

'Whereas me … I just stood there. Watching. Too petrified to do anything. Too ashamed to even come back.'

'Come back now, Jonathan,' Andrea asked him, her voice catching. 'Please.'

'What's the point?' Jonathan sounded hopeless, defeated. 'There isn't any, is there? Not now. I could have killed them. I—'

'They're all fine!' David shouted urgently, seeing Jonathan reel dangerously forwards. 'But Chloe isn't fine, Jonathan,' he pointed out, tempering his tone, moving slowly towards him. 'Hand her to me, yes? Keep her safe.'

Jonathan choked out another sob. 'God!' He glanced heavenwards, then nestling his face close to Chloe's, he pulled her to him. 'Bye, baby.' He pressed a kiss on her cheek – and David stopped breathing. For a split second, it seemed as if the world had stopped turning.

'Daddy will bring you some sweeties, okay?' Jonathan said, and then he turned – and passed her to David.

It took two seconds to swing Chloe around into Andrea's waiting arms.

It was one second too long.

'*Shit!*' The gates shuddering under his feet told David the man had gone over. Riverside. Gone under. Fuck! David stumbled forward, slipped, scraped his ankle, tried to right himself; to block out the noise behind him. Sirens wailing, way too loud in his head, his own heart thundering. Fuck!

'Jonathan!' Andrea screamed as David scrambled shakily from his knees to his feet.

Scouring the swirling black depths beneath him, he was aware of the squad cars screeching to a halt in his peripheral vision. They'd be too late. Much too late. Eden had obviously gone under. 'Where the bloody hell is he?'

'There!' Jake's voice. David's gaze shot towards him, and his stomach turned over. He was too close to the edge. Way too close to the edge. 'Get back! Jake, go back!'

'I've got him,' Ryan yelled, wrapping an arm around Jake and yanking him backwards as David's instincts drove him to protect his son. 'He's there!' Ryan pointed, halting him in his tracks. 'Jonathan, he's up.'

Whirling back round, David saw him. Head and flailing hands only, he was spluttering water, swallowing lungfuls of the stuff back. He wasn't swimming. Why wasn't the stupid bastard—

'He can't swim!' Andrea shouted. 'Sophie, take Chloe.'

'No, Mum. Don't!' Sophie was adamant. 'You need to stay here.'

Dammit. He wasn't going to make it. No way would he survive long enough for the emergency services to reach him in these temperatures. No way. His heart sinking, David watched as Eden went back under and then, closing his eyes, he sucked in a breath and ... *Please God, give me strength* ... moved purposefully towards the edge.

'Dad!' He heard Jake's terrified cry as he went in, and prayed harder: that Ryan would keep a firm hold on him.

He was braced when he hit the water, but still the freezing temperature paralysed him. Move, David instructed himself, his whole body immediately juddering from the inside out. Minutes he'd got. No, more like seconds, before swimming, let alone climbing out would become impossible. Hypothermia would soon start to set in. His blood pressure and heart rate would be increasing. His body would be constricting surface blood vessels – he mentally ran through the symptoms – conserving heat for his vital organs, making him sluggish. *Hard to move.* Calling on all his energy, David turned in the direction Eden had gone under and swam.

A yard or so covered against the tide, his muscles were already tensing. He was shivering, his core temperature already dropping. Eden's would be way down.

Treading water, blinking the rank stuff out of his eyes and spitting it out of his mouth, David scanned the surface. Where the hell was he? There! Floating. Facedown. Arms splayed. Shit. *Move!* He'd be unconscious. Dead if he didn't reach him. *Swim, for fuck's sake.*

Not dead. *Deadweight.* Clothes. Too heavy. *Dammit.* His thought processes were slowing down. Couldn't ... think. Dragging in ice cold breaths that seemed to freeze in his throat, gasping them out, David finally reached Jonathan.

No movement. Face still under the water. *Turn him over*, David's brain urged him. His limbs were slow to obey.

'Dad!' He heard Jake again, his voice raw. The boy was terrified. 'Swim!'

Seizing the man's coat, David wrestled him over, then one arm supporting his head, he kicked back hard. His breathing was laboured, growing more difficult. Eden? Was he alive? David couldn't tell. Keeping the man's head above water, David spat out another mouthful. His limbs felt like lead weights. His clothes, dragging him down. Despite his best efforts, the current was taking him sideways.

Where was the bank?

Too far. No strength left.

'Dad, swim!' Jake's voice, hysterical, desperate.

Hold onto him, Ryan. Hold on.

Gates. David blinked hard, turned, and went under. Spluttering out the foul tasting water, he surfaced, and focussed.

'Dad, this way. You can do it. Swim, Dad!'

Gates. David willed himself on. *Jake* ... please give me strength.

Chapter Twenty-Eight

'Dubai?' David glanced at Ryan, incredulous.

'Apparently,' Ryan said, passing David his coffee. 'He'd booked two tickets.'

One adult, one child, David guessed, taking a sip of the warming drink gratefully.

'The police are here.' Ryan indicated the hospital reception. 'Waiting to interview him.'

David nodded. He'd assumed they would be. No doubt they'd want a statement from him, too. 'Is he okay?' he asked. He shouldn't care, he supposed, but however horrendous Eden's actions were, the man obviously needed some serious psychological help.

'Broken leg. Other than that, yes, thanks to you. I'd have let the bastard drown, myself, but ...' Ryan shrugged.

David wasn't buying it, though. Seeing someone in trouble, Ryan had been ready to leap in himself, which would have just about destroyed Andrea. 'Chloe?' he asked.

'Good. Bit bewildered. Revelling in all the attention and then she fell fast asleep. Sophie and Gran are fine, too. About your counselling suggestion, though, Gran says if you bring a psychiatrist near her, she'll give him a flying kick to the crotch.'

'Back on form then?' David laughed, and then shivered and tried to stave off another bout of the shakes.

'Definitely. Do you need another blanket?'

'You'll be tucking me in in a minute.' David's mouth curved into a smile. He was a good kid. They all were. Eden would get what he deserved, he guessed, but David suspected the man would be punished enough by his conscience.

'How's your mum doing?' he finally ventured to ask.

'Not great,' Ryan answered truthfully. 'Chloe's been discharged, so she's taken her home. She's taken Jake, too. He was a bit reluctant to go, but I assured him you were surrounded by fit looking nurses, and he's happy enough to bunk up in my room for tonight.'

No surprise there. David smiled, but quietly hoped Ryan hadn't mentioned the fit looking nurses in front of Andrea. 'Best idea, under the circumstances.' He drew in a breath, hoping she'd be okay. She was a strong person, David knew that to be true, but there had to come a time when another crisis would be one too many for the strongest of people.

He wished he could have seen her, once he was more compos mentis, spoken to her properly, but an ambulance had whisked him away from the scene and when they reached the hospital he'd been surrounded by medical staff coming and going, trying to get his core temperature up. And Chloe had obviously needed her mum by her side.

He'd check on her, as soon as he could. He wouldn't crowd her, though, he decided. Given what she'd been through, what she had to come to terms with, David imagined the last thing she'd need would be another man invading her space.

'She said she'd try to come back,' Ryan cut through his thoughts. 'As soon as I get home and everyone's settled.'

'Tell her there's no need,' David said, determined Andrea shouldn't come out again tonight. She needed to be home, in the warm, with her family. 'I'm just about finished here. They'll be discharging me soon. Could you tell her … Er, well, you know. I'll give her a call tomorrow, if that's okay.'

'I think she might be pissed if you don't.' Ryan gave him a wily look. 'Right, well, if you're sure you're okay, I'd better get gone. I need to phone Nita and explain why I stood her up tonight.'

Nita? Bloody hell, he was a braver man than David,

bearing in mind the girl's overbearing mother. 'I think you'll have a reasonable excuse as excuses go, Ryan.'

'Yeah, right. You reckon her old battle-axe of a mother will think so?' Ryan headed off, worriedly contemplating his mobile. 'Oh, by the way,' he poked his head back around the cubicle curtain, 'Jake thinks you're a hero. Should try throwing yourself in the river more often.'

'Yes, cheers, Ryan.' David smiled. Jake had looked pretty awestruck, he had to admit. Eyes like saucers, chattering excitedly on about how he could give Iron Man a run for his money. Obviously, he'd gone up in his son's estimation, which felt pretty damn good.

'I take it you know about Sally?' Eva asked, passing Andrea a cure-all cup of tea, then shooing a begrudging Kit-kit from her chair to seat herself back down.

'Sorry, Eva?' Andrea said distractedly, reaching to stroke the black cat, which obviously preferred not to be associated with someone so unlucky and slinked aloofly off out of her reach. Andrea's mind was elsewhere, in Dubai, imagining how bewildered Chloe would have been by the foreign sights, smells and sounds; by her father's uncomprehending behaviour. Andrea still couldn't believe Jonathan had actually intended to flee the country with her, to continue his dubious investment dealings somewhere that didn't have tight financial regulation.

Had he really imagined that Chloe would be better off with him? Taken away from all that she'd known, her family, her brother, her sister, trying to adjust to a climate that would be totally alien to her. How had he hoped to look after her, clothe her, feed her, keep her safe? Where would they have lived? Perhaps he'd already organised the details, Andrea's heart sank to an all-time low. He might have been planning it for months. She didn't know. She wasn't sure she wanted to.

'Sally, I wondered whether you'd heard her news?' Eva pulled Andrea's thoughts back to her kitchen.

Oh, dear, the village drums had been beating, then. It was only a matter of time, Andrea, supposed. 'Yes, Eva, I heard,' she assured her, not quite managing to muster up a smile.

'It's David I feel for.' Eva tsked and shook her head. 'I think he's handled it quite well, all things considered.'

Ye-es. Andrea did smile then, an ironic smile, one dredged up from her oversized charity boots, which she was still filling out with David's socks. Did she really want to hear about him and Sally? As therapeutic as a good gossip might be, Andrea really didn't want to contemplate David's future family arrangements. She was still trying to digest the news that, despite moving out of his house, she was apparently now living in his flat. Eva had glossed it over, saying David had expressed an interest in buying the premises for rental purposes before Andrea's house had burned down. She found that hard to believe. David Adams had been as much an unsociable beast as Eva's cat when he'd first moved to the village, having little to do with the neighbours. It was hardly likely, then, that he would have discussed buying the premises with Eva before it was even up for sale.

True, property prices were moving again, just. And, yes, it was a very desirable apartment. With rented property in increasing demand, he'd have had no trouble letting it, but he'd bought it on impulse, Andrea suspected, with her homeless situation in mind. She was thankful, how could she not be, but she couldn't be beholden to him.

But then, David hadn't intended her to be beholden, had he? He'd obviously sworn Eva to secrecy, but Eva, blushing not-very-convincingly, had 'inadvertently' spilled the beans. 'David said he'd organise intruder and fire alarms,' she'd said, worriedly fussing over her when Andrea had arrived back from the hospital. 'I'll have a word with him and try to hurry it along.'

'David?' Andrea had enquired archly, and thus, to Eva's faux-mortification, she'd found out that David was her landlord.

Beholden Andrea would be then, she supposed, in a way. She was certainly grateful, to David and Eva both. How she'd ever make amends to Eva in regard to her missing investment, Andrea had no idea. The household insurance hadn't paid out, of course. Jonathan had been trying to keep her sweet until he'd gone, Andrea imagined. She wasn't sure the arson investigators were involved yet, but she supposed they would be. She hadn't really believed her mum leaving a pan on had started the fire.

She was still struggling with the idea that Jonathan had, that he might have gone inside the house, and then surely he would have known that the children and her mum were ... An involuntary shudder shook through her. Would he ever admit to more than he had? Did she want to hear it, to then try to understand the workings of the mind of a man who saw his only hope of survival was to burn his family's home to the ground?

'He was an absolute saint, apparently,' Eva chatted on.

To herself, Andrea realised, feeling a bit rude. She really wasn't taking in half of what Eva was saying. 'Who?' she asked, trying to look the least little bit interested. If anyone was a saint, she thought, it was Eva, fussing over her, cooking food for her and her family; going out of her way to be friendly to Dee, who, true to form, was as offensive as ever.

'David,' Eva clarified. 'He was absolutely golden about the whole thing, so Sally said.'

What? Andrea almost spat out her tea. Excuse her, but since when did a man acknowledging he'd fathered an unplanned child make him a saint? She helped herself to one of Eva's custard creams and bit on it huffily.

'I'm not sure many men would be so gentlemanly about it.' Eva sipped her tea contemplatively.

Andrea slurped hers, noisily, hoping to dislodge the crumbs now wedged in her windpipe.

'He's a good man at heart,' Eva continued, with a wistful little sigh. 'He saved her life, according to Sally. Who knows what she'd have done if he hadn't turned up.'

Andrea's eyes boggled. Was she missing something here? Because, despite the fact that David undoubtedly deserved a medal for his heroic actions where Chloe was concerned, unless it had become an Olympic sport, she doubted they gave them out to men for accumulating notches on bedposts.

'Eva,' she started croakily, 'I know he's a good man. I don't dare imagine what would have happened if he hadn't ...' Andrea closed her eyes, because she absolutely could imagine '... but, the fact is, they don't give out knighthoods for inadvertently making women pregnant, as far as I know.'

'But she's not.' Eva blinked at her over her cup. 'I thought you ... Oh, dear, have I done it again?'

Andrea stared at her, incredulous. 'You mean Sally's not ... having a baby?'

'No.' Eva reached for her teapot. 'Never was, so it seems.'

'But ...' Andrea was now really struggling to digest '... David didn't say anything.' She'd popped over this morning, to make sure he was okay; to thank him. She'd wanted to throw her arms around him and kiss him, definitely felt like crying on his shoulder, but both she'd thought better of, given his personal circumstances. He'd never said a word.

'Yes, well, he wouldn't have, would he?' Eva finished pouring the tea and planted the pot down. 'What would he say, Andrea? Oh, by the way, Sally's not pregnant, so I'm available?'

Passing Andrea her cup, Eva held her gaze. 'The man's in love with you, my dear. He doesn't want you to think that he's glib about making another woman pregnant; about not telling you he'd had a ... liaison ... with Sally before you heard it from her.'

Andrea took the cup, and continued to stare at Eva dumbfounded.

'I'm not condoning what he did, but he's a red-blooded man who was searching for the warmth of a woman's embrace having not long lost his wife as far I can ... Andrea close your mouth, dear, you look like a goldfish.'

Eva passed Andrea a napkin. Andrea blew her nose on it.

'And correct me if I'm wrong, but Sally's not really the sort who would be running chastely in the other direction, is she?'

'No, but ...' Andrea started, ready to jump to Sally's defence, but then realised she couldn't. Far from fleeing in the other direction, having just witnessed her husband with another woman, Sally would have welcomed the attentions of someone like David. Encouraged it, knowing Sally. 'She'd just found out Nick was cheating on her.' Andrea knitted her brow, looking confusedly down at her tea, then back to Eva.

'Well, there you go then. She was obviously looking for a man to make her feel better, and pardon me for saying so, but if I was looking for the same, Doctor Adams would do very nicely.'

'Eva ...' Andrea laughed.

'I'd take him over a chocolate éclair any day.' Eva chuckled, helped herself to custard cream and regarded it disappointedly.

'The pregnancy, had there been one,' she went on, biting on the biscuit with a better-than-nothing shrug, 'would have been incidental; fortunate for Sally who did want a baby, but rather unfortunate for David, who is so obviously in love with you even your respective children know it.'

Andrea missed her mouth with her tea. 'They do?'

'Children are very astute, Andrea,' Eva imparted in school ma'amish tones. 'You of all people should know that. I suspect Ryan would quite like to bang your heads together.'

'Ryan?' Andrea wiped a dribble from her chin.

'He looked after Jake while David rushed Sally to the hospital. Found the poor woman in agony, apparently. Wasted no time whisking her off; acted totally professionally and caringly. Her appendix was about to burst, apparently. I gather Ryan asked about her condition when—'

'Appendix!' Andrea clanged her cup down. 'But ...?' She shook her head, more befuddled now than ever. Had Sally thought she might be pregnant? Lied about it? Did it matter, right now, when the poor woman was in ...? She would have to have had an operation! 'I have to go and see her.' Andrea jumped to her feet.

'Splendid idea.' Eva got to hers. 'The whole thing between David and her was obviously a heat of the moment thing and historical, as far as David was concerned. However, he wasn't about to walk away from his responsibilities, that's all I wanted to say.'

'Right.' Andrea nodded dazedly, wondering what on earth had been going through Sally's mind, whether she was all right, whether she might need anything. 'Should I take her something, do you think, Eva? Toiletries? Chocolates?'

'Your friendship?' Eva suggested shrewdly.

David was obviously just about to leave as Andrea arrived. Unable to help herself, she watched through the glass panel in the hospital door. David stood from his visitors chair to smile down at Sally, bent to plant a soft kiss on her cheek then squeezed her hand, before heading for the door, looking pensive.

Andrea stepped away from the room as he came into the corridor, clearly lost in his thoughts. 'Can't keep away from the place, hey?' she joked, knowing that his kiss had been no more than a show of affection. He was a good man at heart. She hadn't really needed Eva to tell her that.

'Andrea, hi.' He looked up, his mouth curving into a smile as he saw her. 'I, er ...' he faltered, his smile fading as he obviously realised she would know why he was here.

'Came to see Sally?' Andrea helped him along.

'Yes.' He nodded and blew out a sigh. 'I thought she could use a friend, to be honest. She's been through a rough time, so ...'

'That's why I came to see her,' Andrea said, aware, now more than ever, just how caring of other people's feelings David seemed to be. 'Assuming she'll want to see me, of course.' She shrugged, glancing worriedly towards the door.

David furrowed his brow. 'Why wouldn't she?'

Caring but naïve, Andrea hid a smile. Because she could see I was in love with you even though I couldn't, she didn't enlighten him.

'How's your ankle?' she asked him.

'How are you?' he said, at the same time.

'Good,' they both said together.

Andrea laughed. 'We're going to have to stop doing this, you know?'

'What? Being awkward in each other's company?' David smiled, a sad reflective smile that really could charm the birds from the trees – and one or two passing nurses.

Andrea noted a pretty young thing's head twizzling on her neck as she passed by, her eyes all but eating David up. Don't walk into any doors, will you, sweetie, and flatten your face. Andrea bobbed around David and beamed the nurse a smile, at which the girl had the good grace to pick her eyeballs up and walk on.

Looking back at David, Andrea pondered. Apparently, he hadn't even noticed the girl openly lusting – and she definitely found that hard to believe. Did he really not know what a catch he was? Good looks aside, the man cared about people, hands-on cared. She quickly dismissed a pelvis-flipping recollection of his hands so tenderly on her, all over her. Did he ever look in the mirror? Obviously he hadn't this morning. She noted a nick where he'd shaved, once again badly, and wished her own caring instinct, her urge to hold him and soothe him; make sweet sensual love to him, wouldn't kick in every time she saw him.

'We need to talk,' she said quickly, and over-brusquely, she realised, in an attempt to disguise her own errant lust.

David flinched, looked physically wounded, as if she'd just slapped him.

'Clear the air, you know,' she added clumsily, glancing down.

'Right,' he said, tugging in a tight breath. 'I, er … When and where?'

Andrea looked back at him. Good question, she thought, as he searched her face, a thousand questions in his eyes. Obviously not here. And not at the apartment with her astute children's ears flapping.

'You could pop over to mine later,' he suggested with a hopeful shrug.

'No, I, um … I'll ring you,' Andrea said. That would be better. She tried to think of somewhere they could actually talk without interruption.

'Okay.' David nodded slowly, looking somewhat deflated. 'I'll wait to hear from you then.'

'I'd better go in.' Andrea nodded past him to Sally's door. 'Is she all right?' she asked, concerned. She had no idea what state she might find her in, physically or emotionally.

'She's had an infection, but she's as well as can be expected.' David nodded again and smiled reassuringly.

'But not pregnant?'

David ran a hand over his neck. 'Not pregnant, no,' he said, his expression now giving nothing away.

'Was she ever?' Andrea had to ask.

David looked at her, down at his shoes, back at her. 'I think you should talk to Sally about that, Andrea. Patient confidentiality aside, I really think anything she wants you to know should come from her, don't you? Sorry.' He shrugged again, apologetically.

'Don't be,' Andrea said, inclined to press a kiss to his cheek, but thought better of it, given they were outside Sally's room. 'You're a very caring man, David Adams,' she said, pressing her hand against his cheek instead.

'But perhaps a little careless sometimes,' he said quietly behind her as she headed for Sally's door.

Andrea looked at him curiously.

'Seems I have an awful habit of losing the things I care about most.' He dragged a hand through his hair and turned to go.

Chapter Twenty-Nine

'Are we talking?' Andrea asked, poking her head around the door.

Sally looked at her, her huge blue eyes glassy, her complexion pale against the starched white of the pillows. 'I didn't think you were talking to me.' She sniffled. 'I didn't think you'd ever want to talk to me again.' She glanced down, fiddling with a tissue then promptly burst into tears.

'Oh, sweetie.' Andrea walked swiftly over to the bed, her heart wrenching inside her. 'Of course, I'm speaking to you. Why on earth wouldn't I be?'

'After the awful things I said?' Sally blinked up at her. 'The awful things I've done. I thought you'd hate me,' she said snottily. 'I was sure David would. I would, wouldn't you?'

'He's not like that, Sally.' Andrea sat down on the edge of the bed and drew her distraught and obviously confused friend to her. 'I don't think he's capable of disliking anyone. Well, apart from Jonathan, possibly. I'm not sure he was overly impressed with him.'

'Oh, Andrea,' Sally pulled her blotchy face from Andrea's shoulder, 'I'm so sorry. Eva told me what happened. I had no idea you were going through all that as well as the fire. God, I'm such a selfish bitch. Poor you.'

'Poor you, you mean.' Andrea relieved her of the tissue, now shredded, and passed her another. 'Do you want to tell me about it?' she asked, once Sally had had a good blow.

Sally pulled in a shuddery breath and ran her hand under her nose. 'I expect David's told you most of it.' She shrugged uncomfortably.

'He hasn't actually.'

Sally blinked her eyelashes, confused.

'Eva told me you weren't pregnant,' Andrea said gently, taking Sally's hand. 'David confirmed it, just now, but he hasn't said any more.'

'He hasn't?' Sally blinked again, bemused.

'He's not one to talk behind people's backs, Sally. He's just concerned for you, that's all.'

A fat tear plopped down Sally's cheek, followed swiftly by another. 'God,' she flopped her head back on her pillow, 'I've been such an idiot, haven't I? Such a cow.'

Andrea glanced away. 'I've brought chocolates,' she said evasively. 'Why don't we open the box and—'

'There never was a baby, Andrea,' Sally said quietly.

'Oh.' Andrea nodded, closing her eyes.

'I bet you don't want to share your chocolates with me now.'

'There's too many for one person.' Andrea forced a smile. 'I'd have to jog to school if I ate—'

'Aren't you going to ask why I did it?' Sally interrupted. 'How I hoped to get away with it?'

Andrea studied the chocolate menu. The vanilla truffle looked tempting. 'Only if you want to tell me,' she said.

Sally drew in a breath. 'I hoped there would be a baby,' she admitted bleakly. 'Maybe not immediately but ... I thought that if we had sex morning, noon and night it was bound to happen.'

Andrea closed the lid. She didn't really feel like chocolate, after all.

'He wasn't interested,' Sally went on as Andrea traced a finger over the embossed lettering on the box. 'Believe me, I tried. I was his for the taking. I even stripped practically naked for him. He turned me down flat.'

Andrea could feel Sally's eyes on her. She didn't look up.

'He wasn't being cruel. I realise that now. He doesn't love me. I thought maybe in time that he might learn to, but ...'

'And if he had been interested?' Andrea met her gaze. 'And you hadn't got pregnant?'

Sally fiddled with her tissue. 'I'd have lied.' She flushed, glancing down.

Told him she'd miscarried his baby? Oh, Sally, Sally ... Had she any idea how devastated he might have been at that news? 'Hoping that by then you'd have established a relationship,' she ventured, 'and David would have stayed anyway?'

'Yes.' Sally nodded, her eyes fixed on her hands. 'At least that was the plan.'

Andrea placed the chocolates on the bedside locker. She should go. She really couldn't digest this piece of news, at least not yet. Did everyone around her live such complicated lives full of secrets and lies? Was anybody ever who they seemed to be?

'Aren't you going to ask why I would do such a thing?' Sally asked as Andrea fell silent.

Andrea wasn't sure she wanted to hear any more.

Sally went on anyway. 'Precisely because he would have stayed, Andrea, don't you see, at least for a while? That's the kind of man he is. A man who couldn't do what most men would do when told they're about to be a father after spending only one night with a woman. I told him it might be my last chance to have a baby. I said I wouldn't consider not having it, not that he suggested I did. That's what we were talking about when you came into the conservatory. He would have been there for his child, if there had been a child,' Sally continued as Andrea felt a tear prickle her eye. 'But he'd much rather have been with you. He loves you, Andrea. He told me, not that he had to. It was as obvious as the nose on my face.'

Andrea nodded slowly, swallowed, and got to her feet.

'You'd better take your chocolates,' Sally suggested as she started towards the door.

Andrea paused. 'I'm not sure I'm in a chocolate mood, Sally,' she said, with some effort. 'I'd better go. I have some things to do.'

'Give David my best,' Sally said sadly behind her.

Not sure what to say to that, Andrea walked on. 'Sally,' she stopped short of the door, 'did David know you were going to tell me all this?'

'*I* didn't know I was going to tell you all this. I wanted to, but I honestly didn't know whether I could. I was so down, that's the only thing I can offer in my defence, so terribly lonely. David's probably the only person who's really understood. I mean, it's just so hard to explain that you've never stopped grieving, when there was never a person to grieve over in most people's minds. You just stop mentioning it after a while. Anyway, he's made me an appointment to see someone and I ...' Sally faltered. 'Can we still be friends, Andrea?'

Andrea didn't turn around, lest her expression belie her emotion. She was angry, furious with Sally. Felt terribly sorry for her. But most of all heartbroken. Did Sally really feel she needed to put on a brave face in front of her? She didn't know whether they could get back to where they had been, but ... If David could find it in his heart to be a friend to Sally, after everything that had happened, then Andrea was going to give it a damn good try. 'Save me the vanilla truffle,' she said. 'I'll see you tomorrow.'

David selected Andrea's number again, then, his thumb hovering over his phone, he aborted the call. She hadn't rung him. He'd felt like a love-struck teenager checking for messages at least five thousand times today. A love-stuck loser, more like.

Dragging his hand through his hair, David sighed and pushed his key into his front door. He couldn't blame her. Her life was complicated enough without him adding to her worries. And he had. The simple fact was, baby or no baby, he had slept with her best friend, albeit he didn't know she was. When he had known, though, he'd chosen not to tell her.

Add to that the web of lies Eden had spun her ... No, Andrea wouldn't want to get embroiled in another relationship with someone she wasn't sure she could trust.

His fault. He'd never imagined he'd fall in love again. Yet he had, and he'd blown it. He was determined to be a friend to her, though, whatever, if that's all she wanted; to be there for her. For her kids, too, Ryan, in particular, who seemed to have become an integral part of his own life. He'd concentrate his energies on Jake, David decided. Get more involved in the daily dog walking routine maybe? Jake might welcome that, Ryan now apparently dating Nita. He could take up jogging, keep himself fit. Take several cold showers a day. He wished he could stop thinking about Andrea, the touch, taste and smell of her.

Letting himself in and dropping his briefcase in the hall, his fantasy of Andrea's sweet lips soft against his was rudely interrupted by the wet snout of a lumbering Labrador in his ear.

'Hi, Homer.' David rolled his eyes and dutifully gave the dog's head a pat, then rolled his eyes again and attempted to extract his trouser leg from Dougal's mouth.

Wait a minute. Dogs on the loose? No owners in sight? That spelled trouble. David plucked the frenziedly yapping Yorkie up and stuck his head around the kitchen door. No Jake. No Ryan. He listened up the stairs, then decided to check downstairs first. 'Anybody home?' he called, heading for the closed lounge door, then pausing, and listening.

'Right, all those in favour?' he heard Eva from inside, followed by several affirmative responses, including Jake's, 'Yup.'

Great. The Kelly Committee had obviously reconvened. David sighed, glanced warily at a tongue-lolling, tail-wagging Homer, and then tentatively pressed down the handle, only to find the door yanked open by Dee.

'You're taking your time, aren't you? My daughter's not

getting any younger, you know,' she imparted, looking him up and down. 'Your tie's skew-whiff. And you're covered in dogs' hairs. You'd better smarten yourself up, young man, if you're hoping to impress anyone.' So saying, Dee walked around him and marched on.

'Ah, David,' Eva said, following in her wake, 'we've been having a little meeting, and you'll be pleased to know the ayes have it, don't they, Jake?'

David glanced past her, to where Jake ambled from the room. 'Yup, I'm cool with it,' he said, looking up at David, his eyes actually full of mischief.

'Er, would someone like to enlighten me?' he asked, peering hopefully around Eva to Ryan, who unfortunately had his hands full, helping Nita back into her chair. And who seemed to also be getting an earful from Thea.

'And while you're delivering the burlesque feather adornments to the shop, you can pop up and ask Andrea whether she'd like to come to dinner, Ryan,' Thea instructed, whilst feeding herself into her faux fur. 'Nothing too formal. I thought we'd start with a nice traditional Kotosoupa Avgolemono, followed by—'

'Ooh, Mum! We've only been going out for ten minutes. Will you just stop with the "meeting his parents" arrangements.' Nita scowled at her mum, and then wheeled herself huffily into the hall.

David tried not to laugh as Ryan collected Dougal and trailed after Nita cross-eyed.

'The course of true love never did run smooth.' David offered Ryan an empathetic smile.

'Yeah, right.' Ryan trudged on, looking definitely put upon. 'Tell me again, why do we do it?'

'Because I'm awesome,' Nita told him.

'Just like her mother.' Thea paused to give David an eyelash flutter on her way out.

'Come along, Thea dear, before the doctor's overwhelmed with your awesomeness.' Eva caught hold of Thea's arm, whisking her onward. 'We don't want Dee wandering off again, do we?'

David shook his head as the two women headed for the front door, Thea's eyes trailing behind her. 'Er, Eva ...?'

'Yes?' Eva turned back.

'Do you want to tell me what it is I'm supposed to be pleased about that apparently got an overwhelming majority?'

'Oh, yes, sorry, Doctor Adams. Head like a sieve, I swear.' Eva slapped a hand against her forehead. Thea coiffed her hair. 'The shop. I've had a word with Andrea and she's absolutely delighted with your offer to allow her the shop on six months free rental.'

Come again? David looked at her askance. 'Er, right,' he said. 'I wasn't aware I had offered it to her.'

'You hadn't? Oh.' Eva had a think. 'Well, not to worry, you have now, haven't you?'

David ran his hand over his neck. 'Apparently, yes,' he said, furrowing his brow. Letting Andrea have the shop wasn't concerning him. He'd be out of pocket in the short term, but David reckoned he'd make a profit on the building in the long term. What this shrewd old woman was cooking up was concerning him, however. She was up to something. He'd bet his life on it.

'Splendid. She's taking six months leave of absence from teaching at the end of this term while she sees how it pans out, so you can use that time to see how other things pan out, can't you?' Eva beamed him a smile and turned to bustle on out.

'What other things?' David scratched his head and glanced at Jake, standing off at a safe distance, in the kitchen doorway with Homer. 'Any ideas?'

'Clueless.' Jake shook his head solemnly.

Too solemnly. David eyed him narrowly. They were definitely up to something. Question was, what?

David had barely closed the front door when Ryan shot back up the drive. 'Just got a call from Sophe,' he said, worriedly. 'Mum's not too well, apparently. I said I'd stay with Jake ...'

'I'm on my way.' David collected his bag and all but fell over Ryan in his haste to get to his car.

'There. You look totally gorgeous.' Sophie stood back to admire her handiwork.

Andrea looked in the mirror, doubting she looked anything near gorgeous. It was an improvement, though, she had to admit. Recent events had taken their toll. Her moisturising and make-up routine had flown out the window, leaving her complexion as dull as dishwater, and her hair would have petrified Medusa. Naturally curly soon ended up naturally knotted without a bit of effort on the conditioning front. Sophie had taken her in hand, however, caking her face in a moisturising face pack and topping her off with hair rescue treatment. Andrea had quite fancied staying under the face pack and turban, but now all was revealed ... Well, it wasn't too bad, actually. Nothing minor surgery or a head transplant couldn't fix anyway.

'Right, I'm off to run you a nice bubble bath,' Sophie said around the grip clenched between her teeth as she pinned up the last few strands of Andrea's hair. 'Then I'm taking Chloe to Maccies with Hannah so you can have a long soak in it.'

Pardon? Andrea's mouth clanged open. Something was wrong with this picture. Either the bodysnatchers had been and swapped Miss Moody for Miss Smiley, or something was wrong.

'What? Problem?' Sophie obviously caught her expression through the mirror.

'No. Nothing.' Andrea turned around, debating whether she should casually enquire whether there might be, though luxuriating in a bubble bath in blissful ignorance seemed the much more inviting option. She cast her mind back, trying to recall if Sophie had hinted at anything being wrong, apart from their lives being turned upside down and inside out, but couldn't think of ... Ooh, no. Condoms! Recalling Sophie's casual mention of them recently, Andrea decided she most definitely should enquire.

'I, um, just wondered whether everything was all right ... with you, I mean?'

'Yes.' Sophie put the final pin in her hair, meaning it might actually stay on top of Andrea's head for once. 'Why?'

'No reason, just wondering.'

'No, I'm fine,' Sophie assured her.

'You don't fancy a bit of girl-talk, then? Just you and me?' Andrea asked nonchalantly.

'Love to, Mum, but Hannah's waiting for me to go over. Another time maybe.'

'Right.' Andrea nodded. 'But there's nothing wrong? Nothing you want to tell me?'

Sophie planted her hands on her hips. 'Mum, I told you, everything's cool. What's your problem?'

'I don't have one.' Andrea shrugged innocently. 'I just thought you might.'

'Why?'

'Well, you are going out of your way to be nice to me, Sophie. You must admit—'

'Oh, charming. Have a go at me for being nice to you now, why don't you? God, honestly!' Sophie folded her arms. 'Going to get Chloe ready. At least there's one person who appreciates me round here.' Sophie twirled around, and stropped huffily off.

Rather than interfere, Andrea left Sophie to see to Chloe

and ran her bath, feeling terribly guilty. Sophie had bought her some coconut bath wash. She must have got that specially, knowing it was Andrea's favourite. She really was just trying to be nice, and she'd openly suspected her motives. What must that say to Sophie about how she generally perceived her?

Hearing Sophie coming back from the bedroom, Andrea dashed out to meet her before she reached the front door. 'Sorry,' she said, meaning it. 'You've been fantastic, Sophie. I really do appreciate it, honestly. I'm just frazzled, that's all, looking for the next problem. Just ignore me.'

Sophie shrugged moodily. 'I do most of the time.'

Not sure what to say to that, Andrea bent down to make sure Chloe's coat was fastened properly. She couldn't get the chill of the cold river air out of her own bones, her natural inclination therefore to make sure everyone was suitably coated and scarfed before venturing out.

'Bye, sweetie.' Andrea pressed a finger to her baby's cute button nose. 'Be good for your big sister, hey?'

'Going Maccies.' Chloe picked up on the teenage vernacular, grinning from ear-to-ear.

'That's because Ronald's all better, so we can go more often now.' Andrea smiled and gave her a hug.

'Be good,' she said to Sophie, standing up.

'I always am,' Sophie said, trailing to the front door, Chloe's hand firm in hers. 'And if I can't be good, I'll be careful.'

'Sophie ...' Andrea's shoulders drooped.

'What?' Sophie turned around. 'Joking, Mum, y'know? I can't do right for doing wrong, can I?' she said, a definite wobble in her voice. 'I was just trying to be nice to you 'cos of all the shit you've been through and even then I seem to get moaned at.'

Oh hell ... Andrea flew over to squish her belligerent big-little girl into a firm hug. 'I know you were, Sophie.' She eased back to look into her daughter's confidently made-up, yet uncertain, eyes. 'And I'm a pain in the bum who keeps banging on all the while, but just so you know, that's because I worry, because I love you. And I love you just the way you are, okay?'

Sophie sniffed and nodded.

'Are we good?'

'We're good.' Sophie managed a smile. 'Go on. You'd better go and have your soak before it goes cold, but be quick. Catchya later.'

'I thought you said I could have a nice long soak,' Andrea said, turning back to the bathroom.

'Oh, um … Yeah, I did, but Gran's probably on her way back by now, isn't she? She'll be fishing you out so she can soak her bunions.'

Well that ruined the romantic bath by candlelight image a bit. Andrea smiled and headed off for a quick dip.

David knocked three times, his concern escalating with each knock. Where the hell was she? And where the bloody hell was Sophie? Hadn't it been her who'd rung Ryan? Deliberating the ethics of letting himself in for all of one second, David fished the spare keys from his pocket. The last he'd heard, Eden was still in the hospital, the femoral fracture sustained when he'd hit ironwork on the way into the river requiring surgery, but David wouldn't put anything past him. That aside, Sophie had obviously gone out, which might mean that Andrea was lying in there too ill to make the stairs to the door. Whatever, David didn't have time for ethics.

'Andrea,' he called, searching room by room, only to find the bathroom door locked. 'What the …? Andrea!'

Why wasn't she answering? Something was wrong. There had to be. David swallowed back a tight knot in his throat and listened. Nothing. Not a sound. 'Dammit!' Panic gripping his stomach, he pressed his shoulder to the door and shoved hard – unfortunately at the exact time Andrea pulled it open.

'David?' she said. 'David! Oh, David! Are you all right?'

Dropping down next to where David was scraping himself disorientated from the floor to all fours, Andrea tried to pull him up by his overcoat – and almost strangled him in the process.

David coughed and shook his head free of stars. 'Erm, yes. I think so.' Cast iron baths in bathrooms, not a good idea, he decided. 'Are you okay?' he asked, wincing as he finally managed to get himself somewhere near sitting.

'Of course.' Andrea blinked at him. 'What on earth were you doing?'

David closed his rapidly swelling eye. Would very much have preferred to keep both eyes open as Andrea was wearing nothing but the skimpiest of towels, but – bloody hell – his head was throbbing. 'Rescuing you?' He shrugged, then, 'Ouch,' winced again.

'Well, that worked,' Andrea said, draping his arm over her shoulders and trying again to heave him up.

David laughed. 'I think you'll need to eat more spinach if you're aiming to become a weightlifter,' he suggested, grabbing hold of the bath with his free hand and levering himself to his feet.

'I wish you'd wear a suit of armour if you're going to insist on being my white knight, David,' Andrea grumbled, his arm still over her shoulder as she helped him to the lounge.

I could get used to this, David thought. 'Your towel's slipping,' he said, unable to resist a peek with his good eye at the pleasing amount of breast revealing itself temptingly above it.

Andrea practically dumped him on the sofa. 'What were you thinking, David?' she asked huffily, hitching her towel up, which revealed an awful lot of thigh.

'That you were in trouble.' David tried to focus his eye and mind where it should be.

'Well, I wasn't!'

David's mouth curved into a smile. 'You might be if you stand there like that much longer.'

'David, be serious.' Andrea hitched her towel down at the bottom, then back up at the top, which had David's mouth curving into a very appreciative smile. 'You scared me to death! Were you actually going to break down the door?'

'You didn't answer,' David said in his defence. 'I thought something was wrong.'

'I was listening to Sophie's iPod!' Andrea pointed at her ears. Bad move, David thought, as the towel slipped. Or maybe not.

'Ooh, David, stop it.' Andrea tugged the towel tighter around herself, blushing furiously, and most definitely beautifully.

'Stop what?' David shrugged helplessly.

'Looking.' Andrea folded her arms over her breasts.

Damn. 'I'm not,' David pointed out. 'I'm half looking.'

'Ho, ho.' Andrea looked away from him, po-faced.

'Come on, sit down for a second,' he said, taking her hand. 'I'm sorry. Scaring you, after all you've been through, was the last thing I wanted to do.'

Andrea slid her eyes back towards him, then, still maintaining po-faced, she sat down on the edge of the sofa next to him. 'Does it hurt?' she asked, finally focusing on him through her understandable fury.

'What, my pride or my eye?'

'David ...' Andrea sighed.

David smiled. 'Yes and yes,' he answered. 'But don't worry. I know a very good doctor.'

Andrea glanced down, but she was smiling, too.

Yep. David dipped his head to glance up at her. Her mouth was definitely twitching up at the corners.

'So do I.' Andrea peered amusedly up at him. 'Thank you, David, for coming to my rescue, even though I didn't actually need rescuing.'

'Flying doctor, at your service.' David saluted ... and winced. Ouch! Definitely a bad move.

'Idiot.' Andrea laughed.

That was better. David much preferred her laughing than crying.

'That looks really sore, David.' Andrea studied his face sympathetically. 'Let me get you some ice.'

'No, stay.' He caught her hand again as she stood up. 'You'll spoil the view if you move.'

Andrea looked at him askew, then cottoned on to the view he was referring to. 'You are bad,' she scolded him.

'I'd like to be.' David sighed, which had Andrea blinking at him wide-eyed.

'Best behaviour, promise,' David assured her. 'Come on, sit with me, please? Just to talk. I don't think we've actually managed more than two minutes on our own.'

Andrea nodded and seated herself back down, demurely, lack of clothing demanding it. 'David, I ...'

'Andrea ...'

'Damn,' they both said together. Then both laughed at the same time, reinforcing David's belief that they were meant for each other. He hadn't expected it to happen. Couldn't explain it. But he was damned if he was going to lose this woman without a fight.

Andrea glanced back down, blushing again under his all too obvious scrutiny – and David's heart constricted. He loved her, absolutely. He wanted her, but he wouldn't force it. To do that would only push her away.

'So, how are things?' Andrea asked awkwardly. 'With you and Sally, I mean.'

Ah. David winced again, this time on the inside. 'I, er ...

I'm not actually sure how to answer that, without knowing how much you know?'

'All of it.' Andrea looked at him, bemusement now in her eyes. 'And yet you still manage to be nice to her.'

David drew in a breath. 'She probably needs all the friends she can get right now.'

'I know. I'm aiming to try to be one, despite …' Andrea trailed off, plucking thoughtfully at a loose strand of terry towelling.

Despite what? David wondered. That Sally's untimely announcement had interrupted something between them? He hoped it was interrupted, rather than finished.

'So, are you going to stay in Hibberton?' Andrea asked him, after a pause.

Which surprised David. He'd had no intention of leaving. 'Yes, definitely. There's no reason not to, is there?'

'You're not worried about the gossiping neighbours making your business their business, then?' Andrea teased him.

David blew out a sigh, immensely relieved she hadn't given him a reason not to want to stay. 'I never thought I'd see the day,' he smiled tolerantly, 'but I think I'm learning to live with them.'

'Good.' Andrea looked at him, a twinkle back in her eyes.

Much better, David thought. Those dancing green eyes should never be clouded with worry. Grazing a thumb lightly over the back of her hand, he held her gaze, wished he could hold all of her. Touch her. Make sweet love to her; slowly this time, savouring every second and every inch of her.

'You're going to take the shop, then?' he asked conversationally as Andrea – as if reading his thoughts – looked away.

Andrea glanced back at him, puzzled. 'I am?'

'Rent free for six months to see how things pan out, so

Eva ...?' David stopped, and furrowed his brow. During which time, he could see how other things pan out? 'I don't believe this.' He shook his head, stupefied. 'I think our gossiping neighbours may very well have been making our business their business.'

Andrea continued to gaze at him, baffled.

'Eva,' he elucidated. 'I suspect she might have been ... manipulating us.' Along with one or two other people, David suspected.

He sat forward to peer at Andrea closely. 'Are you ill?'

'No.' Andrea blinked at him, alarmed. 'Do I look ill?'

'No. No, you look fantastic. It's just ...' David shook his head again, recalling Jake's mischievous expression as he'd come out of the lounge. They were all in on it, he realised, incredulous, Jake included, the little ... David flopped back and laughed out loud.

'What's so funny?' Andrea was now most definitely alarmed.

'They have all been bloody well manipulating us.' David wiped a tear from his eye – and winced, 'Eva, Ryan, Sophie, Jake, Dee probably.'

'Would you like to share?' Andrea said, now sounding miffed.

David held up a hand. 'Don't shoot the messenger,' he pleaded, trying to straighten his face.

Andrea folded her arms, making David laugh all the harder. She really didn't communicate furious very well dressed in a postage stamp towel, even with the scowl.

'Eva,' he finally managed, 'she tells me you're taking the shop, knowing full well I'll ask you about taking the shop, yes?'

Andrea didn't look any the wiser.

'They were all there, at my house, the Kelly Committee, plus Ryan, plus Jake.'

'And?' Andrea cocked her head to one side, and puffed a loose tendril of hair from her face, making her look like the cutest, annoyed woman dressed in a towel David had ever come across.

'So, having imparted the news about the shop, they then leave. But then Ryan comes scooting back, saying Sophie's rung saying you're ill, so here I am.'

'And here they're not.' Andrea glanced bemusedly around an apartment obviously bereft of bodies but theirs.

'I, er, suspect Sophie hoped you might be out of the bath by the time I arrived,' David hazarded hopefully. Either Andrea was going to find the whole thing as amusing as he did, or else she really was going to be furious. David hoped it wasn't the latter.

Andrea didn't say anything. She just looked at him, her expression bewildered. Then she glanced down, again, wrapping her arms about herself as she did. Possibly not a good sign. 'They've been matchmaking, haven't they?'

'That looks about the gist of it, yes.' David sat up, foreboding running through him. If she was going to show him the door, now was the perfect time. 'You're cold,' he said, noticing as a little shiver shook through her.

Andrea looked back at him. 'Do you think they know something we don't?'

'I think it's more likely they know something we do,' David said, his tone now deadly serious. 'At least, I do.'

It was now or never, he realised, feeling as naked as Andrea, but on the inside. He had to know. He'd be lost if she said, she liked him, but ... He had to know though, because sitting here next to her, not touching her, imagining they might never share the intimacy they'd had, physically, emotionally ... David wasn't sure he could cope with that.

Tugging in a breath, he mentally crossed his fingers. 'I'm not sure you know how I feel about you, Andrea. I mean, I hope you do. That what happened between us ... before ... well, that it wasn't ... ahem.'

So far so good, he thought, loosening his collar and wondering whether he should go out and shout it through the front door. That way at least he wouldn't have to read what was in her eyes, if she didn't feel the same.

He sucked in another fortifying breath.

'I love you, Andrea,' he said determinedly, finally. 'I'm not sure it was from the first time I saw you but it was pretty damn close. I, er, just wondered if you, erm … ahem.'

'I know,' Andrea said quietly as David dropped his gaze and debated whether to go and drown himself in the cast iron bath. 'People keep telling me.'

David's eyes shot back to hers. 'The joys of living in a small community.' He smiled, uncertain.

Could she love him? Could she forgive him for being the biggest idiot ever to walk the earth? Probably not. He swallowed, glancing back down. Then swallowed again as Andrea leaned in and kissed him, a soft fleeting kiss, a tender sweet brush of her lips. A brief hesitation and then she pressed her mouth hard against his, her eyelashes closing over her mesmerising green eyes, her delicate tongue sliding into his mouth.

Nothing between her exquisite nakedness and him but that towel.

Closing his eyes, David kissed her back hungrily, his tongue seeking hers, quietly exploring, his hands desperate to do likewise. 'Shall we, er, go somewhere warmer?' he suggested, after possibly the most palatable cure for a headache ever.

David spun around as the apartment door opened behind him. 'I've been trying to ring you,' Ryan said, eyeing him suspiciously as he came into the hall.

He had? David ferreted in his pocket. 'Damn,' he said, extracting his definitely malfunctioning mobile.

'What happened?' Ryan asked.

'Must have smashed it when I—'

'To your eye?'

'Oh.' Hell. He hadn't realised it was that obvious. David looked up to see Ryan squaring up to him, looking most definitely menacing, despite the hip-slung skinny-fit jeans. 'I, er ... Andrea ... Your mum ... She was in the bath when I arrived.'

Ryan rolled his shoulders. 'Oh, yeah?'

He looked about ready to black his other eye. 'I tried to force the door.' Ryan took a step forward. David took a step back.

'It was locked,' he said quickly, his hands raised defensively. 'You said she was ill, Ryan. I had no choice but to force my way in.'

Ryan eyed him rather less suspiciously.

David shrugged. 'She was plugged into Sophie's iPod. Couldn't hear me. The bath broke my fall.'

'Right.' Ryan nodded, his gaze thawing a few degrees. 'So, she's all right, then?'

'Perfect,' Andrea piped up from behind the bedroom door. 'Goodbye, Ryan.'

'Bye, Mother.' Ryan's eyes disappeared under his Emo fringe. 'Be careful with him,' he said, twirling around to head back the way he came.

'Don't worry,' Andrea opened the door and twanged David inside. 'He's in safe hands.'

'Ouch!' David squeezed his good eye closed as Andrea rather over-enthusiastically body-slammed him against the closed door.

'Oops, sorry,' she mumbled through lips now busy with his.

'The course of true love never did run smooth,' Ryan's voice floated from the hall as he made a big show of closing the front door.

Thank you

Thank you for reading *Learning to Love*. I really hope you enjoyed David and Andrea's journey as much as I enjoyed writing it. There's nothing quite like that feeling you get knowing that a reader has connected with your characters, laughed with them, cried with them, screamed at them, or even totally despaired of them. I think all authors would agree, that's why we write, to connect emotionally with people, hopefully leaving them with that all-important feel good factor. All authors, too, really value reader feedback. The road to publication can sometimes be a little bit bumpy and seeing your book finally 'out there' is truly amazing. Knowing people are reading it, though, and taking the trouble to leave a review on Amazon, a book review site such as Goodreads or NetGalley, or the retail outlet site, is equally amazing. Reviews can do so much to up a book's profile, along with that of the author, but they do sometimes truly inspire the author to keep writing and improving.

If you have time therefore, a one line review, or two, or more if you'd like to, would be hugely appreciated.

Please do feel free to contact me anytime. You can find my details under my author profile. And if you like the book enough to go in search of any of my other books, well, there's that amazing feeling again. Meanwhile, I'll keep being inspired and I'll keep writing!

Happy reading all!

Lots of love,

Sheryl

About the Author

Sheryl Browne lives in Droitwich, England with her family. Working part-time in her own business, Sheryl is a mum, a foster mum to disabled dogs and super-pleased to have completed her Masters Degree in Creative Writing at Birmingham City University. She's a member of the Romantic Novelists' Association and was shortlisted for Innovation in Romantic Fiction by Festival of Romance in 2012.

Sheryl has several novels previously published with a small independent. *The Rest of My Life* was Sheryl's first novel with Choc Lit, and *Learning to Love* is her second.

For more information on Sheryl:
www.twitter.com/SherylBrowne
www.sherylbrowne.blogspot.co.uk
www.facebook.com/SherylBrowne.Author/

More Choc Lit

From Sheryl Browne

The Rest of My Life

You can't run away from commitment forever ...

Adam Hamilton-Shaw has more reason than most to avoid commitment. Living on a houseboat in the Severn Valley, his dream is to sail into the sunset – preferably with a woman waiting in every port. But lately, his life looks more like a road to destruction than an idyllic boat ride ...

Would-be screenplay writer Sienna Meadows realises that everything about Adam spells trouble – but she can't ignore the feeling that there is more to him than just his bad reputation. Nor can she ignore the intense physical attraction that exists between them.

And it just so happens that Adam sees Sienna as the kind of woman he could commit to. But can he change his damaging behaviour – or is the road to destruction a one-way street?

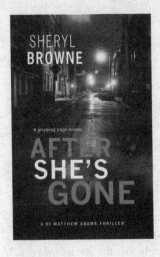

Sins of the Father

Book 2 – Detective Inspector
Matthew Adams series

**What if you'd been
accused of one of the worst
crimes imaginable?**

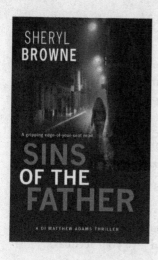

Detective Inspector Matthew
Adams is slowly picking up the
pieces from a case that nearly
cost him the lives of his entire
family and his own sanity too.
On the surface, he seems to be
moving on, but he drinks to forget – and when he closes his
eyes, the nightmares still come.

But the past is the past – or is it? Because the evil Patrick
Sullivan might be out of the picture, but there's somebody
who is just as intent on making Matthew's life hell, and
they're doing it in the cruellest way possible.

When Matthew finds himself accused of a horrific and
violent crime, will his family stand by him? And will he
even be around to help when his new enemy goes after them
as well?

Currently available as an eBook on all
platforms. Visit www.choc-lit.com for
details.

Introducing Choc Lit

We're an independent publisher creating
a delicious selection of fiction.
Where heroes are like chocolate – irresistible!
Quality stories with a romance at the heart.

See our selection here:
www.choc-lit.com

We'd love to hear how you enjoyed *Learning to Love*.
Please leave a review where you purchased the novel
or visit: **www.choc-lit.com** and give your feedback.

Choc Lit novels are selected by genuine readers like yourself.
We only publish stories our Choc Lit Tasting Panel want to
see in print. Our reviews and awards speak for themselves.

Could you be a Star Selector and join our Tasting Panel?
Would you like to play a role in choosing which novels we
decide to publish? Do you enjoy reading women's fiction?
Then you could be perfect for our Choc Lit Tasting Panel.

Visit here for more details...
www.choc-lit.com/join-the-choc-lit-tasting-panel

Keep in touch:
Sign up for our monthly newsletter Choc Lit Spread for
all the latest news and offers: www.spread.choc-lit.com.
Follow us on Twitter: @ChocLituk and Facebook: Choc Lit.

Where heroes are like chocolate – irresistible!